"What are we going to do?" Lauren came out and asked. "What are *you* going to do?" she amended.

He didn't ask her to clarify, but he did look as if he wanted to repeat the question to her. "I wish there was an easy fix for this."

So did she. But there wasn't, and it was breaking her heart. Cameron must have seen that as well, because he said some profanity under his breath and pulled her to him. Lauren didn't resist. Nor did she stop herself from looking up at him. It was a mistake, of course, because they were already too close to each other. Especially their mouths. And that was never a good thing when it came to Cameron and her.

"I should go back into the kitchen," he said.

But he didn't, and Lauren didn't let go of him, either, so he could. Instead, she slipped her arm around his waist, drawing him even closer than he already was.

It was almost too much, and in some ways, it wasn't nearly enough.

Because it made her want more of him.

TEXAS SECRETS

USA TODAY Bestselling Author

DELORES FOSSEN

Previously published as *Lawman from Her Past*
and *Landon*

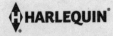

ISBN-13: 978-1-335-42728-1

Texas Secrets

Copyright © 2022 by Harlequin Enterprises ULC

Lawman from Her Past
First published in 2018. This edition published in 2022.
Copyright © 2018 by Delores Fossen

Landon
First published in 2016. This edition published in 2022.
Copyright © 2016 by Delores Fossen

Recycling programs
for this product may
not exist in your area.

For questions and comments about the quality of this book, please contact us at CustomerService@Harlequin.com.

Harlequin Enterprises ULC
22 Adelaide St. West, 41st Floor
Toronto, Ontario M5H 4E3, Canada
www.Harlequin.com

Printed in U.S.A.

CONTENTS

LAWMAN FROM HER PAST   7

LANDON   217

Delores Fossen, a *USA TODAY* bestselling author, has written over one hundred novels, with millions of copies of her books in print worldwide. She's received a Booksellers' Best Award and an RT Reviewers' Choice Best Book Award. She was also a finalist for a prestigious RITA® Award. You can contact the author through her website at deloresfossen.com.

Books by Delores Fossen

Harlequin Intrigue

Mercy Ridge Lawmen

Her Child to Protect
Safeguarding the Surrogate
Targeting the Deputy
Pursued by the Sheriff

Longview Ridge Ranch

Safety Breach
A Threat to His Family
Settling an Old Score
His Brand of Justice

HQN

Last Ride, Texas

Spring at Saddle Run
Christmas at Colts Creek

Visit the Author Profile page
at Harlequin.com for more titles.

LAWMAN FROM HER PAST

Chapter One

Someone was watching him. Deputy Cameron Doran was certain of it.

He slid his hand over the gun in his waist holster and hoped he was wrong about the bad feeling that was snaking down his spine. Hoped he was wrong about the being watched part, too.

But he knew he wasn't.

He'd worn a badge for eleven years, and paying attention to that bad feeling had saved him a time or two.

With his gun ready to draw, Cameron glanced around his backyard. Such that it was. Since his house was on the backside of the sprawling Blue River Ranch, his yard was just a smear of grass with the thick woods only about fifteen feet away. There were plenty of trees and underbrush. The edge of the river, as well. However, there were also trails that someone could use to make their way to his house.

Someone like a killer.

You'll all die soon.

That was what the latest threatening letter had said. The one that Cameron had gotten just two days ago. Not exactly words anyone wanted to read when they opened their mail, but he'd gotten so many now that they no longer held the emotional punch of the first one he'd gotten a couple of months ago. Still, he wasn't about to dismiss it.

Cameron had another look around, trying to pick through the thick clusters of trees, but when he didn't see anyone, he finished off his morning coffee and went inside. Normally, he would have made a beeline to the nursery so he could say goodbye to his nephew, Isaac, before heading off to work at the Blue River Sheriff's Office, but this morning he went to the window over the sink and kept watch.

From the other side of the house, he could hear Isaac fussing, probably because the nanny, Merilee, was changing his diaper. Isaac was only a year old, but he got up raring to go. He objected to the couple of minutes delay that the diapering caused.

Just when Cameron was about to decide that the bad feeling had been wrong after all, he saw it. Someone moving around. Since those particular trees butted right up against an old ranch trail, the movement got his complete attention.

"Merilee," he called out to the nanny. "Keep Isaac in the nursery a little while longer. And stay away from the windows."

Cameron knew it would alarm the woman, but there was nothing he could do about that now. If this turned out to be a false alarm, then he could smooth things over with her. But for now, Isaac's and her safety had to come first.

He drew his gun, and as soon as he opened the door a couple of inches, Cameron spotted more movement. And the person who was doing the moving.

A woman peered out from one of the trees, and even though she was still pretty far from him, he caught a good enough glimpse of her face.

Lauren Beckett.

She stepped out in full view of him so he got an even better look. Yeah, it was Lauren, all right. She still had the same brunette hair that she'd pulled back into a ponytail. The same willowy build. The last time he'd seen her she'd been a teenager, barely eighteen, but the years hadn't changed her much.

If he'd ventured a guess of who might have been lurking around his place, he would have never figured it would be her. Especially since he'd built his house on Beckett land. *Her* family's land. Of course, Lauren hadn't considered her siblings actually family—or him a friend—in nearly a decade.

Cameron felt the punch of old emotions. Ones he didn't want to feel. He and Lauren had parted ways long ago, and he hated that the tug in his body was still there for her.

He looked at her hands. At her wedding ring. She was still wearing it though he knew her husband had died from cancer a year and a half ago when Lauren had been pregnant. Of course, she might still be wearing the ring because she and her late husband had a child together. A son, if he remembered correctly.

Who was he kidding? He remembered, all right. Little details about Lauren just stuck in his head whether he wanted them there or not.

"What are you doing back there?" he asked.

He started to reholster his gun but then stopped when she fired glances all around her. Lauren had her teeth clamped over her bottom lip, and she motioned for him to come to her.

Hell.

He'd been right about that bad feeling. Something was wrong.

"What happened?" he demanded, but she just kept motioning.

Cursing under his breath, Cameron stepped out and locked the door behind him. Judging from Lauren's nervous gestures, someone else could be out there, and he didn't want that person getting into the house. Keeping watch around him, Cameron gripped his gun with two hands and started toward her.

More memories and emotions came. It'd been ten years since he had seen her. Since he'd kissed her. Ten years since their worlds had turned on a dime. Her mother and father had been murdered. Butchered, really, and even though their killer had been convicted and was behind bars, Lauren hadn't thought justice had been fully served.

Because she also blamed Cameron for not doing enough to save her folks.

That was okay because Cameron blamed himself, too.

All of those thoughts vanished for a moment, though, when he made it to her and stopped about two feet away. Still close enough to catch her scent and see those intense blue eyes. She didn't say anything. Lauren just stood there, staring at him, but he could tell from the tight muscles in her face that this wasn't a social visit.

Not that he thought it would be.

No. Lauren had said her final goodbye to him a decade ago, so it must have taken something pretty bad to come to him this way. Unless…maybe she wasn't here for him.

"Your brothers probably haven't left for work yet and are still home," he told her. They didn't live far, either. "Gabriel lives in his old place, and Jameson has a cabin about a half mile from here."

She didn't seem the least bit surprised about that, which meant maybe Lauren had kept up with her family, after all. Good. Because Cameron wasn't the only one who thought of Lauren often. So did her brothers and her sister, Ivy.

"I can't go to them." Her voice was raw and strained.

"Because you broke off ties with them," Cameron commented. "Don't worry about that. You're still their sister, and they'll help you. They love you," he added, hoping that would ease the tension he could practically feel radiating off her.

Lauren blinked, shook her head. "No. Because their houses are on the main road and someone might see me." She turned, glancing around again, and that was when Cameron spotted the gun tucked in the back waist of her jeans.

He cursed again. "What's wrong?"

A weary sigh left her mouth. The kind of reaction a person had when there was so much wrong that she didn't know where to start. But Cameron figured he knew what this was about.

"We've all been getting threatening letters and emails," he volunteered. "I'm guessing you got one, too?"

She nodded and dismissed it with a shake of her head. "You're raising your sister's child?"

Again, she'd managed to stun him. First with her arrival and now with the question. It didn't seem the right thing to ask since this wasn't a "catching up" kind of conversation.

"Gilly's son, Isaac," Cameron clarified. It had been a year since his kid sister's death, and he still couldn't say her name without it feeling as if someone had put a meaty fist around his heart. "What about him?"

Lauren didn't jump to answer that. With her forehead bunched up, she glanced behind her again. "Is he...okay?"

Isaac was fine. Better than fine, actually. His nephew was healthy and happy. That wasn't what he said to Lauren, though. "Why are you asking?"

"I need to see him. I need to see Gilly's son."

That definitely wasn't an answer.

Cameron didn't bother cursing again, but he did give her a flat look. "I'll want to know a lot more about what's going on. Start talking. Why are you here, and if you're in some kind of trouble, why didn't you call your brothers? Because I think you and I both know I'm the last person on earth you'd come to for help."

She didn't disagree with that, but another sound left her mouth. A hoarse sob. And that was when tears sprang to her eyes. "Please, let me see him."

He wasn't immune to those tears, and it gave him a tug of a different kind, one he didn't want. "Tell me what's going on," Cameron repeated.

Lauren frantically shook her head. "There isn't time."

Cameron huffed in frustration. "Then make time. Is someone after you? And what does that have to do with Gilly's son?"

She stared at him, her mouth trembling now, and

those tears still watering her eyes. "Someone tried to kill me."

That put him on full alert, and he automatically caught on to her arm and pulled her behind him. Cameron positioned himself in between her and the area where she kept glancing.

"Keep talking," he insisted. He didn't see anyone out there, but the woods were fairly thick here. "When and where did this happen?"

Again, no fast answer. Which it should have been. After all, a murder attempt should have been fresh enough in her mind that Lauren could have rattled off the details.

"Last night," she finally said. "Two armed men broke into my house in Dallas and shot me."

The profanity flew out of his mouth before Cameron could stop it, and he whirled around just as she pulled back the collar of her dark blue button-up shirt. There was a bandage there. A bandage covering what had to be a sensitive wound judging by the way Lauren winced when she moved her shoulder.

"I'm okay," she added. "Well, physically anyway. The bullet only clipped me, and I was able to get away from them."

Good. But that didn't cause Cameron to feel any relief. "What about your son? Was he hurt?"

"No. There was a panic room in the house, and I had his nanny take him there right after the burglar alarm went off. I didn't manage to get in there in time before they got to me." She paused, choked back a sob. "I heard them say they had orders to kill me. And it wasn't a case of mistaken identity or anything. They said my name."

That did it. He took hold of her hand. "Come on. I'm taking you to Gabriel right now."

But Lauren pulled away from him. "No. Not yet anyway. Not until I know it's safe. I also heard the men say they were cops."

Cameron stared at her. "Cops? Maybe. Criminals don't always tell the truth, but even if they had, your brother's not dirty."

Even though she didn't come out and say it, she'd once suspected Cameron of being just that—dirty. He hadn't been, but Lauren had deemed him guilty by association. Because he'd been friends with the family of the man who'd murdered her parents. If that friendship hadn't existed, then her mom and dad might still be alive.

Somehow, Cameron had never learned to live with that.

"Gabriel and Jameson aren't behind this," she said. "Whatever *this* is," Lauren added in a mumble. "But if those men were really cops and they know all about me, then they must figure I'd go to my lawmen brothers." Another pause, and she dodged his gaze. "This is the last place they'd expect me to come."

True. It wasn't exactly a secret about Lauren's hatred for him. But that wasn't hatred he was seeing in her eyes now. It was fear. Cameron was certain he was feeling some of that, as well. Fear for her. But there were still some very weird things going on.

"Where's your son now?" he asked.

That was concern number one. Once Lauren and the child were safe, then he could work out the rest with her. The *rest* would include bringing in her brothers on this. No way would Gabriel and Jameson want to be left out when someone was gunning for their kid sister, and it didn't matter if they were estranged from Lauren.

She fluttered her fingers in the direction of the trail. "He's in the car with the nanny. That's why I can't stay. I have to get back to him."

Yeah, she did, and Cameron would go with her. "Take me to him, and I can bring all three of you inside while we work this out."

She did more of that frantic head-shaking. "Not yet. Not until I know. Not until I'm sure I can trust you."

Cameron pulled back his shoulders. Trust had indeed been an issue between them in the past. Her trust for him anyway. But from what he could see in the depths of her eyes, this went beyond their past.

"If you didn't trust me, why come here?" he snapped. And he hated how much it stung that this bad blood was still between them.

"I didn't have a choice." Her voice cracked. "I need to see Isaac."

There it was again—something else she'd said that didn't make sense. Or maybe it did. Cameron hadn't been with Gilly when she'd died from a blood clot less than twenty-four hours after giving birth. He'd still been on the road trying to get to her in Dallas. Lauren had been there, though. Maybe had even spoken to her since Lauren and his sister had remained friends. Not only that, they'd lived in the same city.

"Did Gilly tell you something before she died?" It was the same tone he used to interrogate a suspect. Not an especially friendly one, but he wanted answers, and Lauren was going to give them to him now.

Lauren's mouth opened a little to let him know the

question had surprised her. Well, welcome to the club. He'd been surprised by a lot of what Lauren had said.

"No," she answered after several long moments. "This isn't about Gilly. This is about her son. Does he look like her or like his father?"

Now it was Cameron's turn to take a moment before he responded. "I never met his father, Trace Waters. Never wanted to meet him."

She made a sound of agreement, which meant Lauren knew that Trace had been abusive. Something that Gilly hadn't told Cameron until it was too late for him to go to Dallas and beat the living daylights out of the moron for laying a hand on his kid sister. By the time Cameron had heard, Trace had disappeared. Then, several weeks after Gilly had died, someone else had taken it beyond the beating stage and had killed Trace in a drug deal gone wrong.

"Trace's mother, Evelyn, came to the ranch once," Cameron explained. "She pulled a gun on me and demanded her son's baby." He felt his mouth tighten. "I don't like it when people pull guns on me so I had her arrested. The moment she made bail I slapped her with a restraining order."

"And that worked? Evelyn stayed away?"

He shook his head. "She tried to get on the grounds a couple of times, but the hands spotted her and stopped her. After the third time, she ended up in jail, where she's spent the last four months."

Cameron hoped the woman would do something behind bars that would keep her there. He wasn't concerned about losing custody to her. Gilly had made it clear to the hospital staff that she'd wanted Cameron to raise her son. But he didn't want Evelyn to be a free woman so she could try something else stupid.

"Does Isaac look like Gilly?" Lauren pressed. "Or anyone else in your family?"

Cameron nearly said no, but Lauren wasn't getting answers until he had some from her. "Let's get your baby and the nanny into the house, and we can talk."

"He doesn't look like Gilly," she said like gospel. "Or Trace."

Cameron lifted his shoulder. "Lots of kids don't look like their parents. Plus, he's a baby. Only thirteen months old." He huffed, scrubbing his hand over his forehead. "Look, I don't know where this is going, but I can have Gabriel come out—"

Only because he wasn't expecting it, Cameron didn't see Lauren pull that gun from the back of her jeans.

And she pointed it at him.

His heart slammed against his ribs. Damn. He should have been able to stop this before it'd even started, but Cameron fought the instinct to lunge at her and snatch that gun from her hand. He sure as hell wasn't pleased about this, though.

"What do you think you're doing?" he demanded once he got his teeth unclenched.

"I'm saving my son." Lauren used the barrel of the weapon to motion toward the house. "And you'll take me to him. I want to see Isaac now."

Chapter Two

Lauren saw exactly what she'd expected to see in Cameron's eyes.

Anger.

There was plenty of it, too, along with the shock of having her pull a gun on him. This certainly wasn't the way Lauren had wanted all of this to play out, but she hadn't exactly had a lot of options. The seconds were ticking away.

"Move," she ordered Cameron in the strongest voice she could manage. Which wasn't much. She didn't feel strong at all. Just terrified.

This couldn't be happening.

Over the past decade, she'd accepted that she could be in danger from the lunatic who kept sending those threatening letters, but she couldn't accept that two innocent babies could now be in harm's way.

"Put down the gun," Cameron warned her. And it was indeed a warning. Unlike her, he had managed the strong tone, and it had a dark edge to it. An edge that reminded her that she was holding a cop—an experienced one—at gunpoint.

"I can't." She tried to make that sound like an apology and failed at it, too. "I need to see Isaac."

Of course, Cameron would want to know why, and Lauren would tell him. First, though, she had to see the baby.

"Can't?" he repeated, that edge in his voice going up a notch. It went up in his smoke-gray eyes, too.

When she'd been a teenager, the girls had called them bedroom eyes because he was so hot. Still was. With that dark blond hair and natural tan, he'd always had rock-star looks. Those looks were still there in spades, but there wasn't a trace of his bedroom smile.

"Please," Lauren tried. "Just let me see him, and I might be able to clear all of this up."

"You'll clear it up now." Again, it was a warning. "And if you don't, you won't get anywhere near my nephew. However, you will get to see the inside of a jail cell."

She had no idea if that was a threat or not. He certainly had grounds to arrest her, and the fact that they'd once been lovers might not be enough leverage to stop this situation from snowballing.

Cameron still had hold of his gun, but he used his left hand to reach for his pocket. For his phone, she realized. He was going to call one or both of her brothers, and she didn't want them involved in this yet. Not until she could at least try to make things safe.

"No!" she said.

It was the only thing she managed to get out of her mouth, though, because Cameron didn't take out his phone. He lunged at her. Fast. Before Lauren could even react and get out of his way, he rammed into her and sent them both to the ground. While they were still falling, he knocked her gun from her hand.

"Start talking right now," Cameron growled, and he

pinned her hands to the ground so she couldn't reach for her gun. He pinned her, too, with his body since he was on top of her.

Lauren's heart was racing. Along with that, she got a new hit of adrenaline. Something she definitely didn't need since her nerves were already firing in every inch of her.

She looked at Cameron, their gazes colliding, and for a moment she remembered what had once been between them. The intimacy.

The love.

Yes, once she'd loved him, and she thought maybe he'd felt the same way about her, but it was obvious those emotions were long gone. Well, maybe not the heat that had first drawn them together, but he definitely wasn't having any warm and fuzzy feelings about her now.

Lauren struggled, trying to force him off her, but when it was obvious this was a losing battle, she knew she had to say something.

And that something was going to shatter the life Cameron had built here.

"Did I hurt you?" he asked, the question surprising her.

Only then did she remember the wound on her shoulder. That part of her hadn't hit the ground, thank goodness, and since it was a constant throbbing pain, it had become a sort of white noise. Something she was trying to push aside so it wouldn't cause her to lose focus.

"No. I'm not hurt." But in hindsight, she probably should have lied. Maybe then, Cameron would have let her go.

"Talk to me," he snapped. Obviously, he was over his

concern for her injury. Of course, she couldn't blame him when there were so many other things for them to discuss.

"We're in danger," she started. Lauren had to clear her throat and repeat it so it'd have some sound. "Those men who tried to kill me got away, and I believe they'll be looking for me. Maybe for you, too."

Because he was right in her face, it wasn't hard to see the doubt go through his eyes. Despite the doubts, though, he still had a look around them. A cop's look. Good. Lauren didn't want anyone sneaking up on them. Or worse—trying to sneak into the house.

"What do those men have to do with me?" he snarled.

"Maybe everything."

She tried to gather her breath. Couldn't. Cameron wasn't overly muscled, but he wasn't a lightweight, either, and with his chest pressing against her, she couldn't get enough air. He must have realized that, but he didn't move. Probably because he thought she would go for her gun again.

Which she would.

Since there was no easy way to say this, Lauren just blurted it out. "I believe someone swapped my baby with Gilly's."

She gave him a moment to let that sink in, but she couldn't give him the time he needed. She also continued to keep watch as best she could. Hard to do that, though, while on the ground.

He shook his head. "Why would anyone do that?"

"I'm not sure. Please, let's just check on Isaac, and then we can go over all of this."

Cameron didn't answer. Not with words anyway. But his cold, hard stare told her that wasn't going to happen.

"Someone started following me days ago. Two men in a dark car," she added. "I believe those were the same men who broke into my house."

"The men who tried to kill you." Cameron said it as if he didn't believe her. She couldn't blame him. She'd had hours to try to come to grips with it, and part of her still wasn't ready to accept it.

She nodded. "Before they found me, I heard them talking to someone on a communicator, and that's when they said they were cops."

"They could have lied," he reminded her again.

"True. But they still broke in for a reason. And that reason was my son, Patrick. They wanted to kill me and take him." She huffed in frustration because his skeptical look was only getting worse, and she wasn't explaining this well at all. "Just please move off me so we can both keep watch."

She saw him debate that for several moments. Lauren had lost track of how long she'd been out here with him, but Dara, the nanny, would be getting even more worried than she already was.

"If you try anything else stupid, I will put you right back on the ground," Cameron growled.

He finally shifted his body to the side, rolling off her. He also snatched up her gun as he stood. Lauren didn't like not being armed, but at least when she got up, she was able to better keep an eye on the trail behind them.

"Does your nephew look like your sister?" she came out and asked.

He stopped glancing around long enough to shoot her a glare. "That proves nothing. He could have inherited genes from generations ago."

Lauren hesitated a moment. "Does he look like me?"

His quick glare intensified, but what he didn't do was deny it. "First, you have to convince me that a swap even took place before I'll start speculating about who my nephew does or doesn't resemble."

Fair enough. Or at least it would have been fair if time was on their side. She instinctively knew it wasn't.

"I was telling the truth when I said I can't be sure a swap took place, but the men said once they had Patrick, they could do a DNA test and go from there. Go from there," she emphasized. "I believe that means they'll come here next."

Cameron cursed, and it wasn't tame. "That's a big leap to assume the men were talking about Isaac."

"A leap except that I'd already started to get suspicious. Patrick doesn't look like me or my late husband." She swallowed hard. "He looks like you."

She could tell from his slight flinch that Cameron reacted to that. Maybe because he saw something of her face in Isaac's?

"Gilly could have arranged the swap," Lauren went on. "She was afraid of Trace, and if she knew she was dying, this might have been her way of preventing Trace from getting his hands on their child."

Though it sickened her to think that Gilly, a woman she considered her friend, would have intentionally done something like this since it could have put Lauren's own precious son in danger.

"Gilly wouldn't do that," Cameron insisted. "If she was worried about her baby's safety, she would have gotten word to me."

"Maybe. But Gilly was dying. Scared. And they'd had trouble getting in touch with you."

He flinched again, and she knew why. Cameron had

gotten caught up in a lockdown at the prison, where he'd gone to interview a potential witness. He'd been trapped there for hours with no way to leave and get to his sister even though she'd gone into labor.

"But Gilly might not have done this," Lauren added a moment later.

Mercy, she wished she'd rehearsed this or something because it was hard for her to put her line of thinking into words. Equally hard for her to imagine it had happened. "My late husband was Alden Lange, and his business partner or his sister could be the one responsible. They both hate me. Or at least they hate that I have control over Alden's estate."

The flat look Cameron gave her told her he wasn't buying that. And she hoped she was wrong. Because both Alden's sister, Julia, and his partner, Duane Tulley, could be very dangerous. They might have seen this as some sick mind game to watch her suffer. Of course, her suffering could also be profitable for them if it led to one or both of them getting their hands on Alden's money.

"How would Trace or any of these other people have gotten into the hospital nursery to switch babies?" he asked.

Lauren didn't have the answer to that, either. "It must have been an inside job since the babies wear bracelets with security chips that would trigger an alarm if they were carried out of the hospital. I'd just started checking out the medical staff when I was attacked."

He made a sound, a rumble deep in his throat. "And why did you do that? What made you suspicious?"

"I kept thinking it was strange that I would look at my son and see you." She waved that off before he could say anything about it. She didn't want to talk about why the image of Cameron's face was still so clear in her head after all these years and after all the bad stuff that'd gone on between them.

"I had a DNA test done," she went on. "So I could compare Patrick's DNA to mine. I'm supposed to get the results back any day now, but I made the mistake of asking the housekeeper if there was anything still around with Alden's DNA on it." She'd cursed herself for doing that. "I wanted to have the complete DNA results, but I think the housekeeper told Alden's sister what I'd asked for."

At least Cameron hadn't simply dismissed her. He tipped his head to the trail. "We'll get your son and sort this out." Lauren was about to blow out a breath of relief, but then Cameron added, "For the record, I don't believe there was a swap. Isaac is my nephew. But if Duane and Julia are bad news like you think they are, then they could have been the ones behind your attack."

He took her by the arm again to get her moving, but Lauren dug in her heels. "I can't risk bringing my brothers into this yet. Those thugs who attacked me could have connections to Duane and Julia, and they could find out I'm here."

This huff was even louder than his last one. "Look, Gabriel is the sheriff, and my boss. As well as your brother. No way would he risk putting you in danger. I'll just go inside, call him on his personal line and have him come out here."

"No." She couldn't say that fast enough. "I heard those men say if my family got in the way, they would have to kill them."

She hated when his skeptical look returned. Because

she had the same skepticism. "I know those thugs could have wanted me to hear what they were saying, that they could have been feeding me information. But why would they have done that, then shoot me and try to take Patrick?"

"That's what we'll find out—as soon as I call Gabriel." He tightened his grip on her arm and managed to drag her a few steps.

"They could be watching the front of your house from the road. They could be watching Gabriel's and Jameson's places, too. That's why I used the trail. Only the locals know it's there, and it's not easy to spot unless you're looking for it."

Cameron couldn't argue with that, not the last part anyway, even though it looked as if he wanted to dispute something. *Anything.* "We'll go in through the back of my house. Even hired guns won't be suspicious if they see the sheriff dropping by to visit with one of his deputies."

Lauren wasn't so sure of that at all. Anything out of the ordinary might trigger those men to shoot again. And this time, Isaac and anyone else who happened to be around could get hurt. If the gunmen were truly out there, they could be looking for any sign she was there, and Gabriel's visit might give her away.

"I shouldn't have come here," Lauren said under her breath. She lifted her head, making direct eye contact with Cameron. "But I just had to know if Isaac's really my son. Don't get me wrong. I love Patrick with all my heart, but I had to find out the truth."

Cameron hesitated, volleying glances at the house, the woods and her. Just when she thought he was about to give in and let her go inside, she heard something.

Footsteps. Cameron heard them, too, because he pushed her behind him and aimed his gun in the direction of the sound.

Someone was running toward them.

Oh, God. Had something happened to Patrick?

Nothing could have kept Lauren behind Cameron. She snatched her gun from his left hand and would have taken off toward her car, but she finally saw something.

Something that stopped her cold.

Dara. The nanny had Patrick clutched to her chest, and she was running—fast. Probably as fast as she could go.

"They found us," Dara shouted. "Run!"

Chapter Three

Cameron hadn't been sure of what he was going to do, but there was no time left to debate it now. All of his lawman's instincts told him that the stark fear in the woman's voice was real.

So was that baby she had gripped in her arms.

A little blond-haired boy who was about the same size as Isaac.

Cameron forced himself not to think that everything Lauren had told him was real. If this was truly his nephew, anything he felt about that would have to wait. Right now he had to get them to safety.

"Get inside the house," Cameron told Lauren.

She didn't listen, of course. Neither would he if that'd been his child out there. Lauren started to run toward the nanny, but Cameron hurried in front of her. The moment he got to the woman and child, he hooked his arm around them, maneuvering them in front of him, and he got them running again.

"Keep watch around us," Cameron told Lauren.

Maybe that would stop the panic he saw rising in her eyes. It was also something that needed to be done. Because if those two armed thugs were on their tail, then they had to get inside—fast—but they also needed to make sure they weren't about to be gunned down. If necessary, they would have to take cover before they even reached the house.

The little boy wasn't out and out crying, but he was whimpering. Probably because he'd picked up on their fear and because the running was jostling him. Cameron tried to ignore the sounds he was making, and he got them on the porch. He had to fumble in his pocket to get his keys to unlock the door, but the moment he did that, he pushed them inside.

"Get on the floor," he ordered.

Cameron relocked the door, set the security alarm and went to the window to keep watch. He also fired off a text to Gabriel, asking him to come over. Lauren's brother didn't live far and could be there in minutes if he hadn't already left for work. If so, then Gabriel would have to drive back.

A lot could happen in those extra minutes it would take Gabriel to do that.

Cameron still had a much too clear image of the bandage on Lauren's shoulder where she'd been shot. Those goons could be returning now to finish her off.

Lauren scrambled to the nanny, taking Patrick into her arms and pulling him close. There were tears in her eyes again, and she was trembling. The nanny wasn't faring much better. Hell, neither was he. Cameron wasn't trembling the way they were, but he was worried because they had two babies in the house, and he might not be able to protect them if those gunmen started shooting.

"I saw an SUV coming up the trail," the nanny said. Her breath was gusting so hard that it was difficult to understand her. "I couldn't drive off since there were trees blocking the way so I got out and started running with Patrick."

Yeah, there were downed trees back there. Probably shrubs, too, since it wasn't a trail that was often used.

"It could turn out to be nothing," the nanny added in a hoarse whisper. "They might not be the men who were after us."

Judging from her tone, she didn't think that was true. Neither did Cameron. It was too much of a coincidence for someone to show up on that trail so soon after Lauren had been shot.

"Did you get a glimpse of anyone in the SUV?" he asked the woman.

"Barely. I could just make out the outline of the driver behind the tinted glass. I think there was another man in the passenger seat."

Maybe the same two who had attacked Lauren in Dallas. If so, they'd come a long way. And they had probably had some inside help since Lauren had been right about the trail. Not many people outside the area knew it existed. Of course, a police officer might know because they could have tapped into the area maps that were in the database at San Antonio PD.

Hell, he hoped they weren't dealing with dirty cops.

"Is everything okay?" someone called out from the other side of the house. Merilee.

That tightened the knot in his stomach. He could tell Merilee was terrified, as well. She'd been Isaac's nanny right from the start, and since there'd already been two attacks on the ranch, she knew something was wrong.

"Just stay put in the nursery," Cameron settled for saying. He didn't want to unnecessarily alarm the woman even though she was probably well past the alarm stage already.

Cameron also had a second reason for keeping Merilee and Isaac where they were. This way, Lauren wouldn't see Isaac. Of course, she would see him soon enough, but right now he needed her to focus. If Lauren saw him and truly believed he was her son, then she might fall apart.

"Hand Patrick to Dara," Cameron told Lauren. "I need you to keep watch at the window on the side of the house."

He hated to ask her to do that, but right now she was their best bet. Besides, he knew Lauren could shoot since he'd been the one to teach her.

She gave a shaky nod, passed the baby back to the nanny and with a tight grip on her gun, she went to the window near the breakfast table. He didn't have to remind her to stay back. She did. Lauren positioned herself against the side of the glass so she could still peer out.

"Nothing," she relayed to him.

It was the same from his view. That didn't mean the men weren't out there, though. Lauren had been out there for a while before he'd spotted her. Plus, it was possible the men were regrouping, maybe calling for their own backup so they could storm the place and take the baby.

But why?

That was something he intended to find out once they were out of any immediate danger.

Behind him, Patrick started fussing, and he made the mistake of glancing back at the boy. Cameron hadn't been able to see his face earlier when the nanny was running toward them. He saw it now, though.

Oh, man.

It felt like someone had knocked the breath right out of him. The kid had blond hair, and those were definitely the Doran gray eyes. In fact, the resemblance was close enough that Patrick could have been mistaken for Cameron's own son. He wasn't.

But the boy was his nephew.

Cameron silently cursed. This was not what he wanted in his head right now, but it was a fight to keep the thoughts at bay. What the hell was he going to do?

He forced his attention back to the window just as the sound shot through the room. Clearly, everyone was on edge because both Lauren and the nanny gasped. But it wasn't a shot being fired. It was just his phone ringing, and Cameron saw Gabriel's name on the screen. Good. Maybe that meant the sheriff was there.

Cameron put the call on speaker, laying his phone on the counter so his hands would be free in case there was an attack.

"What the hell is going on?" Gabriel demanded the moment he came onto the line.

Since he wasn't going to have time to get into everything, Cameron went with the short version. "Lauren's here, and some men are after her. They tried to kill her."

Gabriel cursed, but he quickly reined it in, no doubt because he realized his kid sister was listening. "Any reason she came to you and not me?"

Gabriel didn't rein in his emotions on that question. Cameron heard the anger come through loud and clear. The emotion was in Lauren's expression, too. Her forehead was bunched up, and she had her still-trembling bottom lip clamped between her teeth. With everything else she was facing, she probably didn't want a show-down with her brother, as well, but it was going to be on the agenda whether she wanted it or not.

"I'll explain it all later," Cameron told him, but he had to raise his voice to speak over Patrick. The baby was fussing even louder now. "The men who are after Lauren will be in an SUV," he added to Gabriel. "It's possible they're on the trail behind my house."

"They're not. I just spotted a black SUV coming up from the back of my folks' old place."

Cameron bit back a groan. The trails coiled all around the ranch, and the men had obviously found a way out of the woods. That meant they could be trying to escape so they could regroup and come at Lauren again. As much as Cameron hated the notion of that, at least it would give him a chance to get the babies, nannies and her to a safe place.

"The SUV isn't moving," Gabriel went on, "and I can't tell if anyone is still inside it. They could have already gotten out and slipped onto the ranch grounds."

Not exactly a comforting thought, but Gabriel was right. Cameron didn't know how long it'd taken the nanny to get to Lauren and him, but the thugs could have driven off the moment she started running. If so, that would have given them plenty of time to get to the old Beckett house, and then the chance to escape.

Or sneak up on Cameron's house.

"I've stopped on the road and am waiting for Jameson," Gabriel continued a moment later. "Once he's here, we can go closer. Why do they want Lauren?" he tacked onto that.

"She's not sure yet." But it gnawed away at him to

think it could be because of his sister's scummy dead boyfriend. "Just give me a heads-up if you see these clowns."

"Will do. Is that Isaac crying?"

"No. It's… Lauren's son." Cameron hadn't meant to hesitate, but it'd just seemed to stick in his throat.

Gabriel's silence let Cameron know it hadn't been easy for him to hear. That was probably because Lauren hadn't bothered to introduce her son to the rest of her family. Even though things had been strained between Lauren and him since their parents' murders, it still had to cut Gabriel to the core. For him, it was all about family, and he'd worked damn hard to bring his siblings back to their birthplace.

Cameron ended the call, and he went to the back door to look out the small windows there. The angle was better for giving him a view of the opposite side of the yard that Lauren was watching. The SUV was the other direction, but it didn't mean the thugs couldn't have brought some help along.

"I think I see something," Lauren said.

That sent Cameron running to her, and he followed her pointing finger in the direction of the far side of his barn. Since the barn was closer to the old Beckett house than Cameron's, it would be a likely place for someone to hide.

But he didn't see anything.

"I'm obviously on edge," Lauren admitted. "It could have been my imagination."

She looked up at him at the exact moment he looked down at her, and it seemed as if there was something else she wanted to say to him. An apology, maybe, but the silence said it all. Because she'd been giving him the silent treatment for the past decade. No reason for this to be any different.

He kept watch, but even though he didn't see anything, it didn't mean someone wasn't out there. Which made him rethink their position. There were way too many windows in this part of the house. Plus, it was hard to hear anything with Patrick crying.

"Stay low," Cameron instructed the nanny, "but take the baby to the nursery. It's the first room off the hall." He tipped his head in that direction. "Go with them," he added to Lauren.

But she shook her head. "You need me to help you keep watch. I don't want those men getting in the house."

Neither did he, but Cameron had figured she'd want to be with her baby. And she probably did. However, like him, Lauren almost certainly knew things could turn on a dime.

"Merilee?" he called out. "A woman and little boy are joining you in the nursery. Once they're in there, lock the door, and all of you get down on the floor."

"What's happening?" Merilee asked. "Are you okay?"

"I'm fine. Lauren is here," he said after a pause.

Merilee would remember Lauren since she'd been the Beckett housekeeper all the way up until the time of the murders. Lauren's mom was a former cop who also worked the ranch, and Merilee had been a pseudonanny to Lauren and her siblings.

He nearly asked about Isaac, to make sure his nephew was all right, but right now Cameron only wanted to focus on what was going on outside. Besides, if something had been wrong in the nursery, Merilee would have let him know.

"Thank you," Lauren whispered.

Cameron was about to tell her not to thank him yet, but the movement stopped him cold. This time he saw what Lauren had almost certainly spotted by the barn.

A man.

He only got a glimpse of him, but the guy was wearing camo. Definitely not a ranch hand.

"He's got a gun," Lauren relayed to Cameron.

Yeah, he'd seen it, too. Again, just a glimpse, but it appeared to be a rifle. Not good because it gave the intruder a longer range that he could use to shoot into the house.

Without taking his attention off the man, Cameron pressed redial on his phone, and Gabriel answered on the first ring.

"Jameson's here," Gabriel explained. "We're going to the SUV now."

"Don't. One of the shooters is here at my place by the side of my barn. I figure he's not alone."

Gabriel made a sound of agreement followed by some profanity. "Okay, we're on the way to your place. I'll also get some of the hands over there."

"Tell them to be careful. The guy is armed, and he's in position to pick off anyone who comes up the road to my house."

And that was probably the reason he was there. Which made that bad feeling inside him go up a significant notch. If these goons knew the trail, maybe they'd watched the place. Perhaps his house. It wouldn't have been hard to do. On any given day there were at least two dozen hands working the ranch along with deliveries and the normal traffic that came with a place this size.

There could be gunmen waiting to ambush Gabriel, Jameson and anyone else who came this way.

Because if their ultimate goal was to get the baby, then it wouldn't matter how many people they killed.

He hated to put something else on Lauren's shoulders, but he needed an extra pair of eyes at the front of the house. That meant he'd have to stay to keep watch of the thug by the barn. Cameron was about to give her instructions as to what to do, but the blur of motion stopped him.

There was a second gunman at the back of the barn.

Unlike his partner, this one didn't immediately duck back behind cover. He lifted his rifle and fired. The shot crashed through the window right where Cameron was standing.

Chapter Four

Lauren shouted for Cameron to get down, but it was already too late. The gunman had fired the shot, the bullet blasting through the window.

In the blink of an eye, she saw a piece of glass slice across Cameron's arm. He was wearing a shirt, and she could immediately see the blood start to spread across the sleeve.

She ran to him, but Lauren wasn't quite able to reach his arm. That was because Cameron took hold of her and dragged her to the floor. But he didn't stay there. He got right back up and took aim out the now gaping hole in the window.

"You're hurt," she said, her breath gusting so hard that Lauren had trouble speaking.

"I'm okay," he grumbled.

But she had no idea if that was true. She couldn't tell if the glass was still in his arm or not because of all the blood.

From the other side of the house, Lauren heard a sound she didn't want to hear. Patrick was crying. Probably because the noise from the gunshot had frightened him. She considered going to him, but she didn't want to leave Cameron alone. She got confirmation that would be a bad idea when two more shots came through the window. These slammed into the side of the fridge.

"Merilee!" Cameron called out to the nanny. "All of you need to get down on the floor and stay there." He glanced at her then, letting Lauren know that applied to her, too.

However, she shook her head. "If I go to the side window, I might have a clear shot and be able to stop the gunman."

"Yeah, and he might have a shot to stop you. Stay down," he repeated, this time through clenched teeth. She couldn't tell if the tight expression was for her or because he was grimacing in pain.

Lauren huffed. She'd forgotten just how stubborn Cameron could be, but this brought it all back. Worse, he didn't stay out of the line of fire. He leaned away from the wall, took aim out the window and pulled the trigger.

The blast echoed through the room. Through the entire house. And Lauren heard both babies cry. She prayed the nannies could keep the boys as calm as possible, but better yet, she just wanted the women to protect them so that none of the bullets could make it to them.

Her son was in danger.

Both her sons.

Because Isaac might be hers by blood, but Patrick was also hers in every way that mattered. Now the babies were at huge risk, and she didn't even know why. That was what cut away at her right now. That, and the bullets that continued to tear into the house.

She thought of what Cameron had said earlier. About Trace's mother, Evelyn, pulling a gun on him. And Lauren wondered if she was behind this. But she couldn't be. For one thing, the woman was in jail, and for another, she wanted custody of her grandson and almost certainly wouldn't put him at risk like this.

But Julia or Duane were capable of that.

They wouldn't have nearly the level of concern for Patrick or any other child that Evelyn likely would. In fact, it would make things easier for Julia or Duane if Lauren and her son were out of the way.

That certainly didn't help her raw nerves.

However, there was a third player in all of this. The idiot who was sending those threatening messages to her and her family. If so, they didn't have a clue who they were dealing with, and that person might not care if everyone inside the house died in a gunfight.

Cameron fired another shot, and he followed it with some profanity. "He's ducked back behind the barn."

Probably because Cameron's shots were getting too close to him. Lauren doubted, though, that the man was retreating. No. He was probably regrouping or else contacting his comrade so he could come at them from a different angle.

Cameron ran to the side of the room where Lauren had been earlier, but the moment he made it to that window, the gunman sent more bullets their way. That created yet another spray of glass over the room and caused Cameron to scramble back. Thankfully, he didn't get cut this time, and the bleeding on his arm seemed to be slowing down. Still, he needed medical attention. That wasn't going to happen, though, until those gunmen were stopped. No way could an ambulance risk coming to the house, since they would drive right into gunfire.

Cameron's phone rang, the sound somehow making it through the deafening blasts. He glanced at the screen and tossed it to her. "It's Gabriel. Let him know what's going on and find out his location."

Lauren cursed her trembling hands because it took her precious seconds to hit the answer button, and she put it on speaker so that Cameron could hear.

"Is everyone okay?" Gabriel asked right off.

"No. Cameron's hurt. His arm is bleeding—"

"I'm fine," Cameron snarled. "I've got a shooter by the barn and another out by the road."

That sped up her heartbeat even more because her brothers would be coming up that road to get to them. She prayed they didn't get hurt, or worse.

"Yeah, I've already spotted the one on the road," Gabriel answered. "That's why Jameson and I stopped. The guy's in the ditch. If he lifts his head enough, Jameson can take him out."

Good. Except that would mean Jameson would have to take a huge risk to do that. Lauren had no idea if that guy was firing at her brothers or not. It was hard to tell with all the bullets flying.

"What about you?" Gabriel continued. "Can you shoot the one by the barn?"

"Haven't managed it so far, but I can't keep letting him fire bullets into the house."

No, they couldn't. Each one was a huge risk to the babies. And that meant she needed to push aside her fears and do something. She was the daughter and sister of a sheriff and had had firearms training. While she certainly didn't have experience in finishing off hired guns, she had plenty of motivation to put an end to this.

"Are there only two of them?" Gabriel asked a moment later.

Good question, and she could tell from Cameron's

frustrated sigh that he didn't know the answer. "Two men attacked your sister last night and shot her in the arm so I'm guessing it's the same pair."

Gabriel cursed again, and Lauren recognized that tone after all these years. He was furious, and that fury wasn't limited to only these men, either. As her brother and the sheriff, he would have expected her to come to him with this. Later, she'd need to explain why she hadn't done that. But that would have to wait.

"I can try to distract the shooter by firing out the kitchen window," Lauren offered. "That way Cameron can try to get him from the front of the house."

That offer didn't please Cameron. It earned her a scowl, but she gave him one right back. "As you said, we can't let him keep firing shots."

She could see the debate Cameron was having with himself about that, but before he could say anything, his phone beeped, indicating he had another call coming in.

"It's from an unknown number," she relayed to him.

"Answer your phone, Deputy," the gunman shouted from outside. The shots also stopped. "We gotta talk."

"The thug by the barn is calling me," Cameron told Gabriel. "While I see what he wants, try to do something about the guy in the ditch. I don't want him getting any closer to the house."

"We'll do what we can," Gabriel assured him.

Lauren pressed the button to take the second call, and she crawled even closer to Cameron so he wouldn't miss a word of what this snake had to say.

"Are you ready to put an end to this?" the gunman asked without any hesitation. "Because I've got a solution that'll make sure your nephew and that other little boy don't get hurt."

"Who are you?" Cameron snapped.

"You don't need to know my name to listen to what I got to say."

"No, but I do need to know who hired you so I can put his or her butt in jail for multiple accounts of attempted murder."

The guy chuckled. "Let's just say that's not gonna happen and move on. You want me to stop shooting up your house, then here's what you have to do. Put Lauren on the phone so the two of us can talk this out."

A chill slid through her. Of course the goon knew she was there, but it was still stomach-twisting to hear him say her name. She opened her mouth to tell him she was listening, but Cameron shook his head and shot her a warning glance.

"Anything you think you need to say to Lauren, you can say to me," Cameron told the gunman.

"I don't think so. Something tells me you're not gonna be nearly as easy to reason with as she'll be." Considering his casual tone, he could have been discussing the weather, but Lauren knew there was nothing casual about any of this.

"You want money, is that it?" she asked.

That didn't please Cameron. No surprise there. He mumbled some profanity and hurried to the other side of the window—probably hoping he could get off a shot while the gunman was talking.

"Money?" the gunman repeated as if it was a joke. "No, sugar. Money ain't gonna fix this."

She hated his flippant attitude and wished she could be the one to silence him. But Lauren wanted that silence only after they'd learned who had hired this monster. Then him, his partner and his boss could be arrested.

"What, then?" she demanded, and Lauren hoped she sounded less shaky than she felt.

"I want you, sugar."

For just a handful of words, they packed a punch along with making her skin crawl. She wasn't sure if he'd meant for it to sound sexual or not.

"All you have to do is walk out the back door," the gunman continued. "Of course, I'm gonna want your hands in the air so I can make sure you don't have a gun. And I'll also want you to tell the deputy that he's out of the picture right now."

"You're not going out there," Cameron told her before the gunman had even finished.

"Figured you'd feel that way, but just think about those little kids. Do I hear them crying? Bet they're real scared, but they're gonna get a lot more scared when I start shooting again. Because once I start, I won't stop until I've ripped your place to shreds. You got thirty seconds, or the bullets start up again."

Lauren sucked in her breath so hard that she nearly choked, and she managed to get to her feet.

"No." Cameron hurried toward her, catching on to her and pulling her down against the fridge. He also took his phone from her and hit the end call button. "He'll gun you down the moment you step outside."

She shook her head, not disputing that since she figured that was exactly what would happen. Someone wanted her dead.

"But if I don't go out there, he'll shoot into the house," she reminded Cameron, though she was certain he hadn't forgotten that.

"He'll do it anyway." He took hold of her chin, lifting it and forcing eye contact. Brief eye contact, just enough for her to see the determination in his eyes before he went back to the window to keep watch. "Think it through. He'll have to kill me, too, so he can escape. In fact, this plan could be about me. A way to draw me out while using you. Because that snake knows I won't let you go to your death."

That last part was definitely true. Cameron wasn't a coward, and he was married to that badge he had clipped to his holster. He would put his own life ahead of hers or anyone else's that he needed to protect.

She tried to figure out if that was indeed what the gunman had in mind, but the thoughts were flying through her head, making it hard to think. The only thing that was coming through loud and clear was that she had to do something, anything, to save the babies.

Cameron glanced around, too, as if trying to sort out what to do, and he finally tipped his head to the front of the house. "Take your gun and go to the window in there. Stay to the side, but if you get a shot, take it."

She didn't thank him. In fact, Lauren didn't say anything for fear he would change his mind. As she was leaving, she heard him make a quick call to Gabriel to tell him to do something to eliminate the guy in the ditch.

Lauren's pulse was thudding so hard now that it was hard to hear, and her feet felt heavy, as if she was trudging through mud. Still, she moved as fast as she could and tried to ignore the sounds of the babies crying. She had to focus, had to do her part to make this right. Then she could deal with the fallout of the baby swap and everything else that her homecoming would cause.

There were three windows in the living room. A huge one that faced the front and two side ones that had a view of the barn. She went to the one that she hoped would give her the best vantage point.

It did.

She immediately caught a glimpse of the gunman, and he was lifting his rifle, pointing it right at the house. That put her heart in her throat. She hadn't needed anything to add to the urgency of their situation, but that did it anyway.

Lauren didn't waste even a second. She broke the glass with the barrel of her gun and took aim. The gunman shifted his position, trying to turn his weapon at her. But it was too late.

She fired.

And she was right on target. The bullet slammed into the guy's chest. He stayed there, frozen and crouched, his rifle ready, but neither he nor his gun moved. So, Lauren shot him again.

He finally dropped like a stone.

Despite the fact that she'd probably just killed a man, she only felt relief and not the emotion of having just taken a life. That was because if he'd been given the chance, he would have killed them all.

She heard the footsteps, hurrying toward her. Cameron. From his angle in the kitchen, he probably hadn't been able to see the fall, but he certainly saw it now. There was no relief on his face, though, because they heard something else.

Another shot.

This one hadn't come from the barn. It had come from the front of the house, and it wasn't a single shot, either. Three more quickly followed.

There was no trace of relief now for Lauren. Because she knew her brothers were in the general direction of that fresh round of bullets. Maybe the gunman's partner had figured out what had gone on by the barn and was now trying to take out anyone that he could.

Lauren turned to run to the front window, but Cameron moved in front of her. "Watch the guy you shot and make sure he doesn't get up."

She was about to tell him that she doubted that could happen, but there was more gunfire. Then Cameron cursed when he looked out the front window.

"Change of plans," he said. "Get down now."

There was more than enough urgency in his voice for Lauren to drop to the floor, but she'd barely had time to do that when Cameron threw open the front door. The security system started to beep, indicating the alarm was about to go off. He ignored that, though, aimed his gun and fired. He got off four rounds before he stopped pulling the trigger.

Lauren waited, praying and afraid to ask what had happened. Several moments later she heard something she actually wanted to hear.

Gabriel's voice.

"Is everyone okay?" her brother called out.

Since the babies were still fussing, Lauren knew they were alive, but she got up to hurry to the nursery to make sure. But she stopped when she saw the chaos in front of Cameron's house.

Two men dressed in camo were sprawled out by the ditch. The one nearest the house was clearly dead, but the other one was still moving around. Both Jameson and Gabriel had their weapons drawn and were closing in on him.

Her stomach sank. Lauren hadn't even known about the third gunman. He could have attacked them from the front while the thug by the barn was keeping them occupied. Thank God Cameron and her brothers had spotted him and stopped him from doing any more harm.

"I had to shoot him," Cameron said. He pressed in the numbers on the security key pad to stop the beeping. "I didn't have a choice."

It took her a moment to realize why that sounded like an apology. It was because two of their attackers were dead, and the third one was injured. Maybe even dying. Dead men wouldn't be able to tell them the person or the reason behind what had just happened.

"Stay inside," Cameron added. "But keep watch to make sure there aren't others."

Lauren hadn't exactly relaxed, but that put her back on high alert again. So did the fact that Cameron hurried outside. Where he could be gunned down like her brothers if there were other thugs hiding.

Even though Cameron had told her to stay inside, Lauren got her gun ready and stepped into the doorway so she'd have a better view of the yard and road. Her brothers were already by the injured man by the time Cameron reached them. She could see them talking, but she couldn't hear what they were saying.

But she had no trouble seeing the alarm on Cameron's face.

Whatever the man had said to him had caused Cameron's shoulders to snap back. Her brothers had similar reactions, and Gabriel took out his phone as he made his way to the house. Cameron and Jameson were right behind him. That was when Lauren realized the injured man was no longer moving.

Gabriel made eye contact with her, and while he continued his phone conversation, he caught on to her arm and maneuvered her back inside the house.

"What about the man?" she asked.

"He's dead," Cameron told her the moment he reached the porch.

The sickening feeling of dread went through her. "Did he say anything?" But Lauren fully expected that answer to be no.

It wasn't.

Cameron nodded. "He gave us the name of the person who hired him." His mouth tightened when he made eye contact with Lauren. "The gunman said it was *you*."

Chapter Five

"I didn't hire those men," Lauren repeated.

It wasn't necessary for her to keep saying that. Cameron hadn't believed it from the moment the thug had tossed out that stupid accusation. Those men had been firing real bullets into the house as well as at Lauren and him, and there was no way she would have put her son in danger that way.

Either son.

Because Cameron was also certain she was already thinking of both boys as hers. They weren't. But that was something they would have to sort out later.

For now, they needed to get to the bottom of why the attack had happened. Gabriel and Jameson were already on that. Lauren's brothers were outside with the medical examiner and the CSIs. The ambulance, too. There'd been no need for medical assistance for the gunmen—they were all dead. But the medics were apparently there for Lauren and him.

Whether they wanted them there or not.

Cameron certainly didn't. He wanted to be outside with the other lawmen, trying to get answers, but instead he was on the sofa in his living room while a medic stitched up his arm. Another medic was checking out Lauren's gunshot wound, as well.

"This isn't necessary," Lauren insisted. It was yet something else she'd been repeating.

Cameron didn't bother to voice his complaint since Gabriel had told him he wouldn't be returning to work until the medic gave him the okay. So far, the guy wasn't okaying anything. He was causing Cameron plenty of pain with each stitch. Of course, that was a small price to pay considering they were all alive and, for the most part, well.

"Is it okay if we come out now?" Merilee called out.

It had been well over a half hour since the attack had ended. If the thugs had brought any other hired guns with them, those guys would probably be long gone. But it still seemed too big of a risk to take.

"Let's call this finished," Cameron told the medic, and even though the guy gave him a hard look, he put in the last stitch and slapped on a bandage.

"Stay put. I'll come to the nursery," Cameron added to Merilee.

That got Lauren moving, too, and despite the fact that the medic was still dabbing something on her arm, she jerked away from him, following Cameron when he started out of the living room and up the hall. Both medics grumbled something that Cameron didn't bother to hear. He needed to see Isaac to make sure for himself that both boys were all right.

Lauren was right on his heels when Cameron knocked on the door. Merilee must have been right there waiting because she opened up right away. She didn't have Isaac in her arms, but Cameron spotted him. He was on the floor, playing with Patrick. Dara was next to both of them.

Cameron felt the punch of relief. Yes, he'd known the boys hadn't been harmed. He'd gotten that reassurance minutes after the attack when he'd been able to talk to Merilee. So had Lauren. But she also must have needed more because she hurried to the boys, kissing them both.

Kisses that got Merilee's attention.

The nanny looked at him, her eyebrow raised. "I'll explain later," Cameron whispered to her. "Thanks for keeping them safe."

"Is it actually safe?" Merilee questioned before Cameron could step away.

"No," he admitted after a pause. "We don't know who hired those men."

And he needed to figure out what to do about that. His house was in too vulnerable of a spot on the ranch since it was backed up against the woods and those trails. Added to that, there were now broken windows, so he would need to move Lauren, the boys and the nannies. First, though, he needed to see Isaac.

The boys were no longer fussing. In fact, they were looking a little confused—Isaac, especially—at the long hug that Lauren was giving them. When Cameron sank down on the edge of one of the chairs, Isaac scooted out of her grip and immediately went to him.

"Nunk," Isaac babbled. It was his attempt at uncle, and it always made Cameron smile. Even more. And while he hugged Isaac often, this hug was especially needed.

Of course, Isaac didn't let the hug go on for long. He was a kid always on the go, and the moment Cameron stood him on the floor, Isaac toddled his way back to Patrick. He dropped down next to him, where there was a huge pile of toy cars and horses.

Seeing them side by side put a knot in Cameron's stomach. If he'd had any doubts about the baby swap, he didn't have them now. He could see his sister, and himself, in Patrick's face, while Isaac was a Beckett. Cameron hadn't seen it before because he hadn't been looking for it.

Hell.

What was he going to do now?

Lauren looked up at him at the exact moment that Cameron looked at her. She didn't say anything, but she seemed to be waiting for something. Maybe for him to offer some perfect solution to fix all of this. But at the moment he was drawing a blank because the one thing he wasn't going to do was give up the little boy he'd been raising for over a year. He couldn't have loved his own son more than he loved Isaac.

Cameron automatically reached for his gun again when he heard someone coming up the hall. He stood, stepping in front of the others, but it wasn't a threat this time. It was Gabriel and Jameson.

Lauren stood, slowly, and she rubbed her hands along the sides of her jeans. Her brothers didn't exactly run to her, either, and Cameron figured they needed some time to hash this out. After all, Lauren had basically abandoned them, but again, that was something that would have to wait.

"Cameron told us about the possible baby switch," Gabriel said, his voice not exactly warm and fuzzy.

She looked at Cameron, probably wondering when he'd had a chance to do that. It'd been in the yard when he'd managed to have a very short conversation with Gabriel while they were waiting for the medics to arrive. And Cameron had indeed added that word—*possible*. But Gabriel and Jameson were no doubt seeing what Cameron had—Patrick's resemblance to them.

Jameson huffed, went to Lauren and pulled her into his arms. "You shouldn't have stayed away," he whispered to her, but since the room was suddenly quiet, Cameron had no trouble hearing.

"I couldn't," she answered. When Lauren pulled back, she was blinking back tears. "Not after what happened to Mom and Dad. I just couldn't stay."

Gabriel didn't argue with that. Not with his voice anyway. But that wasn't exactly a forgiving look in his eyes.

Of course, Cameron hadn't expected there to be. Like Gabriel and Jameson, he'd stayed in Blue River. He'd dealt with the aftermath, had helped put a killer behind bars and then had tried to pick up the pieces and use them to build a new life. Lauren hadn't done that, and it'd cut Gabriel to the core that he hadn't been able to keep the family together.

"Uh, should Dara and I take the boys to one of the other rooms?" Merilee asked after glancing at Gabriel's expression.

"No," Lauren answered without hesitation. Cameron agreed. He didn't want the babies out of his sight for now. If Lauren's brothers were going to have words with her, they'd have to keep it G-rated.

Lauren kissed Jameson on the cheek, and she went to Gabriel. Her steps were tentative and so was the kiss on the cheek she gave him.

"I don't expect you to understand what I did," she

said, her voice a little shaky now. "And I'm sorry for bringing this danger to the ranch."

Gabriel stared at her, the muscles in his jaw battling each other. He seemed to be ready to start that tirade that was bubbling inside him, but he reached out, pulled Lauren to him and kissed the top of her head. It would have been a perfect moment if Lauren hadn't winced. It wasn't from the kiss, though. It was because of the pressure the hug was putting on her injured arm.

She stepped back, both her and Gabriel's gazes going to the fresh bandage, and Cameron figured Gabriel would have cursed if it hadn't been for the little ears in the room.

"You should have come to me when the trouble started," Gabriel insisted.

Lauren shook her head. "I thought the men who did this were cops."

"They weren't," Gabriel said without hesitation. "And I don't need ID's on them to know that."

Jameson made a sound of agreement, went to the babies and sank down on the floor next to them. "The one who accused you of hiring him had a prison tat on his neck. Plus, this wasn't the kind of attack a cop would do. Not a smart cop anyway. If they'd been the real deal, they could have gone to your house, flashed their badges and gained entry that way. You're the daughter and sister of cops, and you would have let them in."

Now it was Lauren who made a sound of agreement after making a soft moan. "I panicked. I didn't want them to get to Patrick."

Gabriel nodded. "Panicking is exactly what they wanted you to do because it caused you to run."

Her brother hadn't come out and said it, but he likely

believed that it'd caused Lauren to run to the wrong man—Cameron. In Gabriel's way of thinking, she should have gone to him, immediately, and that way he could have perhaps prevented this attack.

"So, how did this baby swap happen?" Jameson asked.

It was the question that had been repeating through Cameron's mind. "Gilly maybe orchestrated it," he admitted.

Gabriel looked ready to mumble some more profanity, but he bit it off when he glanced at the boys. "To protect her son from Evelyn and that scumbag boyfriend of hers."

Cameron hated that his sister had been in a position like that, and he also hated he hadn't been there to give her another option.

"We need to start from the beginning," Gabriel continued a moment later. "We'll need DNA tests on the boys—"

"I've already done one on Patrick," Lauren volunteered. "I'm waiting on the results now."

"Good. But we have to do Isaac's, as well, and we should repeat Patrick's, too, and compare it to Cameron's." Gabriel looked at Cameron as if questioning to see if he was opposed to that. He wasn't. What Cameron was opposed to, though, was the fallout.

"I love Isaac," Cameron admitted. He hadn't intended to say that aloud. It was stating the obvious, and that *obvious* was true for Lauren, too. She loved Patrick.

Gabriel didn't need for them to spell out where this would eventually lead. To some kind of custody issues. Maybe a huge legal battle if Lauren tried to go after both boys.

"If the DNA results prove there was a switch," Gabriel went on, "then the next step will be to get hospital surveillance footage to see if we can spot who's responsible. In the meantime, I can get someone to the jail to question Evelyn."

"I can do that," Jameson volunteered, and he stood, taking his cell from his pocket. He was about to make a call, but the ringing shot through the room. Not Jameson's phone, though, but Lauren's.

She looked at her phone screen as if steeling herself up for what she might see there. Probably because she thought this could be another attacker. But she didn't look afraid. She groaned, a sound of frustration.

"It's Julia," she explained. "My late husband's sister."

Good. While it was obvious Lauren didn't want to talk to the woman, Cameron wanted to hear what she had to say. Especially since Julia could be a suspect in this. Of course, the most obvious person was Evelyn, and it didn't matter if she was locked up. People could do all sorts of bad things from behind bars.

"She calls you often?" Cameron asked.

"Rarely. And it's never a pleasant conversation. We talk mainly through our lawyers these days."

Lauren stepped out of the room, but Cameron followed her. Anything that happened right now could be related to the investigation, and he wanted to hear what Lauren's sister-in-law had to say. Lauren obliged by putting the call on speaker. She also moved as far up the hall as she could go.

"What the hell is going on?" Julia immediately demanded. No wonder Lauren had been dreading this. The woman was clearly hostile.

"I was about to ask you the same thing," Lauren

countered without even pausing. "Someone tried to kill me, and I need to know if you had anything to do with that?"

"What? You'd better not be accusing me of something like that."

Cameron considered holding his tongue but then decided against it. "Lauren is fine, by the way. Good of you to ask."

"I don't care if she's fine," Julia spat out. "And who the hell are you anyway?"

"Deputy Cameron Doran," Lauren answered. If she was bothered by Cameron inserting himself into this conversation, she didn't show it. She just gave another weary sigh.

"Your old boyfriend." Julia said that as if Cameron were some kind of disease. "Yes, I know about you. I know everything about Lauren. She moaned out your name when she was under anesthesia after having an emergency appendectomy. *Cameron, Cameron*, she kept saying, so I did an internet search and found out you were a deputy in that hick town she comes from."

Cameron wasn't sure how to respond to that especially since the color began to rise in Lauren's cheeks. Maybe she hadn't wanted him to know that she'd thought about him over the years. It didn't mean anything, though. People in pain said all sorts of things that just happened to fall from their memories.

"Well, Deputy, are you the reason I had two cops at my house last night?" Julia demanded.

Cameron glanced at Lauren to see if she knew anything about that, but she only shook her head. "What cops?" Cameron pressed.

"How the heck should I know? Guys with badges. I

saw them on the security camera outside my house and didn't answer the door. That's because I figured Lauren had sent them."

Lauren huffed. "And why would I do that?"

"To upset me. To try to intimidate me into backing off from the lawsuit. But guess what? I'm not backing off. *Ever.* My brother and I built his company—together. You didn't have anything to do with that. And it should be mine."

"Obviously Alden didn't agree with that because he left the company to Patrick."

Julia cursed, and it was pretty raw. "Because he didn't have time to change his will before he died. You saw to that, I'm sure. Always bad-mouthing me to him."

"I didn't need to bad-mouth you." Unlike Julia, Lauren's voice was practically calm. "Alden knew what you were."

Julia's profanity got even worse. The woman had a temper, and even though Cameron didn't need any more incentive for her to be a suspect, that only made him realize he needed to start digging into Julia's financials.

"Alden was stupid," Julia went on. "You had him eating right out of your hand. Hell, the kid doesn't even look like him, and yet he was willing to hand over a fortune to him."

Everything inside Cameron went still, and he reached out and muted the call for a moment. "Does Julia know about the baby swap?"

"No." But then Lauren shook her head again. "At least she's never given me any indication that she knew."

Well, that comment was definitely some kind of *indication*.

Cameron unmuted the phone. "Did you hire gunmen to come after Lauren?" he came out and asked the woman.

"I'm not going to dignify that with a response. Just tell her to quit sending cops to my house."

"I didn't send them," Lauren insisted, but she was talking to the air because Julia launched into another verbal tirade.

"No one else would have had a reason to send them. It had to be you."

"They might not have been cops," Cameron interrupted. "The men who tried to kill Lauren pretended to be police officers. Your visitors could have come to your house to kill you."

Julia gasped. "Why?"

"I don't know," Cameron answered. "Maybe for the same reason they attacked Lauren. You said you saw the men on your security camera. Do you have footage we can study to see if we can try to identify them?"

"Maybe. I'll look." But she made it sound as if it'd be some big inconvenience. "Have you asked Duane if he has footage?"

Again, Lauren looked puzzled enough by Julia's comment that Cameron knew she was hearing this for the first time.

"Duane?" he questioned. Of course, Cameron had already heard the man's name. He was Alden's business partner, but he wasn't sure how the guy fit into this. Or even if he did fit.

"Duane Tulley," Julia snapped. "He called me about a half hour ago and said cops came to his house, too. He wasn't there. He was staying overnight with his girlfriend, but he has a remote security system and saw the men on the camera."

"Was it the same men who came to your place?" Cameron asked.

"Who knows. Maybe. Lauren, so help me, you'd better not be behind this."

"I'm not—" But that was all Lauren managed to say before Julia continued.

"Just keep me out of your problems. The lawsuit is going before a judge next month, and I don't want you playing games to try to sway this to your side."

Cameron was certain he looked just as puzzled as Lauren did. "You think I'd fake an attack to get sympathy from a judge?"

"Yes, I do." And with that, Julia ended the call.

Lauren stared at the phone for a moment before she gave a heavy sigh and slid it back into her pocket. "Now you know why I thought Julia could be behind this. My sister-in-law hates me."

No way could Cameron argue with that. "Just how much money is at stake in Alden's estate?"

"At least twenty million."

Well, hell. That was plenty of motive for Julia to do all sorts of things. Including hiring someone to murder Lauren. That would definitely get Lauren out of the way and would give Julia control not just of the money but Patrick, as well.

Or rather, Isaac.

It twisted his insides to think of that woman having any kind of claim on the baby Cameron loved.

"I'll have to speak to Duane," Cameron told her. "I not only need the security tapes but I'll also need to question him." Julia, too, of course. "I'm guessing Duane has motive for wanting you dead?"

Lauren nodded, pushed her hair from her face. "It

all goes back to the money. But if he could get Julia, Patrick and me out of the picture, Duane would inherit everything."

Cameron could see how that might play out. And that was playing out in a very bad way. "Duane could have hired those men to kill you with plans to set up Julia. Then he could use DNA proof to verify that Patrick isn't Alden's son."

He watched as Lauren processed that and saw the exact moment she followed that through to what could happen next.

Duane would need to make Isaac disappear.

Because Isaac could indeed be Alden's rightful heir.

Hell, he needed to bring Duane in ASAP, too. But first he had to work on making sure Lauren and the babies were safe.

"I'm sorry," Lauren said, drawing his attention back to her.

The apology irritated him since this wasn't her fault. Well, for the most part anyway. Gabriel was right that she should have gone to him when this had first started, but she certainly didn't need to be feeling any regret about that.

She blinked hard, obviously still fighting those tears, and Cameron had to do some fighting of his own. He wanted to pull her into his arms, to try to reassure her that all would be well. But it was best not to break down the barriers Lauren had put up when she'd left town. Besides, he wasn't ready to forgive himself, either, for letting Travis walk that night of the murders.

"Yes," she said as if she knew exactly what he was thinking.

Lauren touched his arm, rubbed gently and then

headed back toward the nursery. However, she didn't make it far before they spotted Jameson coming out of the room. He had a troubled look on his face.

Hell. What now?

"There could be a problem, and you both need to come back to the nursery," Jameson told them.

That got Lauren and Cameron moving plenty fast, but when they hurried into the room, the babies were fine. They were still playing on the floor, and the nannies were there with them. It looked like nothing was wrong.

Until he made eye contact with Merilee.

Cameron saw the fear again. The concern in Gabriel's expression, too.

"Evelyn's out of jail," Gabriel said. "And one of the hands just spotted her on the road that leads to your house."

Chapter Six

If someone had told Lauren two days ago that she'd be back at Gabriel's, she wouldn't have believed them. Yet, here she was. And not only was she dealing with the old memories of the murders, but she also had some new nightmares to add to the mix.

How was she going to keep the babies safe?

Gabriel had certainly done his part to make sure that happened. They'd moved both boys, the nannies, Cameron and her to his place. He'd assured her that he had a solid security system and that the hands would be patrolling the grounds. But Lauren wasn't sure that would be enough.

Especially with Evelyn out of jail.

Even though one of the hands had seen her near the ranch, she hadn't come to Cameron's or Gabriel's. Maybe because there had been cops and CSIs to scare her off. If she'd been the one behind the attack, she might not have realized all her hired guns had been killed, and she had possibly come with the hopes of snatching Isaac. Thankfully, that hadn't happened, but before Gabriel could get out to the road, the woman hadn't been there, either.

In fact, they didn't know where Evelyn was.

And that only added to Lauren's nightmarish thoughts.

She heard the footsteps outside the makeshift nursery that Gabriel and his wife, Jodi, had set up, and she reached for her gun. Which she no longer had. She'd put it on the top of the fridge because she didn't like the idea of having it on her when she was around the babies. But there was no reason for a gun anyway.

Because it was Cameron.

Like her, he'd spent most of the past two hours in the nursery, only stepping out to take calls. Lauren figured she should be making calls, as well, but she hadn't been able to tear herself away.

"They're still sleeping," Cameron whispered when his attention landed on the quilt where both boys were sacked out.

Hopefully, Dara was getting some rest in one of the guest rooms, as well. Merilee certainly was. She was napping on the daybed not far from the boys. With the high-stress day that they'd all had, Lauren figured the women were having a serious adrenaline crash. She certainly was and felt dead on her feet.

Cameron looked as exhausted as she did, and like her, he was probably having some pain. They'd declined the meds the medics had left for them, though. No way did she want her mind clouded any more than it already was.

"Anything on Evelyn?" She, too, kept her voice at a whisper even though the boys hadn't stirred even when there'd been other noises in the house.

He kept his attention fixed on the boys but shook his head. "But she's definitely out of jail. She was released on parole two days ago, and the board didn't bother to contact me to let me know."

Two days. Enough time to orchestrate all of this. But something about that wasn't right.

"If Evelyn was behind this, why come after Patrick and me?" Lauren asked.

"Maybe because she found out about the baby switch." Cameron answered so quickly that it meant he'd given this some thought. "If she knew Patrick was her grandson, she'd do anything to get him."

Yes. But Lauren was still having trouble thinking of Patrick as anything but her child. He wasn't. He was Gilly's biological son, and that meant Evelyn could have some kind of legal claim to him.

That thought nearly brought her to her knees.

Lauren staggered a little, catching on to the door frame to steady herself. Cameron also caught on to her by slipping his arm around her.

"You can't let this get to you," he said, maybe figuring out what she'd just realized. "Evelyn has a police record. No judge is going to give her custody."

"No clean judge. But Evelyn certainly has the money to pay one off. And hire as many fake cops and thugs as she wants."

The woman was a millionaire many times over, and that was probably why she hadn't spent much time in jail for pulling a gun on a cop. Still…

"If Evelyn wants her grandson so much, then why would she have put Patrick in danger like that?" she pressed.

He lifted his shoulder, and because he still had hold of her, it meant his arm slid against the side of her breast. He noticed, too, mumbled an apology and then eased away from her.

Lauren immediately felt the loss of no longer having him to support her. But it was a loss she shouldn't be feeling. She couldn't take that kind of comfort from Cameron. Not with this fire still simmering between them. A fire he was feeling, as well, she realized when their gazes connected.

He looked away from her, mumbled some profanity and then scrubbed his hand over his face. "Did you ever meet Evelyn?"

It was a good question, but she suspected he was asking to make sure they got their minds off that fire and back where it belonged—on figuring out who was behind the attacks.

"I met her once," Lauren answered. "It was at Gilly's apartment. I was there visiting your sister, and Evelyn showed up. Gilly wasn't pleased, and it wasn't a pleasant conversation. She wanted Gilly to have an amniocentesis done to prove the baby was her grandchild. Gilly refused. The test has risks, and there was no doubt in Gilly's mind that the baby was Trace's."

That gave her another jolt. Because the baby Gilly had been carrying had been Patrick.

"How did Gilly and you reconnect after you left Blue River?" he asked.

Lauren didn't have to think hard to remember that. "Gilly just rang my doorbell one day. She said she'd found me through an internet search and that she was moving to Dallas. We were both pregnant at the time, and she'd heard about my husband dying." Lauren paused. "Did Gilly tell you she'd moved near me?"

"No." His jaw tightened a little. "In fact, she didn't

mention you at all. I knew you were in Dallas. That came up once when Gabriel was trying to get in touch with you."

Yes, Gabriel had tried many times. And early on after she'd left, Gabriel had come to see her every other month or so. There'd been nothing recent, though. Maybe he'd given up on ever bringing her back to the ranch. Ironic that it was danger and not family that had caused her to return.

"You knew Gilly was afraid of Trace?" Cameron continued a moment later.

She nodded. "I think Gilly might have moved to Dallas because it was far away from Trace but close to me. I don't believe she wanted to go through the pregnancy alone, and before my parents' murders, Gilly and I had been close."

Not that she needed to tell Cameron about that. He knew she'd been best friends with his sister because Lauren had spent plenty of time at their house. His folks were no longer around, though. His mom had died when Cameron was only six, and his dad had left shortly after Cameron became a deputy. It hadn't been a huge loss for Cameron or Gilly since their father had spent more time drinking than being a dad. Lauren supposed his father felt Gilly would be in good hands so Cameron had ended up raising his sister.

And now he was raising her son.

Or so Cameron had thought.

Lauren took a deep breath, ready to bring up the subject of what they were going to do, but from the corner of her eye, she spotted Jameson making his way toward them. He was sporting the same serious expression that he'd had since her arrival.

"You have a visitor," Jameson said, motioning toward the front of the house. "Duane Tully. He says it's important."

Cameron groaned. "He's not inside, is he?"

Jameson lifted his eyebrow in a "no-way" expression. "He's parked in the driveway with two hands watching him to make sure he stays put. I told him if it's really that important, he should head straight to the sheriff's office. He's still one of our suspects, right?"

"He has motive to kill me," Lauren verified. "Why does he want to see me?"

"He won't say. That makes me want to arrest him and haul him to jail."

Lauren wouldn't mind the man being in jail, but right now Duane seemed the "safest" of their suspects. As far as she knew, he'd never been in jail, never pulled a gun on a cop and wasn't brimming with venom the way Julia was.

"Gabriel was going to question Duane anyway," Cameron pointed out. "And I'd want to listen to what he has to say. I'd rather not have to leave Lauren and the boys right now to do that. So maybe Gabriel can question him here? After Duane is searched for weapons, that is."

Lauren didn't like the idea of being under the same roof as the man, but it was better than the alternative. Plus, they needed to ask him about the so-called cops that'd come to his house.

"Merilee," Cameron said the moment Jameson gave them the go-ahead nod.

The nanny's eyes immediately flew open, and she sprang to a sitting position. "What's wrong?"

"Maybe nothing," Cameron assured her. "I just need

you to watch the babies while Lauren and I have a chat with someone."

Cameron waited until Merilee had gotten to her feet before he shut the door. Good. Isaac would probably nap for at least another half hour, and he would be cranky if he didn't get those extra minutes.

They went downstairs where Gabriel was waiting in the foyer. "You're seeing him?" he asked right off.

Lauren nodded.

Gabriel huffed. The kind of huff to indicate he wasn't sure this was the right thing to do. Lauren wasn't sure of that, either. But she did want to hear what Duane had to say. Besides, the house was as safe as the sheriff's office would be. Lauren could see armed ranch hands outside, and Jodi was at the front window—her gun drawn. She would no doubt watch to make sure Duane hadn't brought any hired guns with him, and since Jodi was a security specialist, she had nearly as much training as Gabriel.

"I'll frisk him," Gabriel grumbled. He glanced at his wife, a stay-safe warning passing between them, before he headed out.

When Gabriel opened the door, Cameron automatically pulled Lauren behind him, and Jameson stepped in front of her, as well. Again, they were risking their lives for her, and she hated that it'd come down to that. However, despite their quick maneuvering, she still managed to get a glimpse of Duane.

And he got a glimpse of her, too. Duane looked weary and not at all there to do battle with her. That was something, at least. Considering he'd filed a lawsuit against her for Alden's estate, she didn't expect him to be friendly, but maybe he could give them something to help with the investigation.

"Ivy called a little while ago," Jameson told her as they waited for Gabriel.

Ivy, her sister. Like plenty of other things about being at the ranch, her sister's name brought back more of those old memories. Mostly good. Once, Ivy and she had been close. But like Lauren, Ivy hadn't stayed in Blue River, either. She'd left shortly after the murders and had only recently come home.

"Ivy wants to see you," Jameson went on. "Theo and she are down in Houston clearing out her place there, but I told them that for now they should stay put."

Good. Lauren wanted to see her sister, as well, but it was too risky for Ivy to be here since she also had a son. There were already enough people in danger at the ranch.

"I'm sure you remember Theo," Jameson added. "Well, Ivy and he are engaged now."

That created some sudden tension in the foyer. Not because Ivy and Theo were back together. That didn't surprise Lauren. The two had always been in love. But Theo's father, Travis, was in jail for murdering Lauren's parents. Obviously, her sister had gotten past that if she was planning to marry Theo.

Lauren hadn't quite managed to do that, though. And that lack of getting over it involved Cameron. He didn't say anything—he didn't need to—but it was always there. Because he was the lone person who'd had the chance to stop Travis that horrible night, and he hadn't done it. One day Lauren would ask her sister how she'd put that all behind her, and then maybe she could do the same.

Jameson adjusted his stance again, and both Cameron and he slid their hands over their guns as Gabriel approached the house. He had his hand clamped around Duane's arm as if arresting the man.

"Lauren," Duane greeted. The moment he was inside, Gabriel shut the door and armed the security alarm.

Yes, the stress was definitely there, etched around Duane's eyes, and he wasn't the polished businessman that he usually was. He was wearing jeans and a casual shirt rather than the pricey suits that he favored.

"I heard about the attack from Julia," Duane said to her. "I came as soon as I could."

Lauren shook her head. "How'd you get here so fast?" His house was hours away in Dallas.

"I was already on my way. I wanted to talk to you after those cops showed up at my house last night. Julia said you sent them to harass me, but I figured there was more to it than that."

"I didn't send them," Lauren insisted. "And I have reason to believe they could have been hired killers."

"Yes, the sheriff mentioned that to me. You really think someone would want me dead?"

"I don't know," she answered honestly. "I also don't know who hired the men or why they came after me. But you should take precautions just in case."

Duane looked at all three lawmen, maybe to see if they agreed with that, and even though Cameron, Gabriel and Jameson didn't speak, Duane must have seen something on their faces to make him nod.

"I'll look into hiring a bodyguard." He took a piece of paper from his pocket and handed it to Gabriel. "That's the code to access the online storage for the footage from my security system. Maybe you can compare the faces of the men who came to my door to the ones who were killed here at the ranch."

Lauren hoped she was wrong, but the way Duane had said that last part almost made it seem as if he was sympathetic about the thugs who'd attacked them and been shot in the process.

"What about Julia?" Cameron asked Gabriel. "Has she turned over her footage?"

"Not yet." Gabriel looked at the paper and then went into the adjoining living room to use a laptop that was on the coffee table. Jodi stayed at the window, keeping watch.

"Don't expect Julia to just cooperate," Duane muttered. He made a sound of frustration. "Julia's the reason I wanted to come and talk to you face-to-face," he added to Lauren. But he didn't say anything else. He just stood there, glancing around as if trying to figure out what to do.

"Did Julia do something I should know about?" Lauren came out and asked. "Did she hire those men?"

"I honestly don't have any idea about that." Duane paused again. "But I do know she's getting desperate. Did you know she's practically broke?"

Lauren hadn't thought Duane could say anything that would surprise her, but she'd obviously been wrong. "No. And that doesn't sound right. Both Alden and Julia inherited huge trust funds—"

"Julia drained hers to pay off some bad investments," Duane interrupted. "She doesn't want anyone to know," he quickly added, "but a PI I hired learned about it when I had him looking into some background stuff for the lawsuit."

Since Duane had filed that lawsuit against Lauren, she very much wanted to hear this—and especially why he'd included Julia in it.

"How and what did the PI learn?" Cameron asked, taking the words right out of Lauren's mouth.

Duane glanced away from her again. Not a good sign.

"I was looking for something to prove you cheated on Alden," the man finally said. "Yes, I know it's a stretch, but I can't just hand over the company that I helped build."

"You're not handing it over. You still own twenty-five percent. As does Julia."

"And Patrick owns the rest, the majority share," Duane spelled out for her. "You know that Alden wanted me to run the company."

"I know no such thing," Lauren argued. "In fact, at the time of Alden's death, you two were at odds with each other. He didn't approve of some of the investments you'd made. Were they bad investments like Julia's?"

"No," Duane snapped, and he repeated it. "It was just a difference of opinion, something Alden and I would have worked out if he'd lived."

He stared at her as if waiting for her to say something. Maybe something about giving in to him and handing over Patrick's shares. But they weren't hers to give.

Heck, they weren't even Patrick's.

They were Isaac's.

If Duane knew that, he might be trying to get rid of the baby so he'd have a better shot at getting the company. Of course, Julia had an equal motive since she wanted her hands on the money from Alden's estate.

"Alden was my best friend," Duane went on, "and while you and I never really got along, I don't want to see his son harmed."

Lauren pulled back her shoulders so fast that it caused her stitches to pull, and the pain rippled through her. Cameron noticed, too, because he leaned in and made brief eye contact with her before his attention slashed to Duane.

"Explain that," Cameron demanded. "Who would want to harm his son?"

"Julia." This time Duane didn't hesitate. "The PI I hired not only learned she was nearly broke, but he also found out she's in debt to a loan shark. I think she's past being desperate and would do anything to get her hands on her brother's money.

"And the only way Julia could do that would be to kill Patrick and her. If Julia knew there was a possibility of a baby swap, then that could send her after Isaac, too.

"I know about the DNA test you had done on your son," Duane added. "Yes, I know it's snooping, but I'm desperate, too. Not like Julia, but I want to hang on to my company."

Cameron glanced at her, no doubt to see if she was aware that Duane knew about the test, and she wasn't.

"What DNA test?" Lauren asked. Yes, it was a lie for her to pretend she didn't know what he was talking about, but she didn't intend to confirm anything to Duane.

"The PI had someone follow you," Duane admitted. "He saw you go to the lab. He went in after you when the receptionist was logging in the information."

Sweet heaven. If the PI had found out about that, then

Julia could have, too. In fact, it was possible that Julia had had someone watching her, as well.

"The DNA test was for me," Lauren said. Again, it was a lie. "There were rumors my mother had had an affair, and I wanted to be sure that Sherman Beckett was really my father."

Duane couldn't have possibly looked more skeptical. Probably because Jameson and she were side by side, and the resemblance was definitely there. However, Duane hadn't known her folks so maybe he would think they resembled their mother.

"I'll have to send the footage to the crime lab for confirmation," Gabriel said, coming back into the foyer. "But I'm pretty sure the men who paid you a visit are the same ones who tried to kill us."

Some of the color drained from Duane's face. "Julia," he said through clenched teeth. "You have to stop her. Arrest her. Get her to confess."

"Give us everything your PI found out about her," Cameron fired back, "and maybe that'll be enough to get a warrant."

Maybe. Without proof, it would be just hearsay, but it was possible the PI had found something else.

Duane turned as if to leave, but he stopped and made eye contact with Lauren again. "The best way to stop Julia might be to settle the lawsuit with her. That could give her the money to pay the loan shark, and she might back off."

That was true if Julia was the one behind this. But Alden hadn't wanted his sister to have the money, and again, it wasn't Lauren's to give away. Still, it was something to consider if it would keep the babies out of danger.

"I suppose you want Lauren to settle the lawsuit with you, too," Cameron commented to Duane.

Duane shrugged, the answer obvious. "All I'm asking for is enough of the shares so I'll be majority holder. Her son can keep the rest. And it's only fair since it's my company."

That set her teeth on edge because it wasn't only his. And again, she didn't want to barter off Isaac's birthright. One day he might want to run his father's company. It would be easier for Lauren to give up the money since she had plenty of her own that she could pass onto her children, but if she gave Duane the company, she would never be able to get it back.

"I'll think about that and let you know what I decide," she settled for saying.

She expected Duane to look at least slightly optimistic about that. He didn't. He studied her expression as if trying to figure out if she would truly consider it, and then he mumbled something she didn't catch. Lauren didn't believe it was a compliment, though.

With a scowl on his face, Duane motioned for Gabriel to disarm the security system. Her brother did, and he closed the door behind the man. Gabriel also stood at the side windows, no doubt to make sure Duane left.

"Lawsuits?" Jameson repeated.

Lauren nodded. "Both Julia and Duane are suing me. Well, suing Patrick anyway." She paused. "If I can prove a baby swap, then the lawsuits will have to be refiled. That'll cause delays that neither Duane nor Julia will like."

"No," Cameron agreed.

Cameron didn't spell it out, but Lauren figured they were thinking the same thing. That it would be easier for Julia or Duane to eliminate Isaac. Or maybe even both boys.

"You believe what Duane said about Julia owing money to a loan shark?" Gabriel asked.

Lauren had to shrug. "I suppose it could be true. Alden always claimed Julia was irresponsible with money. That's one of the main reasons he didn't want to turn over any part of his estate to her. That, and he wanted Patrick…his son…to have it."

But if it was true about Julia's debts, then that made her even more dangerous.

"I'll get Julia in for questioning," Gabriel assured her.

She was about to tell Cameron and her brothers that they needed to do more to beef up security and they had to make sure neither Duane nor Julia got anywhere near the babies, but Cameron's phone rang before she could speak.

"It's Jace Morrelli," Cameron relayed when he looked at the screen.

Since Jace was another of Gabriel's deputies, that immediately snagged her attention. He could have updates on the investigation, and thankfully Cameron put the call on speaker so she could listen.

"Evelyn Waters just showed up here at the sheriff's office," Jace said without a greeting. "She's demanding to see Lauren and you."

"Is she armed?" Gabriel asked right off. "If she is, arrest her because it'll be a violation of her parole."

"I searched her. No weapons. But she's talking crazy. That's why I called you." It sounded as if Jace blew out a long breath. "She's claiming that Lauren swapped her baby with Gilly's, and Evelyn insists she can prove it."

Chapter Seven

Cameron wasn't sure if this was the right thing to do—bringing Lauren to the sheriff's office. But he'd figured since Evelyn was there and making wild accusations, then Gabriel and he might as well do an interview with not only her but Julia, as well.

Neither conversation would be pleasant.

Still, they were necessary. What wasn't necessary was for Lauren to be there, but she had insisted. Well, she had after Gabriel had assigned two deputies to guard the babies. With Jameson, Jodi and the hands there, as well, Cameron hoped it was enough protection so that hired thugs couldn't get to them.

"You can't go into the interview room," Cameron reminded Lauren when Gabriel pulled to a stop in front of the sheriff's office.

"I'm still going to talk to Evelyn," she insisted. "I want to know how she found out about the baby swap. And why she thinks I'm responsible for it."

Cameron could only sigh. She wanted to confront the woman—he got that—but Lauren had already been through hell and back, and Evelyn wasn't going to make this situation better. Even with that, Cameron doubted he could have stopped Lauren if he'd tried. If he'd been in her shoes, he would have wanted the same thing.

He opened the cruiser door, taking hold of Lauren's hand so he could get her inside as fast as possible. Gabriel did the same. Cameron had hoped they'd have a moment before they had to face the storm, but the "storm" was right there. Evelyn was in the squad room, seated next to Jace's desk, and she stood the moment she laid eyes on them.

Cameron hadn't thought that jail time would ease the hatred Evelyn had for him, and it hadn't. He could see plenty of it in her eyes, but this time the hatred wasn't just for him. No. The woman was aiming some of it at Lauren, too.

"You swapped the babies, didn't you?" Evelyn said, the emotion causing her voice to tremble.

Lauren shook her head. "I don't know what you mean. What swap?"

"You know. You damn well know," Evelyn snapped.

"Uh, you want me to hang around or should I get the interview room ready?" Gabriel asked.

"Definitely get the room ready," Cameron assured him. "Evelyn obviously has a lot to say." Maybe she'd say the wrong thing and implicate herself in the attacks.

Mumbling some profanity under his breath, Gabriel went toward the hall, where there were a pair of interview rooms and his office.

"I do have plenty to say," Evelyn verified. "Plenty to tell you about my grandson being swapped with Lauren's baby."

"Why would I do something like that?" Lauren fired right back at her.

"To keep Trace's son from me, that's why." She

shifted her attention to Cameron. "How long have you known and why didn't you tell me?" Evelyn's voice had gotten louder with each word.

"A reminder," Cameron warned her. "You're on probation. Keep your temper in check, or I will put you back in jail."

She stood there as if daring him to try that, and part of him wanted her to push this so he could lock her back up. Then she might not be a threat to the boys. But first he wanted Evelyn to explain some things.

"Why do you believe someone switched the babies?" Cameron asked.

Evelyn huffed as if the answer was obvious. And maybe it was. Maybe she'd seen a picture of Patrick. The boy didn't look like Trace, but he did resemble the Dorans.

"I got a phone call two days ago," Evelyn said. "The person didn't identify himself, but he said Lauren had done a DNA test on her baby, and the reason she'd done that was because he wasn't hers. He was Trace's."

Now it was Lauren's turn to sigh because she hadn't missed the timing of this. It was when the PI Duane hired had followed Lauren to the lab. Apparently, Cameron needed to have another chat with the man to find out why he'd involved Evelyn in this.

"The DNA test was for me," Lauren said, repeating the lie she'd told Duane. "There was some question about whether or not Sherman Beckett was actually my father."

Like Duane, Evelyn didn't seem to buy that, either. "After I got that call," Evelyn went on, "I did some digging. I found the names of the staff who were working for those three days that both boys were in the hospital nursery."

Since the other deputies were working on the same thing, that piqued Cameron's interest. "And?"

"Dr. Gina Boyer," Evelyn said without hesitation. "I don't have the proof yet, but it all points to her."

Cameron looked at Lauren to see if she recognized the name, and she nodded. "She was an OB resident."

"And in debt up to her eyeballs," Evelyn provided. "She transferred to another hospital less than a week after the babies were born."

Cameron took a notepad from Jace's desk, jotted down the doctor's name and handed it to his fellow deputy. "Find out everything you can about her."

Jace nodded and got right on that, and Cameron turned back to Evelyn. "Did you contact this doctor?"

"I tried. She wouldn't take my calls. Wouldn't see me, either. That alone is suspicious."

"Maybe." Cameron shrugged. "Or maybe she's just busy and didn't want to talk to a stranger."

Evelyn's mouth tightened. "She wouldn't talk to me because she knows I'm onto her. She knows that I found out Lauren paid her to switch the babies."

A weary sigh left Lauren's mouth. "Again, why would I possibly do that?"

"Because of that barracuda of a sister-in-law, Julia. You must have known it would make your boy a target so you decided to make my grandson a target instead."

Since Cameron's arm was against hers, he felt her muscles tense. "I would have never done that," Lauren insisted, but her voice was now a tight whisper.

"No?" It didn't sound as if Evelyn was buying that, either. "Then who switched them?"

"I don't have any proof anyone did," Lauren answered. "And apparently neither do you. Now I have a question for you—did you hire thugs to attack me?"

Evelyn huffed. "Right. Go ahead. Try to wiggle out of this by putting the blame on me."

"You have a history of violent behavior," Cameron reminded the woman. A reminder that earned him a glare.

"I pulled a gun on you because I was desperate." She had to say that through clenched teeth. "Because you wouldn't let me see my grandson. Now I find out he wasn't my blood, after all."

"Does that mean you're about to accuse me of swapping the boys?" he pressed when the woman didn't continue.

Evelyn's eyes narrowed as if she might be considering that, but she shook her head. "I don't think you knew. But she did." She tipped her head to Lauren. "And now that psycho sister-in-law is coming after her."

Cameron's hands went on his hips. "That's your second reference to Julia. How do you know her?"

"I don't. Never met the woman. But I don't have to know her to have her investigated. After I got that phone call about the DNA test, I had my staff drop everything they were doing and start looking into things."

Since Evelyn owned a large public relations firm, she probably did have the manpower to dig up plenty of dirt, but it made him wonder if all of this was meant to cast blame on Julia or even Lauren so the blame wouldn't be squarely on her own shoulders. Yes, Julia and Duane had motives. But so did Evelyn.

Gabriel reappeared in the hall and motioned for Evelyn to follow him. She did. And Cameron and Lauren were about to do the same, but Jace stopped them. He had the landline phone pressed to his ear and was holding his hand over the speaker part.

"I have Dr. Boyer on the line," Jace said once Evelyn was out of earshot. "You want to talk to her now?"

Cameron couldn't take the phone fast enough, and he put it on speaker for Lauren. "Dr. Boyer, I'm Deputy Cameron Doran from the Blue River Sheriff's Office, and I have Lauren Lange with—"

"Yes, this is about that woman, Evelyn Waters," the doctor interrupted. "She's left more than a dozen messages on my work phone, and I believe she has someone following me."

Cameron didn't doubt that, and since it appeared the doctor knew what this was all about, he launched right into his question. "Evelyn believes you might have taken part in a baby swap that happened a year ago. Did you?"

"No," she answered.

He didn't like the doctor's hesitation or the fact that she didn't even add anything to that. In his experience, innocent people tended to protest a lot when accused of a crime. "Did you have contact with Gilly Doran's and Lauren's newborn sons?"

"Of course. I was working at the hospital when they were born. I was one of your sister's doctors and was with her when she died." Another hesitation. "She's the reason I left and went to another hospital. Gilly was one of my first patients. The first one I ever lost," Dr. Boyer added.

So, maybe she wasn't covering up anything and this was just a difficult conversation for her. It was certainly difficult for him. This doctor had been there with his sister, but he hadn't been. That was a wound that was never going to fully heal. Now he had to do what was right by Gilly and make sure her son was safe.

"Dr. Boyer, this is Lauren," she said. "I've had some trouble. Someone's been trying to kill me."

It sounded as if the doctor gasped. "You don't think that has anything to do with something that happened at the hospital?"

"I don't know. That's what we're trying to find out. My son and Gilly's son could be in danger, and you might be able to help."

The doctor certainly didn't jump to offer anything. Finally, though, she asked, "How?"

"Just think back to those two days that our babies were in the hospital nursery at the same time," Lauren continued. "Did Gilly say anything about her son being in danger? Or maybe you saw someone suspicious?"

"You mean someone like Evelyn Waters?"

Cameron saw Lauren go stiff. "Yes. Did you see her?"

"I can't be sure," the doctor said after a long pause. "It's possible. That was over a year ago, and I wasn't getting a lot of sleep. There were so many people in and out, and I didn't really even know the other staff yet."

That sounded like a perfect storm for someone wanting to do a baby swap. But if it'd been Evelyn, why hadn't she just tried to take the child?

If that was indeed her plan, that is.

There was another angle to this.

"Did my sister tell you about her abusive ex, the man who was the father of her child?" Cameron asked.

"Yes." The doc didn't sound so eager to admit to that. "She showed me a picture of him and begged me not to let him get near the baby."

Cameron was thankful for that, but he needed to know if the doctor had taken it past the stage of merely looking out for Trace.

"Did Gilly ever mention anything about swapping the babies to keep them from her ex?" Cameron pressed.

Silence.

The moments crawled by, causing Cameron to curse under his breath.

"No," Dr. Boyer finally answered. "Look, Deputy Doran, I have to go. A patient here needs me."

Before Cameron could say anything else, the doctor ended the call. Cameron stood there, staring at the phone and debating if he should try to call her back. But he doubted she would answer. Besides, he should do a background check on her and see what they were dealing with. First, though, he wanted to hear if Evelyn would give Gabriel anything they could use.

"I don't think Gilly could have done the swap on her own," Lauren said as they walked toward the observation room next to where the interview was taking place.

"If she was desperate enough, she could have figured out a way." Cameron silently cursed that, too. His sister had been so desperate because he hadn't been there to help her.

"Don't put this on yourself." Lauren touched his arm and rubbed it gently.

Cameron didn't like that her touch gave him some comfort—her words, too—but it did. The comfort felt, well, nice, but he needed to focus on what Evelyn was saying. Except she wasn't saying what he wanted to hear.

"I think it's time I brought in my lawyer," he heard

Evelyn say once Lauren and he were in the observation room.

Lauren groaned, and Gabriel looked as if he wanted to do the same. Cameron wasn't sure what'd caused the woman to play the lawyer card, but it meant this interview was over. Or at least it would be until Evelyn's attorney arrived. Thankfully, she took out her phone and made the call that would hopefully get him or her out here ASAP.

"And I'd like some coffee while I wait," Evelyn added when Gabriel stood.

Gabriel didn't agree to get her any, but he left the interview and came into the observation room with them.

"What happened?" Lauren immediately asked.

"I asked her if she had anything to do with those dead gunmen."

It was a question that needed to be asked so Cameron couldn't fault Gabriel for it. Still, this was a frustrating delay. "Did Evelyn say anything before she pulled the plug on the interview?"

"Not really. Just a rehash of what she said in the squad room."

Too bad. And Cameron wasn't going to be able to add anything in the good news department. "Lauren and I talked to Dr. Boyer. I think she's hiding something, so we need to get her in for questioning."

Gabriel gave a weary sigh, nodded and glanced at Evelyn through the mirror. The woman was taking out her phone. "I've got some calls to make so keep an eye on her. She might pitch a fit if she figures out I've locked the door, but I don't like a parolee being able to walk around in the place. Not with Lauren here anyway."

Cameron agreed. Evelyn herself wasn't that formidable, but she could be calling in another round of hired thugs. What they needed was to be able to find a money trail that linked Evelyn to the dead guys. Or to one of their other suspects. Right now all they had were a bunch of pieces and no way to put them together to tell them who was guilty.

"I hate to even bring it up," Lauren continued after Gabriel had left, "but is there any chance Travis Canton could be behind this?"

"You mean because of the threats we've all been getting," Cameron finished for her. "I doubt it." Now, this was something *he* hated to bring up. "Travis hasn't exactly been hostile to me, and he actually liked Gilly. I can't imagine him doing anything to put her boy in danger."

Of course, the man had been convicted of a double homicide so that meant he was pretty much capable of anything. "I'll check with the prison and make sure he hasn't had any unusual visitors," Cameron offered.

Lauren made a soft sound, part frustration, part groan. "This is why I hate being here in Blue River. It always comes back." She squeezed her eyes shut for a moment, and Cameron thought maybe she was fighting back tears again.

He was fighting back some regret. Not just for what he hadn't prevented that night ten years ago but for what he was about to do now. Even though he knew it wasn't a smart idea, Cameron glanced at Evelyn to make sure she had stayed put—she had—then he slipped his arm around Lauren and pulled her to him.

Just like that, time vanished, and they were suddenly lovers again. And it was something his body wasn't going to let him forget.

She leaned back, staying in his arms, but Lauren looked up at him. Yep, he'd been right about those tears. Her eyes were filled with them, and they were threatening to spill down her cheeks. He brushed his mouth over one when it fell.

Not a smart idea, either. But then he seemed to be going for broke in the "making huge mistakes" department. He cupped her chin, using his thumb to catch another tear. Of course, that meant touching her while the air was electric between them. Added to that, Lauren was definitely in vulnerable mode right now. That was probably why she didn't move away from him.

Cameron, however, couldn't explain why he didn't move away from her.

His feet seemed nailed to the floor. So he stood there, volleying glances at the mirror while waiting for either Lauren or him to put icing on this by going in for a kiss. He wanted that. Badly. Judging from the uneven rhythm of Lauren's breath, so did she. And for a couple of moments Cameron had no trouble remembering how her mouth would feel against his. How she would taste.

Since it was obvious neither of them had any sense left to do the right thing, fate got involved and helped them out. The sound of the footsteps, followed by someone clearing their throat, finally got them apart. Lauren practically scampered away from him. That probably had something to do with the fact that Gabriel was in the doorway, and he was scowling at them.

Cameron and he were friends, but that didn't mean Gabriel wanted him to get involved with Lauren again. Especially at a dangerous time like this. Added to that, Cameron really did need to keep his focus on the investigation.

"I just got off the phone with the lab," Gabriel said, his scowl still in place. "The one that Lauren used to do Patrick's DNA."

Cameron felt his stomach tighten, and Lauren caught on to his arm as if to steady herself.

"It's not good," Gabriel added. "Someone stole the test results."

Chapter Eight

Lauren rocked Patrick in the chair in the nursery. Across from her, Merilee was doing the same thing to Isaac in another rocker that Cameron had brought over from his house.

Cameron wasn't in the room, though. Since they'd returned from the sheriff's office hours earlier, he was in the kitchen making calls and working the case. Something Lauren wanted to be doing, as well, but she didn't even know what else she could do. She'd called the lab immediately after Gabriel had told her the test results had been stolen, but she hadn't gotten much of an explanation.

Simply put, the lab tech didn't know what'd happened. According to him, he'd run the test, but when Gabriel had called to press him for the results, it wasn't there. Someone had deleted it from the computer log. Now Cameron was trying to figure out who'd done that since the same person was likely responsible for the attacks.

But why would someone want the results hidden?

Lauren didn't have an answer for that—though part of her wished there was some way for both boys to be biologically hers. Then she would have a claim on them. Of course, Cameron was perhaps wishing the same thing.

Eventually, they would have test results, though, since Gabriel had taken DNA not only from the boys but also from Cameron and her. Soon they would have confirmation of what Lauren already knew. No. It was more than that. She felt it all the way to her bones.

"It's funny how the boys are on the same schedule," Merilee whispered. She smiled down at Isaac. "They eat, nap and wake up around the same time." She got up and eased Isaac into the crib.

Lauren made a sound of agreement, and since Patrick was completely sacked out for his nap, she put him in the crib next to Isaac. Despite the nightmare that was going on, it soothed her to see them so peaceful like this.

"I'll be in the kitchen helping Dara with dinner," Merilee added. "Wouldn't be a good idea to rely on Cameron or Jodi to fix anything."

So Lauren had heard. Apparently, sandwich-making was the limit to their culinary skills. Lauren still had some baby food in the diaper bag she'd brought with her, but Dara had insisted on cooking something from scratch. Now the nanny was making the rest of them dinner.

Since the boys would likely sleep through the night, Lauren took the baby monitor so she could find a quiet place to start making some calls to friends who might have heard something, anything, about Julia or Duane. Then she planned on sleeping in the nursery. It wouldn't be as comfortable as the guest room that Jodi had fixed up for her, but she didn't want to be far from the boys.

In case more of those hired guns tried to come after them again.

Gabriel probably wouldn't like it, but Lauren wanted to hire some extra security. Maybe some bodyguards. And that was going to be the first call she made. However, she'd barely had time to go into the hall when she saw Cameron making his way toward her.

He glanced in at the boys, then at the monitor she was holding before he motioned for her to follow him. He didn't go far, just into the foyer. The overhead light was on there. Unlike the nursery, where all the blinds and curtains had been closed all afternoon. Lauren had realized it was already dark outside.

When Cameron stopped and turned to her, he opened his mouth. Closed it. As if he'd changed his mind about what to say.

"Are you okay?" he asked.

Lauren didn't want to know how bad she looked for him to say that. Probably about as bad as she felt. "Just tired and frustrated."

"Yeah." She heard the frustration in his voice, too. But that wasn't only frustration in his eyes.

Maybe Cameron was remembering the near kiss that'd happened at the sheriff's office. Lauren hadn't thought for a minute that she was fully over Cameron, and that moment between them had proven it.

He glanced away as if knowing what she was thinking. "You want the good news or the bad news first?" he asked.

Lauren sighed. "The good." Since she wasn't ready for anything else bad, she figured she needed something—anything—positive first. And this attraction between them definitely didn't fall into the positive category.

"I found out more about Dr. Boyer," Cameron explained. "No red flags whatsoever. She left the hospital where the babies were born so she could move to Austin to be near her family. Her mom has late-stage cancer."

So the doctor hadn't fled after doing a baby switch. "But why did she sound, well, suspicious when she was talking to you?"

He lifted his shoulder. "My guess is that she got too close to Gilly, and she blamed herself in some way for Gilly's death."

The doctor shouldn't do that because Gilly had died from a blood clot. It wasn't common, but it did happen, and in Gilly's case, there was nothing anyone could have done to stop it.

Lauren took a deep breath and tried to steel herself up. "What's the bad news? And please don't tell me we're about to be attacked again."

"No attack. The hands are guarding the road and checking anyone coming in and out of the ranch. Jameson even has a couple of his Ranger friends helping."

Good. But she still wasn't nixing the idea of bodyguards just yet.

"Evelyn is making waves," Cameron said a moment later. "As soon as she left the sheriff's office, she had her team of lawyers petition a judge for custody of Patrick."

Lauren shook her head. "But she doesn't even have proof that Patrick is her son's baby."

"Oh, she's petitioning to get DNA results, too." He rubbed his hand over the back of his neck. "The thing is—Evelyn stands no chance of getting custody unless she can prove in some way that you or I hid her grandson from her. She'll want to make the judge believe we obstructed justice in some way."

Well, it definitely wasn't good news, but Lauren wasn't sure it was enough of a threat to put that troubled expression on Cameron's face. "There's no proof because we didn't do anything like that."

But then it hit her.

"While we're being investigated, a judge could put the babies in foster care." Just saying it aloud caused Lauren to stagger back, and she caught on to the wall.

"Isaac would be fine, probably," Cameron added. "Because a judge would likely give temporary custody of him to one of your siblings. But Evelyn and I are the only living relatives that Patrick has."

That nearly knocked the breath out of her and made Lauren even more unsteady. Cameron noticed, too, because he slid his arm around her. "They can't take Patrick. I won't let them."

"Neither will I," he assured her.

Cameron said that with such confidence that she looked up at him to make sure he wasn't lying. He wasn't. "He's my nephew, and I'll hide him if I have to."

He'd break the law—which no doubt would cut him to the core. But the cut would be even deeper if Patrick was taken away from her. She'd break plenty of laws to keep him. Of course, Evelyn and the law weren't her only threats.

Cameron was, too.

"What are we going to do?" Lauren came out and asked. "What are *you* going to do?" she amended.

He didn't ask her to clarify, but he did look as if he

wanted to repeat the question to her. "I wish there was an easy fix for this."

So did she. But there wasn't, and it was breaking her heart. Cameron must have seen that, as well, because he said some profanity under his breath and pulled her to him. Lauren didn't resist. Nor did she stop herself from looking up at him. It was a mistake, of course, because they were already too close to each other. Especially their mouths. And that was never a good thing when it came to Cameron and her.

"I should go back into the kitchen," he said.

But he didn't, and Lauren didn't let go of him, either, so he could do that. Instead, she slipped her arm around his waist, drawing him even closer than he already was.

Cameron said more of that profanity before his mouth came to hers. The jolt was instant, a reminder of all those feelings and memories she'd been battling since she'd come back to the ranch. It was almost too much, and in some ways, it wasn't nearly enough.

Because it made her want more of him.

Cameron must have known that because he deepened the kiss, sliding his hand around the back of her neck and angling her so that she got an even stronger dose of those old feelings. New ones, as well. Cameron had always known how to set her body on fire, and he clearly hadn't forgotten that. But there was something different, too. The kind of intensity between two people who were no longer kids.

The stakes were sky-high, and that seemed to make the kiss even better. And worse. Worse because it was so good and made her wish that it wouldn't end with just a kiss.

However, it did end.

Cameron snapped away from her, and in the same motion, he pushed her behind him and drew his gun. Because the kiss had clouded her mind, it took Lauren a moment to realize why he'd done that. Because someone was out on the porch.

"It's one of the hands," Gabriel said.

Lauren also hadn't known that her brother was so close, and she wondered if he'd seen that kiss. If so, she was certain she would catch some flack about it later.

Lauren quickly looked out the window so she could see the ranch hand. She recognized him. Allen Colley. He'd started working for her family when she was a kid.

"Two San Antonio cops just showed up," Gabriel added. "Not alone, either. They have Julia with them."

Lauren immediately looked at her brother for an explanation, but Gabriel didn't give her one. "Step to the side," he instructed.

Lauren didn't want to do that. She wanted to see what was going on, but she did move into the adjoining living room. She wasn't in the direct line of the door, but she could still see from the window.

"The babies," she said, glancing down at the monitor.

"They'll be fine," Gabriel assured her. "These guys don't have a court order or search warrant so they're not getting in the house."

Good. But if they didn't have those things, then she wondered why Gabriel had allowed them onto the ranch.

Her brother disarmed the security system and opened the door. That was when Lauren spotted the SAPD cruiser parked in front of Gabriel's house. The two uniformed officers were already out of their vehicle, and Julia was between them.

"What do they want?" Cameron asked.

"Julia supposedly has some info that's critical to our investigation." Gabriel slid his hand over his gun, and that was when Lauren realized this could all be some kind of hoax. More fake cops. Ones that Julia herself could have hired.

"I checked with SAPD," Allen said, not looking any more comfortable about this than Gabriel, Cameron and she were. "The lieutenant confirmed these guys were his and that he'd sent them out here."

Lauren still wasn't breathing easier just yet because the lieutenant could be dirty, too. She hated that she could no longer trust everyone with a badge, but it was too risky to let down her guard.

"I'm Sergeant Terry Welker," the officer on the right greeted them. He was yet someone else who didn't look especially pleased about this visit. He tipped his head to the other cop. "This is Detective Miguel Rodriguez. I'm pretty sure you know Ms. Lange."

"They know me, all right, and they're trying to smear my name," Julia promptly snapped.

Cameron reholstered his gun and huffed. "It's not a smear if it's the truth. You're desperate for cash because you're in debt to a loan shark." He shifted his attention to the sergeant. "Did she tell you that?"

Julia certainly didn't jump to deny it, which meant she probably thought they had some kind of proof. They didn't. Well, other than Duane's accusations, but since he was a suspect, too, Lauren wasn't about to accept everything he'd told them. But in this case, it appeared Duane had been right.

Lauren moved back to the edge of the foyer, coming into Julia's view. The woman aimed a scowl at her, but Lauren gave the woman one right back. Because owing money to a loan shark was plenty of motive for the attacks. It sickened Lauren to think the babies could be in danger because of money.

"This visit doesn't have anything to do with that," Julia insisted. "Believe it or not, I've come to help you. Not for your sakes. But so you'll leave me the hell alone."

Cameron didn't ask how she'd come to help. Instead, he looked at the sergeant for answers. "She demanded we escort her out here. Said you might shoot her if she just showed up."

"Not if she'd shown up at the sheriff's office. This is my home," Gabriel reminded them, and it wasn't a friendly reminder, either. Her brother obviously didn't want Julia anywhere near the ranch.

"We went there first," the detective answered. "When neither you nor Deputy Doran were there, Ms. Lange wanted us to bring her here so she could give you something. She's not armed—we checked—and she wouldn't give the info to us."

"Because I don't want this to fall into the wrong hands."

Lauren had no idea what Julia had, or rather what the woman claimed to have, but she shook her head. "You couldn't force her to turn it over to you?"

The sergeant grunted as if he wished he could have done that. "Ms. Lange's not under arrest." He shot Julia a hard glance. "That was before we knew about the loan shark, though. I'll be looking into that."

Good. Lauren hoped SAPD dug until they got to the truth.

"Anyway," the sergeant went on, "your brother-in-law, Theo Canton, and I are old friends, and I thought

I'd bring her here as a favor to him. I know he's worried about what's going on with the trouble you had here, and he'd like to put a stop to it. I figured if Ms. Lange could help in any way, that it'd be worth the drive."

Maybe it would be. If not, Lauren was certain that Cameron and Gabriel would put a quick end to this little visit.

Julia gave Cameron a piece of paper that she took from her purse. Lauren looked at it from over his shoulder, but it appeared to be some sort of code.

"That's the password for the computer files," Julia explained. "Files for Alden's business."

Lauren had a closer look, but she didn't recognize the site for the online storage, the password or the files. "I manage my late husband's company," Lauren said to the cops. "These aren't my files, and—"

"No, they're Duane's," Julia interrupted. "He's been keeping secret books from you. No good reason I can think of for doing that, but if you go through those files, you can see there's money missing. Enough to pay some thugs to kill you so he can get the company he believes he should have had all along."

Lauren felt her breath go thin. Of course she'd known Duane could be behind this, but it put an icy chill through her to hear it spelled out like that.

"How did you get this?" Cameron asked her.

Julia pulled back her shoulders. "I was looking for any kind of files or notes my brother might have left before he died."

Translation—Julia wanted to find something she could use for her lawsuit to get Alden's money.

"You hacked into Duane's files," Lauren concluded.

"Company files," Julia corrected. She pointed to the

paper. "And I got you something that'll not only clear my name, but you can also use to arrest Duane."

The sergeant turned to Gabriel. "Since the company is in Dallas and the computer hacking happened there, that's out of our jurisdiction. You want to call in your brother Jameson to handle this?"

Since Jameson was a Texas Ranger, he didn't have a set jurisdiction. He could basically do whatever local law enforcement asked him to do.

Gabriel nodded. "I'll have Jameson check it out. If he finds anything, he'll let you know. And if there's nothing else, I'd like for you to get Ms. Lange off Beckett land."

The cops made sounds of agreement. The detective started back to the cruiser with Julia, but Sergeant Welker stayed behind. However, he didn't look at Gabriel but rather Cameron.

"I made some calls on the way over here," the sergeant said. "Just so I could figure out what the devil was going on with Ms. Lange. Anyway, I discovered Evelyn Waters was out of jail. I remembered all the trouble you had with her a few months back."

"Yeah," Cameron verified, "she's out on probation."

"I heard." The sergeant huffed. "I thought you might want to know that she got out early thanks to Judge Wendell Olsen. They're old friends—belong to the same country club and such. Anyway, the only reason I'm bringing it up is because Evelyn's looking to have her record expunged. Then it'll be as if she never even committed the crime."

"Can she do that?" Lauren immediately asked.

"Not without friends in high places," the sergeant answered. "This might not amount to anything, but I heard that Evelyn plans to have Judge Olsen help her get custody of her grandson. Just thought you'd want to know," he added before he walked away.

The chill inside her got even colder. So cold that it caused Lauren to shudder. "I won't let that woman have Patrick or Isaac."

"No," Cameron quietly agreed.

Gabriel shut the door, reactivated the security system and went to the window to watch—making certain that Julia did indeed leave. Lauren headed straight to the nursery, and even though she was moving pretty fast, Cameron caught up with her.

"It's time for us to hide the boys," she insisted. Yes, she was panicking, and she couldn't make herself stop.

Cameron took hold of her arm and stepped in front of her. "Not yet. But there is something we need to do."

"What? Because I'll do anything to keep them safe."

"So will I." Cameron looked her straight in the eyes when he continued. "And that's why you and I need to get married."

Chapter Nine

Cameron hadn't been sure what Lauren's reaction would be when he proposed to her. Or rather when he had *insisted* they get married. He had figured she would be shocked.

And she was.

He had also expected her to need some time to think about it.

And she had.

But what he hadn't counted on was that her thinking time would last through the night. She hadn't even brought it up when Patrick had awakened around two in the morning, and Cameron and she had ended up in the nursery together. Lauren had rocked the baby back to sleep while she hummed to him. What she hadn't done was given Cameron an answer. Or for that matter, she hadn't even talked that much to him. Granted it was an ungodly hour, but still he'd expected something—including a flat-out no answer.

Now it was causing his own round of thinking time as he sat in the family room with his third cup of coffee and went through the latest emails about the investigation. Cameron had been certain that Lauren would jump on the idea since it might be necessary to stop

Evelyn's claim to custody. Even a dirty judge would have trouble explaining why he would deny custody to a married couple and then hand the baby over to a grandmother with a criminal record.

Of course, nothing they did might be enough to stop Evelyn, who seemed hell-bent on raising her grandson. Since she'd done such a bad job raising Trace, Cameron didn't want the woman to have a second chance to screw up another child's life. Especially when that child was Gilly's son.

He downloaded the next round of emails, scowling at the one that caught his eye. It was from Sergeant Welker, SAPD. It was an account by an informant that Welker identified only as a "credible source," who basically repeated what Welker had already told them. Evelyn was gearing up for a fight. Maybe that wouldn't include another attack, but just in case Evelyn did have that on her agenda, Cameron had added even more to their security measures.

Gabriel and he had posted hands on the old trails that coiled around the ranch. It wasn't foolproof since gunmen could still go through the woods to get to them, but there was no way they could watch every acre of land. Cameron could only hope that if thugs did get near the house, then the other hands and reserve deputies would see them and stop them.

The next email didn't cause Cameron's scowl to fade. It was from Jameson, who was now handling the so-called evidence Julia had given them. The Rangers' computer guys had gotten into the files without a hitch, and it did indeed appear that Duane was keeping a second set of books, but it could be something that Julia had set up to incriminate the man. It was going to take time to unravel everything, and time wasn't something that was on their side.

Cameron had a bad feeling in the pit of his stomach.

The feeling eased up a lot, though, when he heard the chatter. Baby talk. He'd seen both boys when they'd gotten up about an hour earlier, but Lauren, Jodi and the nannies had whisked them away for baths and breakfast. That was probably like therapy for them and a good way to get their minds off the danger that seemed to be skulking right up to their doorsteps. That potential danger was the reason Gabriel was working in his home office. Jameson would be returning soon, too, after he finished up some things in Dallas.

The chatter got louder, and Cameron expected to see all the women, including Lauren, come into the room. But it was only Lauren. She had a baby on each hip, and she was smiling. *Really* smiling.

Her happiness faded some, though, when her attention landed on his face. Probably because of his somber expression after reading those emails. Cameron quickly tried to fix that, though. He put his laptop and coffee aside and got to his feet.

"Nothing new on the investigation," Cameron told her right off, and he went to them.

They were a welcome sight, that was for sure. Both boys had obviously had their baths and been fed because they looked ready to do some serious playing. They were squirming to get down—probably because there were some plastic toy blocks on the coffee table.

However, the squirming shifted to a different direction when Isaac reached out for Cameron. He took the boy, brushing a kiss on the top of his head, but Patrick must have wanted a part of that because he reached for

Cameron, too. Cameron quickly found his arms filled with babies. Patrick gave him a sloppy kiss on the cheek while Isaac bopped Cameron on the nose.

Lauren laughed.

It was silky and soft, but it faded, though, just as the smile had done.

Lauren picked up two of the blocks and handed both of the boys one. Of course they went straight in their mouths, but it would keep them occupied for a couple of seconds while he chatted with Lauren.

"In case you missed it last night, I did bring up the subject of marriage," Cameron reminded her.

She nodded, then dodged his gaze. On a heavy sigh, Lauren dropped down into the chair next to the sofa. "When I was a teenager, I used to plan our wedding," she said. "You knew that, of course."

He did. He'd heard her talking to Ivy about it. It'd scared the heck out of him, too, because Lauren had been just seventeen. If her father had caught wind of it, he probably would have fired Cameron, punched him or both. Back then, marriage hadn't even been on his radar, but he had been attracted to Lauren. Wisely, he'd held back on the attraction, though, until she had turned eighteen. They'd had just a couple of short weeks together before the night that changed everything.

"Old water, old bridge," she added in a mumble.

Cameron wished that hadn't felt like a slap. Or a lie. It might be old baggage, but the attraction was still just as strong and new as it had been when she'd discussed marrying him with her sister.

As he'd predicted, the boys started to squirm, and he stood them on the floor next to the coffee table so they could reach the rest of the blocks.

"I just thought it would be easier to fight Evelyn if we had a united front," Cameron told her.

Lauren didn't argue with that. In fact, she didn't say anything for several long moments. "I agree. We should get married."

Cameron snapped toward Lauren and stared at her. She didn't look convinced this was the right thing to do, but then, Cameron wasn't so sure it would work, either. Right now they didn't have a lot of ammunition to fight custody with anyone. Not with the DNA results not in yet, and he wasn't going to allow either boy to be placed into foster care.

"I talked this over with Gabriel," Lauren added.

Cameron hadn't figured anything else she could say would surprise him, but that sure did. "And?"

Lauren lifted her shoulder, and without missing a beat, she caught Isaac when he wobbled and nearly fell. She steadied the baby before she looked at Cameron. "He understands."

Yeah, but that was a whole different thing than approving of it. He was reasonably sure that Gabriel no longer held any resentment for Cameron's screwup ten years ago, but he would still want to protect his sister. Lauren's husband had only been dead a year and a half, and Gabriel probably thought it was too soon for her to get married.

And it might be.

But their options were limited here.

"Anyway, I can get started," she went on. She stood, rubbing her hands along the sides of her jeans. "I mean, I can call the courthouse and see about putting a rush on a license."

"I've already done that. Just in case you said yes. I

know the clerks who work there, and one of them can bring it over this morning. The justice of the peace can come out, as well, and marry us."

She dragged in a long breath, nodded again. "You've been busy."

"I wanted to save time. My guess is that Evelyn will be visiting her judge friend today if she hasn't already."

Cameron hadn't expected this to be a romantic moment. After all, they were devising a plan to save the children they both loved, but Lauren looked as if she was bracing herself for a huge disaster. Not exactly a way to stroke his ego. Especially after that hot kiss that'd happened just yesterday.

Lauren finally looked him straight in the eyes. "If this marriage arrangement goes south," she said, "please promise me that you won't try to keep either of the boys from me."

"Of course. You'll make the same promise to me?"

"Yes." She stood and fluttered her fingers to the back of the house. "I'll tell the others. Any idea how soon you can get the clerk and justice of the peace out here?"

He took out his phone. "ASAP."

"Good." She took another of those long breaths and repeated it before she scooped up the babies.

Cameron was about to tell her to leave them while she did whatever it was she needed to do, but his phone rang before he could do that. When he saw the name on the screen, he decided it was a call he should take.

Duane.

He showed her the screen, and Lauren put the boys back on the floor. No doubt so she could listen.

"Duane knows the accusations Julia made against him?" she asked.

"He knows. Jameson called him last night." Which meant this probably wasn't going to be a pleasant conversation. Still, Cameron wanted to know what the man had to say about those files.

He didn't put the call on speaker in case Duane started cursing. Even though the boys were too young to understand it, Cameron still didn't want them hearing it. However, he held out the phone between Lauren and him so that she could lean in and listen. She moved to the sofa next to him.

"Why did you have the Texas Rangers come after me?" Duane said without a greeting. Unlike his other conversation with Cameron and Julia, this one did not have a respectful tone to it. "You know anything Julia said about me would be a lie."

"She had computer files," Cameron reminded the man.

"Files that she concocted to make me look guilty." And yes, Duane peppered that with some profanity. "If she gets me out of the way, she has an easier path to getting her brother's company. I can't believe she convinced you that what she found was real."

"She didn't convince us," Lauren said. "But it had to be investigated. That's why Jameson was called in. If the files are bogus, then he'll figure that out."

Duane made a sharp sound of disagreement. "Innocent people get railroaded all the time. In fact, there are plenty who believe Travis Canton was wrongfully convicted of murdering your parents."

That caused the skin to crawl on the back of Cameron's neck, and Lauren didn't seem to fare much better. She clamped her teeth over her bottom lip for a moment, as if trying to keep her composure. Despite the sudden bad turn of mood in the air, the boys thankfully didn't seem to pick up on it. They continued to play with the blocks, banging them against the hardwood floor.

"Why would you bring up Travis?" Cameron demanded from Duane.

"Because it's true. Travis never confessed. Heck, he doesn't even remember if he's guilty. You didn't lock him up that night when you found him drunk, and that made him an easy patsy for someone who needed a scapegoat."

All of that had been in the newspapers, so it wasn't surprising that Duane would know those details. What Cameron wanted to know was why this man was even interested in the old murders.

"How long ago did you file the lawsuit against Lauren and Patrick?" Cameron asked.

Duane hesitated, maybe because he realized he'd just spilled something he shouldn't. "Are you accusing me of something?"

"Just asking a very simple question."

Of course, it wasn't that simple. Cameron wanted to know if the lawsuit was somehow tied to the threatening letters they'd been receiving. Lauren, included. Maybe Duane was trying to intimidate her or send her running by making her believe her parents' "real" killer was going to come after Patrick and her.

"About six months ago," Duane finally answered. Definitely not a trace of friendliness in his voice. "Why?"

"Because shortly after that, Lauren started getting death threats. Did you have something to do with that?"

"No!" No hesitation that time. "Hell, I called you to try to clear up the lies Julia told, and now you accuse me of this?"

"I'm not accusing. Again, I'm just asking a simple question."

"No," Duane repeated, though it sounded as if he'd spoken through clenched teeth. "I didn't threaten Lauren. And I didn't do any creative bookkeeping so I could steal money from the company. I sure as hell didn't hire any gunmen to go after Lauren."

Well, Cameron had gotten his answers, but he wasn't sure if they were the truth or not. There was no way Duane would just confess his wrongdoing, since it could land him in jail. Especially if Jameson could connect any missing funds to the bank accounts of those hired thugs who'd been killed at the ranch. That would be a charge of conspiracy to commit murder and would give Duane plenty of time behind bars.

"Why did you really call?" Cameron pressed.

He expected Duane to shout out his innocence again. He didn't. "Evelyn Waters called me first thing this morning."

Judging from the way Lauren's eyes widened, that surprised her as much as it did Cameron. "What did she want?"

"To invest in my legal fund to fight Lauren. In exchange, she'll want a piece of the company once I reclaim it."

Hell. Evelyn was really on the offensive, and Cameron thought he knew why she'd gone about it at this angle. Maybe Evelyn thought she could cause Lauren to go broke with a long legal battle. Or maybe just wear Lauren down. It wasn't going to work. Cameron didn't come from money, but Lauren did. And the Becketts would join forces to make sure she had whatever funds she needed. Plus, she could always tap into her trust fund.

"A word of advice about Evelyn," Cameron warned the man. "She could be looking to use you as a patsy. If she breaks the law again, and it sounds as if she's very close to doing that, then she'll want someone to take the fall for her. She could have you in her sights for that."

"I'm not worried about Evelyn," Duane insisted the moment Cameron had finished. "Julia's the snake in all of this. You'd better hope she doesn't team up with Evelyn. With Evelyn's seemingly unlimited supply of cash and Julia's desperation, it could be an unholy alliance."

Yeah, one that could have already happened. Evelyn could have given Julia the cash to pay those gunmen. That way, if Evelyn managed to kill both Lauren and him, she'd have a better shot at getting her hands on the baby.

"If Julia's the snake you think she is," Lauren said, "then we need proof to stop her. Do you have anything we can use? Something more than just her owing money to a loan shark."

"That should be enough," Duane snapped. But then he huffed. "I'll look and see what I can find. I have some incentive now that Julia's set the dogs on me with those fake files."

Cameron jumped right on that. "If they're truly fake, then figure out a way to prove that. The Rangers are looking into it, of course, but they could use your help."

He wasn't so sure of that. In fact, Jameson might not want any interference from a suspect, but it could keep Duane busy. Of course, if Duane was behind the attacks, then this was all just a ruse anyway. The man could have called them just to keep the focus on those files rather than the fact that someone was trying to kill them.

"Find something to put Julia behind bars," Cameron repeated to Duane, and he ended the call.

During the conversation, Cameron had glanced at Lauren a few times while also keeping an eye on the boys, but he really looked at her now. There were no tears in her eyes, but he saw that this was taking a serious toll on her. It was the same for him, too.

"Marrying you might not help," she said, her voice a whisper.

"It might not." Cameron had thought about all angles of this, and there was one angle that he needed to mention. "If we're married and one of us dies, then the other one would have a legal claim to the boys. We'd need to do guardianship paperwork, of course. And wills."

Hell, that caused Lauren to go way too pale, and he reached for her, pulling her into his arms. The embrace didn't last, though. Isaac lost his balance again, and Lauren bolted from the sofa. This time she didn't get to him in time, and the baby fell. He didn't hit hard, but it was enough to cause him to start crying. The commotion must have upset Patrick because he started to cry, as well.

Lauren scooped up both boys, kissing them, and Cameron went to her to help. He didn't get far, though, because his phone rang again. The sound of it only caused the babies to cry even louder. Lauren motioned for him to take the call while she took the babies in the direction of the kitchen.

Cameron figured this might be Duane calling back, but it wasn't a name or number he recognized. He pushed the answer button and hoped it wasn't someone from the press wanting a story. There'd already been a couple of those calls, and he didn't want another. Especially since he had "wedding" arrangements to make.

"Deputy Doran," he answered.

But the caller didn't say anything, and it put a knot in his stomach. Was this another hired gun?

"What do you want?" Cameron snapped.

"Uh, I'm Maria Black," the caller finally said.

He mentally repeated the name, and it rang a bell, but Cameron couldn't make the connection of why it seemed familiar.

"I was a nurse at the hospital where your sister, Gilly Doran, had her son," the woman added several moments later.

Bingo. Now he remembered. He'd spoken to her briefly after learning Gilly was dead. Other than her name, Cameron couldn't recall anything else about her. But just the fact that she had gotten in touch with him piqued his interest.

"Is something wrong?" he asked. Because it was possible that Evelyn was harassing her in some way.

"Yes." Her voice cracked, and it sounded as if she was crying. "I think someone's trying to kill me."

That was not what Cameron wanted to hear. "You need to go to the cops now. Where are you?"

"I'm on my way to the Blue River Sheriff's Office right now, and I need to see you. Lauren, too. God, I'm so sorry, Deputy Doran."

The knot in his stomach got worse. "Sorry for what?"

The sound of her sob was loud and clear. "I wouldn't have done it, but your sister begged me to help her. She was dying, and she begged me to do it. Please forgive me. I'm the one who switched the babies."

Chapter Ten

Lauren sat in the back of the cruiser, staring out the window but not really seeing anything. She felt numb. Of course, she'd known in her heart that the boys had been switched, but she hadn't prepared herself to hear the proof of that.

If it was the truth, that is.

She hadn't gotten a chance to speak to the woman who'd called Cameron, but there had indeed been a nurse named Maria Black who had worked at the hospital where Lauren and Gilly had had their sons. And while it wouldn't have been easy, Maria would have been in a position to make the switch. That didn't mean she had, though.

"Evelyn could have put the nurse up to doing this," Lauren said to Cameron and Gabriel. Her brother was behind the wheel of the cruiser, and Cameron was in the backseat with her.

Judging from their quick sound of approval, the two had already come to that conclusion. "Do you remember Gilly ever mentioning this nurse?" Cameron asked.

"No. But she was on the ward where we were. And Gilly was desperate to keep her baby from Trace. He was still alive then, and she was terrified of him."

That caused a muscle to flicker in Cameron's jaw. It was obviously a sore subject that his kid sister had been in an abusive relationship. One that he hadn't been able to stop. But then, Gilly had kept a lot from him because she'd been worried that Cameron might kill Trace if he learned that Trace made a habit of beating her up.

"When we get to the sheriff's office, I'll ask Maria to take a polygraph," Gabriel said. "It's not conclusive, but if she's lying, it might spur her into telling the truth." He paused. "You do know I'll have to arrest her, right?"

Lauren nodded. She was torn between hating the woman and wanting to thank her for trying to keep Gilly's child safe. Of course, by doing that, Maria had put their lives in a tailspin.

"I can't think of a reason why Julia or Duane would do a baby switch," Lauren tossed out there.

"They could have hoped to prove Patrick wasn't Alden's child," he reminded her. "That might help Julia's lawsuit to get her brother's estate. It might help Duane's cause, too."

True, but that seemed a stretch. Not for Evelyn, though. She might have thought it would be easier for her to kidnap Patrick since Lauren wouldn't have been on the lookout for the woman. Still, it might not have been anything that complicated. Because Maria could be telling the truth.

"I'm guessing you two will go through with this marriage while you're here?" Gabriel asked.

Lauren hadn't been expecting his question. Though she should have. She knew that Cameron had told Gabriel about their plan to wed. She also knew her brother didn't approve. To him it probably seemed like a knee-jerk reaction, one that Cameron and she might regret later. And they might. But doing something—anything—felt better than just spinning her wheels.

"What the hell?" Gabriel mumbled, and he slowed the cruiser.

Since they were still a good mile from town, that put Lauren's heart in her throat, but it took her a moment to figure out what had caused her brother to say that. There was a car just ahead, parked on the shoulder. The driver's door was wide-open.

"You recognize the car?" she asked.

"No," Gabriel and Cameron answered together.

Definitely not good. This wasn't a heavily traveled section of the farm road. In fact, the only traffic was usually from people who lived nearby, but there was a way to access the road from the interstate so occasionally people would take the wrong exit and then look for a turnaround.

"Get down on the seat," Cameron told her.

Lauren had already felt the surge of adrenaline, and that caused her to feel even more. Her breathing was already too fast. Her heart was throbbing in her ears. She did start to move lower but not before she got a glimpse of someone slumped behind the wheel of the car.

A woman.

One Lauren thought she recognized.

"I think that's Maria Black," she managed to say before Cameron pushed her down on the seat.

"There's blood," Gabriel grumbled.

That sent her heartbeat up another notch, and Lauren immediately thought the worst. Easy to do since Maria had said someone might be trying to kill her. Mercy, had some hired thugs gotten to her before she could make it into town?

After Gabriel called for an ambulance, he stopped directly next to Maria's car, and Lauren had another look just to make sure it was indeed the woman. It was.

And, yes, there was blood.

It was on the side of her head. Maria's face was turned toward them with her head resting on the steering wheel. Lauren was about to ask if she was dead, but then she saw the woman move.

"Stay in the cruiser with Lauren," Gabriel told Cameron.

Lauren could tell he didn't want to do that. Cameron wanted to be out there helping his boss, but he stayed put. However, he did open the door a fraction and drew his gun.

Because the person who'd injured Maria could still be around.

Keeping low, Lauren glanced around, trying to spot anyone else in the area. There weren't many trees on this stretch of land, only pasture, so it would be hard for someone to hide. But then she remembered one of the goons at the ranch who'd hidden in the ditch outside Cameron's house. There were plenty of ditches, including one that was just to the right of Maria's car.

"Be careful," she warned her brother.

Gabriel also drew his gun and went to Maria. Lauren couldn't hear what he said to her or vice versa, but she did see the woman's lips move. Maria didn't seem strong enough, though, to lift her head, and she didn't open her eyes. Lauren couldn't tell if that was because the woman was dazed or if she was dying. Yes, there was blood, but it didn't seem like there was enough to indicate she was bleeding out. It was possible she'd had to slam on her brakes and hadn't been wearing her seat belt. Her head could have hit the steering wheel. She certainly had seemed frantic when she'd called them, and people in a panic made mistakes.

"Maybe it won't take long for the ambulance to get here," Lauren muttered. And while she was hoping, Lauren added that whatever Maria was saying to Gabriel, that it would help them figure out what the heck was going on.

Gabriel took Maria's hand and had her press it to her side. Maybe that meant she was injured there, as well, and her brother had done that to make sure the wound didn't bleed too much. After Gabriel had done that, he came by the side of the cruiser.

"She says someone rammed into the rear end of her car," Gabriel explained. He wasn't looking at them, though. Like Cameron, he was keeping watch around them. "A big bulky guy got out of the other vehicle, came up to her and shot her at point-blank range."

Oh, mercy. Lauren had to put her hand to her chest to try to steady her heart. "How is she still alive then?"

"My guess is she won't be for long. The bullet appears to have grazed her head, but she was shot in the chest, too."

Cameron cursed. "What did Maria say to you?"

"She only said one word, and she kept repeating it." Gabriel paused. "Julia."

The air was suddenly so still that it felt as if everything was holding its breath. Everything including Lauren.

"Julia's behind this," Lauren heard herself whisper.

"Or someone wanted Maria to believe she was," Cameron quickly pointed out.

Yes, that was possible. Julia had perhaps tried to set

up Duane, and now he could be doing the same to her. But why would he, or Julia for that matter, hire someone to murder Maria?

Gabriel's head whipped up, his attention going in the direction of the road behind him, where she heard the sounds of someone slamming on their brakes. Lauren hoped it was just someone who belonged out here, someone who was stopping to see if they could help.

But judging from Gabriel's expression, he didn't think that.

Neither did Cameron. He pushed Lauren all the way down on the seat, and Gabriel ran back to the cruiser. However, before her brother could get back in, Lauren heard another sound.

Someone fired a shot.

CAMERON DIDN'T HAVE much time to react. In the blink of an eye, the shooter leaned out from the SUV, sent a bullet slamming into the cruiser and ducked back behind the heavily tinted glass. Almost immediately, the driver sped up, and Cameron knew they were about to slam into them.

He didn't have to tell Gabriel to hurry. He was. But Cameron did have to warn Lauren again to keep down. She was obviously terrified for her brother. And she should be. Gabriel was literally out in the open, and another shot could kill him.

However, the gunman didn't fire again. That was because the SUV did plow right into them, jolting them forward.

Cameron's shoulder smacked into the back of the seat, the impact so hard that the pain jackknifed through him. But that was the least of his worries. The impact also caused the cruiser to collide right into Gabriel. Lauren shouted out to him as he fell to the ground.

Now more shots came. Three of them, and Cameron had to fight to regain not only his balance but his aim, too. Hell, he was hurting, but he pushed that aside and threw open the door that had slammed shut during the collision. He had to return fire. Had to keep these thugs from killing Gabriel.

Cameron leaned out of the cruiser, took aim at the SUV's front windshield and started firing. The glass was obviously bulletproof, but his shots were doing some damage. They were causing the glass to crack, and maybe that would be enough to obstruct the driver's view.

It wasn't enough for the gunman, though.

The thug's hand came out from the passenger-side window, and he fired at Cameron. Cameron had to scramble back, and in the same motion, he pushed Lauren onto the floor in case the glass on the cruiser gave way.

"My brother," she said on a rise of breath.

He couldn't see Gabriel, which meant he was probably pinned down in front of the cruiser. He couldn't stay there because Cameron needed him back in so they could get the heck out of there. That meant trying to get Maria into the cruiser, as well.

Cameron took out his backup weapon from the side holster in his jeans and handed it to Lauren. "This doesn't mean I want you getting up and returning fire," he warned her. "I want you to have it just in case."

What he meant was in case all else failed and those goons made it to her. If that happened, it would mean they would have already shot Gabriel and him.

"What are you going to do?" Her voice was shaking like the rest of her.

Something that wouldn't be particularly safe, but then, nothing was safe right now. He gave her his phone, as well. "Make sure we have some backup on the way out here."

That wasn't just busywork, either. Cameron wasn't sure if Gabriel had requested assistance when he'd called the ambulance, and if he hadn't, Cameron needed more deputies on the way now.

"They're coming," Lauren relayed to him a few seconds later. "But the ambulance can't get in here as long as shots are being fired."

Yeah, he'd known that would be the case, but he had to try.

"Don't get up," he told Lauren one last time.

He threw his door all the way open, using it for cover. Not just for him but for Gabriel, too.

"We need to get Maria," Cameron said to Gabriel.

Cameron didn't shout it because he didn't want to telegraph his moves to the gunmen, but they likely couldn't have heard anyway because the bullets were slamming nonstop into the cruiser. It wasn't only the passenger firing, either. The driver had gotten in on the shooting.

Gabriel came around the side of the cruiser. He didn't appear hurt—thank God—and he opened the front door. Cameron didn't lean out far enough to make himself a target, but he fired some shots at the gunmen, hoping he would get lucky and hit one of them. He didn't, but at least it caused them to pull their hands back into the SUV. That gave Gabriel and him a few precious seconds to rescue Maria.

Even though Gabriel had said the nurse probably wasn't going to make it, Cameron couldn't leave her there to die. The thugs would likely just shoot her again, and this time, they would finish her off.

Cameron and Gabriel both took hold of Maria, dragging her out of her car and into the front of the cruiser. Gabriel climbed over her, getting behind the wheel, and Cameron scrambled to get in the backseat. He almost made it, too.

But the SUV slammed into them again.

Cameron heard Lauren call out to him. He heard Gabriel curse, too, but he couldn't respond. That was because the impact caused the still open back door to smack against his head. His arm and shoulder were still hurting, but this was a whole new level of pain. Worse, it dazed him enough so that it blurred his vision.

The shots started coming at him again, the bullets tearing through the metal in the door. Cameron groped around, trying to orient himself, but he was pretty sure he was failing. Until someone caught on to his arm and pulled him onto the backseat of the cruiser. He landed against the seat and came up, ready to fire.

But Lauren fired first.

That was when he realized one of the thugs was right there. Just a few feet away from him. The guy had obviously gotten out of the SUV with plans to get close enough to kill him. And that was exactly what he would have done if Lauren hadn't put a bullet in his head.

The shooter dropped to the ground.

Seeing his partner fall must have enraged the driver because he slammed the SUV into them again.

"Hold on," Gabriel warned them a split second before he gunned the engine and sped off.

The jolt tossed Cameron and Lauren around again, and it didn't help that the SUV managed to ram them one more time.

Cameron got his door shut, and he pivoted in the seat to try to figure out what he could do. Not much. The front of the SUV had almost certainly been reinforced, but there wasn't much damage to it. That meant the driver had no trouble coming at them again. Gabriel pushed the accelerator even more, trying to get them out of there.

Despite the ringing in his ears, Cameron heard a welcome sound. Sirens. Backup had arrived. But the thug in the SUV no doubt heard them, as well, because he slammed on his brakes. The road wasn't that wide, but he managed to get turned around in just a few seconds.

And he drove off.

Cameron wanted to go after the SOB and beat the truth out of him. He wanted to find out who'd hired him and his dead partner to try to kill them. But it was too risky to do that. Instead, Gabriel instructed the backup to go after the SUV while he continued to drive toward town. It didn't take long for the SUV to disappear from sight.

Lauren's hands were shaking hard, but she was able to use his phone to call the ranch. "The SUV might go there," she said.

That upped his concern a couple of notches. Even though he knew there were plenty of security measures in place, Cameron didn't release the breath he'd been holding until he heard Jameson tell Lauren that all was well at the ranch. The babies were fine.

Two cruisers went flying past them, heading in the same direction as the SUV. Cameron only hoped they could catch up with him and bring the snake in alive for questioning.

Gabriel kept volleying glances in the rearview mirror and at Maria, but he also made a call to the sheriff's office.

"Are you okay?" Cameron asked Lauren.

She nodded. "But you're not. Your head is bleeding."

"I'm fine." That was possibly the truth, and even if it wasn't, Cameron had no plans to do anything about it.

He cupped Lauren's face, checking for any injuries but didn't see any. However, there was a new level of fear in her eyes. Of course, she had just killed a man. Her second one in two days. It would only add to the other nightmares she already had.

"How about you?" he asked Gabriel. "Are you hurt?"

"Just some bruises." He tipped his head to Maria. "She can't say the same, though."

No. Now that the woman was in the cruiser, Cameron had no trouble seeing that the front of her dress was drenched in blood. Cameron pulled off his shirt and held it to her chest wound. It wasn't much, but maybe it would help until they could get her to the hospital.

"What about the ambulance?" Lauren asked. "How soon can it get here now that the shots have stopped?"

"It's just about a half mile up," Gabriel answered. "I talked to Jace at the office, and he said they're waiting for us."

Good. That would mean Maria would soon get the medical attention she needed.

"Julia," Cameron heard Maria mumble. Her voice was too weak, and he wasn't sure if she could manage more than just that one word, but Cameron had to try.

"Did Julia hire the men who did this to you?" Cameron asked.

Maria opened her eyes, and it was as if she was surprised he was there. "Deputy Doran," she said. Her gaze drifted to Lauren. "I'm so sorry."

"The apology can wait." Cameron hated to sound harsh, but hearing that wasn't going to help them. "Why do you keep saying Julia's name?"

Maria dragged in a shallow breath. "She came to see me."

Probably not a good thing especially since Julia was desperate for money. "You told her about the baby swap?"

Maria nodded, and her eyes drifted down. "Be careful."

It was definitely a warning, but Cameron didn't get a chance to press her for more. That was because Gabriel hit the brakes again. This time, though, it was for the ambulance. He pulled to a quick stop right next to it, and the medics rushed out to take Maria.

"I'll ride with her to the hospital," Cameron insisted.

With the seconds ticking away, he figured he only had a few minutes at most to get what he needed from Maria. The truth. And then maybe he could finally put an end to this once and for all.

Chapter Eleven

Lauren sat at Gabriel's desk and waited. Something she'd been doing since they'd arrived at the sheriff's office over an hour ago. There wasn't much else she could do until Cameron called with news from the hospital.

Maybe the news would be good. Maybe Maria would survive surgery and be able to tell them what was going on. Until then, Cameron had no plans to leave.

At least the boys weren't anywhere near the danger and the aftermath. Lauren hadn't been able to stop herself from calling Dara three times to make sure all was well there. It was. And now she had to pray it stayed that way.

She heard the footsteps heading toward her, and Lauren practically jumped to her feet. But it wasn't Cameron. It was Gabriel. He had a foam box in one hand, a bottle of water in the other, and he was sporting a very concerned look.

"A sandwich from the diner," he said, putting the box and water on the desk in front of her. "You need to eat."

Yes, she probably did, but she wasn't hungry. In fact, her stomach was churning. Still, she would try to keep something down. It wouldn't do any of them any good if she got light-headed.

"Anything from Cameron?" she asked, but she already knew the answer. If there had been, Cameron would have texted her. He knew she was on pins and needles while she waited.

He shook his head and opened the foam box when she didn't touch it. Lauren sat down and took a small bite of the BLT. There wasn't just one sandwich, though, but two. Gabriel must have thought she was starved. Or just eager to sample something she hadn't had in a long time.

"You remembered this was my favorite," she said. He'd even gotten a bag of her favorite chips to go with it.

"Of course I remembered. You're my sister."

There was some emotion that went with that comment, and Lauren knew they were talking about a lot more than just the sandwich.

She looked up at him, their eyes connecting. "I can't apologize for leaving Blue River. I *had* to go."

If he agreed with that, he didn't show any signs of it. "Now you're back." He paused, a muscle flickering in his jaw. "With plans to marry Cameron."

There was definitely no hint of agreement for that, either. "We don't want any chance of the boys being sent to foster care."

Gabriel nodded. Finally, they'd found some common ground. "And then what? What do you do when we stop the person behind the attacks?"

At least he'd said *when* and not *if*. This had to stop. They couldn't keep going on like this.

"I don't know," she answered honestly. "When the DNA tests prove there's been a swap—"

"There was," Gabriel interrupted. "I just got the results back. I texted Cameron, too, so he knows."

Obviously, Lauren had known the swap had taken place, but it still felt like a shock. A violation, really. Someone—Maria, probably—had swapped the babies, and in doing so had robbed Lauren of being with her son for the first year of his life. She'd done the same to Cameron.

"I love Patrick just as much as I do Isaac," she said, pushing the sandwich aside. No way could she take another bite.

"I know. Cameron feels the same way."

He did. Lauren had no doubts about that, either. "That's another reason for the marriage. Neither of us can give up the babies we've been raising."

Gabriel stayed quiet for a moment. "So you…what? Try to make a real go of it?" He didn't wait for an answer. "Because if you're not, then that's not right for Cameron or you. Especially Cameron. You've had a marriage, a real one, but Cameron's never had that. He deserves it."

Lauren was already reeling from the DNA news and everything else that'd happened, but that only added to the feeling. She hadn't expected her brother to have that objection.

But he was right.

Cameron did deserve better. He deserved a real wife who loved him and wanted to build a family with him. Lauren could give him the family—that was already in place—but she wasn't sure she could handle the rest. A real marriage to Cameron would mean her staying in Blue River. It would mean forgetting her past. And she wasn't sure she could do that just yet.

"What are you suggesting?" she came out and asked.

"That you hold off on saying I do at least for a day or so until you've had time to give it more thought."

Good advice. But it wasn't advice she could take. "It would crush me if the boys were taken away. In fact, I couldn't let that happen, and that means Cameron and I could end up breaking the law."

Gabriel gave her a snarled look that only a lawman big brother could manage, and he made a suit-yourself sound. Since she'd obviously ruffled his feathers, Lauren went to him and brushed a kiss on his cheek. She hadn't expected it to help and was surprised when it did. It soothed his expression a bit anyway.

"I love you," he said. "I only want the best for you. For Jameson, Cameron and Ivy, too."

She knew that. So did they. But there were no easy ways for her to get "the best." Right now she'd just settle for keeping the babies and the rest of them safe.

"I love you, too," Lauren answered.

They had a nice moment, one that felt like old times before Gabriel tipped his head to the sandwich. "You should finish eating. You're going to need your strength. Duane and Julia are on their way here now."

That wouldn't be fun, but it was necessary. "They agreed to come?"

Gabriel gave her a flat look. "I didn't exactly ask. I told them I'd put out warrants for their arrests if they didn't show up. I want to question Julia especially."

Yes, because Maria had kept repeating the woman's name.

"I thought if I had Julia and Duane here together, that one of them might blurt out something when they started arguing with each other," Gabriel went on. "There seems to be enough bad blood between them that it brings out the fangs."

It did. And the two had had no trouble incriminating

each other in their other conversations. Too bad nothing had panned out on those so Gabriel could make an arrest. There'd been no proof that Julia had hired those gunmen, and the Rangers hadn't had any luck confirming that the files Julia gave them were real and not some attempt to set up Duane.

"And Evelyn?" she asked. "Are you bringing her in, too?"

Gabriel got that hard look again. "She's not answering her phone, and according to her housekeeper, she didn't come home last night."

Lauren thought about that for a moment. "Could she be with her *friend*, Judge Olsen?"

Gabriel shook his head. "I called him. He didn't know where she was, either. I pressed him for some info about his relationship with Evelyn." He put relationship in air quotes. "But he got huffy and reminded me that I was a small-town cop who had no right to question him."

"That sounds like something a guilty man would say. Please tell me there's something that proves Evelyn has bought off Judge Olsen?"

"Nothing. So far," he quickly added. "I'm hoping either Julia or Duane will have something to say about that, too. All three—Duane, Julia and Evelyn—seemed to be coiled around each other like a family of snakes."

They did. And that was unsettling. It was bad enough if only one of them was behind this, but if they'd teamed up…well, Lauren didn't want to go there.

She heard more footsteps, and Lauren hurried to get past Gabriel so she could peer out into the hall. Gabriel didn't let her get far, though. He stepped in front of her, probably because he thought it was one of their suspects. It wasn't.

It was Cameron.

He was wearing a bandage on the side of his head near his right temple, but even seeing that didn't diminish the relief she felt. It flooded through her, and Lauren practically ran to him. She hadn't intended to do it, but she put her arms around him and kissed him.

Cameron's muscles tensed, probably because he hadn't been expecting it. And because Gabriel was almost certainly watching them. Still, Cameron didn't push her away. He let the kiss linger until Lauren eased back.

And that was when she saw the weariness in his eyes. Lauren was pretty sure she knew what it meant, too.

"Maria's dead?" she asked.

He nodded and brushed a kiss on her cheek. Not a kiss of relief as hers had been. Also not one of passion. That had been meant to comfort her, and much to her surprise, it worked.

She'd been right about Gabriel watching them. He was in the doorway, but he walked out, stopping directly in front of them. "Did Maria say anything else?"

"No." Cameron scrubbed his hand over his face and blew out a long, frustrated breath. "She was unconscious by the time she went into surgery, and she died on the operating table."

Lauren reminded herself that the woman's chances of surviving hadn't been that good, but it was still a blow. Not just because they wouldn't be able to get answers from her but also because a woman was dead. Maria hadn't exactly been innocent since she was the one who'd switched the babies, but she didn't deserve to die because of what she'd done.

"Whoever's behind this can now be charged with murder," Gabriel said.

He was right, but the trick would be to catch the person.

As if waiting for something, Gabriel glanced at both Cameron and her. Maybe he wanted to discuss the marriage, but he didn't get a chance to do that. That was because his phone rang. When he glanced at the screen, he mumbled something about having to take the call, and he went into the squad room.

"Make sure she eats," Gabriel told Cameron from over his shoulder. "Her lunch is on my desk."

Cameron immediately took her back into her brother's office, and she was about to remind him that he needed to eat, too, but he sat across from her and helped himself to some of the chips. She handed him half the sandwich, and he started in on that, as well.

"You know about Duane, Julia and Evelyn?" she asked.

He nodded, then drank some of her water, too. It seemed…intimate or something. Which her body thought was good. Of course, her body often had thoughts like that around Cameron.

"SAPD is looking for Evelyn," he explained, which meant Cameron had been keeping up with the case even when he'd been at the hospital. "The justice of the peace will be here soon, too."

He took something from his shirt pocket and handed it to her. A marriage license.

"I had the clerk bring it to the hospital," Cameron added. He ate more of the chips and stared at her. "Having second thoughts? Or did Gabriel talk you out of doing this?"

"He tried," she admitted. And paused. "FYI. You deserve better, though. Better than a marriage of convenience."

The corner of his mouth kicked up in a slight smile, and he leaned across the desk to drop a kiss on her cheek. "Lauren, there's nothing convenient about you," he drawled.

There it was. The heat that always went to flames. It set off red flags in her head. Because the heat could lead her to do things that shouldn't be happening. At least not now anyway. Cameron and she had too much without adding sex to the mix.

The heat faded considerably when she heard the voices in the squad room. Julia and Duane had arrived. And they'd brought their lawyers from the sound of it. Someone—a man—was talking about this being harassment.

"I haven't started to harass you yet," Gabriel growled, his voice low and dangerous as only Gabriel could manage. "Trust me, you'll know when I've started."

Cameron and she stepped into the hall just as she saw Gabriel motioning for Duane and Julia to follow him. Lauren had been right about the lawyers. There was a man and woman, both wearing business clothes, and they fell in step behind Gabriel as he led them toward the interview room.

Julia stopped to give Lauren a glare.

Lauren glared back and hoped she wouldn't lose her temper and punch the woman. Julia had been a thorn in her side for years, and Lauren had reached her limit. So that her brother wouldn't have to arrest her for assault, she stayed just slightly behind Cameron when they went into the interview room with the others.

"They're going to stay for this?" the female lawyer balked.

"Yes," Gabriel said without hesitation. "And rein in your attitude. Just a short while ago, the three of us had thugs shoot a lot of bullets at us. They killed a woman. And before that woman died, she said one thing—the name of your client. I think Cameron, Lauren and I deserve a few answers about that."

"What?" Julia had just sat down, but that brought her right back to her feet. "That nurse said I did this?"

Obviously, Julia knew plenty about this situation, and judging from her lawyer's scowl, she didn't like that her client had just admitted as much.

Gabriel put his hands on the metal table and leaned in, his face getting very close to Julia's. "Tell me everything you know about *that nurse*."

Duane huffed. "I don't know why I got called in for this. Obviously, this is Julia up to her old tricks again." He got up to leave, too, but Cameron shot him a glare that could have frozen Texas in August.

"Sit," Cameron said through clenched teeth.

Duane sat, but his lawyer—the bald guy in a gray suit—rattled off a legal protest. He didn't mention the word *harassment*, though.

"Your client has the means, motive and opportunity to be behind that attack," Gabriel reminded the lawyer. "That's why he's here. And that's why he's staying here until I get answers. Don't," he added when the lawyer opened his mouth. "I have enough to arrest your client, and I'm in a bad enough mood to do it. Just let Deputy

Doran and me ask the questions, and we might be able to get to the bottom of this."

Maybe it was the badass looks on Cameron's and her brother's faces, but the lawyers, Duane and Julia didn't say anything.

Gabriel waited a couple of seconds, and he turned back to Julia. *"That nurse,"* he repeated. "Start talking."

Julia didn't do that right away. She took a deep breath first. "I went to see her. You already knew I was suspicious about Patrick. Because he doesn't look like Alden or me. Or Lauren, for that matter. I'd hoped Lauren had cheated on my brother, that the baby was someone else's. Like *his*." She motioned toward Cameron. "It's obvious Lauren still has feelings for him."

It probably was obvious. Lauren sighed. This old attraction was hard to hide.

"Anyway, Maria didn't admit it at first," Julia went on, "but she finally said she'd switched the babies. She claims she did that because of his sister, Gilly." She pointed to Cameron again. "Gilly was afraid of her baby's father, Trace Waters. Well, I thought that was a stupid reason to do the switch because Trace could have gone after the wrong kid. He could have gone after my nephew."

Julia probably wanted them to think that she cared if that happened or not. She didn't. It would make Julia's lawsuit a little easier if Alden's son wasn't around to be his rightful heir.

"Did Maria happen to say how she did the switch?" Cameron asked.

"I didn't ask about that, but Maria claimed she never intended to put my nephew in danger. She said Gilly had told Trace that the baby wasn't his, and that she would prove it with a DNA test. She had Maria do a test on Alden's son and was having the results sent to Trace. That way, he wouldn't try to take the baby."

That helped soothe Lauren's nerves a bit. At least Gilly had had a plan to protect Isaac. And if Trace had insisted on repeating the DNA test, he would have assumed Gilly had been telling the truth about the boy not being his. Still, there was something not right about this.

"Why didn't Maria tell us what she'd done after Gilly's boyfriend was killed?" Lauren pressed.

"How should I know?" Julia snarled. "I only saw the woman once."

"Yet she kept repeating your name when she was dying." Gabriel stared at her, clearly waiting for an explanation about that.

But an explanation didn't come from Julia. It came from Duane.

"Julia met with Maria more than once," Duane said. Julia opened her mouth as if to shout out a denial, but Duane added, "I have proof."

"You can't possibly have proof—" But Julia stopped, her eyes narrowing. "You had me followed."

"I did," Duane readily admitted. "I wish I'd had you watched 24/7 because that way you wouldn't have had the chance to set up those fake books to try to get me in hot water."

"You had no right," Julia spat out as if she was completely innocent in all of this, and she looked ready to launch herself at Duane.

Cameron got in between them. He pointed to Julia. "How about telling us the truth? Not just about Maria but everything else."

"I have told the truth," she insisted. She paused.

"Other than the number of times I met with Maria. What does it matter if I met with her once or three times? It doesn't," she quickly concluded.

Cameron huffed. "It matters because you lied. Now, I want to know why."

Julia made a sound of outrage, and she pushed away her lawyer when she tried to whisper something to Julia.

"I didn't see the point in Maria telling Lauren and you what happened," Julia finally explained. "I mean, you were both raising the babies, and it would only send things into a tailspin."

It didn't take long for Lauren to figure out what Julia had done. And what she'd intended to do. "You paid Maria hush money. Or you could have silenced her by threatening to turn her in to the cops. Of course, you didn't plan to keep it a secret. My guess is you were going to spring the DNA results during the lawsuit. That way, it would negate Patrick's claim to Alden's money."

"Bingo," Duane agreed. "And the reason Julia didn't spill the news sooner was because she didn't want to give you time to figure out what was going on. She was counting on you being stunned enough to just hand over the money to her."

"And it might have worked," Lauren said over the profanity Julia was aiming at Duane. "Except I also got suspicious and had a DNA test done. I would have known the results and had time to figure out what they meant long before the lawsuit."

"That's why Julia hired the gunmen." Duane, again.

Julia went after Duane, this time slamming into Cameron. Her lawyer caught on to her, and between Cameron and her, they managed to get Julia back in her seat.

"My client shouldn't have to sit here and listen to these allegations," the lawyer snapped.

"They're not allegations," Duane responded without hesitating. "Julia came to me months ago and wanted us to team up against Lauren. She thought there was something I could do to drive Lauren back into Cameron's bed. That way, Lauren might decide the lawsuits weren't worth fighting. I mean, it's not like Lauren needs the money or anything."

Gabriel glanced at Lauren, and even though he didn't come out and say it, this was probably what he'd had in mind when he wanted them all in the room together. Obviously, Duane and Julia had been trying to figure out how to get their hands on Alden's money and company.

Julia was glaring. Not just at Duane, either. She shared that glare with Cameron and Lauren. "You have no proof I've done something wrong."

"But we do," Cameron assured her. "You met with a criminal suspect—Maria. You knew she'd committed a crime, and you didn't tell the cops. That definitely falls into the 'done something wrong' category."

Julia sputtered out some angry sounds and slid back her chair, scraping the metal legs against the floor. She got to her feet. "Duane doctored the company books, and I don't see you harassing him like you're doing to me."

"Oh, I'll get to him," Gabriel said. His phone dinged with a text message, and he glanced at the screen before returning his attention to Julia. "Duane knew about Maria's crime, too, and didn't report it. That means both of you are going to stay for a while as my deputies take your statements. I'll have a little chat with the DA to see if he wants me to go ahead and arrest you."

That started more protests from Julia, Duane and their attorneys. They were all so loud that it was nearly impossible to hear what any of them were saying. Gabriel ignored them all and turned to Cameron and her.

"Wait here," Gabriel added to Julia and Duane, and he motioned for Cameron and Lauren to follow him into the hall. Her brother didn't say anything, though, until he'd shut the interview room door. "Maybe they won't kill each other before I get Jace in there to take their statements." He tipped his head to the squad room. "By the way, you two have a visitor."

So that was what the text had been about. And Lauren soon saw who the visitor was. Henry McCoy. He'd been the justice of the peace for as long as Lauren could remember.

Cameron looked at her. The kind of look that implied he was trying to figure out what she was thinking. Was she still up for this? Or was she having second thoughts?

The answer to both questions was yes. Lauren wasn't sure this was the right thing to do, but she was going through with it. She gave Cameron a nod. Her brother must have known what that meant because he huffed. However, Gabriel didn't try to talk her out of it. He walked on ahead of them, making his way to Jace's desk. No doubt to tell the deputy to get started with those statements.

"Thank you for coming," Cameron told Henry. He went to the man and shook his hand.

"Cameron, Lauren," Henry greeted. The man was in his early seventies now, and he seemed frail in a suit that practically hung off him. His smile seemed genuine, though. "Always figured you two would tie the knot." His smile faded. "I hate that it's under these circumstances, though."

It didn't surprise Lauren that Henry knew about the attacks. Or that Cameron and she had once had a thing for each other. Heck, he might even know about the baby swap.

Henry looked around. "You want to say the vows out here or in one of the offices? Oh, and you don't need a witness, but maybe you'd like Gabriel to be there."

Lauren wasn't so sure Gabriel would want to do that, but she turned to ask him. Before she could do that, though, Cameron's phone rang, and she saw Jodi's name on the screen. It gave her another jolt of adrenaline, and it must have done the same to Cameron because he quickly answered it and put the call on speaker.

"Cam, you need to get back to the ranch ASAP. There's been some trouble." Jodi paused. "Evelyn's here."

Chapter Twelve

Cameron hated that he was having to rush Lauren out of the sheriff's office. When they were in a panic, it was hard to think straight, and with a mind-set like that, it could make them easy targets for those hired guns who were still out there. Still, Cameron didn't have a choice.

He couldn't let Evelyn get anywhere near the babies.

"Where's Evelyn now?" Cameron asked Jodi.

"I'm holding her at gunpoint. I had Jameson stay inside with the boys."

Good. Even though Gabriel had plenty of work to do, he must have heard what Jodi said because he grabbed the keys for the cruiser that was parked right out front. He motioned for them to go with him.

"How the hell did Evelyn get on the ranch?" Cameron hurried Lauren into the vehicle, and the moment they were in, Gabriel took off.

"We think she came in on that trail at the back of your house."

The one that Lauren had used. Lauren shook her head, maybe to let him know that she hadn't told the woman about the trail, but her headshake wasn't necessary. Cameron knew she wouldn't do that.

"Here's the thing, though," Jodi continued a moment later. "There's no vehicle on the trail. The hands checked. When they found Evelyn, she was in your yard. She looks dazed or something. I think someone might have drugged her."

Well, hell. Cameron certainly hadn't expected that. "Was she armed?"

"No. And she has some cuts and scratches on her hands. They look like defensive wounds to me."

Cameron looked at Lauren to see if she was making sense of this, but she seemed just as baffled as he was. Maybe, though, this was some kind of ruse.

Or trap.

That put his heart in his throat. "Are you outside with her?" he asked Jodi. Cameron met Gabriel's gaze in the rearview mirror and saw the concern in his eyes.

"Yes. The hands brought her here, but I didn't want her in the house."

Neither did Cameron. But he didn't want Gabriel's wife being gunned down. "Move her to the porch." It wasn't ideal, but at least it would give Jodi a little cover, and she wouldn't be so out in the open.

"Make sure the hands keep watch," Gabriel added. "We're already on the road and will be there soon."

"Hurry," Jodi said. "I got a bad feeling about this."

Since Lauren, Gabriel and he had been attacked just hours earlier, Cameron wasn't feeling so easy, either. Of course, Evelyn usually brought trouble with her wherever she went.

Cameron ended the call so he could keep watch around them. After all, they were going to have to drive right past the place where Maria had been shot.

And where Lauren had killed a man.

It wouldn't be a good thing for her to see—since

she'd be reliving that latest nightmare—but it was the shortest route to the ranch, and they would have to take it. The minutes counted now, and he wanted to get to Jodi so that she wouldn't have to be in harm's way. Judging from the way Gabriel was speeding, he felt the same.

"Why would Evelyn have done this?" Lauren said, but she seemed to be talking more to herself than to him.

"Maybe she's desperate." Or worse. She could have gone off the deep end.

Cameron's phone rang, the sound causing Lauren to gasp. It got Gabriel's attention, too. Probably because he thought it was his wife calling back with bad news. But it wasn't a number that Cameron recognized.

That bad feeling skyrocketed. Because this could be one of the gunmen. Cameron answered it, putting it on speaker, but he didn't say anything.

"Deputy Doran?" the caller asked. "I'm Judge Wendell Olsen. I'm a friend of Evelyn—"

"I know who you are," Cameron interrupted. "Did you put her up to trespassing onto the Beckett Ranch?"

The judge made a slight gasping sound. "Trespassing? No, Evelyn wouldn't do that."

Cameron didn't groan, but that was what he wanted to do. "Yes, she would, and she's there now."

"Not by choice. Something must have happened."

Either that or the judge didn't know just how loony his friend could be. "Why are you calling?" Cameron didn't bother to make his tone sound even marginally pleasant because he didn't like this clueless clown distracting him.

"I was worried about Evelyn. And her housekeeper just called. SAPD found Evelyn's car in a parking lot at a bar in south San Antonio. It's not an area where Evelyn would go. I think she was kidnapped."

That would mesh with the defensive wounds that Jodi thought the woman might have. Still, Cameron wasn't buying this. Evelyn could have something up her sleeve.

"Why would a kidnapper take Evelyn to the ranch?" Cameron came out and asked the judge.

"To make her look guilty of violating her restraining order. And you're the person who'd gain the most from that." The judge also wasn't tossing out any friendly vibes.

It took Cameron a moment to get his jaw unclenched. "You just accused me of a felony. Want to rethink that?"

Silence. For a long time. "I don't want you railroading a woman who simply wants to see her grandson."

"Evelyn doesn't want to *see* him," Cameron corrected. "She wants custody of him. Big difference, and from what I'm hearing, you think you're going to try to make that happen."

More silence from the judge. Then he said, "I'll get Evelyn's lawyer and the San Antonio cops out to the ranch."

"SAPD has no jurisdiction in Blue River," Cameron reminded him.

"Then I'll get the Rangers."

Olsen really wasn't going to like this. "No need. There's already one at the ranch. Jameson Beckett. I suppose you'll threaten us with the FBI next, but they have to be invited to an investigation. I'm not inviting them. Not for this anyway. However, I wonder what they would think about a judge pressuring local law enforcement to do his bidding because his friend with a criminal record just committed another crime."

Cameron figured that put a scowl on the judge's face. "I just want to make sure Evelyn's treated fairly." And with that, he ended the call.

Great. Now he had a meddling judge added to this mix. It made Cameron rethink the idea of staying at the ranch. It was time for him to look into a safe house for Lauren and the babies.

Gabriel took the turn to the ranch so fast that Cameron was surprised he didn't lose control of the cruiser. He grappled with the steering wheel, keeping it on the road, and he sped toward his house.

The hands were definitely out and about. Cameron spotted six of them, and one of them had to open the cattle gate so that Gabriel could drive through. The moment the house came into view, he saw the reserve deputy, Mark Clayton, in the front yard. And he also saw Jodi. She was indeed on the porch by the front door and was holding a gun. She had it aimed right at Evelyn, who was sitting on the top step a good eight feet away from Jodi.

Gabriel braked to a stop and threw open the door. In the same motion, he drew his gun. "Go inside," he told Jodi.

Cameron rarely heard that kind of emotion in his boss's voice, but it was definitely there now. Gabriel loved Jodi, and it was obvious he'd been worried about her. Cameron was, too, but he was just as concerned for Lauren and the others in the house.

"I told Jodi I'd keep an eye on the woman," Mark said, "but she insisted on doing it herself."

That didn't surprise Cameron. He'd known Jodi his whole life, and her stubborn streak was just as big as her heart. Since she was a security specialist, she had the training to hold someone at gunpoint. The training to protect herself, too, but Gabriel almost certainly hadn't wanted the woman he loved in danger.

"Wait inside with Jodi," Cameron told Lauren.

She hesitated, then shook her head. "I don't want Gabriel and you out here. It's too dangerous."

Lauren was right. A good sniper might be able to pick them off. That was why he had to hurry this along. He brushed a kiss on her cheek and gave her a nudge to get her moving. He gave her a different kind of nudge when he whispered, "Check on the boys. Make sure they're not near the windows."

Her eyes widened, and she practically ran inside. One down, one to go. Plus, he really did want to make sure the boys were in the safest place possible. Lauren would see to it that they were.

Gabriel, however, didn't go in. He went onto the porch, blocking the door with his body. Probably in case Evelyn tried to bolt inside.

"Your wife said she would shoot me if I moved," Evelyn told Gabriel.

"She would have. And if you move, I'll shoot you if Cameron doesn't beat me to it first."

It was an empty threat. Well, the shooting part was anyway. Jodi had told them that Evelyn wasn't armed, so they couldn't use deadly force on her, but Cameron would stop her if she tried to get in the house.

"Start talking," Cameron demanded. "Why are you here?"

Evelyn looked him straight in the eyes. "Because you set me up."

Cameron huffed and tried to rein in his temper. "Let's deal in reality and not fairy tales. I haven't had time to set you up. I've been too busy dodging bullets from hired guns. And if I did want to frame you for something, the ranch is the last place I'd bring you."

She kept staring at him as if trying to figure out if he was telling the truth. She must have decided he was because Evelyn finally looked away and touched her fingers to her mouth. The gesture muffled a sob. For the most part anyway. Cameron still heard it. Normally, he had a soft spot for a crying woman, but he wasn't feeling anything more than wariness when it came to Evelyn.

"Start from the beginning," Gabriel said. "Tell us what happened."

Since this could go on for a while and he was still in the yard, Cameron joined Gabriel by the door.

"I was leaving my office to go home when a cop pulled me over," Evelyn explained. "It wasn't a cop car, but he had a blue flashing light. And a badge. He showed me his badge." She pressed her fingers to her mouth again. "I lowered the window to ask him why he'd pulled me over, and he pulled a stun gun out. I fought him, but he hit me with it."

Evelyn turned, showing them her neck. There were indeed two wounds there that looked like the kind of marks a stun gun would make.

"Did you get the cop's name?" Gabriel asked.

"No. In fact, I don't remember much after the stun gun. I think he must have drugged me. When I woke up, I was out in the middle of nowhere. The woods," she clarified. "My car wasn't there. Neither was my phone or purse. So I started walking on a path. I ended up in your backyard."

"Convenient," Cameron mumbled.

She lifted her head, the anger flashing through her

eyes. "No, it wasn't. I was attacked by a cop and brought here."

"By a fake cop," Cameron corrected. "Lauren, Duane and Julia all had fake police officers go to their homes. In Lauren's case, the guy shot her in the arm."

Evelyn gasped. "Was my grandson there when that happened?"

Cameron nodded. "He was in the house."

And he carefully watched Evelyn's expression. The color drained from her face, and she seemed horrified. But Cameron didn't know if that expression was because her grandson had been in danger or because Evelyn had hired those thugs and they'd gone against her order to make sure the baby was safe.

It took several moments before Evelyn regained her composure. "May I see him? May I see Patrick?"

Cameron didn't even have to think about this. "No. Not as long as you're a suspect in these attacks."

Even though that was a serious accusation he'd just made, Evelyn didn't lash out. "But you'd let me see him if there was no chance of his being in danger, if the fake cops and hired guns were caught?"

Now he had to think about it. "I'd consider it if I knew beyond a shadow of a doubt that you had no part in any of this. That includes Maria Black's murder."

Her mouth dropped open, and she got to her feet. "Maria's dead?"

Cameron wasn't going to get into how she knew the nurse. Apparently, everyone connected to this had known her.

"She's dead," Gabriel verified. "A gunshot wound to the chest at point-blank range. My guess is a fake cop who someone hired did that to her."

Evelyn shook her head and looked genuinely distressed about that. She glanced around as if trying to figure out what to do. Cameron hoped she didn't try to run because he didn't want to have to go after her.

"Will you be taking me to the sheriff's office?" she asked Gabriel.

Gabriel tipped his head to Mark. "No, he will be." He motioned toward Allen Colley, one of the hands who was close to the house. "And he'll go with you, too. I'll be there later when I've made sure things are okay here."

Both Cameron and Gabriel waited on the porch until Mark, Allen and Evelyn were in the cruiser and Mark had driven away.

"You believe her?" Gabriel asked him as they went inside.

"No." But then Cameron had to shrug. "Maybe she's telling the truth. Julia or Duane could have set her up because they needed a patsy." And Evelyn would have made a great patsy because of her police record.

Lauren and Jodi were right there waiting in the foyer for them. Gabriel reset the security system, hooked his arm around Jodi and moved her away from the door. They went toward Gabriel's office.

"I heard most of what Evelyn said," Lauren volunteered. "First, though, I checked on the boys. They're okay."

Cameron didn't doubt that, but he wanted to see for himself so he made his way to the nursery. The relief came when he spotted them napping on a quilt on the floor. The disappointment, too, because he'd wanted to hold them. He certainly needed something to ease the tension he was feeling.

Lauren helped with that when she gave his hand a gentle squeeze.

Both Dara and Merilee were in the room, sitting on the floor next to the boys. The curtains were drawn, and the lights were off.

"Everything should be all right now," Cameron told them, and he hoped that was true.

Merilee gave a shaky nod and made her way to a chair where she picked up her e-reader. Dara said something about getting a snack and headed to the kitchen. He doubted she'd be eating, though, since she didn't look very steady.

Cameron hated what this was doing to Dara and Merilee. Hated what it was doing to all of them. Thankfully, the only ones who didn't seem to be aware of the danger were Patrick and Isaac.

He looked at Lauren, taking her back into the hall so their conversation wouldn't wake the boys. But Lauren spoke before he had a chance to say anything.

"We're leaving the ranch?" she asked.

They were obviously on the same wavelength. He nodded. "It'll take me a while to set up a safe house, but I should have it ready by tomorrow."

She didn't question that. Didn't argue. But then, Lauren knew full well that the hired guns were still at large, and another attack could happen despite all their security measures.

"We'll also need to postpone the marriage plans," Cameron continued. "I don't want to take you back into town, and I don't think it's a smart idea to have the justice of the peace come here."

Lauren made a sound of agreement. "The thugs could maybe use him to get to us."

Yep. Heck, the thugs could use anyone, and that was why it was best if they were away from here. Every minute they stayed at the ranch, they put Lauren's family and the ranch hands in danger.

Cameron was about to find a quiet place to work so he could start on making the arrangements for the safe house, but he heard footsteps, and a moment later Jameson came into the hall. He looked in on the boys before he motioned for them to follow him into the foyer.

"I got some news on the loan shark Julia owes," Jameson explained. "The guy's name is Artie Tisdale, and he's bad news. He wouldn't say much to me on the phone. I think he was afraid I was recording it, but one of the other Rangers is headed over there now to talk to him."

It didn't surprise Cameron one bit that the guy was wary of talking to law enforcement. He probably wouldn't say much to the other Ranger, either, but they had to try.

"Did he admit Julia owed him money?" Lauren asked her brother.

"He chose his words carefully, said that he'd *helped Julia out* when she was short of cash, but of course he didn't admit to being a loan shark. He also didn't say anything about what he would do if Julia didn't pay back the cash soon."

Cameron thought about that. "Tisdale could have paid for the hired guns. Heck, they could be on his payroll. Is there anything to link Tisdale to the dead gunmen?"

"There's no money trail, but yeah, I could see Tisdale doing that to protect his investment. If Julia gets her brother's estate, then she could pay back Tisdale's loan along with all his other expenses."

Lauren shuddered, rubbing her hands along the sides of her arms. She winced a little, too. A reminder of her injury. Cameron wanted to kick himself for not having a medic check her out when they'd been at the sheriff's office.

"I'll let you know if the Ranger gets anything more from Tisdale," Jameson went on. "In the meantime, I'll look for any connection between Tisdale and the thugs. Something might turn up."

Cameron wanted that to happen, but a loan shark had probably covered his tracks.

Jameson turned to walk away, but Gabriel came hurrying into the foyer. One look at his face, and Cameron knew something was wrong.

"Please tell me there aren't gunmen on the ranch," Lauren said.

Gabriel shook his head. "No, but gunmen just attacked Allen and Mark. And they took Evelyn."

Chapter Thirteen

Lauren stared out the window of the guest room. She wasn't standing directly in front of it, though. Cameron's orders. He'd also told her to keep the curtains shut, which she had, but she could still look out through the small gap on the side where the curtains met the wall. She could see part of the ranch and her parents' old house.

It was a view she'd seen a lot as a kid since Gabriel's place had once belonged to their grandparents.

She'd come here plenty of times and stayed in the rambling big house. Had actually stayed in this very room even though in those days it had been her gran's sewing room. But this was a first for her to stand at the window and keep watch for hired guns.

And Evelyn.

Everyone was on the lookout for the woman. For the thugs, too. But the ranch had over a thousand acres. That made it nearly impossible to watch every part of it. The gunmen could take advantage of that. Maybe Evelyn, too.

Since that only caused Lauren to feel more depressed, she turned her attention to the makeshift bed on the floor where the boys were sleeping. Dara and

Merilee had volunteered to sleep in the nursery with them, but Lauren had thought it was safer for them to be on the second floor. Plus, she hadn't wanted them near her. That way, if something went wrong, she could grab them and try to escape.

At least Mark and Allen hadn't been hurt when the gunmen had attacked the cruiser. In fact, Mark had said the men hadn't even seemed interested in them. The goons had rammed into the cruiser, running it off the road. When that happened, they'd opened the door, dragged out Evelyn and put the woman in their SUV before they sped away.

Lauren had no idea if Evelyn was still alive or if this had been some ruse to make it look as if she'd been taken. Either was possible. Heck, the judge could have even helped her do this so she could escape.

Lauren sank down on the floor not far from the boys, and she leaned the back of her head against the bed. Her body needed sleep, but her mind was still racing too much for that to happen. Maybe, though, she'd be able to get in a nap since they would likely be moving to the safe house in the morning. That would bring a whole new set of worries since they'd have to take the boys out in the open, but maybe once they were in place, there'd be some peace of mind, too.

All of their suspects and the hired guns knew the location of the ranch. They almost certainly knew Cameron, the boys and she were in Gabriel's house. That was why they had to move, and Lauren only wished they didn't have to go through the long night before that happened.

She'd left the door open, so she had no trouble hearing someone walking toward the bedroom. It was Cameron. Not a surprise. He'd been checking on them and giving her updates every half hour or so. Since he'd been keeping his footsteps light—hard to do with cowboy boots on a wood floor—he probably hoped that he would find her asleep. At least the boys were, and that was enough for now.

Even though the lights were all off, there was still enough illumination coming from downstairs that she could see his weary expression. Of course, that weary expression was on a very hot face, so she saw that, as well. As she usually did when she had eyes on Cameron, she felt that tug in her belly. Felt it lower, too. But she figured they were both way too tired for tugs or kisses.

"Anything on Evelyn?" she whispered. Best to get her mind on something else other than Cameron's face.

He shook his head, went to her and sank down next to her on the floor. Not touching her exactly, but he sat close enough for her to catch his scent. He'd showered, probably because he'd had blood on his shirt from the earlier attack. Now he was not only wearing clean clothes, he also smelled like soap and the leather from his boots.

That didn't help the tug.

Normally, she wouldn't have considered those scents a turn-on, but her body suddenly seemed very interested in that combination.

"There's been no ransom demand," Cameron said. "And she hasn't turned up dead. Judge Olsen thinks we're behind it, of course. I think Evelyn wants to play the victim card because she thinks it might stop her from being arrested. It won't," Cameron assured her.

Good. Well, maybe good. If Evelyn was guilty, Lauren definitely wanted her in jail, but the truth was, the woman could be a pawn in all of this. A pawn who could now be in grave danger if those thugs weren't actually working for her.

"Gabriel did find out more on the cooked books that Julia claims she found," Cameron went on. "There's definitely some money missing from the accounts. Not a lot, considering the company has over ten million in assets." He turned to her. "Did you know it was worth that much?"

She nodded. "Isaac is the heir to all of that."

He stayed quiet a moment, a muscle flexing in his cheek. "I'd give away every penny to keep him safe."

So would she—along with every cent in her own personal accounts. But even that wouldn't ensure he was safe. Those thugs could still come after them.

"How much money was missing?" she asked.

"About thirty grand. Enough to fund the attacks and then some."

Yes, it was. "I'm guessing Duane is saying he's innocent, that he didn't take it?"

He nodded, but his forehead bunched up when he looked down at her. Not her face. But her shoulder. Cameron mumbled some profanity, reached out and unbuttoned her shirt. Since this didn't seem to be his version of hasty foreplay, Lauren figured he was checking her wound.

"I meant to change the bandage for you," he said, peeling it back and having a look at it.

She'd already had a look, and while the sight of it turned her stomach, it wasn't serious. "I changed it after my shower," she told him. "Jodi gave me some antibiotic cream to use on it."

He made a sound, sort of a disapproving grunt.

Maybe because the wound turned his stomach, too. Or maybe he thought the home doctoring wasn't nearly enough.

Since he was examining her, Lauren did the same to him. She eased back the bandage on his forehead and had a look. It was clean but would probably leave a scar. It would just give him some more character on his face.

As if Cameron needed more of that.

"You're scowling," he pointed out. "Does the cut look that bad?"

She lowered her gaze, making eye contact with him, and Lauren wasn't sure what he saw, but the corner of his mouth lifted for a moment. "Oh, *that*," he said.

Yes, that. She looked away, but it didn't help. She was already caught up in the moment. Lauren would have liked to blame it on spent adrenaline and the fact that she didn't know if she was going to live long enough to see another day. Realizing something like that had a way of making every moment seem as if it might be her last. But she couldn't lie to herself. What she was feeling had to do with the attraction and nothing else.

"I kissed you in this room once," he said, glancing around.

He had, and she was a little surprised he remembered. She'd been seventeen then. Her grandparents had already passed away and Gabriel had moved in. Lauren had come to get her gran's sewing machine so she could mend the seam on her favorite shirt. Cameron had walked with her there so he could help her carry it back to her house.

"Apparently, a chore like that was fuel for a kiss back then," she joked.

"Breathing was fuel for a kiss," he joked back.

Except it was the truth. Still was. And that caused Lauren to sigh.

She should just get up, move away from him and keep watch again. There were so many reasons for her not to be with him. She didn't want it to cloud her mind. She shouldn't jump into that kind of intimacy until she was certain of her feelings for him. Plus, the boys were in the room.

But those good reasons turned to dust when Cameron leaned in and kissed her.

Despite his being so close, she hadn't seen the kiss coming, but Lauren had no trouble feeling it. One touch from his mouth, and the heat trickled through her. Head to toe.

He lingered a moment, deepening the kiss, before he pulled back and looked at her. Maybe to gauge her reaction. It must have gauged well because it caused him to give that hot half smile again.

"I guess breathing is still a fuel," he said, his voice low. Husky. A Texas drawl that pulled her right in.

Lauren figured either walking out or staying would be the wrong thing to do. Staying would lead to sex. Walking out would no doubt give her plenty of regrets. That was why she slid her hand around the back of Cameron's neck and pulled him to her for another kiss.

And she made sure it was plenty long and deep.

Enough to rid them of the breath that was apparently fueling some of this. Of course, the kiss did its own share of fueling, too.

"Give yourself some time. Think about it before you do anything," she said.

Cameron looked up at her, and she had no trouble seeing the surprise on his face. Lauren figured that

surprise increased a lot more when she got to her feet
and headed for the door.

CAMERON WASN'T SURE what was going on in Lauren's
head, but he sure as heck knew what was going on in
the rest of her. That'd been heat he'd seen in her eyes.
Plenty of it. And the heat had been in her kiss, too.

So why was she leaving?

The simple answer to that was she wasn't, and he
would make certain of that. He got up as fast as he
could and hurried to her. She'd already made it into the
hall by the time he caught up with her, but she was just
standing there—as if trying to figure out what to do.

"Is this about having second thoughts?" he asked.

A soft breath left her mouth. "No. Second thoughts
happened hours ago. I'm on third and fourth thoughts
now."

Yeah, he'd been there, done that. And all those doubts
hadn't solved a thing. He still wanted Lauren, and she
felt the same way about him. Cameron proved that in a
really stupid way. He hooked his arm around her waist,
hauled her to him and kissed her.

Obviously, if Lauren needed some thinking time, this
was not the way to go about it. So he didn't kiss her for
long. Just enough to rid her of more of her breath. And
he stepped back. Cameron figured she was either about
to chew him out or—

She went with the *or*.

She took hold of the front of his shirt, gathering it
up in her hand as she pulled him closer. Lauren kissed
him, and this time it wasn't a kiss to prove anything. It
was scalding hot and meant to send them straight to bed.

Cameron responded, all right. He put his arms

around her, dragging her right against him. Not that it took much effort. Lauren was already headed in that direction. Her breasts landed on his chest while the kiss raged on.

Cameron did his own version of raging. He slid his hand beneath her top, touching the bare skin on her stomach. It was hard to think, but he forced himself to remember the gunshot wound on her shoulder. He didn't want to hurt her.

If the injury was bothering her, Lauren showed no signs of it. She also showed no signs of the timid teenager who'd become his lover over ten years ago. No. This was a woman's kiss. A woman's touch. And this woman apparently knew exactly what she wanted.

She wanted him.

Lauren turned him, putting his back to the wall, holding him in place while she made the kiss even deeper. Cameron did more touching, too, sliding his hands into the cups of her bra. She must have liked that because she made a sound of pleasure. It wasn't loud, but it gave him another reminder.

They were in the hall of her brother's house. Gabriel or the others could come walking up at any second.

Cameron silently cursed and started maneuvering her back into the bedroom so he could shut the door. Of course, there was a problem here, too. The babies. Yeah, they were asleep, but if much more moaning and grappling went on, Lauren and he could wake them.

When he stopped kissing her, Lauren looked to see what'd caught his attention. She glanced at the boys. Then, back at Cameron. All the while she was nibbling on her bottom lip. Maybe she was realizing the logistics of having sex wasn't going to be easy.

But it wasn't impossible.

Cameron looped his arm around her and got her moving. He grabbed the baby monitor along the way but put it on the counter as soon as they were in the adjoining bathroom. Lauren was the one who shut the door, and she immediately launched into another kiss.

The overhead light was off, and Cameron kept it that way, though there was a night-light by the sink. It was just enough for him to see the heat and the determined look in her eyes.

He was still having doubts about whether this should happen or not, but the longer the kiss went on, the more the doubts faded. Soon, he quit thinking and went with it. He pulled Lauren back to him, and this time he had more than kissing on his mind. Well, more than just kissing her mouth anyway.

She made another of those pleasure sounds when Cameron pushed up her top and kissed her breasts through the lace cups of her bra. It was good, but it got a whole lot better when he opened the front clip. That way, he could kiss her without the thin layer of fabric between them. She must have liked that, as well, because she fisted her hand in his hair and held on.

As he went lower.

Cameron got in some kisses to her stomach. Got her unzipped, as well, but Lauren seemed to want to kick up the pace. She achieved that by sliding her hand down into the waist of his jeans.

Yeah, she was kicking this up, all right.

He got rock-hard. And desperate to have her. Not exactly a good combination when he needed to make sure he didn't hurt her while he also listened to the baby monitor.

"Please tell me you have a condom," she said.

"Wallet, back pocket," he managed to answer.

She went after it, doing some clever touching along the way. It felt more like foreplay than looking for something they needed for safe sex. Of course, there were a lot of other "unsafe" things about this, but Cameron chose not to think about that right now. That probably had plenty to do with Lauren unzipping him.

Since there wasn't exactly anywhere else to go, Cameron lowered her to the floor. His back landed on the hard tile, but he barely noticed.

That was because Lauren landed on him.

Straddling him, she took out the condom and tossed his wallet aside.

Cameron did a little tossing, too. Even though he liked seeing Lauren on top of him, he had to move her to get her out of those jeans. Not easy to do. The bathroom wasn't that big, and Lauren wasn't making things easier because she was fighting to get his jeans off, too.

Everything suddenly felt way too urgent, and it was taking an eternity to rid them of their clothes. Cameron finally managed it, and Lauren moved back on top again. It was the best position so that her shoulder didn't get hurt, though he certainly didn't see any trace of pain on her face.

But he did see the pleasure.

Cameron was certain there was plenty of that on his face, too, because he was feeling a whole lot of it in his body. The feeling went up significantly when she got the condom on him and took him inside her.

Lauren went still, as if savoring this for a moment, and in the milky light, she made eye contact with him. It was as if the past ten years just vanished. They were young lovers again before the tragedy that had torn them apart. The ache came. The reminder of just how much he'd lost that night.

And then it was gone.

Because Lauren started to move. That rid him of the ache but created a different kind of one. His need to pleasure her. The need for release.

He caught on to her hips, guiding the movement that was taking him in and out of her. Not that she needed any guidance. Lauren was doing just fine on her own. Better than fine, actually. She was taking them both to the only place that either of them wanted to go.

She put her hands on his chest, anchoring herself while she leaned down and kissed him. Her mouth was still on his when she pushed against him one last time and shattered. That was all Cameron needed, and with the taste of her roaring through him, he gave in to the release and went with her.

Chapter Fourteen

The sound woke Lauren, and she jackknifed in the bed. It was a loud boom. And for several heart-stopping moments, she thought they were under attack, that one of those hired thugs had made it onto the ranch and fired a shot at them.

"A storm moved in," Cameron said. He was close to the bed. Very close. Right by the nightstand just a couple of inches from her. "It's thunder."

She heard the words, but it took a while for them to register. It was indeed storming. Lauren could hear the rain hitting against the windows and the tin roof. There was even a crack of lightning. But she wasn't sure how she'd managed to sleep through that or Cameron getting out of the bed.

Actually, she wasn't sure how she'd managed to sleep at all.

She had, though. She had apparently fallen asleep after Cameron carried her to the bed, and now it was morning. *Late* morning. Well, late for her anyway. It was seven thirty.

"I took the boys downstairs when they woke up about a half hour ago," Cameron said as he made an adjustment to his shoulder holster. "Dara and Merilee changed them and are feeding them breakfast."

Good grief. She'd slept through the babies getting up, as well. Obviously, sex with Cameron was an amazing stress reliever for her to be able to do that. She hadn't slept through the night since she'd become a mother.

"You should have gotten me up sooner," she grumbled.

He shrugged. "I had some things I had to work out. Things to do with the investigation," he added. "Besides, I wanted you to get some rest."

She wanted him to have some rest, too, but she was betting he hadn't gotten much. They'd gotten in bed together, but before she'd fallen into a deep sleep, she'd remembered him getting up to go to the window to look out. Keeping watch to make sure those thugs didn't come back for another round.

She threw back the covers, only to remember that she was stark naked. Cameron noticed, too, and he gave her one of those lazy smiles that reminded her of why she'd landed on the bathroom floor with him in the first place.

"We need to talk, so you should probably get dressed."

"Talk?" she questioned.

"About the safe house. About some other things." He was obviously keeping it vague, and she might have pressed for more, but he leaned down, brushing a kiss on her mouth. Coming from any other man, it would have qualified as a peck, but even a brief kiss was potent when it came from Cameron.

"I'll meet you in the kitchen," he added and headed for the door. But then he stopped and looked back at her.

"By the way, Gabriel knows we were together last night. He came to the room at around five to check on you."

Lauren groaned. She didn't mind Gabriel knowing, but it wasn't something she wanted to discuss with him. Gabriel wouldn't feel the same way, though. She'd get another big-brother lecture from him about guarding her heart.

And it was a lecture she needed to hear.

She should do some heart-guarding, but considering she'd had sex with Cameron—amazing sex at that— that ship had already sailed.

The moment Cameron was out of the room and had shut the door, Lauren hurried from the bed and to the shower. She didn't even wait for the water to reach the right temperature. She just rushed through it and tried not to think of what could go wrong with the move to the safe house. They'd already been through so much, and she didn't want anything else bad to happen.

Lauren changed her bandage, got dressed and was ready to rush out of the room when she spotted something on the floor to the side of the vanity. Cameron's wallet. She'd tossed it there after she'd taken out the condom, and Cameron must not have seen it. She picked it up, the wallet falling open. And that was when she saw it.

The edge of the photo.

It was tucked in one of the slots normally used for credit cards. Without thinking, she lifted it out and got a shock. It was a picture of Cameron and her. They were smiling, and he had his arm slung over her shoulders.

She instantly remembered when it'd been taken. They'd been outside the barn at her house, and Ivy had just walked in on them making out. They'd been fully clothed, thank goodness, but Ivy had insisted on snapping the shot with her phone. Her sister had sent them both the picture, but Cameron must have had his printed out.

Strange that he would have kept it all these years. It seemed like something a man would do when he was in love, and Cameron had never come close to saying the L-word to her. Of course, maybe he'd put the photo there way back then and had forgotten about it.

Lauren headed downstairs, hoping to find Cameron alone so that she could give him the wallet without anyone noticing. No such luck. He was in the kitchen and so was everyone else who was staying in the house.

Like all the other rooms, the curtains and blinds were drawn here. Merilee and Dara were at the table eating breakfast. Jameson was holding Patrick, and Cameron had Isaac. Jodi was at the back window, peering out the side of the blinds. And Cameron and Gabriel were going over a map that was on the laptop computer screen.

They all stopped what they were doing and looked at her.

Gabriel's eyebrow lifted, and since it seemed as if everyone in the room knew what had happened in the guest room bath, she went to Cameron, kissed his cheek and handed him his wallet. What he didn't do was smile or kiss her back. For a moment she thought that was because Gabriel was standing there, but everyone else was looking somber, as well.

"What happened?" Lauren immediately asked.

Cameron put his wallet in his pocket and touched the map. That was when Lauren realized it wasn't an ordinary map. It was the ranch. It showed not only some of the trails but also the nearby roads.

"About two hours ago, one of the hands spotted a suspicious vehicle here. A black SUV." Cameron tapped the road that was only about a quarter of a mile from Gabriel's house. "The hands were down by the cattle gate and used binoculars to read the license plate." He paused. "It was bogus. There's no vehicle registered with those plate numbers."

Well, there went any trace of that dreamy morning-after feel from sex. Lauren glanced at the others and realized they'd already learned this bad news. And it was bad. That vehicle had been way too close to the house. Obviously, this is what Cameron had meant by needing to talk to her, but Lauren had figured it was going to be a discussion about arrangements for the safe house.

"Two hours," she repeated. "Why didn't you come up and wake me?"

"I woke Cameron instead," Gabriel said, looking straight at her.

Good grief. She wasn't normally such a sound sleeper, but that did explain why they'd had the time to come up with this plan. They'd probably been talking about it for the past two hours, and that meant Cameron hadn't just rolled out of bed when she'd awakened. He'd probably come up just so he could have her get dressed.

There was a loud boom of thunder, and Patrick started to fuss. Lauren took him, cuddling him close to her and hoping he didn't pick up on the fear that was starting to crawl through her.

"The SUV was gone by the time I made it to the road," Jameson said, obviously taking up where Cameron had left off. "I looked around but didn't see it."

What he didn't say was that didn't mean it was gone. The SUV could be on one of the trails or a side road.

"I have a reserve deputy posted here." Gabriel tapped the road that led from town to the ranch. "About an hour ago he saw a black SUV. It had different license plates from the one that was near here. But the plates were fake, too. The deputy went in pursuit, but the vehicle got onto the main highway before he could reach it."

If there were hired thugs in the second SUV, they could have doubled back. Or while the deputy was out chasing them, more hired guns could have gotten in place to launch an attack. That spelled out the bottom line for Lauren.

"It's too risky to take the babies out on the road," she said. "We can't take them to a safe house."

Gabriel, Jodi and Jameson all made sounds of agreement. Cameron groaned. "That doesn't mean they'll be safe here, either. You saw how easily Evelyn got through the trails. So could these guys."

That panic and fear weren't just crawling now. Both emotions were at a full sprint. Their situation sounded hopeless, but it couldn't be. They couldn't just stand by waiting for another attack.

"We need to do something." Lauren knew she sounded desperate because she was.

Cameron nodded, then paused. He looked as if he wanted to curse. "I don't like even asking you to do this, but I can't think of another way. Our first priority has to be to keep the babies safe."

"I agree," Lauren said without hesitation. "What do we need to do?"

Cameron looked her straight in the eyes. "We're going to have to force the gunmen to come after us. We'll have to make ourselves bait."

"For the record, I don't like this plan," Gabriel spat out.

Neither did Cameron, but he couldn't stomach the thought of the babies being caught up in another attack. Apparently, neither could Lauren.

"So, how do we do this?" she asked. Again, no hesitation. "How soon can we make it happen?"

She probably had doubts, just as Cameron and Gabriel did, but Cameron knew something that was much worse than doubts and fear, and that was having the babies they loved in danger.

"The cruiser is already parked out front," Cameron explained. "You and I will pretend to get into it with the babies. What we'll be carrying are blankets that will hopefully look as if we have the boys. Since it's pouring rain, it shouldn't seem suspicious that we'd have them covered up like that."

"Where will the babies be?" Lauren asked him. Patrick was still fussing a little so she rocked him gently, brushing a kiss on the top of his head.

"Patrick and Isaac will stay here at the house with Gabriel, Jodi, the nannies and Mark, the reserve deputy. Jameson and Jace will come with you and me."

Cameron took a deep breath before he continued. Here was the part that was going to make Lauren very uneasy. "The gunmen probably have the place under surveillance, so we need to make them believe the babies are truly gone from the ranch. That means sending the hands back to the bunkhouse and to the barns. We need them out of sight."

She shook her head. "But what if gunmen come here after we leave?"

That was a question that had bothered Cameron right after he'd learned about the SUV being in the area. "The ranch hands will be close enough to respond." Not immediately, though. And that in itself was a risk.

"Merilee and Dara will be in the hall bathroom with the boys," Gabriel added. "It's the safest place in the house since there are no windows. Jodi, Mark and I will stand guard. If there's a sign of trouble, we'll sound the alarm and get all of you back here."

And there was the other concern that was eating away at Cameron. If there was trouble, then Lauren and he could be right in the line of fire. That was better than having the babies at risk, but it was nowhere near ideal.

Simply put, Lauren could be hurt.

Heck, Jace and Jameson could be, too.

"If we see the SUV once we're on the road," Cameron continued, "then it'll almost certainly follow us. We'll lead them here." He pointed to one of the larger trails that was about five miles from Gabriel's house. "Or here." Cameron moved his finger to another trail. "It's far enough away from the ranch—"

"Wait," Lauren interrupted. "Why lead them there? There are woods. The river, even."

"There'll be some hands, reserve deputies and even Rangers hidden on those trails." He checked his watch. "They'll be in place by now."

And with some luck, the hired guns hadn't spotted them. If they had…well, Cameron didn't want to go there.

"We also recorded this shortly before you came downstairs." Jameson hit a button on his phone to play the sound of the baby whimpering. It was almost identical to what Patrick had been doing just moments earlier, but this had come from Isaac when Merilee had stopped him from spilling his sippy cup of milk.

"Why would you need that?" she asked, turning first to Jameson and then to Cameron.

"In case the attackers call us." Cameron patted his phone. "They have my number because they've called me before. This way, they'll hear the recording and believe the babies are with us."

Lauren stood there, her forehead bunched up. She was obviously processing all of this, and Cameron wished he could give her more time, but he couldn't.

"If you can think of a safer way to do this," Cameron said to her, "I'd love to hear it."

Lauren rocked Patrick some more and shook her head. "Would we leave now?"

Cameron nodded. "The sooner the better. We need to put some distance between the boys and us."

She blew out a breath, kissed Patrick again and then did the same to Isaac. Lauren handed Patrick to Dara. "Please take care of them," she whispered, and she included Gabriel and Jodi in the glances she gave the nannies.

"I'll get the blankets ready," Jodi said, passing Isaac to Merilee. She headed out of the room.

Gabriel handed Lauren a gun that he took from the top of the fridge, and she tucked it in the back waistband of her jeans. "I've already given Cameron some extra ammo," Gabriel explained. "And make sure your phone is with you. Just in case."

Yeah, in case this plan went south and those goons tried to kill them. If that happened, then Lauren would be the one who'd probably have to make the call since Jameson, Jace and he would be returning fire.

Lauren checked to make sure, and she already had

her phone in her front pocket. That meant they were as ready as they could be.

Jameson certainly didn't seem so eager to get out the door. He huffed and grabbed two Kevlar vests that he'd gotten from Gabriel's home office. "My advice is to lay this on top of the blankets. So it looks as if you're protecting the babies. Then, once you're in the cruiser, put them on." He tapped his chest. "Jace and I are already wearing ours."

That was something Jace and Jameson had done because they'd thought they would be taking the babies to the safe house. Now they would be doing backup for Lauren and him, and the vests might come in handy.

It didn't take Jodi long to return with the blankets, and she'd already rolled them up in such a way that it did look like bundled babies. She handed one to each of them, and while Lauren took it, holding it against her shoulder as she'd done to Patrick, she also gave both boys another kiss.

Cameron kissed them, too, and he draped the vests over the blanket bundles, but he didn't linger. "Go ahead and take them to the bathroom," Cameron instructed the nannies.

No need to stretch out this goodbye. For one thing, it wasn't the safe thing to do, and besides, there were tears in Lauren's eyes. Best not to have her break down. Not until they were in the cruiser, at least.

Cameron waited until he heard the bathroom door shut with the nannies and the boys inside, and Jameson, Lauren and he headed to the front door where Jace was waiting.

"Move fast," Gabriel instructed.

Lauren probably hadn't needed anything else to put

more alarm in her eyes, but that did it. Because it was a reminder that there could be snipers.

Gabriel turned off the security system so they could get out the door, but Cameron was certain he would reset it. There wasn't anyone else he trusted more to protect Patrick and Isaac, but Cameron prayed it would be enough.

The rain seemed to be coming down harder now, and the lightning was close. So close that the thunder boomed almost immediately after the strikes. Definitely not a good time to be out driving, but they couldn't wait it out. The storm was supposed to last most of the day.

Cameron took hold of Lauren's arm to help her down the slippery steps, and Jace and Jameson ran ahead of them to open the doors. The moment they were inside, Jace drove away.

Lauren looked back at the house, tears watering her eyes, and even though Cameron doubted it would help, he kissed her. Her gaze came to his then, and even though she didn't say anything, he knew her heart was breaking.

She'd been through way too much in the past couple of days, and he certainly hadn't helped matters by having sex with her. Yeah, it'd felt necessary at the time, but it had caused them both to lose focus. Had been confusing, as well. But that was something he could dwell on another time.

"Go ahead and put on the vest," Cameron instructed.

He lay the blankets on the seat next to her and helped her into the Kevlar before she put on her seat belt. Cameron got on both his jacket and his seat belt, and then he immediately drew his gun. That didn't help with the alarm in Lauren's eyes, either.

"It's just a precaution," he told her. A necessary one.

As they'd discussed, Jace drove away from town and in the direction of one of the trails. It was hard to see much of anything because of the rain sheeting over the windows. Still, Cameron kept watch. So did Jameson and Jace from the front seat.

"So what's put Gabriel in a snit?" Jameson asked. He glanced back at his sister. "And it's not a snit because of the danger. I'm pretty sure this one's more personal."

Lauren frowned. "Gabriel found me with Cameron."

Jameson laughed. "Like old times. I seem to remember him not approving of you two way back when."

He hadn't. Gabriel had thought Cameron was too old for Lauren. And he had been. But that age difference no longer seemed like an obstacle. A good thing, too, because they had plenty of other obstacles to get in their way.

"Want my advice?" Jameson said, but he didn't wait for Lauren to answer. "Just let Gabriel know you're in love with Cameron, and he'll back off. Love cures a lot of ill will between siblings."

Lauren made a sound of surprise that was borderline outrage. That meant she didn't love him. Not that he thought she did. Lauren had fallen out of love with him years ago, and heck, it probably hadn't even been real love then. He'd been her crush.

A thought that made him frown.

Was that all it'd been?

The attraction had definitely been there, now and then. But maybe her feelings for him hadn't gone beyond basic lust.

"You were more than a crush to me," Cameron mumbled under his breath, but it was obviously loud enough for Lauren to hear because she practically snapped toward him.

However, she didn't blurt out anything to reassure him that he'd just babbled the truth. "You have a picture of us in your wallet," she said.

Now she was the one who looked alarmed at saying something she hadn't meant to say. He nodded, admitting that he did indeed have a picture. One she must have seen when he'd left his wallet on the bathroom floor. But Cameron didn't get a chance to add anything to his nod. That was because Jameson spoke first.

"A black SUV just pulled out of the side road behind us." Jameson drew his gun and turned in the seat. "And it's following us."

Chapter Fifteen

The plan was working. Now Lauren had to hope that was a good thing and that they could truly lead these thugs away from the ranch.

"Speed up," Cameron instructed Jace. "They'd expect us to do that if we actually had the babies in the car."

Cameron gave an uneasy glance behind them at the SUV, followed by an equally uneasy one at the sky. Going fast on these roads wasn't a safe idea, but he was right. They needed to make this as realistic as possible. That meant taking risks.

More than the ones they'd already taken.

She prayed that whatever they would do, it would make Patrick and Isaac safe. Lauren didn't want these goons anywhere near the boys. Still, it was a chance that could happen. While Cameron and she were luring the gunmen, the gunmen could be playing a cat-and-mouse game to get them away from the house.

"They're speeding up, too," Jace relayed.

Lauren got a glimpse of that, and yes, the SUV was much closer now, but Cameron took hold of her arm and lowered her to the seat. "Pick up the blankets," he instructed. "Hold them as if you'd be holding the boys.

The cruiser windows are tinted, but they still might be able to see inside."

True, and again they had to make this look believable. Lauren gathered up the blankets in her arms, making sure they stayed rolled up.

"How much farther is the trail where we'll be turning?" she asked.

Cameron didn't jump to answer, and she saw the renewed alarm on his face. "Hold on," he warned her. "They're going to hit us."

It wasn't a second too soon because the jolt came. So hard that even with her seat belt on, it slung her forward. The strap caught her wounded shoulder in the wrong place and caused the pain to shoot through her. She made a sharp gasp that she tried to muffle, but she failed because Cameron looked at her. But he didn't look for long.

That was because the SUV rammed into them again.

The cruiser went into a skid on the wet pavement, and she could see Jace fighting with the steering wheel to keep control. The cruiser tires clipped the gravel area just off the asphalt and sent a spray of rocks banging against the doors and undercarriage. It sounded like gunfire.

"Hold on," Cameron repeated, and this time he took hold of her.

The SUV rammed into them again. And again. Obviously, the front end of the vehicle had been reinforced because the engine was still roaring behind them.

"Let me see if I can do something about this," Cameron said when Jace finally got the cruiser back on the road surface.

He lowered his window, the rain immediately dampening the backseat. Despite the summer temperatures, the spray of water was cold, and Lauren started to shiver. Part of the shivering, however, was because Cameron was about to make himself an easy target for those hired killers.

Cameron leaned out enough so he could take aim, and he sent two shots in the direction of the SUV. Since Lauren was down on the seat, she couldn't tell if he hit anything, but at least the SUV didn't ram into them.

But the gunmen did something worse.

They returned fire. The shots slammed into the roof of the cruiser. The bullets didn't tear through it, but Lauren could hear them slice across the metal.

"Why would they be shooting with the babies inside?" she asked, the question meant more for herself than the others. "Why would they risk that?" It didn't make sense if they wanted the boys alive.

If.

"They're not firing kill shots," Cameron answered. "If they were, they'd be shooting into the window. I think they're just trying to run us off the road."

Yes, but even that could hurt Patrick and Isaac. Maybe that meant these thugs didn't care if the babies were harmed or not. Or they could have figured out the boys weren't in the cruiser.

That thought didn't make her breathe any easier.

Lauren tried not to panic, but it was hard to rein in the fear. Not only were their precious babies in danger, but these goons could end up killing Cameron and her in a car wreck, too. Of course, that could be what the person behind this wanted. If it was Julia or Duane, they wanted her dead. Evelyn probably felt the same way about Cameron. She didn't want to think of what would happen to Patrick and Isaac if these thugs succeeded in carrying out whatever orders they had.

"How long before we get to the trail?" Lauren repeated.

"A minute, maybe." Jace was volleying glances between the road and the rearview mirror.

The SUV rammed into them once more, but this time Jace managed to keep control. There was no other traffic, thank goodness, so Jace swerved into the oncoming lane to stop them from being hit again.

"Let me try to hold them off." Jameson lowered his window as Cameron had done, and he sent three shots at the SUV.

Maybe those shots would buy them some seconds until they could get to the trail. Of course, the SUV would follow them. That was the plan, after all. The driver could still ram into them. But they wouldn't be going at such a high speed on the trail, and there'd be an ambush waiting for the thugs. Maybe they'd be able to capture at least one of them alive so they could get some answers.

"Everyone hold on," Jace said. "The turn is just ahead."

Lauren pulled in her breath and held it. There were wide ditches on each side of the trail, and if the SUV hit them again, they could land in one of those. They were filled with water and mud, and the cruiser would likely get stuck.

There was another thing that could go wrong, too. Simply put, the gunmen might not follow them. They might recognize this could be a trap and just speed away so they could regroup and come after them again.

Jace had to hit the brakes to slow down for the turn, but he was still going pretty fast when he took it. The trail was a mixture of gravel, dirt and grass, and judging from the way Jace had gripped the steering wheel, he must have expected them to go into another slide.

And they did.

The back of the cruiser fishtailed, slinging them around again, but Jace got them back on course. He didn't speed up right away, though, and Lauren knew why. He was waiting for the gunmen.

She lifted her head to look out the back window. It seemed to take an eternity, but it was only a few seconds before she finally saw what she needed to see. The SUV made the turn, as well, and came after them. Jace hit the accelerator again.

"The reserve deputies and the Ranger should be about a half mile up," Jameson explained. He kept his eyes on the SUV but motioned for Lauren to get back down on the seat.

She did. But she hated she was being protected like this when all three of the men were high enough in the seats that they could be shot. Of course, the gunman's bullets would have to get through the glass first.

That thought had barely crossed her mind when there were more shots fired. These slammed into the trunk of the cruiser. Definitely not as "safe" as those on the roof since the trunk was right next to the backseat.

"What the hell?" Jace mumbled.

That put her heart right in her throat, and Lauren lifted her head again so she could see what'd caused his reaction. There was a motorcycle, and it was parked just beneath some trees just off the left side of the trail.

"Is that the Ranger?" Jace asked.

Jameson shook his head. "Maybe it's one of the reserve deputies. I'll ask Gabriel."

He took out his phone, no doubt to call their brother, but Jameson didn't get a chance to do that.

Because there was a blast.

It was deafening. Lauren couldn't be sure, but she thought maybe it'd come from the direction of the motorcycle. She was sure of something else, though. It hadn't been the sound of a bullet. No, this was something much, much bigger. And whatever it was, it hit them.

Hard.

Jace still had hold of the steering wheel, but it didn't seem to do any good. That was because whatever had hit them exploded into the front end of the cruiser. There were ditches here, too. Ones almost as wide as those on the road. And that was exactly where the blast sent them.

CAMERON DIDN'T KNOW what the guy by the motorcycle had shot at him. He'd barely had time to spot the man before he'd fired something. Not a grenade. The blast hadn't been big enough for that, but it'd been some kind of explosive device.

Jace cursed when the cruiser pitched to the left, and the deputy had no control when the tires on that side went into the ditch. Because of the rain, it was more of a small stream, and they instantly went into the bog.

Trapping them.

They were much too close to the motorcycle guy, since he was on the same side of the trail.

Cameron glanced down at Lauren to make sure she hadn't been hurt in the impact. She hadn't been, but she'd already pulled her gun and was about to sit up. He pushed her right back down.

Behind them, the SUV came to a stop. Not a fast one, either, which meant they'd slowed down enough, probably because the driver had known this was going to happen. And what had happened was the worst-case scenario for this plan. Because now they were trapped.

"I'll call the backup," Jameson said. He, too, still had his weapon drawn, and he was looking all around them.

Cameron was looking, too, but he could no longer see the man by the motorcycle. He'd likely slipped into the woods, and there were plenty of hiding places for him. The trees and underbrush were thick here.

"How far away is backup?" Lauren asked. She was shaking some, but not nearly as much as Cameron had expected her to be doing. Good. Because he might need her to help him shoot their way out of this.

He hated that she was in this position. Hated even more that he was the reason she was here. But Lauren and he were of a like mind on this. They'd wanted to do whatever it took to protect Patrick and Isaac.

And maybe that could still happen.

Cameron had to hold on to that hope. Unless the thugs had brought an army with them, then they might not be able to get to them in the cruiser. Added to that, backup was almost certainly on the way here, and they shouldn't be that far away.

"Backup's coming," Jameson verified when he finished his call.

Cameron looked back at the SUV again. No movement there. The men were staying inside. There was also no movement from anywhere in the woods, but he was dead certain more men were out there.

Hell.

"This could be a trap for the backup," Cameron told Jameson.

Jameson cursed, too, and made another call. Of course, backup would have anticipated that the thugs would be on the lookout for them, but they probably thought they'd be coming to a gunfight. There hadn't been a shot fired, though, since the blast that'd disabled them. That didn't mean, however, that more shots wouldn't come soon.

Cameron's phone rang, the sound knifing through the silence. Lauren gasped, and then she groaned when she saw *Unknown Caller* on the screen. It was almost certainly their attackers. Cameron answered and put it on speaker, but he didn't say a word.

"Deputy Doran," the caller said. "Looks like you and your woman are in a tight spot. I think this is what folks mean by sitting duck."

The thug was stating the obvious, but it still put a knot in Cameron's gut to hear it. "What do you want?" Cameron snapped, and he motioned to Jameson to play the recording on his phone. Within seconds, there was the sound of Isaac fussing.

"I want you and your woman, of course. Those kids, too," the thug said. "Good to know the little fellas weren't hurt during the blast."

"What if they had been?" Lauren snarled. "You could have hurt them. Is that what your boss wants you to do—hurt babies?"

There was plenty of anger in her voice, but Cameron figured it was also a stall tactic. The longer they kept him talking, the more time backup would have to arrive.

"Don't have a clue what my *boss* wants to do to them, and it falls under the heading of I don't care. I just want my money. And no, don't bother to start offering me a payoff. I'm more or less committed to this, you see."

Which meant he could be being blackmailed or coerced in some way. So Cameron tried a different angle.

"If you want immunity, you've got it." That was a lie. As a deputy he couldn't make an offer like that unless he cleared it with the DA. "All you have to do is tell us who hired you."

"No more talk about that," the gunman growled. "Just shut up and listen." He sounded impatient now. Probably because he knew they would have already requested backup, and that time was running out for him. "You and your woman need to get out of the cop car."

"And the babies?" Cameron asked. "Which one do we bring?" Because that would narrow down the identity of the person responsible for this. If the man said to bring Isaac, then it was either Duane or Julia. But Evelyn would want Patrick since he was her grandson.

"I would say just bring one of them, but since I don't know which one," the gunman snarled, "I'll be needing you to step out with both of them. And I'm not gonna do a countdown or anything. You come out with them now."

Cameron doubted the man would want to hear this, but he didn't have a choice. He couldn't take Lauren out there for her to be gunned down. "It's too risky for the babies."

"Hell, it's too risky for you!" the goon practically shouted. "Now, move. I'd better see that door opening right now."

Cameron looked at Jameson and Jace to see if they were ready for whatever was about to happen. They were. Jameson had turned off the recording, put his phone back in his pocket and he had a firm grip on his gun. So did Jace.

And Lauren.

"They'll come to the cruiser after us, won't they?" she asked.

As a minimum. And they didn't have to wait long for that minimum, either.

"Time's up," the gunman said, but the words had hardly left his mouth when Cameron saw something he didn't want to see. It was the guy who'd been by the motorcycle. This probably wasn't the one they'd been talking to since this man didn't have a phone.

However, he did have some kind of launcher.

And he aimed it at the cruiser.

Before Cameron could even react, another explosive came their way. It crashed into what was left of the front end of the cruiser, tearing the metal and engine apart. It also knocked out the front windshield. They had to shelter their eyes from the flying glass and debris.

"Still not convinced you should get out?" the goon on the phone said. "The next one goes right into the cop car where y'all are sitting."

It was a bluff. Possibly. But Cameron couldn't call him on that bluff, and he didn't have time to come up with a plan. They were going to have to run for it, and there was only one direction to go. To the right, away from the thug with the launcher. That meant they'd have to run directly in front of the SUV.

Cameron looked at Lauren, who'd just followed his gaze out the window. Judging from her expression she knew what was about to happen.

"Take both blankets, one in each arm," he instructed. That might save her from being gunned down.

Lauren gave a shaky nod and gathered them up. "When do we start running?" she asked.

"Now."

Cameron threw open the door and started shooting.

Chapter Sixteen

Lauren hadn't had nearly enough time to steel herself up for this, but maybe there was no chance of that happening anyway. Not with the strong possibility that they were all about to die.

Cameron got out ahead of her, took aim at the man by the motorcycle and sent several shots his way. Lauren didn't look back to see if that had pinned down the guy or sent him scrambling. She just ran as fast as she could while trying to keep hold of the blankets. Despite the rain and the slick, muddy surface, she raced across the narrow trail, went several yards into the woods and dropped behind a tree.

She had her gun. She was holding it in a death grip beneath the blankets. But no way did she have a clean shot. That was because Cameron, Jameson and Jace were in between the motorcycle thug and her.

"Run!" she called out to them.

They did, but they weren't hurrying as much as she'd done, and they were volleying their attention between the motorcycle and the SUV. Good thing, too, because it was only a handful of seconds before both SUV doors opened, and the armed men leaned out. They stayed in the SUV and behind the doors, using them for cover.

While they sent round after round of bullets at Cameron and the others.

Lauren didn't have a clean shot of them, either, so she could only pray that they reached safety.

Cameron and Jameson did. They ran toward her, but they only made it a few feet off the trail and ducked behind the first tree they reached. It was still much too close to the SUV, but at least they were no longer in a direct line of fire.

Unlike Jace.

He wasn't nearly as lucky.

Lauren watched in horror as a bullet slammed into Jace's arm.

She heard him make a sharp sound of pain, and he scurried to the front of the cruiser. It was a wreck, but at least he was out of the path of the men in the SUV. Not from the motorcycle guy, though, or anyone else who happened to be out here in these woods. That was why Lauren tried to keep watch for him.

Soon, very soon, Jace would need an ambulance, but there was little chance of getting one out here unless they stopped these hired guns. That meant killing them, since she figured they hadn't come out here with plans to surrender.

The thugs from the SUV continued to fire at Cameron and Jameson, forcing them to stay put, though Cameron did look in her direction. Just a glimpse. And she saw the same worry on his face that was no doubt on hers.

She caught some movement from the corner of her eye. It wasn't by the motorcycle, where she'd last seen the guy with the launcher. It was a good fifteen feet past that. But it was the same man, all right. He was behind some dense shrubs, and he lifted something. Not a launcher this time. But rather a gun.

And he aimed it at Jace.

"Look out, Jace!" she yelled.

But Lauren did more than just shout out a warning. She dumped the blankets on the ground and shot at the guy. She missed. Cursed herself for doing that because the man dropped back out of sight. She had no doubt, though, that he was still there, waiting for a shot where he could finish off Jace.

Her phone dinged with a text message, and while Lauren hated to take her eyes off her surroundings, she knew this could be important. It was. It was from Cameron.

Stay put and keep holding the blankets, he texted. Backup can't get to us right away.

Lauren did pick up the blankets, but her breath froze. The fear wedged there in her throat that'd clamped shut.

No.

That wasn't what she'd wanted to hear.

They needed backup. Worse, it could mean the Ranger and reserve deputies had been hurt or killed. Obviously, these hired guns had known they were trying to lead them to a trap. If they'd spotted the lawmen, then they could have taken them out before Jace had even driven onto the trail.

She forced herself to breathe. To think. Hard to do with the bullets still flying all around, not just from the SUV shooter but also from Cameron and Jameson.

Plus, she had to watch for the man with the launcher. He could send another one of those explosives at Jace. Or at Cameron and Jameson, for that matter. Lauren didn't think he would aim at her, though. Not as long as he thought she had the babies in her arms. It didn't make her feel better to know that she was safe while Cameron, Jace and her brother weren't.

Lauren adjusted her gun, holding it beneath the blankets, and she continued to keep watch. The gunman who'd had the launcher finally leaned out from cover again. Like before, he took aim at Jace. But this time, Jace must have seen him because he fired first. Unlike her shot, Jace's didn't miss, and the guy fell to the ground.

Good, one down and at least two to go.

It wasn't safe for Jace to try to make his way across the trail to her, but he did drop lower to the ground. She could see that he was grimacing in pain. However, he was also looking around to make sure there weren't others who could pick him off.

Even over the noise of the gunfire, Lauren heard another sound. A car engine. Someone was coming up the trail and would soon be behind the SUV. She hoped it was Gabriel or another cop, but she couldn't count on that. She had to do something to help.

Now that Jace was out of immediate danger, Lauren started moving. She stayed crouched as low as she could manage while still carrying the blankets, and she began to make her way to Cameron.

Jameson and he had almost certainly heard the car and knew that it could mean more trouble. If they had to fend off more gunmen, she wanted to be in a position to help.

Lauren kept moving. Kept checking her, too, to make sure Jace was all right. He was still in the same spot, and she didn't see any other hired thugs trying to get to him.

"Stay down," Cameron snapped when he spotted her. "Don't come any closer."

"I can help you return fire."

He didn't answer her, not with words, but he gave her a stern look while he continued to trade shots with the gunmen. Lauren did get down, but she went several more feet first and then took cover behind a tree. All in all, it wasn't a bad position because she had line of sight of Cameron and Jameson as well as Jace.

There was blood on his shirt.

The rain was soaking him, but the blood continued to flow. She saw him grimace again, and he pressed his hand over it. Probably to try to slow the bleeding.

In the distance she heard something else to let her know that things had gone wrong. More gunfire. It seemed to be coming from two areas—both up the trail and back by the road. The gunfire was probably why the backup couldn't get to them.

She kept her attention on their surroundings, but Lauren took out her phone again so she could try to text Gabriel. He almost certainly knew what was going on, but she wanted to make sure the babies were all right. Before she could press his number, though, her phone rang.

Unknown Caller.

Her heart thudded against her chest. Because the gunman was calling her. Maybe because Cameron was too busy shooting to answer. But it did make her wonder how he'd gotten her number.

She hit the answer button, but as Cameron had done earlier, Lauren didn't say anything. It didn't take long, though, before she heard the voice.

"Lauren," the caller said. "There's only one way for

your brother and Cameron to get out of this alive. And that's for you to bring me the babies now."

CAMERON HAD HEARD Lauren's phone ring, and he'd hoped it was Gabriel calling to reassure her that he had a plan to rescue her. But after one look at her face, Cameron knew it wasn't that.

Something was wrong.

Of course, the worst possible scenario came to mind. That something bad had happened at the ranch; that they were under attack. There were plenty of people at Gabriel's to protect Patrick and Isaac, but that didn't mean one of the boys couldn't have been hurt.

He wasn't close enough to Lauren to hear what she was saying, but she was definitely responding to something the caller had said. Not a good response, either. Lauren cursed the caller, and then her gaze flew to him.

Yeah, something was definitely wrong, but he didn't think it was fear that he saw. Cameron thought she was angry. So angry that every visible muscle was tight.

Even though Cameron had insisted that she stay put, Lauren started toward him. She didn't exactly stay down, either. She hurried, but at least she was continuing to hold the blankets to her chest. Unfortunately, they no longer looked much like babies because the rain had soaked the blankets. It had soaked Lauren, too. The rain was dripping off her face.

When she was still several feet away, Cameron ran to her, pulling her behind the tree with Jameson and him. He was about to ask her what'd happened, but she just handed him the phone. Her hand was shaking. *She* was shaking. But her eyes were narrowed almost to slits.

"It's Julia," she said.

Cameron doubted the woman was calling to check on them or declare her innocence for the umpteenth time. No. She was the person behind this. Probably the person in the car that'd just come to a stop in back of the SUV.

Hell.

Of course, she was one of their main suspects, but it sickened him to think of this witch putting Lauren and everyone else in danger. And he figured Julia was doing that because she needed money. Now Cameron could feel his own surge of anger, and he hoped he got a chance to settle the score with this woman.

"What do you want?" Cameron snapped when he finally spoke to her. Jameson moved closer so he could hear over the drone of the rain.

"Lauren and Isaac," Julia said without hesitation. "Have them come to my car, and you, Patrick and anybody else you brought with you will be safe. You can even get an ambulance out here for your deputy friend."

Cameron wanted the ambulance for Jace, but that was too big of a price to pay. Jace would feel the same way about it, too.

"You really think I'll just allow Lauren and Isaac to go to you?" Cameron asked. "You'll kill them."

Now Julia hesitated. "No. I'm not about to kill my brother's son. Lauren and Isaac will be taken to an undisclosed location, and once I have the money from Alden's estate, I'll release them."

"Right." And he didn't bother to take the skepticism out of his voice.

Lauren was plenty skeptical, as well, and he didn't think her trembling was all from the cold rain. It was also from the rage she was feeling right now. Cameron had to make sure that rage didn't cause Lauren to do something stupid. Like try to go after Julia.

"You don't believe me," Julia remarked. She sounded so calm she could have been discussing the weather, but Cameron figured the woman was also feeling loads of emotion. Fear being one of them. Julia had to know that so many things could go wrong now.

That applied to Lauren and him, as well.

"You should believe me," Julia went on. "I'll disappear after I have the money and settle my debts. I plan to move overseas. A place where I can't be extradited back here."

There were many countries that didn't have extradition treaties with the US, but Cameron still wasn't convinced.

"I figure you'll stay put, right here in Texas," Cameron said. "And you'll probably set up Duane or Evelyn to take the fall for this."

Silence. Which meant he was probably spot-on with his theory. No way would Julia take the blame for any of this.

"You need to hurry," Julia warned him, her voice crisp now. "Don't count on help from your lawmen friends, either, because my men are holding them off on the road."

Cameron didn't like the sound of that, and he hoped none of them had been hurt. The injury to Jace was enough. "You've hired an awful lot of thugs for someone who's flat broke."

"Funded with money from Alden's company," she admitted. "And a little help from the person who loaned me money."

So the thugs belonged to the loan shark. That was

why none of them had been willing to negotiate a deal with Cameron. Their boss wouldn't have killed them. And this way, the loan shark ensured that he'd get not only the money Julia owed him but then some, too. Heck, the loan shark might end up taking most of the entire estate. Along with killing Julia. But the woman probably hadn't realized that.

"Your deputy might have managed to take out the person who was manning the launcher," Julia went on. "But there's someone else out there who can do the same job. He has orders to fire if Lauren doesn't come to me with Isaac. You've got a minute to send her out here."

"I'll go," Lauren whispered.

Cameron cursed and muted the call. Even though Lauren already knew this, he thought it was worth repeating. "She wants you dead."

"Yes, but when I get to the car, she'll want to take a look at Isaac, to make sure I've brought the right baby. When she does that, I can escape."

There were way too many things that could go wrong—especially since Julia would have at least one hired gun in the car with her. Still, they didn't have a lot of options here. If the guy with the launcher fired at them, then they'd all die.

Cameron forced himself to think, and there was no completely safe way to handle this. But maybe he could do something to ensure that Lauren made it out of this alive.

"Make sure there's not another launcher," Cameron told Jameson.

Jameson nodded, and he started moving. Unlike Lauren had done, he kept low. Obviously trying to stay out of sight while he made his way closer to the cruiser and the area where they'd last seen the launcher.

"Give me thirty seconds before you start walking out to Julia," Cameron added to Lauren. "I'll try to get as close to Julia's car as possible so I can be in place to help you escape."

He gave one of the blankets an adjustment and gave her a quick kiss. Cameron wished there was time to say more. Exactly what, he didn't know. But he hated to think that these might be his last moments with her.

"Thirty seconds," he repeated, and Cameron started moving.

Thankfully, there was plenty of underbrush so he could keep hidden, but Julia had probably figured he'd be trying to do something exactly like this.

He counted off the seconds in his head, and once he was close to that thirty-second mark, Cameron stopped and got ready to fire. He considered just shooting into the windshield of Julia's car with the hopes he'd hit her or her goons. But then the guy with the launcher would no doubt retaliate.

Cameron felt the punch of dread go through him when Lauren stepped out. Right out in the open. Of course, that'd been the plan, but still, he hated that she had to be in harm's way like this.

"I'm coming," Lauren called out to Julia.

She had a bundled blanket in the crook of her right arm. And she also had her gun. It wasn't hidden nearly enough, but there was no way Cameron could warn her now. Lauren was walking directly to the car.

The car doors opened. Both on the driver's and front passenger's side, and even though no one got out, Cameron figured these were the hired goons. Julia was probably in the backseat, but he couldn't see her.

"You'll want to drop that gun," one of the thugs told Lauren.

Lauren stopped, hesitating, and she let go of it so that it fell to the ground. She started walking again. Only making it a few steps.

Before the shot blasted through the air.

LAUREN HEARD THE sound and braced herself for the bullet to hit her. The old saying was true. Her life did flash before her eyes. The pain and the happiness. She'd known that Cameron had been a big reason for a lot of her happiness, and she regretted that she had never told him that.

But the bullet didn't hit her.

Stunned, she stood there a moment before she realized the guy on the driver's side of Julia's car had fired the shot at Cameron. Lauren's stomach went to her knees, and she called out for him.

No response.

The anger came, quickly replacing the stunned fear, and Lauren charged toward the gunman.

"Don't shoot her," Julia yelled. "Not until we have the kid."

Lauren had figured all along that Julia had no plans to let her live, and Julia had just confirmed that. Since holding the baby gave Lauren some protection, she kept running. Except she didn't go to the driver. She ran to the other side of the vehicle, where she hoped to get her hands on Julia.

Behind her, she heard the explosion. Mercy, that was where Jameson had been going, and she prayed he hadn't been hurt. Maybe he'd managed to get out of the path before that blast went his way, but she couldn't risk even glancing over her shoulder to check on him.

There was another shot.

The bullet slammed into the driver, and it'd come from Cameron's direction. She prayed that meant he hadn't been hurt and added the same prayer for her brother.

The thug on the passenger's side took aim at Cameron, and he started shooting. One shot right after the other. And Cameron wasn't returning fire.

Lauren kept moving, pushing aside all the gunfire and the possibility that the gunman would turn his weapon on her. In case he tried that, she held the blanket even higher so that it would make it harder for her to kill him.

When Lauren reached the car, the thug stopped shooting at Cameron, and he reached out to grab her. She didn't give him a chance to do that, though. She used the entire weight of her body to ram into the car door, which, in turn, rammed into him. He cursed her and howled out in pain. But Lauren ignored him and threw open the back door.

Julia.

The woman sat there, alone on the backseat, and she had a gun aimed right at Lauren.

"Give me the kid," Julia snarled.

Her sister-in-law had never been friendly to her, but now Lauren saw the pure hatred in the woman's eyes. She was certain there was hatred in her own eyes, too. Hatred that she aimed at Julia.

Yelling at the top of her lungs, Lauren tossed the blanket at her. She caught just a glimpse of Julia's stunned look before Lauren launched herself at the woman. Pinpointing all of her rage into her fist, she punched Julia right in the face.

Julia didn't just sit there and take that, though. She let out her own feral yell, and she came at Lauren, grabbing her by the hair and shoving her back. They fell out of the car and onto the ground. Unfortunately, Julia landed on top of Lauren, and she whacked her gun across Lauren's jaw.

The pain slammed through Lauren so hard and nearly robbed her of her breath. Still, that didn't stop her from fighting back. Nor did the shots that she heard being fired all around them. Cameron and maybe Jameson were in a fight for their lives, but Lauren was in her own fight. One that she had to win so that she could help Cameron and the others.

Lauren managed to catch on to Julia's wrist to stop the woman from hitting her with the gun again, but Julia only punched her with her left hand. That one wasn't nearly as hard as the first one had been, but it still dazed her for a moment.

"You should have just brought the kid!" Julia shouted. "They'll kill me now, but first I'll make sure you're dead."

Lauren had no intention of just letting her do that. While she still had a grip on Julia's wrist, Lauren shoved up her hand—and Julia's gun slammed into the woman's chin. Julia cursed her again.

And pulled the trigger.

The gun was close to Lauren's ear. Too close. Because the blast from the bullet was so loud that it deafened her. But she had no trouble feeling, and even though Julia's shot had missed her, that didn't stop her from head-butting Lauren.

Enough of this. Lauren wasn't just going to lie there while Julia beat her into unconsciousness. Then she'd be an easy kill. She didn't intend to make any of this easy for Julia.

Lauren mustered as much energy as she could, and she threw Julia off her. She moved fast to pin the woman's hands to the ground by throwing her body over Julia's.

"Kill Cameron," Julia shouted out to her hired thug. "Kill him now." And the thug fired some shots.

That was not the right thing for Julia to say, and it caused a new wave of anger to wash through Lauren. She slammed her forearm into Julia's face, causing the woman's head to flop back. Lauren took full advantage of that. She ripped the gun from Julia's hand, turned toward the thug.

Lauren fired.

But her shot wasn't necessary. The thug was already in the process of falling to the ground. That was when she saw Cameron. Alive, thank God. And with his gun aimed right at the fallen man.

Beneath her, she felt Julia's body tense. The woman was probably about to gear up for another round of the fight. She didn't get a chance to do that, though. Cameron raced toward them, and he pointed his gun at Julia.

"Please move so I can shoot you," he said through clenched teeth.

Julia went limp, her hands dropping to her sides. Lauren didn't relax, though. She got up and took aim at the woman, as well.

Lauren risked a glance at Cameron to make sure he

was okay. He seemed to be. No blood anyway. She was certain she was bleeding, though, from the punches she'd taken from Julia.

The sound of running footsteps sent Cameron snapping in the direction of the cruiser. Lauren looked there, too, and saw a welcome sight.

Jameson.

Her brother seemed fine, too.

"The guy with the launcher's dead," Jameson said. "I don't see any other hired guns around, but we need to get out of here." He glanced down at Julia. "We can get that piece of slime behind bars."

Julia had a strange reaction to that. She looked up at Lauren and laughed. "It's not over," the woman said. "I had a backup plan in case something went wrong. In case you didn't bring the babies with you, after all."

"What do you mean?" Lauren asked, and she reminded herself that anything that came out of the woman's mouth could be a lie.

But this didn't feel like a lie.

Not with that sick smile on Julia's face.

"Evelyn didn't want any part of the violence," Julia continued. "She didn't want to get her hands dirty. But she's at the ranch now to get her grandson. And I sent enough hired guns with her to do just that."

Chapter Seventeen

Cameron couldn't get to his phone fast enough, and he prayed that Julia's threat was all just a bluff. But he also knew Evelyn. Knew that she was desperate to get her hands on Patrick, so she might indeed have fallen for something like this.

"Hurry," Lauren said. She was firing glances all around, no doubt looking for a way to get to the ranch ASAP.

"I'm calling Gabriel," he told her, and he pressed the number. It rang and then went to voice mail.

Hell.

That was not what Cameron wanted to hear. Apparently, neither did Lauren, because she hurried to Julia's car. "The keys are in the ignition."

If they took it they could leave immediately, especially since the cruiser had been disabled. "Jace..." Cameron mumbled.

"Go," Jameson insisted. "I'll stay with him and see if I can get the ambulance out here. If not, I can take the gunmen's SUV."

Cameron figured there were some concerns about the plan, but his bigger concern was getting to the boys.

He ran to the car, motioning for Lauren to get in, but she had by the time he got behind the wheel.

There was no place to turn around, so he threw the car into Reverse. "Look for any kind of tracking devices," he added to Lauren.

He figured Julia wouldn't have put anything like that on the vehicle, but it was possible the loan shark had. That was just one possible obstacle. The next one was the hired guns that Julia said were at the end of the trail—the very place they needed to go to get back on the road to the ranch.

"I don't see anything," Lauren said. She shook her head, the panic in both her expression and her voice. "But if it's small enough, it could be hidden underneath something."

Yeah, and it probably wouldn't be that small. Still, it wasn't something he could worry about right now, especially since there was the biggest worry of all— possible gunmen at the ranch. And Gabriel was short some hands and deputies because they'd been at the sites where they were supposed to trap the gunmen.

They'd failed at that.

But Cameron couldn't fail at getting to Isaac and Patrick.

"Try calling Gabriel again," Cameron told her.

She did, all the while she was mumbling something. A prayer from the sound of it. Cameron said a few himself.

"Voice mail," Lauren relayed to him, and she groaned. Not an ordinary one but the kind that sounded as if she was about to cry.

"Keep trying," he pressed. "And get down on the seat."

He knew that was only going to cause her more

alarm, but there was nothing he could do about it. They were approaching the end of the trail, and while he didn't hear any gunfire, that didn't mean the shooters weren't there. Added to that, the car probably wasn't bullet resistant like the cruiser.

While she kept redialing Gabriel's number, Lauren did sink lower in the seat, but she kept her head high enough to keep watch. Cameron was watching, too, and that was why he had no trouble spotting the three vehicles at the intersection of the trail and the road. One was a black SUV, identical to what the other hired guns had driven. There was also a cruiser and a truck that he knew belonged to one of the ranch hands.

"I don't see any gunmen," Lauren said on a rise of breath.

Other than Allen, the ranch hand, neither did he. He had the butt of a rifle resting against his hip. There was a Texas Ranger next to him and a reserve deputy on the other side of the trail. Cameron slowed down and lowered his window.

"The gunmen are dead," Allen said to Cameron. He tipped his head to the trail. "How about up there?"

"Dead. There could be trouble at the ranch. Lauren and I are headed there now, but you should go check on Jameson and Jace. Jace will need an ambulance. Is the road clear?" he asked without pausing.

"As far as I know. I'll follow you," Allen volunteered.

Cameron thanked him but didn't wait for the man. He backed out onto the road, and now that there was room to turn around, that was exactly what he did. Fast. And he sped toward the ranch.

The rain had slowed some, but there was still plenty of water on the road. It was a risk, but Cameron didn't slow down. Everything inside him was yelling for him to get to the boys as fast as he could.

"Gabriel," Lauren said.

Finally. But Cameron didn't breathe easier just yet. "Put the call on speaker. Are the boys okay?" Cameron asked the moment Lauren did that. "Julia said there could be gunmen at the ranch."

"Yeah to both. The boys are fine, but we've definitely got some armed thugs."

The panic slammed through Cameron. Through Lauren, too, because he heard her make a hoarse sob.

"That's why I couldn't answer your call," Gabriel continued. "I'm out by the barn where I just took out two of them."

Two. But Cameron was betting there were more than that. Heck, Julia could have sent a dozen of them.

"Julia sent them," Cameron explained. "And Evelyn will be with them."

"We have Evelyn in handcuffs, facedown on the porch, but we haven't managed to round up a final gunman yet. He's somewhere near the front of the ranch. Maybe by the road. If I thought it would do any good, I'd tell you two to wait until—"

"We'll be there in about a minute," Cameron interrupted.

"I figured you'd say that. Just be careful because this guy has a rifle with a scope." Gabriel ended the call, probably because he had his hands full making sure the house was safe. Which was exactly what Cameron wanted him to do.

"I'm not staying down on the seat this time," Lauren said. "I want to stop this guy."

Like Gabriel, Cameron knew he didn't stand a chance

of winning that argument with her. Besides, he might need her. Lauren had proven herself to be a good shot, and he wanted all the backup he could get. No way did he want this guy firing anywhere near Gabriel's house.

Cameron slowed when they approached the turn for the ranch, and he drew his gun, keeping it in his hand, but he didn't see anyone. Well, no one that he didn't recognize anyway. There were two ranch hands, both armed, and they were in a truck parked on the side of the road. He pulled to a stop next to them and lowered his window again.

"We lost sight of the guy," the hand said. "But he came this way, and he's wearing all black."

That wasn't an especially good camouflage color, but he could be hiding in the trees that were nearby. Of course, that would be the first place someone would look for him. And maybe this man knew that.

"Check the ditch on your side," Cameron told Lauren.

He kept his window down and moved the car up so the hands' truck wouldn't be obstructing his view. He angled his head to get a better look. Like the ditches on the trail, these were filled with water. Water that was almost black under the iron-gray sky and rain.

Cameron crept along at a snail's pace, searching, while Lauren did the same on the other side. He was a good twenty yards from the ranch hands before he spotted something.

The gunman.

The guy was squatting chest-deep in the water. And yes, he had a rifle. One that he immediately started turning toward Cameron.

Cameron didn't even bother telling Lauren to watch out. There wasn't time. He just took aim and fired. Not one shot but three. The bullets slammed into the guy's chest, and they must have killed him instantly because the thug didn't even get the chance to pull the trigger.

Lauren sat there, frozen for a moment. She'd seen way too much death in the past couple of days, but she didn't leave her attention on the dead gunman for long. She looked at Gabriel's house. She didn't need to tell Cameron to hurry there now. He did. Because they both had to see for themselves that the boys were truly okay.

"Cameron shot the gunman," she said to Gabriel when she called him. "Yes, he's dead. Was anyone hurt at the ranch?"

Since she hadn't put this call on speaker and because his heartbeat was drumming in his ears, Cameron didn't hear what Gabriel said. However, the news must have been good because Lauren released the breath she'd been holding.

"No one's hurt," she relayed to Cameron when she ended the call.

Cameron was glad for that, but he wasn't feeling any relief yet and wouldn't until they were inside.

He went too fast again, the tires shimmying over the slick surface, but he managed to get them to Gabriel's. Before he'd even brought the car to a full stop, Lauren was out and running to the porch. Cameron was right behind her. There was no sign of Evelyn, thank goodness.

When Cameron went through the front door, he expected Lauren to already be on her way to the bathroom or wherever they'd moved the boys. But she wasn't. She was in the foyer with Jodi.

"Where's Evelyn?" Cameron asked, hoping the woman wasn't in the house.

"One of the Rangers took her into town to lock her up," Jodi answered. "I'm thinking this will pretty much put an end to any challenge she might have for custody."

Yes, it would. That was the silver lining in this. The other silver lining was Lauren.

Lauren whirled around to Cameron when he shut the door, and before he even saw it coming, she was in his arms. She kissed him. Not one of those passion-laced kisses that'd led to sex. This one seemed to be from pure relief.

"You saved my life," she said, her voice cracking.

There were tears in her eyes. And bruises and small cuts on her face from where Julia had punched her. It made him want to go back and throttle the woman. But Cameron didn't want to give Julia another moment of his time.

"And you saved mine," he answered.

Lauren nodded, managed a half smile and brushed another kiss on his mouth. "Good. Because I'm in love with you. Now, wipe the blood off your chin so we can see Isaac and Patrick."

He automatically reached to take care of the blood, but then her words sank in. It was too late, though, for him to respond because Lauren took off running toward the hall bathroom.

Jodi just shrugged. "I think the only person surprised by that I-love-you is *you*."

What? Cameron shook his head. That certainly wasn't common knowledge.

Was it?

Again, there was no time to dwell on it because he hurried after Lauren. And he found her, all right. She was on the bathroom floor and had both boys in her arms.

She was showering them with kisses. Isaac liked it because he was giggling, but Patrick was fussing and trying to get away from her so he could get to his toy horse.

Cameron scooped up both the boy and the horse in his arms, and Patrick rewarded him with a sloppy kiss on the cheek. That kiss went a long way to soothing the adrenaline that was still surging through him.

"Is it okay for us to leave the bathroom?" Merilee asked. "Because it seems as if Lauren and you should have some family time with the boys." Dara added a sound of agreement.

Family time. That made it sound as if their marriage—a real marriage—was a done deal.

Cameron nodded. "Just stay inside and don't go near any windows," Cameron instructed. He needed to go out and check on Gabriel, to make sure the danger had passed before things could start getting back to normal.

Well, his new normal anyway. Whatever that would be.

He sank down on the floor next to Lauren, and Patrick and Isaac must have taken that as playtime because both boys went to the stash of toys that was all over the bathroom floor and started bringing them to Lauren and him.

Lauren turned to Cameron, and she eked out another smile. "Everything considered, you don't look shell-shocked."

Then he was covering it well, because he was. Shell-shocked about the attack, about how close they'd come to dying and Julia's obsessive greed. But what Lauren had told him was at the top of that list of surprising things.

I'm in love with you.

Cameron was about to ask her if it was true, but she leaned in, and with that smile still in place she kissed him. It wasn't a relief kiss this time. No, this one had some heat to it. When she finally broke away, his breath was a little thin, but he was ready to launch into the conversation they needed to have.

But the footsteps stopped him.

Since the boys were right there, Cameron drew his gun and pivoted in the direction of the doorway. However, it wasn't a gunman. It was Gabriel. He glanced at all of them before his attention settled on his sister.

"Are you okay?" he asked.

Lauren nodded. She touched a bruise on her cheek that had obviously gotten Gabriel's attention. "Trust me, Julia looks worse. I got in some punches, too."

Gabriel winced a little, probably because he hated having to hear about his kid sister being in a fistfight with a would-be killer. It would certainly give Cameron some nightmares for years to come. They'd gotten damn lucky that Julia's shot had missed.

"Jameson has Julia on the way to jail," Gabriel continued. "And I think we got all the hired guns, not just here at the ranch but also the ones on the trails," Gabriel added to Cameron. "But everyone should stay in for a while until we've searched the grounds."

Good. Cameron didn't want to take any more risks with Lauren or the babies. "Has Julia said anything else?"

Gabriel shook his head. "She just yammered about wanting her lawyer. She'll want a plea deal but won't get one. I'll make sure of that. And we have enough from what Julia said to arrest the loan shark."

"That would hopefully keep the guy off the streets

for the rest of his life. After all, he'd supplied the hired guns who'd killed Maria."

Lauren shook her head. "I still don't know why Julia sent those men to my house. She knew about the swap so why didn't she just try to take Isaac?"

"Because I think she wanted concrete proof of the swap," Gabriel answered. "If she'd managed to get you out of the picture, she would want to be able to prove that she had Alden's son in her custody."

True, but Cameron seriously doubted Julia would have kept Isaac around any longer than necessary. Only until she'd gotten her hands on the money.

Gabriel hitched his thumb to the front of the house. "I need to go out and check on the hands."

"I can help," Cameron volunteered.

"No," Gabriel said without hesitation. "You should stay here and work things out with Lauren." He paused and lifted an eyebrow when Cameron just stared at him. "Jodi mentioned what she'd heard in the foyer."

Great. Now Gabriel might want to punch him. Except he didn't make any move to do that. However, Gabriel did glare at him some.

"Just make Lauren happy," Gabriel growled. "Because if you don't, you'll have to answer to me."

Lauren huffed. "Let Cameron get his footing first before you go all alpha on him." Then she added a wink to her brother.

It seemed, well, such a light moment, considering they were only minutes out of an attack. But then it was hard to stay gloom and doom with the boys crawling all over them. Even Gabriel was smiling when he strolled away.

"My footing?" Cameron asked.

"Yes. I figured you'd need some time to come to terms with me telling you I love you."

He opened his mouth, closed it and tried to come up with a good answer to that. "You meant it?"

Her eyebrow came up. "Of course I did. You thought it was some heat of the moment thing?"

"I didn't know," he admitted. "I thought maybe you said that because of the boys."

She didn't say, "What?" but that expression was all over her face.

"You know, because you want us to have a life together with the boys," he clarified. And he was obviously not gaining any ground here. She was frowning now.

Lauren huffed again, slipped her hand around the back of his neck and kissed him. Really kissed him. This one had much too high of a heat level considering they weren't alone.

"Do you know now?" She kept her mouth right next to his as if ready to convince him again.

Cameron didn't need convincing, but he kissed her anyway. There it was. More than the heat. More than this insane attraction that had been brewing for years. It was deeper than that, and now Cameron could finally tell her.

"I love you," he said, taking Lauren into his arms. "Not because of the boys, either—though they're a sweet bonus. I love you because of us. Because of you and me."

That was the right thing to say because Lauren smiled and pulled him to her for another kiss.

* * * * *

LANDON

Chapter One

Deputy Landon Ryland was looking for a killer.

He stood back from the crowd who'd gathered for the graveside funeral, and Landon looked at each face of the fifty or so people. Most he'd known since he was a kid, when he had visited his Ryland cousins here in Silver Creek, Texas.

But today he had to consider that one of them might have murdered Emmett.

Just the thought of it felt as if someone had Landon's heart in a vise and was crushing it. Emmett and he were cousins. But more like brothers. And now Emmett was dead, and someone was going to pay for that.

Especially considering how, and why, Emmett had died.

Landon knew the how, but it was the why that was causing his sleepless nights. He intended to give the killer a whole lot worse than just lack of sleep, though.

He glanced out of the corner of his eye when he sensed someone approaching. Landon didn't exactly have a welcoming expression, and everybody had kept their distance. So far.

Since he was on edge, he slid his hand over his gun,

but it wasn't necessary. It was Sheriff Grayson Ryland, yet another of his cousins.

Grayson, however, was also Landon's new boss.

The ink was barely dry on his contract with the sheriff's office, but he was the newest lawman in Silver Creek. Newest resident, too, of the Silver Creek Ranch since he'd moved to the guesthouse there until he could find his own place. Landon just wished his homecoming had been under much better circumstances.

"You see anything?" Grayson said. He was tall, lanky and in charge merely by being there. Grayson didn't just wear a badge—he was the law in Silver Creek, and everybody knew it.

Grayson was no doubt asking if Landon had seen a killer. He hadn't. But one thing was for certain: *she* wasn't here.

"Any sign of her yet?" Landon asked.

Grayson shook his head, but like Landon, he continued to study the funeral attendees, looking at each one of them from beneath the brim of his cowboy hat. Also as Landon had done, Grayson lingered a moment on Emmett's three brothers. All grief stricken. And that didn't apply just to them but to the entire Ryland clan. Losing one of their own had cut them each to the bone.

"Tessa Sinclair might not be able to attend, because she could be dead," Grayson reminded him.

Yes. She could be. But unless Landon found proof of that, she was a person of interest in Emmett's death. Or at least, that was how Grayson had labeled her. To Landon, she was a suspect for accessory to murder since Emmett's body had been found in her house. That meant she likely knew the killer.

She could even be protecting him.

Well, she wouldn't protect that piece of dirt once

Landon found him. And old times wouldn't play into this. It didn't matter that once she'd been Landon's lover. Didn't matter that once they'd had feelings for each other.

Something that didn't sit well with him, either.

But despite how Landon felt about her and no matter how hard he looked at the attendees, Tessa wasn't here at the funeral. With her blond hair and starlet looks, she would stick out, and Landon would have already spotted her.

Grayson reached in his pocket, pulled out a silver star badge and handed it to Landon. It caught the sunlight just right, and the glare cut across Landon's face, forcing him to shut his eyes for a second. He hoped that wasn't some kind of bad sign.

"You're certain you really want this?" Grayson pressed.

"Positive." He glanced at his cousin. Not quite like looking in a mirror but close enough. The Ryland genes were definitely the dominant ones in both of them. "You haven't changed your mind about hiring me, have you?"

"Nope. I can use the help now that I'm short a deputy. I just want to make sure you know what you're getting into."

Landon knew. He was putting himself in a position to catch a killer.

He clipped the badge onto his shoulder holster where once there'd been a different badge, for Houston PD. There he'd been a detective. But Landon had given that up when Emmett was murdered, so he could come home and find the killer.

Too bad it didn't look as if he would find him or her here.

"I'll see you back at the sheriff's office," Landon

said, heading toward his truck. It was only about a fifteen-minute ride back into town, not nearly enough time for him to burn off this restless energy churning inside him.

This is for you, Landon.

The words flashed through his head and twisted his gut into a knot so tight that Landon felt sick. Because that was what the handwritten note had said. The note that had been left on Emmett's body. Someone had killed Emmett because of Landon.

But why?

Landon had thought long and hard on it, and he still couldn't figure it out. Since he'd been a Houston cop for nearly a decade, it was possible this was a revenge killing. He'd certainly riled enough criminals over the years, and this could have been a payback murder meant to strike Landon right in the heart.

And it had.

Somewhere, the answers had to be in his old case files. Or maybe in the sketchy details they'd gotten from witnesses about the hours leading up to Emmett's death. Something was there. He just had to find it.

He took the final turn toward town, and Landon saw something he sure as hell didn't want to see.

Smoke.

It was thick, black and coiling from what was left of a barn at the old Waterson place. The house and outbuildings had been vacant for months now since Mr. Waterson had died, but that smoke meant someone was there.

Landon sped toward the blaze and skidded to a stop about twenty yards away. He made a quick 911 call to alert the fire department, and he drew his gun just in case the person responsible for that blaze was still around. However, it was hard to see much of anything, because of the smoke. It was stinging his eyes and making him cough.

But he did hear something.

A stray cat, maybe. Because there shouldn't be any livestock still inside that barn.

Landon went to the back of the barn, or rather what was left of it, and he saw something that had his heart slamming into overdrive.

Not a cat. A woman.

She had shoulder-length brown hair and was on her side, moaning in pain. But she was only a couple of feet from the fire, and the flames were snapping toward her.

Cursing, Landon rushed to her just as the gust of the autumn wind whipped some of those flames right at him. He had to put up his arm to protect his face, and in the same motion, he grabbed her by the ankle, the first part of her he could reach, and he dragged her away from the fire.

Not a second too soon.

A huge chunk of the barn came down with a loud swoosh and sent a spray of fiery timbers and ashes to the very spot where they'd just been. Some of the embers landed on his shirt, igniting it, and Landon had to slap them out before they became full-fledged flames.

The woman moaned again, but he didn't look back at her. He kept moving, kept dragging her until they were finally away from the fire. Well, the fire itself, anyway. The smoke continued to come right at them, and it sent both Landon and her into coughing fits.

And that was when he heard that catlike sound again.

Landon dropped down on his knees, putting himself between the woman and what was left of the fire.

Part of the barn was still standing, but it wouldn't be for much longer. He didn't want them anywhere near it when it finally collapsed.

"Are you okay?" he asked her, rolling her to her back so he could see her face. Except he couldn't see much of her face until he wiped off some of the soot.

Ah, hell.

Tessa.

He felt a punch of relief because she was obviously alive after all. But it was a very brief punch because she could be hurt. Dying, even.

Landon checked her for injuries. He couldn't see any obvious ones, but she was holding something wrapped in a soot-covered blanket. He eased it back and was certain his mouth dropped open.

What the heck?

It was a baby.

A newborn, from the looks of it, and he or she was making that kitten sound.

"Whose child is that?" he asked. "And why are you here?"

Those were just two other questions Landon had to add to the list of things he would ask Tessa. And she would answer. Especially answer why Emmett's body was found in her house and where the heck she'd been for the past four days.

"You have to help me," Tessa whispered, her voice barely audible.

Yeah, he did have to help. Just because he didn't like or trust her, that didn't mean he wouldn't save her. Landon didn't want to move her any farther, though, in case she was injured, so he fired off a text to get an ambulance on the way.

Both the baby and she had no doubt inhaled a lot of smoke, but at least the baby's face didn't have any soot on it, which meant maybe the blanket had protected him or her.

"Did you hear me?" he snapped. "Why were you near the burning barn? And whose baby is that?"

He wanted to ask about that dyed hair, too, but it could wait. Though it was likely a dye job to change her appearance.

Landon couldn't think of a good reason for her to do that. But he could think of a really bad one—she was on the run and didn't want anyone to recognize her. Well, she'd picked a stupid place to hide.

If that was what she'd been doing.

She stared up at him. Blinked several times. "Who are you?" she asked.

Landon gave her a flat look. "Very funny. I'm not in the mood for games. Answer those questions I asked and then tell me about Emmett."

"Emmett?" she repeated. She touched her hand to her head, her fingers sliding through her hair. She looked at the ends of the dark strands as if seeing them for the first time. "What did you do to me?"

Landon huffed. "I saved your life. And the baby's."

At the mention of the word *baby*, Landon got a bad feeling.

He quickly did the math, and it'd been seven months, more or less, since he'd landed in bed with Tessa. And he hadn't laid eyes on her since. Seven months might mean…

"Is that our baby?" he demanded.

As she'd done with her hair, she looked down at the newborn who was squirming in her arms. Tessa didn't gasp, but it was close. Her gaze flew to his, the accusation all over her face.

"I don't know," she said, her breath gusting now.

That wasn't the right answer. In fact, that wasn't an acceptable answer at all.

He didn't hold Tessa in high regard, but she would know who'd fathered her child. If it was indeed Landon, she might also be trying to keep the baby from him. After all, they hadn't parted on good terms, and those *terms* had gotten significantly worse with Emmett's murder.

Damn.

Were Tessa and he parents?

No. They couldn't be. The kid had to be Joel Mercer's and hers, and even though Landon had plenty of other reasons for his stomach to knot, just thinking of Joel's name did it. That night, seven months ago, Tessa had sworn she was through with Joel, but Landon would bet his next two paychecks that she had gone right back to him.

She always did.

In the distance, Landon heard the wail of the sirens from the fire engine. It'd be here soon. The ambulance, too. And then Tessa would be whisked away to the hospital, where she could pull another disappearing act.

"Start talking," Landon demanded, getting right in her face. "Tell me everything, and I mean *everything*."

The baby and the ends of her brown hair weren't the only thing she looked at as though she'd never seen them before. Tessa gave Landon that same look.

"Who are you?" she repeated, her eyes filling with tears. "Whose baby is this?" Tessa stopped, those teary blue eyes widening. "And who am *I*?"

Chapter Two

She couldn't catch her breath. Couldn't slow down her pulse. Nor could she fight back the tears that were stinging her eyes. Her heart seemed to be beating out of her chest, and everything inside her was spiraling out of control.

Where was she?

And who was this man staring at her?

Except it wasn't only a stare. He was glaring, and she could tell from the tone of his voice that he was furious with her.

But why?

With the panic building, she frantically studied his face. Dark brown hair. Gray eyes. He was dressed like a cowboy, in jeans, a white shirt and that hat. But he also had a gun.

God, he had a gun.

Gasping, she scrambled to get away from him. She was in danger. She didn't know why or from what, but she had to run.

She clutched the baby closer to her. The baby wasn't familiar to her, either, but there was one thought that kept repeating in her head.

Protect her.

She knew instinctively that it was a baby girl, and she

was in danger. Maybe from this glaring man. Maybe from someone else, but she couldn't risk staying here to find out. Somehow she managed to get to her feet.

"What the hell do you think you're doing?" the man snarled.

She didn't answer. It felt as if all the muscles in her legs had disappeared, and the world started to spin around, but that didn't stop her. She took off running.

However, she didn't get far.

The man caught her almost immediately, and he dragged them to the ground. Not a slam. It was gentle, and he eased his hands around hers to cradle the baby. While she was thankful he was being so careful, that didn't mean she could trust him.

She heard the sirens getting louder with each passing second. Soon, very soon, there'd be others, and she might not be able to trust them, either.

"I have to go," she said, struggling again to get away from him.

But the man held on. "Tessa, stop it!"

She froze. *Tessa?* Was that really her name? She repeated it several times and knew that it was. Finally, something was clear. Her name was Tessa, and she was somewhere on a farm or ranch. Near a burning building. And this man had saved her.

Maybe.

Or maybe he just wanted her to think that so she wouldn't try to run away from him.

"How do you know me?" she asked.

He gave her that look again. The one that told her the answer was obvious. It wasn't, not to her, anyway. But he must have known plenty about her, because he'd asked if the baby was theirs.

She didn't know if it was.

Mercy, she didn't know.

"You know damn well who I am," he snapped. "I'm Landon Ryland."

That felt familiar, too, and it stirred some different feelings inside her. Both good and bad. But Tessa couldn't latch on to any of the specific memories that went with those feelings. Her head was spinning like an F5 tornado.

"Landon," she repeated. And she caught on to one of those memories. Or maybe it was pieces of that jumble that were coming together the wrong way. "I was in bed with you. You were naked."

That didn't help his glare, and she had no idea if she'd actually seen him without clothes or if her mind was playing tricks on her. If so, it was a pretty clear *trick*.

A fire engine squealed to a stop, the lights and sirens still going, but Tessa ignored them for the time being, and she gave the man a harder look. She saw the badge then. He was a lawman. But that didn't put her at ease, and she wasn't sure why.

"Can I trust you?" she came out and asked.

He grunted, and then he studied her. "Is this an act or what?"

Tessa shook her head. Not a good idea, because it brought on the dizziness again. And the panic. "I don't remember who I am," she admitted, her voice collapsing into a sob.

He mumbled some profanity and stood when one of the firemen hurried toward them. "An ambulance is on the way," the fireman said. "Is she hurt?"

"Maybe. But there's also a baby with her."

That put some concern on the fireman's face. Concern in her, too, and she pulled back the blanket to make sure the baby was okay. Something she should have done minutes ago. But it was just so hard to think, so hard to figure out what to do.

The baby was wearing a pink onesie, and she appeared to be all right. Her mouth was puckered as if she were sucking at a bottle, and she was still squirming a little but not actually fussing. Tessa couldn't see any injuries, thank God, and she seemed to be breathing normally.

"I'll tell the ambulance to hurry," the fireman said, moving away from them.

And he wasn't the only one rushing. The firemen were trying to put out the rest of the blaze, not that there was much to save. There were also other sirens, and she saw the blue lights of a cop car as it approached.

She caught on to Landon's hand when he got up and started toward that car. "Please don't let anyone hurt the baby."

That seemed to insult him. "No one will hurt her. Or you. But you will tell me what I need to know."

Tessa didn't think this had anything to do with that memory of them being in bed, but she had no idea what he expected from her. Whatever it was, he clearly expected a lot.

Landon pulled his hand out of her grip and started toward the man who stepped from the cop car. The second man was tall, built just like Landon.

A brother, perhaps?

The second man and Landon talked for several moments, and she saw the surprise register on the other man's face. He kept that same expression as he made his way to her.

"Tessa," he said. Not exactly a friendly greeting. "I'm Deputy Dade Ryland. Landon's cousin," he added, probably because she didn't say anything or show any signs of recognizing him. "We need to ask you some questions before the ambulance gets here."

Tessa nodded because she didn't know what else to do. The baby and she were at the mercy of these men. Her instincts told her, though, that she should get away, run, the first chance she got.

Maybe that chance would come soon. Before it was too late.

But it wasn't Dade who asked any questions. It was Landon. He put his hands on his hips and stared down at her. "We need to know what happened to Emmett."

"He's dead," she blurted out without even realizing she was going to say it. "And so is his wife, Annie. Annie was killed in a car accident."

Where had that come from?

"That's right," Dade said, exchanging an uneasy glance with Landon. "Emmett and Annie are both dead." As Landon had done earlier, Dade knelt down, checking the baby. Then Tessa. Specifically, he looked into her eyes. "She's been drugged," he added to Landon.

"Yeah," Landon readily agreed.

The relief rushed through her. That was why she couldn't remember. But just as quickly, Tessa took that one step further.

Who had drugged her?

The drug had obviously messed with her head. And maybe had done a whole lot more to the rest of her body.

She had a dozen bad possibilities hit her at once, but first and foremost was that if someone had drugged her, they could have done the same to the baby.

The panic came again, hard and fast. "Did they give the baby something, too?"

"I don't think so," Dade said at the same moment that Landon demanded, "Tell me about the baby."

Tessa latched on to what Dade said about the baby, but she had to be sure that the newborn hadn't been drugged. It was something they'd be able to tell her at the hospital.

It's not safe there.

The words knifed through her head, and she repeated them aloud. And something else, too. "Don't trust anyone."

They weren't her words but something someone else had said to her. Important words. But Tessa didn't know who'd told her that.

Or why.

Obviously, that didn't make Landon happy. He said some more profanity. Added another glare. "She keeps dodging questions about the baby."

That caused Dade to give her another look. This time not to her eyes but rather her stomach. Not that he could see much of it, because she was holding the baby, but he was no doubt trying to see if she had recently given birth.

"Did you set this fire?" Dade asked her, easing the baby's legs away from Tessa's belly.

Tessa flinched, and Dade must have thought he'd hurt her, because he backed off. But that wasn't the reason she'd reacted that way. She'd winced not from pain but from his question.

"Someone set the fire?" she asked.

Landon didn't roll his eyes, but it was close. "Take a whiff of the air."

She did and got a quick reminder of the smoke. The breeze was blowing it away from them now, but Tessa could still smell it. And she could also smell something else.

Gasoline.

"Someone, maybe you," Landon continued, "used an accelerant. Based on how the fire spread, I'm guessing it was poured near the front of the barn and was ignited there."

And the person had done that while the baby and she were still inside.

Oh, mercy. That was a memory that came at her full force with not just the smells but the sensation on her skin. The hot flames licking at her. Her, running. Trying to get away from…someone.

She also remembered the fear.

"Someone tried to kill me," she said.

Dade didn't argue with that, but it was obvious she hadn't convinced Landon. Well, she didn't need to convince him. There weren't many things Tessa was certain of, but she was positive that she'd just come close to being murdered. Or maybe the person who'd set that fire had been trying to flush her out.

But why would she have been hiding in that barn?

Tessa didn't get to say more about that, and maybe she wouldn't have anyway, because the ambulance came driving toward them. The moment the vehicle stopped, two paramedics scrambled out, carrying a stretcher, and they headed straight for her and the baby.

She studied their faces as they approached, trying to see if she knew them. She didn't, but then, no one looked familiar. Well, except for Landon, and she didn't have enough information to know if she could trust him.

Don't trust anyone.

But if she hadn't trusted Landon, why had she landed in bed with him?

After cutting his way past Dade and Landon, one of the medics checked her. The other, the baby. And they asked questions. A flurry of them that she couldn't answer. How old was the baby? Any medical history of allergies? Were either of them taking medications?

"She claims she doesn't remember anything," Landon snarled. "Well, almost nothing. She knows Emmett's dead."

Yes. She did know that. But that was it. Heck, she wasn't even sure who Emmett was, but even through her hazy mind, it was obvious that these two lawmen believed she knew a whole lot more than she was saying.

Or maybe they believed she was the reason he was dead.

While Tessa kept a firm hold on the baby, the paramedics lifted them both onto the stretcher. "Will you be riding in the ambulance with them?" one of them asked Landon.

Landon stared at her, nodded. "Please tell me once these drugs wear off that she'll be able to remember everything."

"You know I can't guarantee that. She's been injured, too. Looks like someone hit her on the head."

Landon glanced back at the barn. "She could have gotten it there. When I got here, she was on the ground moaning. Maybe something fell on her."

The paramedic made a sound of disagreement. "It didn't happen today. More like a couple of days ago."

"Around the time when Emmett was killed," Landon said under his breath, and he looked ready to launch into another round of questions that Tessa knew she couldn't—and maybe *shouldn't*—answer.

However, one of the firemen hurried toward them,

calling out for Landon before he reached him. "You need to see this," the fireman insisted.

Landon cursed and started to walk away, but then he stopped and stabbed his finger at her. "Don't you dare go anywhere. I'm riding in the ambulance with you to make sure you get there."

It sounded like some kind of threat. Felt like one, too.

The paramedics lifted the stretcher, moving the baby and her toward the ambulance, but they were also carrying her in the same direction Landon was headed. Tessa watched as the fireman led him to the front of what was left of the barn.

Whatever the fireman wanted Landon to see, it was on the ground, because both men stooped, their attention on a large gray boulder. Dade did the same when he joined them.

She saw Landon's shoulder's snap back, and it seemed as if he was cursing again. He pulled his phone from his pocket and took a picture, and after saying something to Dade, he came toward her. Not hurrying exactly, but with that fierce expression, he looked like an Old West cowboy who was about to draw in a gunfight.

"What do you know about this?" Landon demanded. "Did you write it?" He held up his phone screen for her to see.

With everything around her swimming in and out of focus, it took Tessa a few seconds to make out the words. When she did, she felt as if a Mack truck had just slammed into her.

Oh. God.

Chapter Three

While he waited on hold for Dade to come back on the line, Landon glanced around the thin blue curtain to check on Tessa again. Something he'd been doing since they arrived at the Silver Creek Hospital. She was still sitting on the examining table, feeding the baby a bottle of formula that the hospital staff had given her.

Tessa was also still eyeing Landon as if he were the enemy.

That probably had plenty to do with the message that'd been scrawled on the boulder back at the barn. *This is for you, Landon.*

The same words as in the message that'd been left on Emmett's body. Except this time, there was a little more. *Tessa's dead now because of you.*

Reading that obviously hadn't helped lessen the fear he'd seen in Tessa's eyes. Hadn't helped this knot in Landon's stomach, either. He had to find out what was going on, and that started with Tessa.

She'd insisted on the baby staying with her, so they had both been placed in the same room, where the doctor was checking them now. Maybe the doc would be able to give her something to counteract whatever drug Tessa had been given.

Or taken.

But Landon had to shake his head at that thought. Tessa wasn't a drug user, so someone had likely given it to her. He needed to know why.

This is for you, Landon.

Someone clearly had it out for him. And that someone had murdered Emmett and had maybe now tried to do the same thing to Tessa and that innocent baby.

The baby had to be cleared up for him, too. If she was his child… Well, Landon didn't want to go there just yet. He already had enough to juggle without having to deal with that. The only thing that mattered now was that the baby got whatever medical attention she needed, and Landon could go from there.

"There were no prints on the boulder," Dade said when he finally came back on the line.

Landon groaned, but he really hadn't expected they would get that lucky. The person who'd set all of this up wouldn't have been stupid enough to leave prints behind. But he or she had left a witness.

One whose memory was a mess.

"The crime scene folks will do a more thorough check, of course," Dade went on. "Something might turn up. Anything from Tessa yet?"

"Nothing. The nurse drew her and the baby's blood when they got here. Once we have the results of the tox screen, we'll know what drug she was given. And if that's what is affecting her memory."

Of course, there was still that lump on her head.

The doctor had examined it, too, right after checking the baby, but like the paramedic, the doc said it was an injury that Tessa had gotten several days ago. In the doctor's opinion, it was the result of blunt-force trauma.

Landon figured the timing wasn't a coincidence.

"I don't think she's faking this memory loss," Landon added to Dade.

Tessa must have heard that, because her gaze slashed to his. Of course, her attention hadn't stayed too far away from him since this whole ordeal started. And after seeing that message on the rock, he knew why.

"All of this is definitely connected to me," Landon said to Dade. "The second message proves it."

Or at least, that was what someone wanted him to believe—that both Emmett's murder and this attack were because of something Landon had done.

"Did you find anything else in the old arrest records you've been going through?" Dade asked.

Landon had found plenty. Too much, in fact. It was hard to narrow down a pool of suspects when Landon could name several dozen criminals that he'd had run-ins with over the years. But there was one that kept turning up like a bad penny.

"Quincy Nagel," Landon answered. The name wouldn't surprise his cousin, because Landon had discussed Quincy with Grayson, Dade and the other deputies in Silver Creek.

Landon had put Quincy behind bars four years ago for breaking and entering. Quincy had sworn to get even, and he was out on probation now. That made him a prime suspect. Except for one thing.

Quincy was in a wheelchair.

The man had been paralyzed from the waist down in a prison fight. It would have taken some strength to overpower Emmett and to club Tessa on the head. Strength or a hired thug. But while Quincy had plenty of money from his trust fund to hire a thug, there was no money trail to indicate Quincy had done that.

"I'll keep looking," Landon said to Dade. Though the looking would have to wait for now, because the doctor stepped away from Tessa, and that was Landon's cue to go in the room.

Landon knew the doctor. Doug Michelson. He'd been a fixture in Silver Creek for years, and while Landon had moved away when he was a kid, he still remembered the doc giving him checkups and tending to him on the various emergency room trips that he'd had to make.

"The baby's fine," Dr. Michelson said right off. "But I want to get a pediatrician in here to verify that. I'm guessing she's less than a week old since she still has her umbilical cord."

Since Landon didn't have a clue what to say about that, he just nodded.

"Is she yours?" Dr. Michelson asked.

Landon didn't know what to say about that, either, so he lifted his shoulder. "I'm hoping Tessa can tell me."

The doctor scratched his head. "Probably not at the moment but maybe soon she can do that. I can use the baby's blood test to run her DNA if you give me the go-ahead."

"You've definitely got the go-ahead for that. And put a rush on it just in case Tessa's memory doesn't come back."

"Will do. I did manage to get Tessa to let a nurse hold the baby so I could get an X-ray of her neck," the doctor continued, but he stopped, obviously noticing the renewed surprise on Landon's face.

"What's wrong with Tessa's neck?" Landon asked.

"She's got a small lesion." The doctor pointed to the area where his neck and shoulders met. "It's too big for it to be an injection site for the drugs she was given. Besides, I found the needle mark for that. Or rather the needle *marks*. There are two of them on her arm. One is at least a couple of days old, and there was bruising involved."

"Bruising that probably happened around the same time she was hit on the head?" Landon asked.

"Yes. The other is more recent. I'd say an injection given to her within the last couple of hours."

So she'd been drugged twice. "Then what's with the lesion?"

The doctor shrugged. "I might know once I've had a chance to look at the X-ray. For now, though, I need to get an OB in here to examine Tessa."

Landon heard something in the doc's voice. Concern maybe? "You think something's wrong?"

"She doesn't trust me, so I'm thinking she might not trust an OB to do an exam, either. But an exam is a must since we have to rule out problems other than just the head injury." The doctor patted Landon's arm. "Talk to her. Convince her we're the good guys."

He'd have an easier time convincing Tessa that the sun was green. Still, he'd try. Plus, the doctor didn't give him much of a choice. He headed out, no doubt to round up the OB and pediatrician, leaving Landon alone with Tessa and the baby.

"Tell me what's going on," Tessa demanded.

Since that was what Landon wanted to ask her, they were at an impasse. One that he hoped they could work through fast. While he was hoping, he needed those drugs to wear off—now.

"Tell me," she snapped when he didn't jump to answer.

He didn't jump because Landon wasn't sure where to start. The beginning seemed like a lifetime ago.

"Stop me at any point if this is old news," he began. "A year ago, you moved to Silver Creek to open a private investigations office. We met shortly afterward, had a few dates, and I ran into you again at the Outlaw Bar when I was in town visiting my cousins."

He paused, waiting for her to process that. "Is that when you were naked in bed with me?" she asked, setting the baby bottle down beside her.

Of course she would remember *that*. But then, if the baby was his, she probably had it etched in her memory. Landon had it etched in his for a different reason. Because of the white-hot attraction that'd been between them.

But that wasn't something he needed to remember now. Or ever.

"Yes. The following morning, you told me you couldn't get involved with me," Landon continued. "And then your scummy boyfriend showed up. Joel Mercer. Remember him?"

She repeated the name, shook her head. "If I had a boyfriend, why did I sleep with you?"

Landon had asked himself that many, many times. "You said he was an ex, but he sure didn't act like it." He stopped, huffed. "Look, are you sure you don't remember simply because you'd rather not be talking about this with me?"

"I'm not faking or avoiding this conversation. Now, tell me about Joel. Why did you say he's scummy?"

"Because he is. He's a cattle broker—at least, that's what he calls himself, but it's really a front for assorted felonies, including gunrunning and money laundering. That's why I was surprised when he showed up and said you two were together."

Judging from her expression, Tessa was surprised, too. But it wasn't the same kind of surprise that'd been on her face that morning seven months ago. Landon had seen the shock, and then she'd changed. Or something. She'd become all lovey-dovey with Joel and told Landon to leave.

But Landon hadn't forgotten the look that'd gone through her eyes.

After he'd walked, or rather stormed, out, he'd gone back to Houston and hadn't seen her since. And apparently neither had any of his cousins. Tessa had closed her PI office, and while she'd kept her house in Silver Creek, she rarely visited it.

That was maybe why no one had known she was pregnant.

Because if his cousins had known, they would have told Landon. Plenty of people, including a couple of his cousins, had seen him leave the Outlaw Bar with Tessa that night.

"What does Joel have to do with Emmett?" she asked.

Everything inside him went still. Until now he hadn't considered they could be connected.

But were they?

Landon decided to try something to jog her memory. "Four nights ago, someone murdered Emmett in your house." Man, it was still hard to say that aloud. Just as hard to think about his cousin dying that way. "Your cleaning lady found his body. He'd been shot three times, and there was a note left on his chest."

"'This is for you, Landon,'" she whispered.

"How the hell did you know that?" He hadn't intended to raise his voice, and the baby reacted. She started to whimper.

"I'm not sure. But I saw your reaction when Dade showed you what was on the boulder. I guessed it must have been something to do with Emmett since the majority of your questions had been about him." She rocked the baby, kissed her forehead. "And her."

Yeah. And he would have more questions about *her* when he was finished with this.

Landon took out his phone, and even though he knew the picture was gruesome, he searched through his pictures and found the one he'd taken at the crime scene.

Emmett's body in a pool of blood.

There'd been blood on the note, too.

"Does this look familiar?" Landon asked, putting the phone practically in her face.

She gasped, turned her head and closed her eyes for a moment. "No." And she repeated it in a hoarse sob.

Landon didn't have a heart of ice. Not completely, anyway, and whether he wanted to or not, he was affected by that look on her face. Affected, but not to the point where he was stopping with the questions.

"Why was Emmett there at your house, and how did you know he was dead?" he pressed.

She shook her head. "I honestly don't know." Tessa paused, swallowed hard. "There's something about that photo that seems familiar, but I don't know what."

Good. Because if it was familiar, then it meant she was possibly there and might have seen who had done this.

Landon went to the next picture. A mug shot this time of Quincy Nagel. "Recognize him?"

Tessa moved closer for a long look and gave him an-other head shake. "Who is he?"

"A person of interest." Too bad Landon hadn't been able to find him yet. "A thug I arrested who might have wanted to pay me back by killing my cousin."

Tessa kept her attention on the baby, but because Landon was watching her so closely, he saw the small change in her. Her mouth tensed. A muscle flexed in her cheek. He hoped that was because she was concerned for the baby rather than because she was withholding something about Quincy. The little girl went beyond the whimpering stage and started to cry.

"So I slept with you, got pregnant." Tessa stood and rocked the baby. "Or maybe you believe she's Joel's daughter? You're not sure, but you'll demand a test so you can be certain."

He nodded. Though he would be surprised if she was Joel's. Yes, Tessa had been more than just friendly with Joel, but Landon didn't think she was the sort to go from one man straight to another. But he'd been wrong about stuff like that before. He didn't think so this time, though.

"Or maybe she's not my baby at all," she added. Tessa shuddered, dodged his gaze.

Landon lifted her chin, forcing eye contact. "Are you remembering something?"

"No."

Her answer came much too fast, and Landon would have jumped right on that if his phone hadn't buzzed. It was Grayson, which meant it could have something to do with the investigation. Since the baby was still crying, Landon stepped just into the hall so he could hear what the sheriff had to say.

"We found something," Grayson said the moment Landon answered. "A car on a ranch trail not far from the barn. The plates are fake, the VIN's been removed, but it has some baby things in it. A diaper bag and some clothes."

Tessa's car.

Or one that she'd "borrowed."

"We'll process it, of course," Grayson went on, "but something really stuck out. The GPS was programmed to go to your house in Houston."

Landon wanted to say that wasn't right, that there'd been no reason for her to see him, but if the baby was indeed his, maybe Tessa had been on the way to tell him. Of course, that didn't explain the other things: the dyed hair, the hit on her head, fake tags, no vehicle identification number on the car. Those were all signs of someone trying to hide.

Landon stepped out of the doorway when he saw Dr. Michelson approaching. There were two other doctors with him. The pediatrician and the OB, no doubt, and maybe one of them could talk Tessa into having the examination.

"What about the area leading from the car to the barn?" Landon asked Grayson. "Were there any signs of a struggle?"

"None, but something might turn up. In the meantime, ask Tessa why she was going to see you. Hearing about the GPS might trigger her memory."

He ended the call, intending to do just that, but Dr. Michelson pulled back the blue curtain and looked at him. "Where's Tessa and the baby?"

Landon practically pushed the doctor aside and

looked into the room. No Tessa. No baby. But the door leading off the back of the examining room was open.

Damn.

"Close off all the exits," Landon told the doctor, and he took off after her.

He cursed Tessa, and himself, for this. He should have known she would run, and when he caught up with her, she'd better be able to explain why she'd done this.

Landon barreled through the adjoining room. Another exam room, crammed with equipment that he had to maneuver around. He also checked the corners in case she had ducked behind something with plans to sneak out after he'd zipped right past her.

But she wasn't there, either.

There was a hall just off the examining room, and Landon headed there, his gaze slashing from one end of it to the other. He didn't see her.

But he heard something.

The baby.

She was still crying, and even though the sound was muffled, it was enough for Landon to pinpoint their location. Tessa was headed for the back exit. Landon doubted the doctor had managed to get the doors locked yet, so he hurried, running as fast as he could.

And then he saw her.

Tessa saw him, too.

She didn't stop. With the baby gripped in her arms, she threw open the glass door and was within a heartbeat of reaching the parking lot. She might have made it, too, but Landon took hold of her arms and pulled her back inside.

As he'd done by the barn, he was as gentle with her

as he could be, but he wasn't feeling very much of that gentleness inside.

Tessa was breathing through her mouth. Her eyes were wide. And she groaned. "I remember," she said.

He jerked back his head. That was the last thing Landon had expected her to say, but he'd take it. "Yeah, and you're going to tell me everything you remember, and you're going to do it right now."

But she didn't. Tessa just stood there, her attention volleying between him and the parking lot.

"Please, just let me go." Her eyes filled with tears. "It's not safe for you to be with me."

"What the hell does that mean?" Landon snapped.

She closed her eyes, the tears spilling down her cheeks. "I'm not who you think I am. And if you stay here with me, they'll kill you."

Chapter Four

Tessa tried to move away from Landon again, but he held on to her.

"Explain that," he demanded.

She didn't have to ask exactly what he wanted her to tell him. It was about the bombshell she'd just delivered.

If you stay here with me, they'll kill you.

There were plenty of things still unclear in Tessa's head, but that wasn't one of them.

She glanced behind her at the parking lot on the other side of the glass door. "It's not safe for us to be here. Please, let's go somewhere else."

Landon stared at her, obviously debating that, and he finally maneuvered her to the side. Not ideal, but it was better than being in front of the glass, where she could be seen, and at least this way she had a view of the hall in case someone came at her from that direction.

"Now that the drugs are wearing off, I'm remembering some things about Emmett's murder," Tessa admitted.

His eyes narrowed. "Keep talking."

"I didn't see the killer's face." Though Tessa tried to picture him, the bits and pieces of her memory didn't cooperate. "I came into my house, and this man wearing a ski mask attacked me. Emmett was there, and they fought."

Landon stayed quiet for a long time, clearly trying to process that. "Why was Emmett there?"

She had to shake her head. "I don't know. I don't know why the other man was there, either. Maybe he was a burglar?"

That didn't sound right at all, though. No. He wasn't a burglar, but clearly there were still some blanks in her memory. And because he was wearing a ski mask, she didn't have even fragmented memories of seeing his face.

Tessa looked down at the baby. Did that man have something to do with the newborn?

"A *burglar*," Landon repeated, "wouldn't have left a note like that on Emmett's body. His killer was connected to me and obviously to you since the murder happened in your house." He tipped his head to the baby. "And where was she the whole time this attack on you was going on?"

"In my arms." Tessa was certain of that. "She was also in my arms when I ran from the man. No, wait." More images came. Then the memory of the pain exploding in her head. "He hit me with his gun first." That explained the bump on her head. "Emmett tried to stop him, and that's when I think the man shot him."

Landon dropped back a step, no doubt taking a moment to absorb that. Those details were still fuzzy, and Tessa was actually thankful for it. She wasn't sure that right now she could handle remembering a man being murdered. Especially so soon after nearly dying in that barn fire.

"You were close to Emmett?" she asked but then

waved off the question. Of course he was. And apparently she had been, too.

After all, Emmett had been at her house.

"I think his killer might have been a cop," Tessa added.

Landon huffed. "First a burglar, now a cop?"

She didn't blame him for being skeptical, but her mind was all over the place, and it was so hard to think, especially with that warning that kept going through her head.

That it wasn't safe here. That she couldn't trust anyone.

That she was going to get Landon killed.

"The killer held his gun like a cop," she explained. "And he had one of those ear communicators like cops use."

"Criminals use them, too," Landon was just as quick to point out.

True enough. "But he said something about a perp to whoever he was talking to on the communicator. That's a word that cops use." Tessa paused. "And when I saw your badge, I got scared. Because I thought maybe… Well, it doesn't matter what I thought."

"You thought I had killed Emmett," he finished for her. Landon added a sharp glare to that. "I didn't, and I need you to remember a whole lot more than you just told me."

So did she, but before Tessa could even consider how to make that happen, she saw some movement in the hall. Landon saw it, too, because he moved in front of her. From over his shoulder, Tessa saw Dr. Michelson and a security guard. But there was another man with him. Tall and lanky with blond hair. Wearing a suit. It took her a moment to get a good look at his face.

Her heart jumped to her throat.

"Joel," she said. Even with the dizziness, she recognized him.

Landon looked back at her, a new round of displeasure in his expression. "So you remember him now?"

She did. And unlike the other memories, these were a lot clearer.

Oh, God.

This could be bad.

Joel kept his attention on her, obviously studying her dyed hair, but she soon saw the recognition in his eyes, and he picked up the pace as he made his way toward her.

"Tessa?" Joel called out. "Are you all right?"

Landon didn't budge. He stayed in front of her. "Someone tried to kill her. What do you know about that?"

Until Landon barked out that question, Joel hadn't seemed to notice him. But he noticed him now. "What are *you* doing here?" Joel snapped.

Landon tapped his badge. "What I'm doing is asking you a question that you *will* answer right now."

Despite the fact that Landon's tone was as lethal as his expression, Joel made a sound of amusement when he glanced at the badge. "What happened? Did you lose your job as a Houston cop and have to come begging your cousin for work?"

That jogged her memory, too. Yes, Landon had been a detective with the Houston PD, but Tessa doubted he'd lost his job. He had likely come back to Silver Creek to solve Emmett's murder. Good thing, too, or else there might not have been anyone to save her from that barn fire.

But he couldn't help her get out of this.

"How did you know I was at the hospital?" Tessa asked Joel.

Obviously, that wasn't what he wanted to hear from her. He probably expected a much warmer greeting, because he stepped around Landon and reached out as if to hug her.

Landon, however, blocked his path. "How did you know she was here?" he pressed.

Joel looked at her. Then at Landon. And it must have finally sunk in that this was not a good time for a social visit. If that was indeed what it was.

"What happened to you?" Joel asked her.

"I'm not sure." That was only a partial lie. "Someone drugged me and then tried to kill me."

Joel nodded. "In the barn fire. My assistant got a call from a friend who works at the fire department. He told her that you'd been brought here to the Silver Creek Hospital. I came right away."

"Why?" Landon demanded.

Joel huffed as if the answer were obvious, but he snapped back toward Tessa when the baby made a whimpering sound. He peered around Landon, and Tessa watched Joel's face carefully so she could try to gauge his reaction.

He was shocked.

She hadn't thought for a second that the baby was his, because Tessa was certain she'd never slept with Joel. She definitely didn't have any memories of him being naked in her bed. But she'd considered that he might have known if she'd had a child.

If she had, that is.

Joel stepped back, the shock fading, and in his eyes, she saw something else. The raw anger, some directed at her. Most of it, though, was directed at Landon.

"You two had a baby," Joel snapped. "That's why I haven't heard from you in months."

Months? Had it been that long? Mercy, she needed to remember.

"I didn't think things were serious with you two," Joel added. "You said it was just a one-time fling with him."

She figured Joel had purposely used the word *fling* to make it seem as if what'd happened between Landon and her had been trivial. Of course, that was exactly what she'd led Joel, and even Landon, to believe.

Tessa needed to settle some things with Joel, but she couldn't do that now. Not with the baby here. And not until she was certain that this jumble of memories was right.

"I want the name of the person from the fire department who contacted your assistant and told her about Tessa," Landon continued.

It took Joel a few moments to pull his stare from her and look at Landon. "I'll have to get that for you. My assistant didn't mention a name, and I didn't think to ask."

Well, it was a name that Tessa needed so she'd know if Joel had someone in the Silver Creek Fire Department who was on the take.

"I'll want that information within the next half hour," Landon added. "And now you'll have to leave because Tessa and the baby have to be examined by the doctors."

Joel turned to her as if he expected her to ask him to stay. And she might have if Tessa had had the energy to keep up the facade so she could try to get what info she could from Joel. She didn't. It was time to regroup and tell Landon what she'd remembered, but she couldn't do that in front of Joel.

"Landon's right. The baby and I need to be examined," Tessa stated to Joel. "Please just go."

She could see the debate Joel was having with himself, but Tessa also saw the moment he gave in to her request. "Call me when you're done here," Joel said. "We have to talk." And he walked away as if there were no question that she would indeed do just that.

Tessa and Landon stood there watching him, until Joel disappeared around the hall corner.

"I'll need a minute with Tessa," Landon told the doctor and security guard.

The doctor hesitated, maybe because Landon's jaw was clenched and he looked ready to yell at Tessa. But Tessa gave the doctor a nod to let him know it was okay for him to leave. As Landon and she had done with Joel, they waited until both men were out of sight.

Since she knew that Landon was about to launch into an interrogation, Tessa went ahead and got started. "I don't think the baby is ours," she said. "And I'm certain she's not Joel's."

"How would you know that?"

She got another image of Landon naked. Good grief, why was that so clear? It was a distraction she didn't need. Especially since the man himself was right in front of her, reminding her of the reason they'd landed in bed in the first place.

"I just know," she answered. An answer that clearly didn't please him.

"Then whose baby is that?" Landon snapped.

Even though Landon wasn't going to like this, she had to shake her head. "Memories are still fuzzy there, but I don't have any recollection of being pregnant. I think I would have remembered morning sickness, the delivery…something."

"And you don't?"

"Nothing." She wasn't certain if he looked relieved, disappointed or skeptical. But she wasn't lying.

"The doctor will be able to tell once he examines you," Landon reminded her.

She nodded. "I do have plenty of memories about Joel, though." Tessa had to lean against the wall when a new wave of dizziness hit her. "And some memories about me, too. I'm not a real PI."

Landon stared at her as if she were lying. "But you have a PI's license. A real one. I checked."

Of course he had. Landon probably wouldn't have asked her out unless he'd run a basic background check on her. And he definitely wouldn't have slept with her.

Then she rethought that.

The sex hadn't been planned, and it'd happened in the heat of the moment. Literally.

"Yes, I have a license." Best just to toss this out there and then deal with the aftermath. And there would be aftermath. "But I had it only because of Joel. He said he wanted me to get it so I could help him vet some of his business associates. It's easier for a PI to do that because I had access to certain databases."

She got the exact reaction she expected. Landon's eyes narrowed. Tessa wasn't sure of all of Joel's activities, but there were enough of them for her to know the kind of man she was dealing with. Landon had called him scummy, but he was much worse than that.

Because Joel was a dangerous man.

With that reminder, she looked around them again. Tessa could still see the parking lot and the hall, and Landon made an uneasy glance around, too.

"You'll want to keep going with that explanation," Landon insisted. "But remember, you're talking to a cop."

The threat was real. He could arrest her, but it was a risk she had to take right now. She needed Landon on her side so he could help her protect this baby. Maybe from Joel.

Maybe from someone else.

Mercy, it was so hard to think.

Tessa had to clear her throat before she could continue. "I think Joel might have murdered someone."

His eyes were already dark, but that darkened them even more. "Who? Emmett?"

But she didn't get a chance to answer.

Landon stepped in front of her, drawing his weapon. That was when she saw the man in the hall.

He was coming straight toward them.

And he had a gun.

Chapter Five

Landon had a split-second debate with himself about just shooting at the armed man who was coming right at them.

But he couldn't.

It would be a huge risk to start shooting in the hospital around innocent bystanders.

A risk for Tessa and the baby, too.

The man obviously didn't have a problem doing just that. He lifted his gun and took aim. Landon hooked his arm around Tessa and yanked her out of the line of fire.

Barely in time.

The bullet smacked into the concrete block wall where they'd just been standing. The noise was deafening, and the baby immediately started to cry.

Landon pulled Tessa and the baby to the side so that he could use the wall for protection, but it wouldn't protect them for long, because the idiot fired another shot and sent more of those bits of concrete scattering.

"Tessa?" the man called out. "If you want the bullets to stop, then hand the kid to the cowboy cop and come with me."

Because Landon still had hold of her, he felt her

muscles turn to iron, and she held the baby even closer to her body.

"Oh, God," she whispered.

Landon mumbled something significantly worse. This was not what he wanted to happen.

Of course, Landon had known there could be another attack since someone had tried to kill Tessa in that barn fire, but he hadn't thought a second attempt would happen in the hospital with so many witnesses around. Plus, the guy wasn't even wearing a mask. That meant he either knew no one would recognize him or didn't care if they did. But whoever he was, one thing was crystal clear.

This thug wanted Tessa.

Later, Landon would want to know why, but he figured this had something to do with one of the last things she'd said to him before the guy started shooting.

I think Joel might have murdered someone.

Landon didn't doubt it for a second. Nor did he doubt this armed thug was connected to Joel. But why exactly did Joel want her? Had she learned something incriminating while she was working for him vetting his "cattle broker" associates?

"Tessa?" the man called out. "You've got ten seconds."

"He knows you," Landon whispered to her. "You recognize his voice?

"No," she answered without hesitating.

"Think about it," the guy added. "Every bullet I fire puts that kid in danger even more. Danger that you can stop by coming with me."

"He's right," Tessa said on a rise of breath.

She moved as if preparing herself to surrender, but Landon wasn't going to let that happen.

"Stay back," he warned her.

Landon leaned out, trying to time it so that he wouldn't get shot, and glanced into the hall. The guy was no longer out in the open. He'd taken cover in a doorway.

Hell.

Hopefully, there wasn't anyone inside the room where this man was hiding or he would no doubt shoot them.

On the second glance, Landon took aim and fired at the moron. The guy ducked back into the room, and Landon's bullets slammed into the door.

He couldn't stand there and trade shots with this guy, because sooner or later, the gunman might get lucky. Certainly by now someone had called the sheriff, and that meant Grayson would be here soon. Although it might not be soon enough.

"Let's go," Landon told her.

He leaned around the corner and fired another shot at the man, and Landon hoped it would pin him in place long enough to put some distance between those bullets and Tessa.

Staying in front of her while trying to keep watch all around them, Landon maneuvered her down the back hall toward the other end, where there was another line of patients' rooms. He prayed that all the patients and staff had heard the shots and were hunkering down somewhere.

The baby was still crying, and even though Tessa was trying to comfort it, her attempts weren't working.

Too bad. Because the sounds of the baby's cries were like a homing beacon for that shooter.

Landon had no choice but to pause when he reached the junction of the halls, and he glanced around to see if there was a second gunman waiting to ambush them.

Empty.

Thank God.

But his short pause allowed the shooter to catch up with them. The guy leaned around the corner where Landon had just been, and he fired at them.

Since it was possible for the gunman to double back and come at them from the other end of the hall, Landon needed better protection. Again, it was a risk because he didn't know what he was going to find, but he opened the first door he reached.

Not empty.

And the young twentysomething woman inside gave him a jolt until he noticed that she wore a hospital gown and was hanging on to an IV pole. She was a patient.

He hoped.

"Go in the bathroom," he ordered the woman. "Close the door and don't come out."

She gasped and gave a shaky nod but followed his instructions. Landon would have liked to have sent Tessa and the baby in there with her, but he couldn't risk it. Anyone bold enough to send this gunman could have also planted backups in the rooms.

"Keep an eye on the woman," Landon whispered to Tessa.

Tessa's eyes widened, probably because she realized this could be a trap. Of course, that was only one of their problems. The baby was still crying, the sound echoing through the empty hall.

Landon heard the footsteps to his right. The gunman, no doubt. And he readied himself to shoot when the man rounded the corner. But the footsteps stopped just short of the hall junction.

He glanced back at Tessa to make sure she was staying down. She was, and she was volleying glances between him and the bathroom door. In those glimpses that Landon got of her face, though, he could see the stark fear in her eyes. He would have liked to assure her that they'd get out of this alive, but Landon had no idea how this would play out.

"Tessa?" the guy called out. "Time's up."

Landon braced himself for more shots. And they came, all right. The guy pivoted around the corner, and he started shooting right at Tessa and him. Landon had no choice but to push her deeper into the room.

"Deputy Ryland?" someone called out. It was the security guard, and judging from the sound of his voice, he was on the opposite end of the hall from the shooter. "The other deputies are in the building. They're on the way now to help you."

Good. Well, maybe. It could be a bluff since it'd been less than ten minutes since the shooting had started, and that would be a very fast response time for backup. Still, even if it was a bluff, it worked.

Because the shots stopped, and Landon heard the guy take off running.

His first instincts were to go after the guy, to stop him from getting away, but Landon had no way of knowing if the security guard was on the take. Hell, this could be a ruse to lure them out of the room so that Tessa could be kidnapped or killed.

Landon waited, cursing while he listened to the thug

get away, but it wasn't long before he heard another voice. One that he trusted completely.

Grayson.

"Landon?" his cousin called out. "Don't shoot. I'm coming toward you."

It seemed to take an eternity for Grayson to make it to them, and when he reached the door, Landon could see the concern on his face. Concern that was no doubt mirrored in Landon's own expression.

"Come on," Grayson said, motioning for them to follow him. "I need to get the three of you out of here right now."

TESSA'S HEART WAS beating so hard that she thought her ribs might crack. Her entire body was shaking, especially her legs, and if Landon hadn't hooked his arm around her for support, she would have almost certainly fallen.

She hated feeling like his. Helpless and weak. But at the moment she had no choice but to rely on Landon and Grayson to get the baby and her away from that shooter.

The sheriff led them up the hall, in the opposite direction of where the gunman had fired those last shots. Since that back hall also led to the parking lot, Tessa suspected he was getting away.

That didn't help slow down her heartbeat.

Because if he escaped, he could return for a second attempt. But an attempt at what? He obviously had wanted her to go with him. Or maybe that was what he had wanted her to believe. If she'd surrendered, he could have just gunned her down, done the same to Landon. Heaven knew then what would have happened to the baby.

"This way," Grayson said, and he didn't head toward the front but rather to a side exit.

The moment they reached it, Tessa spotted the cruiser parked there, only inches from the exit and apparently waiting for him. When Grayson opened the door, she saw Dade behind the wheel.

Even though she now believed she could trust the Ryland lawmen, seeing him and Grayson still gave her a jolt. If she'd been right about Emmett's killer being a cop, then it was possible the killer worked at the Silver Creek sheriff's office.

Landon hurried her onto the backseat, following right behind her, and the moment he shut the door, Dade took off.

"Are you all okay?" Dade asked, making brief eye contact in the rearview mirror.

Landon nodded but then checked her face. Tessa did the same to the baby. The newborn was still making fussing sounds, but she wasn't hurt. Thank God. That was a miracle, what with all those bullets flying.

When she finished examining the baby, Tessa realized Landon was still looking at her. Or rather he was staring at her. No doubt waiting for answers.

Answers that she didn't have.

Someone had attacked her twice in the same day. Heck, maybe even more than that since her memories were still hazy.

"Maybe he's one of Joel's hired thugs?" Landon asked.

She had to shake her head again. Then Tessa had to stop because a new wave of dizziness came over her. It was so hard to think with her head spinning. "I only got a glimpse of him before you pulled me back, but he didn't look familiar. I don't know why he came after me like that. Do you?"

"No," Landon snapped. "But I want you to guess why he attacked us. And the guessing should start with you telling me everything you know about Joel. The baby, too."

His tone wasn't as sharp as it'd been before, and his glare had softened some. Maybe he was starting to believe that this wasn't her fault.

Well, not totally her fault, anyway.

Tessa tried to concentrate and latch on to whatever information she could remember. It was strange, but the memories from years ago were a lot clearer than the recent ones. In fact, some of the recent ones were just a tangle of images and sounds.

"Tell me about Joel," Landon pressed, probably because she was still trying to figure out what to say.

"Joel," she repeated. And Tessa went with what she did remember. "I started working for him two years ago as a bookkeeper. I didn't know what he was," she added. "I was an out-of-work accountant, and he offered me a job. Later, he wanted me to be a PI so I could run background checks for him."

"But you soon found out what he was," Landon finished for her.

Another nod. "But I didn't know how deep his operation went, and he was hiding assets and activities under layers of corporate paperwork." Tessa had to pause again, brush away the mental cobwebs. These next memories were spotty compared to the ones of her starting to work for Joel.

"Back at the hospital, you said you thought Joel

had killed someone," Landon reminded her. "Who? Emmett?"

Tessa closed her eyes a moment, trying to make the thoughts come. Finally, she remembered a piece of a memory. Or maybe it was just a dream. It was so hard to work all of this out.

"No. Not Emmett. I think the murder might have had something to do with the baby's mother," she said. "But…no, that's not right." She touched her fingers to her head. "It's getting all mixed up again."

"Her mother?" Landon questioned. "So you're positive she's not yours…ours?"

"Yes, I'm certain."

She couldn't tell if Landon was relieved about that or not. He didn't seem relieved about anything. Neither was she. The child might not be theirs, but Tessa still needed to protect the newborn.

But who was after the baby? And why?

Her gaze dropped to the baby. "I think I know the reason I have her, though. Because a killer was after her mother, and she left the baby with me for safekeeping."

"A killer," Landon said. "You mean Joel?"

"I just don't know." Tessa groaned softly. "If I could just rest for a while, maybe that would help me remember?"

"You'll get some rest later. For now, tell me what happened to the baby's mother," Landon demanded.

Tessa had no idea. But this wasn't looking good. If all of this had happened four days ago, then the mother should have come back by now. If she was able to come back, that is.

Landon cursed. "Is the mother dead or hurt?"

But before she could even attempt an answer, Dade

was on the phone, and she heard him ask if there was any information on the baby's mother that would match the sketchy details she'd just given them.

"Is it possible the woman who had this baby didn't have anything to do with Emmett?" Landon pressed.

"I just don't know." She paused. "But maybe Emmett was helping me find some evidence against Joel?"

As expected, that didn't go over well with Landon. He didn't come out and say that she should have contacted him instead of Emmett, but she knew that was what he was thinking.

"But why would Emmett have been helping me?" Tessa asked.

Neither of the men jumped to answer that, maybe because they didn't have a clue, but it was Landon who finally responded. "Emmett was a DEA agent in Grand Valley, and Joel had a business there."

The memories were coming but too darn slow. She huffed and rubbed the back of her neck. Or rather she tried to do that but yanked back her hand when her fingers brushed over the sensitive skin there.

"Does it hurt?" Landon asked. He leaned closer, lifted her hair and looked for himself.

"Some." Not nearly as much as her head, though. "Why? How bad does it look?"

"It looks like a wasp sting or something. But the doctor took an X-ray. If it's something serious, he'll let us know."

Now that the drugs were partially wearing off, she tried to remember what'd happened to cause this particular injury. But nothing came. Everything was still so jumbled in her head, and that couldn't last.

There were secrets in her memories, secrets that had

caused someone to try to kill her, and until she unlocked those secrets, she wouldn't be able to figure out who had sent that gunman after the baby and her.

And figure out who'd killed Emmett and why.

"Good news, *maybe*," Dade said when he finished his call. "There have been no reports of a seriously injured or dead woman who gave birth in the past week, but Josh will keep calling around and see if something turns up."

"Josh?" she asked, hoping it was someone she could trust. Of course, at the moment Tessa wasn't sure she could trust anyone.

"Our cousin," Landon explained. "He's a deputy in Silver Creek."

Like Landon. Tessa prayed this Josh was being mindful of those calls and that he didn't give away any information that could put the baby's mother in further danger. Of course, it was possible the woman was dead. Just because the cops hadn't found a body didn't mean there wasn't one.

Oh, God.

Another wave of dizziness hit her, and Tessa had to lean her head against the seat. She closed her eyes, hoping it would stop. Hoping, too, that the car would soon stop, as well.

"Where are we going?" she asked. And better yet— how soon would they be there? But the moment she asked the question, Tessa got yet another bad feeling. That feeling only increased when neither Landon nor Dade jumped to answer.

"Where?" she repeated.

"Someplace you're not going to like," Landon grumbled.

Chapter Six

Landon had told Tessa that he was taking her some-place she wouldn't like. Well, it wasn't a place where he especially wanted her to be, either, but his options were limited.

And that was why Tessa was now sleeping under his own roof.

Or at least, the roof of the guesthouse at the Silver Creek Ranch where Landon had made his temporary home. Until he could come up with other arrangements, it would be Tessa and the baby's temporary home, too. With more than a half-dozen lawmen living on the grounds, it was safer than any other place Landon could think to take them.

Landon poured himself a fourth cup of coffee, fig-uring he'd need a fifth or sixth one to rid him of the headache he had from lack of sleep, and checked on the baby again. She was still sacked out in the bassinet his cousins had provided. Maybe Tessa was asleep, as well, because he didn't hear her stirring in the bedroom.

Since Tessa had been the one to do the baby's 2:00 a.m. feeding, Landon had brought the infant into the living-kitchen combo area with him so that Tessa could sleep in. Of course, he'd done that with the hopes that he might get in a catnap or two on the sofa—where he'd spent the night—but no such luck. His mind was spinning with all the details of the attack. With Tessa's situation. With Emmett's murder. And despite all that mind spinning, Landon still didn't have the answers he wanted.

But maybe Tessa would.

By now, those drugs she'd been given should have worn off, and that meant maybe she would be able to tell him not only who was behind the attack at the hospital but also who'd murdered Emmett.

Landon had more coffee and checked outside. Something he'd done a lot during the night and yet another of the reasons he hadn't gotten much sleep. No signs of gunmen. Thank God. But then, the ranch hands had been told not to let anyone other than family and ranch employees onto the grounds. Maybe that would be enough to stop another attack.

However, the only way to be certain of no future attacks was to catch the person responsible. Joel, maybe. He was the obvious person of interest here, but Landon wasn't ruling out Quincy. Too bad neither Landon nor any of his lawman cousins had been able to find any evidence to make an arrest for either man.

Landon heard the two sounds at once. The baby whimpered, and Tessa moved around in the bedroom. He didn't wait for Tessa to come out. Since it was time for the baby's feeding, Landon went ahead and got the bottle from the fridge and warmed it up, just as the nanny had shown him when they'd arrived yesterday. Thankfully, there were three full-time nannies at the ranch now, so he hadn't had to resort to looking up bottle-warming instructions on the internet.

He eased the baby from the bassinet, silently cursing
that his hands suddenly felt way too big and clumsy. The
baby didn't seem to mind, though, and she latched on
to the bottle the moment it touched her mouth.

Without the baby's fussing, it was easier for Landon
to hear something else. Tessa's voice. She wasn't talking loud enough for him to pick out the words, but it
seemed as if she was having a conversation with someone on the phone. The guesthouse didn't have a landline, but there was a cell phone on the nightstand for
guests—something that apparently Tessa had decided
to make use of. But before Landon could find out who
she was calling, Tessa quit talking, and a moment later
the bedroom door opened.

And there she was.

Landon hated that slam of attraction. Yeah, he felt
it even now, and it was proof that attraction was more
than just skin-deep. Because despite the bruises on her
face, the fatigued eyes, and the baggy loaner jeans and
shirt, she still managed to light fires inside him that he
didn't want lit.

She opened her mouth, ready to say something, but
then her attention landed on the baby. "You're feeding
her," Tessa said in the same tone someone might use
when announcing a miracle. Maybe because he didn't
look like the bottle-feeding type.

"The nanny talked me through how to do it," he explained. "And since you'd done the other feedings, I
figured it was my turn."

Tessa glanced around as if expecting to see Rose, the
nanny, standing there, but the woman hadn't returned
after she'd gotten them settled in the night before. That
was Landon's doing.

"I didn't want to disrupt the nannies' routines any more than we already have, so I told her to go home," he explained. "My cousins have a lot of kids."

Thirteen at last count. Or maybe fourteen. Sometimes the ranch felt a little like a day care.

"I remember," Tessa said.

Two words, that was all she said, but those two words caused Landon to release the breath he didn't even know he'd been holding. Because she wasn't just talking about remembering that his cousins had plenty of children. She was talking about the memories the drugs had suppressed.

"You know who killed Emmett?" Landon asked.

His relief didn't last long, because she shook her head. "No. I don't know the person's name, but I remember what happened." Tessa lifted her shoulder. "Well, some things are still fuzzy, probably because of the drugs, but I remembered about the baby. Her name is Samantha."

"Whose child is this?" he pressed when Tessa didn't continue.

"She belongs to a friend, Courtney Hager. She wanted me to keep the baby while she made arrangements to move. The baby's father was abusive, she said, and Courtney didn't want him anywhere near Samantha or her. She told me not to trust anyone, because the father had connections."

Landon would want to know more about those connections and the father, but for now he stood and handed Tessa the baby so he could fire off a text to his cousin Holden. Holden was a marshal and would be able to do a quick background check on this Courtney Hager. Of course, Grayson and the other deputies could do it, as well, but they were already swamped with the investigation.

In a way, Landon hated to ask Holden to do this, too. Because Emmett and Holden were brothers, and Landon knew that he and Emmett's other brothers were sick with grief over their loss. But Landon also knew that Holden and the others would do whatever it took to find Emmett's killer and that Tessa and this baby could be a connection.

"How long were you supposed to keep the baby?" Landon pressed.

"Courtney said it would only be a day or two. She's probably looking for us right now. Probably frantic, too."

Probably. Well, unless something had happened to her. "Was it Courtney you just called?"

She got that deer-caught-in-headlights look. A look that didn't please Landon one bit. "No. I called a friend," she said. "I didn't have Courtney's number memorized. It was on my cell, but I lost that somewhere in the last day or so. I wanted to try to figure out if this friend knew anything about what was going on, but he didn't answer the call."

She didn't remember Courtney's number, yet she remembered the number of this other "friend." Landon wanted to know a lot more about that, too, but it wasn't at the top of his list of questions.

"Did Courtney have anything to do with Emmett's murder?" he asked.

"No," Tessa jumped to answer. Then she paused. "But maybe her abusive boyfriend did. I don't know his name," she quickly added. "I've only known Courtney a couple of months, and I never met Samantha's father. She didn't talk about him much, but I know she's afraid of him or else she wouldn't have told me not to trust anyone."

That was something Holden might be able to uncover in the background check. Maybe this abusive guy had killed Emmett when Emmett was trying to protect the baby, though that didn't explain the note left on Emmett's body.

Tessa glanced down at the baby, brushed a kiss on her cheek. "Anything new on the attack? Did they find the gunman?" she added before he could press her for more information.

Landon would indeed press her for more, especially more about that "friend" she'd called, but for now he went with the update on the investigation. Unfortunately, he wasn't going to be the bearer of good news.

"Grayson and the deputies didn't catch the man," he said and paused the bottle-feeding just long enough so he could hit the button on his laptop. "It's surveillance footage from the hospital, and I want you to take a closer look. Tell me if you recognize the man who attacked us."

Maybe she would be truthful about that. Maybe.

Landon didn't look at the screen. He didn't need to, since he'd studied the footage frame by frame. Instead, he watched Tessa, looking for any signs that she knew the man who'd been trying to gun them down.

She shook her head, moved closer to the laptop. In doing so, she moved closer to Landon, her arm brushing against his. She noticed. Also noticed the scowl he gave her as a result, and Tessa inched away from him.

"I'm not positive," she said, her attention back on the screen, where she froze one of the frames, "but I think that might be the same masked man who attacked me at my house. The man who killed Emmett." Tessa pointed to the guy's hand. "See the way he's holding his gun, the way he's standing. He looks like a cop."

Could be, but Landon wasn't convinced. He could just as easily be a trained killer or a former cop.

"Who is he?" she asked.

"We still don't know. But I don't believe it's a coincidence that Joel was there just minutes before this clown showed up."

Tessa made a sound of agreement. "Has anyone questioned Joel yet?"

"Grayson did last night. Of course, Joel claims he had nothing to do with the attack. He also came up with that name of the fire department employee who told his assistant. It was the dispatcher, Valerie Culpepper, and she confirmed she did tell the assistant."

"You believe her?"

"Not sure. Of course, it's possible Joel paid the dispatcher to say that. He could have known you were at the hospital because he or his hired gun was at the scene of the fire and saw you'd been taken away in an ambulance."

Since there was only one hospital in Silver Creek and it wasn't that big of a building, Tessa wouldn't have been hard to find.

Landon's phone buzzed, and when he saw Holden's name on the screen, he stepped away to take the call. Not that he could step far. The guesthouse wasn't that big, but he went into the living room area.

"Dade told me what happened at the hospital," Holden said the moment Landon answered. "Any reason I didn't hear it from you?"

"I've been busy. I'm with Tessa."

"Yeah. I heard that, too." Even though Holden didn't come out and say it, Landon heard the disapproval in his cousin's voice. Probably because Holden knew how Tessa had treated him. "I'm guessing Tessa's the reason you wanted me to find out about Courtney Hager?"

"She is. The baby that Tessa had with her belongs to Courtney." Landon nearly added some *maybes* in that explanation since he wasn't sure if Tessa was telling him the truth. Not the whole truth, anyway. But Holden would have automatically known that Landon had doubts about his former lover.

"I'll do a more thorough check," Holden continued a moment later, "but here's what I got. Courtney Hager is twenty-nine, unmarried and is a bookkeeper. Her address is listed in Austin."

"Have someone sent out there to do a welfare check on her," Landon suggested. That was only an hour away, but the local cops there could do that ASAP.

"She's in danger?" Holden didn't hesitate with that question.

"Possibly." And that was, sadly, the best-case scenario here. If she truly did have an abusive ex, then it was possible she was already dead. "If she's home, the locals need to take her into custody and bring her here to Silver Creek."

"Got it," Holden assured him. "What about Tessa? You want me to arrange a safe house for her?"

"Thanks, but I'm already working on it." Landon paused. "Are you…okay?"

It wasn't something he'd normally ask his cousin. Holden wasn't exactly the type to want anyone to ask that, either, but Landon wanted to make sure he wasn't pushing Holden too hard this soon after his brother's death.

"I just want to find the bastard who killed Emmett," Holden answered. "I won't be okay until then."

Landon knew exactly how Holden felt. He finished the call and turned to face Tessa.

"I'm going to a safe house?" she asked. Clearly, she'd heard the conversation.

Landon nodded. "The baby will, too. As long as the gunman's out there, you'll need protection."

She didn't disagree with that, but she made a weary sigh and sank down onto the chair. "Joel," was all she said. "It has to be him. He must have been the one who hired that guy who killed Emmett and attacked me. I've been hiding from him all these months, but he must have found me and sent a thug after me."

If Landon followed this line of reasoning, then it was also a thug who'd killed Emmett. "Do you remember why Joel would want you dead?"

She nodded, and since Samantha was finished with the bottle, Tessa put the baby against her shoulder to burp her. "I found out…something." She swallowed hard, and when her gaze met his, Landon saw the tears shimmering in her eyes. "I told you I believed Joel had murdered someone. It was a man named Harry Schuler."

The name didn't mean anything to Landon, but like Courtney, he'd soon find out everything he could about him. "How long have you known about this murder?" he asked.

"Several months."

Landon cursed. Then he bit back more profanity since it seemed wrong to curse in front of a baby.

"Months? Why didn't you come to me with this? Or to anybody in law enforcement?"

"No proof. Not just about that but any of the other illegal things that I'm certain Joel was doing."

Landon was certain of those illegal things, too, and he motioned for her to continue.

"By the time Harry Schuler was killed, I'd stopped working for Joel," she went on after taking in a long breath. "But I pretended to stay friendly with Joel so I could keep digging into his business dealings."

"Define *friendly*," Landon snapped.

She flinched a little. "Nothing like that. But I didn't want Joel to know I was on to him."

"Good thing. Or he would have killed you, too. What kind of dirt did you have on Joel?"

Tessa shook her head. "Everything I found was circumstantial at best. Vaguely worded emails and part of a phone conversation I overheard. That's really why I jumped at the chance when Joel wanted me to become a PI, so I'd have the resources and contacts to look for something concrete that could be used for an arrest. I wanted to get some proof because I knew if I accused him and he didn't go to jail, that he would kill me."

Landon tried to process that while he fired off yet another text to his cousin. This time he asked Holden to get him more info on Harry Schuler.

"You said Joel wanted you to be a PI," he reminded her. "You think that's because he could use you in some way? Maybe so he could get access to those data bases you mentioned?"

"Could be, but he never asked me for any specific info from them. He only wanted me to vet potential clients to make sure they had the finances to cover whatever deal he was making with them."

But Joel was smart, and he might have been giving Tessa just enough rope to hang herself. "When specifically did this possible murder happen?"

Silence.

Oh, man. He didn't like this at all.

"That same week we slept together," she finally said. "*Before* we slept together," Tessa clarified.

That made the cut even deeper. She'd had sex with him while withholding something as huge as an alleged murder.

"If you believed Joel was capable of murder, then why leave with him that morning after you were with me?" Landon asked.

Oh.

He saw it in her eyes then. "You thought Joel would try to kill me," Landon concluded.

She nodded. "Maybe even kill both of us."

Landon had to bite back more profanity, and it took him a moment to get his jaw unclenched so he could speak. "Protecting me wasn't necessary, and it was stupid for you to go off with him like that."

"I thought if I went with him, then I'd be able to find the proof that he'd murdered Harry Schuler."

Landon jabbed his finger in her direction. "There's no argument, *none*, that you can make that'll have me agreeing with what you did." He tapped his new badge. "I'm a cop, and I could have handled this the right way."

And there was no chance she could refute that this had been anything but the right way. Now Emmett was dead, Courtney was heaven knew where, and Tessa had a killer after her.

"I was planning to come to you," she said after several quiet moments. "I got your address in Houston and had put it in my GPS, but then the baby kept fussing, so I decided to make a detour to my house here in Silver Creek."

Landon didn't have to tell her that the second part of that wasn't such a good idea. Even though her house was in town and near the sheriff's office, someone could have been watching it.

"Is that how the gunman found you?" he asked. "Were you going to your house?"

She nodded. "I didn't see him following me until it was too late. I tried to outrun him, and that's how I ended up near the barn. The memories are sketchy after that, though. I don't have any idea how I got from my car to the barn."

Because she'd been drugged a second time, that was why. While Landon hoped she would recover all her memories, including those, recalling an attack that'd nearly left her dead wouldn't help her sleep at night. Still, the devil was in the details of those memories.

Emmett's killer was.

And anything she could tell him might help him figure out who'd sent that ski-masked thug after Emmett and her. Or if it was indeed the same thug who'd committed this crime spree.

She stayed quiet a moment, her own jaw muscles stirring. "Tell me about that picture of the man you showed me. Quincy Nagel."

Since Landon was still trying to rein in his temper, it took him a moment to switch gears. "He's someone I arrested. And yes, it's possible he's the one who had

Emmett murdered, but right now Joel is looking like my top suspect."

What he needed now was proof. And more answers. Landon thought he might get at least one of those answers on the bedroom phone that Tessa had used to call her friend.

He excused himself without telling Tessa what he was going to do, and he went into the bedroom. Landon went through the cache of recent calls, but Tessa had obviously cleared the one she'd made. There wasn't a good reason for her to do that, and he went back into the living room, ready to demand a full explanation as to what was going on. However, before he could do that, Landon's phone buzzed, and it wasn't his cousin this time.

It was Dr. Michelson.

Since it was barely 6:00 a.m. and nowhere near normal office hours, Landon figured it had to be important, so he answered it right away.

"I just got back the results of Tessa's tests," the doc said, skipping any greeting. "You need to bring her back to the hospital immediately."

Chapter Seven

Tessa couldn't stop herself from thinking the worst. Easy to think the worst after everything she'd been through. But it wasn't the memories of the attacks that troubled her most right now.

It was what she couldn't remember.

Those hours right after she'd been given the drugs were still a blur, and she needed to recall every second of what'd happened to her. Maybe then she would know who had done this to her.

"Any idea what it is?" Dr. Michelson asked Landon. They were looking at what the doctor had just extracted from her neck. It was only about a quarter of an inch long and looked like a tiny bullet.

"I think it's a tracking device," Landon answered.

Tessa's stomach dropped. To think she'd been walking around with that in for heaven knew how long, and she couldn't even remember how she'd gotten it. Of course, it wasn't very big, but she still should have known that something wasn't right, and it sickened her to think of what else this unknown monster could have done to her.

"I'll need it bagged as evidence," Landon instructed the doctor, and he glanced back at her. "You okay?"

Tessa lied with a nod, and even though Landon likely

knew it was a lie, he also understood something else. It could have been much worse.

Now that she'd had a thorough exam, Tessa knew she hadn't been sexually assaulted and that her captor had given her a powerful barbiturate cocktail. She also knew that she hadn't given birth, but then, she hadn't needed an exam to confirm that. Her memories of Courtney calling her and asking her to come and get the baby were clear.

She also had clear memories of how afraid Courtney had been.

Tessa had hurried next door to Courtney's rental house when she'd heard that fear in the woman's voice, and when Courtney had begged her to take the baby for safekeeping, Tessa had done it. After she'd tried to talk Courtney into going to the authorities, that is. Courtney had flat-out refused that, though.

"Why would someone have injected Tessa with a tracking device?" the doctor asked Landon.

"Probably in case she escaped. That way her captor could find her."

Oh, God. "The baby." Tessa tried to get off the table, despite the fact the nurse was still bandaging her neck. "Someone could have used the tracking device to follow us to the ranch."

Landon motioned for her to stay down, and he made a call to the ranch, where they'd left Samantha with a nanny and several of his lawman cousins. The ranch had security, but it wasn't a fortress, and a gunman might be able to get onto the grounds and hurt the baby.

"Everything's fine," Landon relayed after he finished his short call. "The ranch hands are all on alert, and they'll let one of my cousins know if they see anyone suspicious." Landon walked closer to her. "Besides, this tracking device was on you, not the baby."

Yes, he was right. Maybe that meant the gunman wasn't after Samantha at all but just her. That didn't help with the tangle of nerves she was feeling. The newborn could be in danger all because of her.

"Will you be able to tell who was getting information from the tracking device?" she asked once the nurse was out of the room. It wasn't that Tessa didn't trust the woman, but she wasn't sure she fully trusted anyone right now.

Landon lifted his shoulder. "We'll try, but it's probably a microchip that can be tracked with a computer. It does make me wonder, though, why someone would go to the trouble of injecting you with it."

Tessa gave that some thought but had to shake her head. She didn't know why, either, but it was obvious whoever had attacked her had wanted to be able to find her if she escaped.

Unless…

"Maybe this person wanted me to come to you," she said on a rise of breath.

"I'm not a hard man to find," Landon pointed out. "But this could mean the person didn't want you dead. Not when he or she put that tracker device on you, anyway."

True. If someone had gotten close enough to do that to her, they could have easily just killed her. Not exactly a comforting thought.

Dr. Michelson put the tracking device in a plastic bag and looked at Landon. "You want me to have Grayson or one of the other deputies pick this up?"

"No. I'll take it. When will she be free to go?"

The doctor looked at her. "She can leave now but keep an eye on her. The barbiturates have worn off, but she still could experience some dizziness."

Yes, the dizziness was there, and her head still felt a little foggy. Still, it was better than not knowing who she was. At least now she could start to look for the person behind this.

Either Landon had noticed she was wobbly or else he was just being cautious, because he took hold of her arm and helped her from the examining table. "Come on. I can drop off this tracking device at the sheriff's office, and we can give our statements about the attack."

That wasn't exactly a surprise for Tessa. She knew they needed to do the paperwork, but that meant facing yet more Ryland lawmen who wanted answers she didn't have. Even after regaining most of her memories, she didn't know who'd murdered one of their own.

With Landon's grip still firm on her arm, they made their way to the exit. Since Dade had driven with him, she expected to see him waiting in the cruiser just outside. But Tessa stopped in her tracks when she saw the scowling man. Not Dade.

But Deputy Mason Ryland.

None of the Rylands had been especially friendly to her, but Mason had a dark and dangerous edge to him, and right now he was aiming some of that intensity at her.

"Dade had to leave for a parent-teacher thing at the school," Mason growled. "I drew the short straw."

Clearly, he wasn't happy about that, but then, she'd never actually seen Mason happy. "Thank you," Tessa told him, but that only intensified the scowl.

"As soon as you drop us off at the sheriff's office,

you can head back to the ranch," Landon told him Landon's eyes met hers as they got into the backseat of the cruiser. "Mason's retiring as a Silver Creek deputy. That's why Grayson offered me the job."

Tessa knew Mason pretty much ran the sprawling ranch and had done so for years, so that was probably why he was giving up his deputy duties. But she also suspected that Landon had pressed for the job. So he could catch his cousin's killer.

"Who did you call this morning?" Landon asked out of the blue. Except it probably wasn't out of the blue for him. He was like a dog with a bone when he latched on to anything to do with the investigation. And sadly, this might have something to do with it. Of course, it wouldn't be a simple explanation.

Or one that Landon would like.

"His name is Ward Strickland," she said and tried to figure out the best way to spill all of this.

"A boyfriend?" Landon didn't hesitate. He also continued to glance around, no doubt to make sure that they weren't being followed or that the gunman wasn't nearby, ready to launch another attack.

"Hardly. I haven't had a boyfriend since you." She hadn't meant to blurt that out, and it made her sound even more pathetic than she already was. Telling him about Ward wouldn't help that, either. "He's a Justice Department agent." Tessa paused. "But I'm not sure I can trust him."

She hadn't thought anyone's scowl could be worse than Mason's, but she'd been wrong. Landon beat him. "Explain that now," he demanded.

Tessa took a deep breath first. "You already know I was looking for dirt on Joel. Well, Ward said he was, too, and he contacted me to see if I had anything he could use to make an arrest. I didn't, but Ward kept hounding me to dig deeper. He wanted me to tell him anything I found out about Joel."

Landon fired off a text, no doubt to have one of his cousins run a background check on the agent. "Why aren't you sure you can trust him?" Landon asked.

"Gut feeling." She braced herself for Landon to groan. He didn't. "Once I found an email that Joel had sent. It possibly connected him to some illegal arms. *Possibly*," she emphasized. "Anyway, the day before Emmett was killed, I gave Ward a copy of the email, but a few hours later, I noticed the email had been deleted off Joel's server. I'd been checking for things like that, hoping to find something to use to have Joel arrested."

Landon stayed quiet a moment. "You think this agent could be working for Joel and just wanted to figure out if you were on to anything? Or maybe he wanted to make sure you didn't find something?"

There it was in a nutshell. "If Ward is on Joel's payroll, maybe he's the one behind the attacks."

No quiet moment this time. Landon cursed. "So why did you call him this morning? And I'm guessing it wasn't because you thought he could help you find Courtney."

"No. He doesn't know Courtney. I told you that because I didn't want to explain who he was. Not until I'd found out more about what was going on."

Landon made a circling motion with his finger to indicate he wanted this explanation to continue. He also hoped she understood that he wasn't happy with the lie she'd told him.

"I called Ward to feel him out, to try and see if he had

anything to do with this. But he didn't answer. The call went straight to voice mail, so I left a message just to tell him I'd been attacked. And before you tell me that it was risky, that I could have led Ward straight to the ranch, I remember Dade saying it was a prepaid cell, so I knew Ward wouldn't be able to trace it."

More profanity from Landon, and Mason even grumbled some, as well. "If you're that worried about this guy, you should have said something before now. I'm trying to find out who came after us, and I need the names of anyone who could have been involved. *Anyone*," Landon emphasized.

Tessa couldn't argue with that. "I just didn't think you'd want to rely on my gut feelings."

"A disappearing email is more than a gut feeling," Landon verified as Mason pulled to a stop in front of the sheriff's office. "Anyone connected to Joel is a suspect."

No argument there, either. "But Joel doesn't need to hire a federal agent to come after me. I'm sure he already has plenty of hired thugs."

Landon didn't answer. In fact, he was no longer looking at her. Instead, his attention was on the two men who were entering the sheriff's office. One of the men was in a wheelchair, and the other, much larger man was helping him through the door.

"Did Grayson call him in for questioning?" Landon asked.

"No," Mason snarled. "He was going to wait until after he questioned Joel again later this morning. Maybe I should take Tessa back to the ranch while you deal with this?"

Tessa wasn't sure why Mason had said that until she

got a better look at the man in the wheelchair. Landon had shown her his mug shot. Quincy Nagel.

And he was yet another suspect.

Quincy had barely made it into the office when Landon stepped from the car. Quincy turned his wheelchair in their direction, and much to Tessa's surprise, the man smiled.

"Thank God you're here," Quincy said. But he wasn't looking at Landon when he spoke. He was looking at Tessa. "Where's the baby? I'm here to take my daughter home."

LANDON HADN'T BEEN sure what exactly Quincy would say to him, but he hadn't expected *that*.

Clearly, neither had Tessa, because she got out of the cruiser to face the man. In case this was some kind of ploy to get her out in the open so someone could gun her down, Landon hooked his arm around her and maneuvered her into the sheriff's office. Mason followed.

The place wasn't exactly quiet. Two deputies were at their desks in the open squad room, and Landon spotted Grayson in the hall outside his office. Like the deputies, he was in the middle of a phone call, but when he spotted them, he disconnected and headed for them.

"Trouble?" Grayson immediately asked.

Probably. Trouble and Quincy often went together.

"No trouble, Sheriff," Quincy insisted. He didn't sound like the thug that Landon knew he was. Didn't look like one today, either. He was wearing a dark blue suit and so was the linebacker-sized guy behind his wheelchair.

"You said something about a baby?" Tessa asked.

Quincy smiled. "Samantha. I understand you've been keeping her for Courtney."

Landon looked at her to see if this was yet something else she'd kept from him, but she looked as shell-shocked as Landon felt. That precious little girl was Quincy's?

"So where is she?" Quincy asked.

"I don't know what you're talking about," Landon said before Tessa could speak. No way was he handing over a newborn to this man.

Quincy's thin smile didn't stay in place for long. "But you do know." His jaw tightened. Eyes narrowed. "Quit playing games with me and give me my daughter. I know that Courtney gave Tessa the baby, but that's only because she couldn't find me. Well, I'm here now, so give Samantha to me."

Landon needed to stall him until he could either get in touch with Courtney or find out what the heck was going on.

"Tessa and I don't have your daughter," Landon said. "The baby we have is ours."

The squad room suddenly got very quiet. Grayson knew Landon had just lied through his teeth. Mason, too.

Quincy looked Tessa over from head to toe. "You expect me to believe that you just had a baby?"

Even though Tessa was wearing loose loaner jeans, they skimmed her body enough to show her flat stomach. But Tessa didn't panic, and she stepped right into the lie by taking hold of Landon's arm and leaning against him.

"Tessa kept the pregnancy from me," Landon added. "But she had no choice but to come to me when someone tried to kill her. What exactly do you know about that?"

Quincy shook his head as if trying to figure out what was going on, but then Landon saw the moment the man pushed his surprise aside to deal with the accusation. "Nothing. You believe I tried to hurt Tessa?"

"Did you?" Landon didn't even try to sound as if Quincy might be innocent. Plain and simple, Quincy hated him, and he hated Emmett, too, for testifying against him. That hatred could have bubbled over to Tessa.

Except Quincy might not have gone after Tessa because of any ill will he was feeling for Landon. This could indeed be connected to the baby.

"Where's Courtney?" Landon asked.

Quincy shook his head again, and Landon got a flash of the thug behind the newly polished facade. "You tell me. Are you hiding her from me?"

"Is there a reason I'd do that?" Landon countered.

Oh, Quincy did *not* like that. The anger slashed through his eyes. "You have no right. Courtney is my lover, the mother of my child. Tessa knows that."

"No, I don't," Tessa argued. "Courtney's never even mentioned you, but she did tell me that Samantha's father was abusive."

"That's a lie!" Quincy shouted. "I never laid a hand on Courtney."

The goon behind his wheelchair leaned down and whispered something to him. Landon didn't know what the guy said, but it caused Quincy to rein in his temper.

"I want my daughter, and I want her now," Quincy insisted. "And don't say you don't have her, because I know you do."

Landon lifted his shoulder. "You're mistaken." And Landon left it at that. "Now, let's talk about Emmett. About his murder."

The rein on Quincy's temper didn't last long, and Landon could practically see the veins bulging on the man's neck. "I had nothing to do with that."

"I don't believe you. I think you killed him to get back at me."

The goon whispered something else, or rather that was what he tried to do, but this time Quincy batted him away. "You have no proof linking me to Emmett's death."

"Wrong." Landon decided to test out his latest theory. "You went to Tessa's, looking for Courtney and the baby, and Emmett was there. You got violent, Emmett tried to stop you, and you killed him."

Despite his tense muscles, Quincy managed a smile. "I didn't know you believed in fairy tales. I've never stepped foot in Tessa's place, and that means there's not a shred of physical evidence to link me to it or Emmett's murder." He made a show of gripping on to his wheelchair. "Besides, how could I overpower Emmett when I can't even walk?"

"You don't need to walk to shoot someone," Landon argued. "Or to hire a thug to shoot someone. With the trust fund your parents left you, I'm betting you've got plenty of funds to hire plenty of thugs."

"Prove it," Quincy snapped. He motioned for his goon to get him moving. "In the meantime, I'll work on getting a court order to force you to turn over my daughter to me. Neither Courtney nor you will keep her from me."

Landon considered holding Quincy for questioning, but the man would just lawyer up. It was best if Landon backed off, regrouped and figured out exactly how Quincy was involved in this.

Quincy's goon wheeled him out of the sheriff's office, but Landon didn't stand there and watch them leave. He moved Tessa away from the windows in case Quincy or his hired gun started shooting. Since Landon didn't have a private office, he took her down the hall to one of the interview rooms.

"I didn't know Quincy was involved with Courtney," Tessa said the moment they were inside. "I told the truth when I said she'd never mentioned him."

Landon believed her. "Quincy could have been lying about Courtney."

Tessa blinked. Shook her head. "But why would he do that?"

"I'm not sure." But Landon intended to find out. He took out his phone, and this time he didn't text his cousin Holden. He called him, and he put it on Speaker. Mainly because he knew Tessa would want to hear this, and he didn't want her standing too close to listen. "Please tell me you found out something, anything, about Courtney Hager."

"Bad morning?" Holden asked, probably because Landon hadn't even bothered with a greeting.

"I've had better. I just had a visit from Quincy Nagel claiming he's the father of the baby Tessa was protecting. Courtney Hager's baby."

"Quincy, huh? Haven't found a connection between Courtney and him. Uh, can Nagel even father a child?"

"His paralysis is in his legs, so yes, I'm guessing he could. But that doesn't mean he did. What did you find out about Courtney?"

"Not much at all. She has no criminal record, and she did have a baby just last week. She also moves around a lot. I mean like every couple of months. The local cops did a welfare check for me, but she wasn't home, and her neighbors said they hadn't seen her in days."

That was possibly because she was on the run, hiding out from Quincy, but it was just as possible that she was hurt. Or dead. Quincy could have gotten to her before he came looking for his baby. If he had a baby, that is.

"Did you have DNA tests run on the baby?" Holden asked.

"Yes," Landon answered. "But I did that in case the child turned out to be mine. Now we could look for a match with Quincy, and it'll speed things up because Quincy's DNA is already in the system."

"I'll get to work on seeing if it's a match. And I'll keep looking for a connection between Quincy and her," Holden went on. "By the way, did Tessa remember anything else that could help us find Emmett's killer?"

"Nothing so far, but Grayson is questioning Joel later this morning. I'll be here for that—after I take Tessa back to the ranch."

Tessa's gaze flew to his. "I want to be here for Joel's interview, too," she insisted.

His first reaction was to say no, that she didn't need to go another round with Joel, but if Landon had been in her place, he would have wanted to hear what the creep had to say about the attack.

"I'll let you two work that out," Holden grumbled. "If I find out anything else, I'll call you."

Landon put his phone away and stared at her. "Tell me everything you know about Courtney. How did you meet? How long have you known her?"

"Like I already told you, I've only known her a few months. She moved into the rental house next to me, and while she was waiting on her internet to be connected, she came over and asked to use mine." She paused. "I did a computer check on Courtney, to make sure she wasn't someone Joel hadn't sent over to spy on me. I didn't find anything."

Good. Because a connection to Quincy was bad enough. Still, that didn't mean this wasn't all stirred together somehow. But at the moment Landon couldn't see how. If Quincy had arranged for Courtney and Tessa to meet, what could he have gained by that? It was the same for Courtney. If the woman had known about his affair with Tessa or Landon and Quincy's bad blood, why wouldn't she have said anything about it?

Landon was still trying to piece together some answers when his phone buzzed, and he saw the name on the screen of someone who just might be able to help him with those answers.

Ward Strickland.

Tessa must have seen it, too, because she pulled in her breath. "I want to talk to him," she insisted.

"For now, just listen," Landon instructed. Whether she would or not was anyone's guess. Like his, her nerves were sky-high right now.

"Deputy Ryland," Ward said the moment Landon answered. "Your cousin Holden told me you needed to speak to me. Is this about Tessa? Do you know where she is?"

Landon took a moment to consider how to answer that. "She's in protective custody. Someone's been trying to kill her," he settled for saying.

"Yes, I heard. She left me a message but didn't give me any details. Is she all right?" The man's tone sounded sincere enough, but Landon wasn't going to trust him merely on that.

"For now. But I need proof as to who's behind these attacks. I'm hoping you can help with that."

Even from the other end of the line, Landon heard the agent's weary sigh. "I'm sure Tessa would say it's Joel."

"Is it?" Landon pressed.

"Maybe, but I've been investigating Joel for a year now, and I haven't found any evidence to arrest him for a misdemeanor, much less the felonies that Tessa claims he's been committing."

Tessa shook her head and looked ready to launch into an argument about that, but Landon motioned for her to keep quiet.

"You believe Joel's innocent?" Landon came out and asked Ward.

"No, not totally, but I'm not sure I believe what Tessa said he did. In fact, I'm not sure I can trust Tessa."

Thankfully, Tessa didn't gasp or make a sound of outrage, though there was some anger going through her eyes.

"I need to talk to Tessa," Ward went on. "I tried to trace the call she made to me, but it came from a pre-paid cell, and she didn't leave a number where she could be reached."

"You want to talk to her even if you don't trust her?" Landon snapped.

"Of course." The agent paused. "Because I'm not just investigating Joel. I'm also investigating her. I believe they're working together, or else Tessa could be using Joel as a front man for several illegal operations. Specifically, gunrunning and money laundering."

Tessa no longer looked angry. But rather defeated. Landon couldn't blame her. She'd been attacked at least three times and had been drugged, and someone had injected her with a tracking device. Now here was a federal agent accusing her of assorted felonies.

"I want to take Tessa into custody," Ward continued. "If she's truly in danger, I can protect her. And if she's helping Joel, maybe I can learn that, too. When can I pick her up?"

Landon's first instinct was to tell his guy to take a hike, but there was no sense showing Ward his hand. "I'll get back to you on that. Gotta go." And Landon ended the call.

Tessa was shaking her head before Landon even slipped his phone back into his pocket. "I'm not going with Ward. He could be trying to set me up to cover for Joel."

She turned as if to bolt out of there, but Landon took hold of her shoulders to stop her. "You're not going anywhere with Ward."

Her breath rushed out. Maybe from relief, but her eyes watered. "I'm not helping Joel," she said, her voice more breath than sound. "And I'm not a criminal."

Landon wasn't made of ice, especially around Tessa, and seeing those fresh tears in her eyes melted the ice he wished were there. Cursing himself, cursing Tessa, too, he slid his arm around her waist and eased her closer.

She melted against him. As if she belonged there.

His body seemed to think she belonged, not just in his arms. But other places. Like his bed. Still, Landon pushed that aside and tried to do what any de-iced human would do—comfort Tessa. It seemed to work, until she looked up at him.

Hell.

He didn't want another dose of this, but he wasn't

exactly moving away from her, either. In fact, Landon thought he might be inching closer.

Yeah, he was.

And he didn't just inch with his body. He lowered his head, touched his mouth to hers. Now would have been a really good time for her to come to her senses and push him away. Thankfully, she did. Tessa stepped back.

"I'll bet you're already regretting that," she said, pressing her lips together a moment.

"I regretted it before I even did it." Regretted even more that it would happen again.

Landon wanted to think he could add a *probably* to that—that other kisses would probably happen—but he wasn't a man who approved of lying to himself. The *probably* was a lie. If he was around Tessa, he would kiss her again. And that was a really good reason to come up with other arrangements for her protective custody.

Definitely not Ward. But maybe he could arrange for her to stay with Holden for a while.

There was a knock at the door, and even though Tessa was no longer in his arms, she moved back even farther. The door opened, and Grayson stuck his head inside. His attention went to Tessa, not Landon.

"There's a woman lurking across the street," Grayson said. "I haven't been out there, because I didn't want to spook her, but it's possible it's Courtney."

That got Tessa moving, and Landon had to hurry to get in front of her. "I don't want you outside," Landon reminded her.

He wasn't even sure she heard him, because Tessa was already looking out the window. Landon did the same, and it didn't take him long to spot the woman.

Lurking was a good description since she was in the narrow alley between two buildings, and she was glancing over at the sheriff's office.

Landon had seen Courtney's driver's license photo, but it was hard to tell if it matched this woman. The hair color was right, but she was wearing a baseball hat that she'd pulled low over her face. Also, with the baggy dark blue dress she was wearing, he couldn't tell if she had recently given birth.

"It could be her," Tessa said, shaking her head. "But I'm not sure."

"I'll go out and talk to her," Landon volunteered. "Wait here," he warned Tessa. "And I mean it."

Grayson stepped beside her and gave Landon a glance to assure him that Tessa was staying put. Good. One less thing to worry about.

Landon went outside, but he didn't make a beeline toward the woman. If this was Courtney, then she probably wouldn't trust him just because he was a cop. He first wanted to make sure it was her, and then he could try to coax her into going inside.

But the woman surprised Landon by calling out to him. "Are you Landon Ryland, the cop Tessa told me about?" she asked.

"I am." Landon went a little closer, wishing he could get a better look at her face.

And he did.

The woman moved out from the alley, not onto the sidewalk but just enough for him to see her.

Hell.

It wasn't Courtney. Landon didn't have a clue who she was, but when she lifted her hand, he saw the gun.

The gun she pointed right at him.

Chapter Eight

Tessa got just a glimpse of the woman taking aim at Landon before Grayson shoved her behind him.

"Get down!" Tessa managed to shout to Landon. But it was already too late.

The woman fired at him.

Landon dropped down, and the bullet slammed into the window. The glass was reinforced, so the shot didn't go through into the squad room, but Landon wasn't behind the glass. He was out there in the open.

Oh, God.

It was happening again. Someone was trying to kill them, and Landon was in danger because of her.

It was hard for Tessa to see around Grayson, and it got even harder when the other two deputies stepped up, as well. All three of them took aim, but it was Grayson who stepped out. He delivered a shot that had the woman ducking back into the alley, and the sheriff continued to shoot at her until Landon could scramble back inside.

"It's not Courtney," Landon relayed to her.

Tessa heard him, but she couldn't respond, because she had to make sure he wasn't hurt. There'd been a lot of shots fired, but Landon appeared to be unharmed.

And riled to the core.

"I don't want her to get away," Landon growled. "I'll go out back and see if I can get her in my line of sight."

"I'll do it," Grayson insisted. "In the meantime, take Tessa to my office. This could be some kind of trap."

Tessa hadn't even thought of that, but he was right. There were four lawmen in the building, and their instincts were no doubt to go in pursuit of the shooter. That might be exactly what their attacker wanted, and he could use this to come after Tessa again. Still, she didn't want Grayson hurt, either.

"Be careful," Tessa called out as the sheriff and one of the other deputies hurried toward the back exit.

Landon didn't waste any time taking her to Grayson's office, but he didn't go inside with her. He stayed in the hall with his gun ready while he volleyed glances at both the front and back of the building.

Another shot.

But Tessa didn't know if the woman had fired it or if it was Grayson.

"She wanted us to think she was Courtney," Tessa said, thinking out loud.

"Yeah. I believe she was sent here to draw you out."

And it'd nearly worked. If Landon hadn't held her back, Tessa would have indeed gone out there. But which of their suspects would be most likely to use a Courtney look-alike to do that?

Quincy Nagel.

Plus, the man had just left the building, so he could be out there somewhere watching his "handiwork." It sickened her to think of Courtney being involved with a man like that. Sickened her even more that Quincy might have already found Courtney and killed her.

"Hell," Landon growled. "I don't need this now."

Tessa could see why he'd said that, but it sent her heart pounding, and a moment later she heard a voice she didn't want to hear. Joel.

"What the hell's going on?" Joel spat out.

She heard some kind of struggle, maybe between Joel and the deputy, but Landon didn't budge. However, he did take aim in that direction, and every muscle in his body was primed for a fight.

"Keep your hands where I can see them," Landon ordered, and a moment later Joel scrambled into the hallway. He dropped down onto the floor, his back against the wall.

"If you demand a man come in for an interrogation," Joel snapped, "then you should make sure the place is safe first. Who the hell is shooting?"

"I thought you might know something about that," Landon countered. Now he was including Joel in those volleyed glances, and the man who crawled to Joel's side. His lawyer, no doubt.

Tessa knew that Joel was indeed coming in for an interview, and judging from the timing of the attack, this could make him appear innocent. Appear. But it was just as likely that Joel had orchestrated it just for that reason. If so, it was still risky since Joel could have been hit by a stray bullet.

More shots came.

These didn't seem as close as the others, but they still sliced through Tessa as if they'd been fired at her. Then everything stopped, and she held her breath, waiting and praying.

"Grayson's coming back," Landon relayed to her,

but he still didn't budge. He stayed in front of her like a sentry.

Tessa managed to get a glimpse of Joel to see how he was dealing with this, but he was checking his phone. Obviously, being caught in the middle of an attack hadn't caused him to go into the panic mode, which only supported her notion that he could have set all of this in motion.

"I had to shoot her," she heard Grayson say. "She's dead." He didn't sound any happier about that than Landon was, and Tessa knew why. A dead shooter couldn't give them any answers.

"Get into the interview room and close the door," Landon told Joel and the lawyer, and he didn't say anything else until they had done that. "Did she say anything?" he added.

Grayson joined them in the hall, and he shook his head. "She had no ID on her, but she did have a phone. Josh is looking at it now."

Good. Maybe they'd find something to tell them who she was and who had hired her. Maybe.

Grayson tipped his head to the interview room. "Let Joel know it's going to be a while before I can talk to him. Then, you can go ahead and get Tessa out of here if you want."

She could see the debate Landon was having with himself about that. He no doubt wanted to be part of this investigation, but that wouldn't happen if he was with her at the ranch.

"As long as the baby's safe, I'll be okay here for a while longer," she offered.

"My cousins will call if there's a problem at the ranch," he said. Landon looked at the interview room.

"But now that Quincy and Joel both know you're here, this is probably the last place you should be."

Ironic because it was a sheriff's office, but Tessa could see his point. As long as she was in danger, so were Landon and his cousins.

He went across the hall and opened the door of the interview room. Joel and his lawyer were huddled together, talking, but they hushed the moment Landon stepped in.

"You're going to have to wait for the interview," Landon insisted. He certainly didn't offer Joel the opportunity to reschedule.

"Who fired those shots?" Joel asked. "And don't bother accusing me, because I didn't do it. Nor did I hire someone. Was it Quincy Nagel?"

Because she was standing so close to Landon, she felt his muscles go stiff. Tessa was certain some of her muscles did the same thing. She stepped in the doorway next to Landon so she could face Joel.

"How do you know Quincy?" Landon asked, taking the question right out of her mouth.

Joel looked as if he was fighting a smile. "Really? You don't think I've made it my business to learn everything I can about both Tessa and you? I know you crossed paths with Quincy, and I know he wants to get back at you. I saw him and some guy in a suit just seconds before the shots started. Why was he here?"

"As you said, he wants to get back at me," Landon answered. Not exactly the truth, but she didn't want to discuss Quincy's possible paternity with Joel. "What'd you learn about Quincy?"

Joel stared at him as if trying to figure out if this

was some kind of trick. It wasn't, but it was a fishing
expedition.

"I know you arrested him," Joel finally answered,
"that he's paralyzed because of a prison fight. But I
have no idea if he's the one who murdered Emmett."

"Anything else?" Landon pressed.

Joel did more staring. "What are you looking for
on Quincy?"

"You tell me."

Joel chuckled. "It must make your hand really tired,
holding your cards so close to the vest like that. Well,
no need. I really don't know anything about Quincy."

Landon made a sound to indicate he didn't buy that.
Neither did Tessa. Joel knew something…but what?
Tessa would have definitely pressed for more, but from
the corner of her eye, she saw Grayson motioning for
them. Landon shut the door of the interview room and
headed toward his cousin.

"We might have found something," Grayson said
the moment they joined him. "Josh looked through the
shooter's recent calls, and there's a name you'll recognize."

Tessa figured Grayson was about to say Joel's or
Quincy's name. But no.

Grayson lifted the phone and showed them the
screen, and Tessa had no trouble seeing the name of
the caller.

Agent Ward Strickland.

WAITING HAD NEVER been Landon's strong suit, and this
time was no different. Where the hell was Ward Strickland and why wasn't the agent returning Landon's calls?

One way or another, he would find out why, but for now he had to wait it out.

Along with keeping Tessa and the baby safe.

That was the reason he'd brought Tessa back to the ranch, but at the time he'd done that, Landon had thought it would be only a couple of hours, but here it was nearly nightfall, and they still had nothing.

Tessa stared at him from over the dinner that the cook had brought from the main house. Fried chicken, some vegetables and homemade bread. Landon had eaten some of it. Tessa, too. But judging from the way she was picking at her food, her appetite was as off as his. Nearly being killed could do that.

"You think Ward could be dead?" she asked.

Landon had gone over all the possibilities, and yeah, that was one of them. The person behind this could have set up Ward with that phone call to the dead shooter and then murdered Ward. Without a body, it would certainly look as if Ward was guilty. And maybe he was. But Landon wanted to make sure. Tessa's and the baby's safety depended on it.

As if on cue, Samantha stirred in the bassinet. Since she'd probably want another bottle soon, Landon figured she'd wake up and start fussing, but she went back to sleep.

"So how long do we stay here?" Tessa asked.

Good question. Landon had gone over all the possibilities and for now had put the safe house on hold.

"I figured we'd need at least one of my cousins to go with us to a safe house, and that would mean tying up a deputy, one Grayson will need," he explained. "At least by being at the ranch, the hands can help with security."

She nodded but didn't look especially pleased about

that. Maybe because she just felt as if she were in hostile territory here because of her connection to Emmett's death. Or maybe it was him.

Or rather that stupid kiss.

Their gazes met, and Landon knew which one it was. Definitely the kiss. Clearly, Tessa wasn't any more comfortable with the attraction than he was, because she looked away and stood. Too bad Landon did the same thing at the exact same time, and in the small space they nearly bumped into each other.

The corner of Tessa's mouth lifted in a short-lived half smile. "It's a good thing we don't have time for this," she said in a whisper.

If he'd wanted to be a jerk, he could have asked her what she was talking about, but Landon knew. It was the attraction—the reason that kiss had happened. And she was right. They didn't have time for "this."

He had things he could be doing to try to move the investigation along. Calls to make. Of course, none of those calls had resulted in anything so far, but now that they'd finished eating, he needed to get back to it. So far, they'd yet to find a number for Courtney. There wasn't a phone in her name anyway, but she could have been using a prepaid cell.

But he didn't get back to the calls.

Like in the sheriff's office, his feet seemed anchored to the floor, and he couldn't take his eyes off Tessa. What else was new? He'd always had that trouble around her, but unlike at the sheriff's office, Landon didn't pull her to him. Didn't kiss her. Instead, he took out his phone to start those calls, but before he could make the first one to Grayson, there was a knock at the door.

Landon automatically put his hand over his gun, but when he looked out the window, he realized it wasn't a threat. It was his cousin Lieutenant Nate Ryland, a cop in the San Antonio PD, and he wasn't alone. He had four kids with him. The oldest, Kimmie, was Nate's eight-year-old daughter, but the other three were Nate's nieces and nephew.

"Supplies," Nate said after Landon opened the door. He had two plastic bags, one with disposable diapers and the other containing formula.

"And a dolly for the baby," Kimmie added. She held up a curly-haired doll for Landon to see.

The four kids came in ahead of Nate and made a bee-line for the bassinet. Tessa stepped back as if clearing the way, or maybe she was just alarmed by the sudden onset of chattering, running kids. Her nerves probably weren't all that steady yet, and Landon wasn't even sure she had much experience being around children.

Kimmie looked in at the baby, putting the doll next to the bassinet, but one of the other girls, Leah—at least, Landon thought it was Leah—hurried to him and hugged him. Since Leah and her twin sister, Mia, were only six years old, that meant the little girl ended up hugging his legs. Landon scooped her up and kissed her cheek.

"Are all these your children?" Tessa asked Nate.

Nate smiled. "Just that one." He pointed to Kimmie, who had her face right against Samantha's. "The boy is Grayson's son, Chet. He's five. And the twins belong to my brother Kade and his wife, Bree."

"And Uncle Landon," Leah corrected, snuggling against Landon. Landon was her cousin, not her uncle, but since Nate had five brothers, Landon figured the kids gave the uncle label to any adult Ryland male.

"Yep. I'm yours," Landon agreed, and that seemed to surprise Tessa, too. Or maybe the surprise was just because he was smiling. Landon certainly hadn't done much of that in the past couple of weeks.

"Can we keep her?" Chet asked, looking down at Samantha.

Nate didn't jump to answer, which meant he probably didn't know the situation. He knew that Samantha wasn't Landon's daughter, of course, but with the baby's mother missing, it was possible she might be at the ranch for a while.

"Don't you have enough cousins?" Nate teased the boy. He ruffled his dark brown hair.

Chet shook his head. "I don't have a sister. Once I get a brother or sister, it'll be enough."

"You'll need to talk to your mom and dad about that. Grayson and his wife, Eve, are thinking about adopting since they can't have any more children of their own," Nate added to Tessa.

Landon set Leah back down on the floor so she, too, could go see the baby, and once all four kids were gathered around the bassinet, Nate went closer to Landon and Tessa.

"I got a call from the crime lab a few minutes ago," Nate said, and he kept his voice low. Probably so the kids wouldn't hear. "Grayson asked me to try to cut through some red tape so he could get the baby's DNA test results and the tracking device the doctor took from Tessa. It's not good news on either front."

Tessa groaned softly. "Is Samantha Quincy's baby?"

"The results aren't back on that yet, but Quincy does

have a fairly rare blood type, and it matches Saman-tha's."

Yeah, definitely not good. "Quincy said he was going to get a court order," Landon told Nate.

Nate nodded. "He's already started proceedings. Of course, his record won't work in his favor, but since he's served his time, a judge probably wouldn't block a demand for custody. That's why Grayson's pushing so hard to find the baby's mother. Still no sign of her, though."

Hell. It sickened Landon to think of Quincy getting anywhere near the newborn, much less taking her. If Courtney was still alive, Quincy could use the baby to force her to come back to him.

"What about the microchip taken from Tessa?" Landon asked.

"It's not traceable. There were thousands of them made, and the techs can't work out who, if anyone, was even monitoring it." Nate paused. "Though I'm guess-ing someone was monitoring it and that's how Tessa ended up in that burning barn."

Tessa made a sound of agreement. "And I don't re-member who did that to me. In fact, I still don't re-member much about the hours after the two times I was drugged."

That was too bad, but the doctor had already warned Landon that those memories might be lost for good.

"Are you two, uh, back together?" Nate came out and asked.

"No," Tessa said even faster than Landon.

Maybe it was the fast answers. Maybe their body language was giving off some signs of the attraction. Either way, Nate just flexed his eyebrows.

"All right, kids, let's go," Nate said.

That got varied reactions. The twins were already bored with the baby, probably because they had a baby sister of their own at home, but Chet lingered a couple of extra seconds.

"Can't we wait until she wakes up?" Kimmie begged.

"Afraid not. I gotta get ready for work, but maybe you can come back in the morning with Uncle Mason when he stops by."

Despite Mason being the most unfriendly looking guy in the state, that pleased Kimmie. Probably because she had her uncle Mason wrapped around her little finger.

Landon got hugs from all four of them, but just as he was seeing them out, his phone buzzed, and he saw Grayson's name on the screen. Landon looked up while he answered it.

"We found Ward," Grayson greeted, but Landon could tell from the sheriff's tone that this wasn't good news. "Someone ran his car off the road, and he's banged up. He said he spent most of the afternoon at the hospital and that's why he didn't answer his phone."

"Could his injuries have been self-inflicted?" Tessa immediately asked. Landon hadn't put the call on Speaker, but she was close enough to hear.

"Possibly. I'll ask him about that when he comes in for questioning in the morning." Grayson paused. "But you should know that Ward is saying that Tessa's responsible, that she hired the person who tried to kill him." Another pause. "Ward is demanding that I arrest her."

Chapter Nine

Tessa's nerves were still raw and right at the surface, and walking into the sheriff's office didn't help. Neither would coming face-to-face with Ward, since he was accusing her of a serious crime that could lead to her arrest. Still, she wanted to confront him, wanted to try to get to the truth. But there was a problem with that.

Landon.

He didn't want her anywhere near Ward when the agent was being questioned. It had taken some doing for Tessa to talk him into allowing her to go with him and that had been only after she'd agreed she wouldn't take part in the interrogation. However, she would be able to listen and she was hoping Landon could convince Ward that she'd had no part in running him off the road.

"Move fast," Landon reminded her the moment they stepped from his truck.

He'd parked it directly in front of the sheriff's office, so it was only a few steps outside, but considering the hired gun had fired those shots just the day before, with each step, she felt as if she were in a combat zone. No way would Tessa mention that, though, since Landon was no doubt leaning toward the idea of having someone escort her back to the ranch so she could stay with the baby, his lawman cousins and the rest of his family. They'd left the baby with Mason and the nanny, and while she didn't want them to be inconvenienced for too long, this meeting was important.

"Is Ward here yet?" Landon asked Grayson the moment they were inside. Landon also moved her away from the window. Not that he had to do much to make that happen, since Tessa had no plans to stand anywhere near the glass.

Grayson nodded. "Ward's in the interview room. He still wants you arrested for hiring the person who ran him off the road," he added to Tessa.

Tessa had figured Ward wouldn't have a change of heart about that, but she had to shake her head. "Has he said why he believes I did that?"

"Not yet, but he's claiming he has proof."

Since Tessa knew she was innocent, there was no proof. But Ward might believe he had something incriminating.

"Well, we have proof of his connection to the dead woman who tried to kill us," Landon countered.

But there was something in Grayson's expression that indicated otherwise. "We checked the phone records. Ward didn't answer the call from her."

Tessa groaned because she knew that meant Ward could claim not only that he didn't know the woman but also that the call had been made to set him up.

And it was possible that was true.

Heck, it was possible that the same person was trying to set up both of them. Joel maybe? Or Quincy? Tessa knew why Joel or even Quincy might want to set her up, but what she needed to find out was if and how Ward was connected to this.

"Quincy's lawyer has been pestering us this morning," Grayson went on. "He's trying to find a judge who'll grant him temporary custody."

Landon cursed under his breath. "Then I need to find a judge who'll block his every move." He tipped his head to the interview room. "Speaking of our some-times-warped legal system, did Ward manage to get a warrant for Tessa's arrest?"

Grayson shook his head. "But he claims he's work-ing on it."

"I am," someone said.

Ward.

The lanky sandy-haired agent was standing in the doorway of the interview room and stepped into the hall. His attention stayed nailed to her.

It didn't surprise her that Ward had heard Landon and her talking with Grayson. In fact, he'd no doubt been listening for her to arrive so he could confront her with the stupid allegation that she'd tried to kill him.

"Tessa," Ward greeted, but it wasn't a friendly tone.

He walked closer. Or rather he limped closer. In addi-tion to the limping, there was also a three-inch bandage on the left side of his forehead and a bruise on his cheek. It was obvious he'd been banged up, but Tessa figured she beat him in the banged-up-looking department.

Grayson tipped his head to the interview room. "You and I will go back in there and get started."

But Ward didn't budge. "Why do you want me dead?" he asked Tessa.

"I could ask you the same thing," she countered. It was obvious that neither Grayson nor Landon wanted her to confront Ward, but Tessa couldn't stop herself.

Ward scowled at her. "If I'd wanted you dead, I wouldn't have hired some idiot gunwoman who just happened to be carrying a phone that she used to call me. Lots of people know my phone number. Even you."

That was true, but that didn't mean Ward was innocent. It could have been a simple mistake, or else done as a sort of reverse psychology.

"Why do you think I'm trying to kill you?" Tessa asked.

Ward glanced at Landon. Then Grayson. "That was something I'd planned on telling the Texas Rangers. I figure the Silver Creek lawmen are a little too cozy with you to make sure justice is served."

Landon stepped closer, and he had that dangerous look in his eyes. "I always make sure justice is served," he snarled. "And you'd better rein in your accusations when it comes to me, Tessa and anyone else in this sheriff's office."

The anger snapped through Ward's eyes, and she could tell he wanted to challenge that. But he wasn't in friendly territory here, and he was indeed throwing out serious accusations that Tessa knew he couldn't back up.

"Let's take this to the interview room," Grayson said, and it wasn't a suggestion. He sounded just as dangerous as Landon.

"You're not joining us?" Ward asked when she didn't go any farther than the doorway.

While she wanted to know answers, she didn't want to compromise the interrogation that could possibly help them learn about a killer. "I just want to hear whatever proof you claim to have against me."

Ward didn't say anything, but he took out his phone and pressed a button. It didn't take long for the recorded voice to start pouring through the room.

"Tessa Sinclair can't be trusted," the person said. "She paid my friend to try to kill you."

That was it, all of the message, and the voice was

so muffled that Tessa couldn't even tell if it was a man or a woman. But it didn't matter. Someone was trying to frame her.

"Is there any proof to go along with that?" Grayson asked, taking the question right out of her mouth.

Ward's face tightened. "No. And the call came from a prepaid cell that couldn't be traced."

Even though Tessa already knew there wouldn't be real proof, the relief flooded through her. "Someone's trying to set us up."

"Why would you think Tessa had done something like this?" Landon asked as soon as she'd finished speaking.

Ward lifted his shoulder. "I figured it was all connected. Emmett's murder. Joel. And what with Tessa being involved with Joel—"

"I wasn't involved with him," Tessa interrupted. "At least, not involved in the way you're making it sound. I was trying to find proof to send him to jail. So was Emmett. That's why he was at my house the night someone killed him."

Ward shifted his attention to Landon. "And that someone left that note tying you to the murder?"

Landon just nodded, but Tessa could tell from the way his back straightened that the connection not only sickened him but was also the reason he'd moved back to Silver Creek.

"What do you know about Quincy Nagel?" Landon asked.

Ward just stared at him. "He's involved in this?"

Landon stared at Ward, too. "I asked first."

Ward clearly didn't care for Landon's tone, but Tessa didn't care for Ward's hesitation on what was a fairly simple question.

"Word on the street is that Quincy wants to get back

at you for arresting him. He blames you for being paralyzed." Ward paused again. "But I don't know whether
or not he's connected to any of this." He huffed and
scrubbed his hand over his face. "In fact, I don't know
what the hell is going on."

Tessa felt relief about that, too. At least he wasn't
yapping about trying to have her arrested.

"I'm shaken up, I guess," Ward went on a moment
later. But then there was more of that anger in his eyes
when he looked at her. "Swear to me that you didn't
have anything to do with trying to kill me."

This was an easy response for her. "I swear. Now I
want you to do the same. That gunwoman fired shots
into the building. I don't want Landon or anyone else
hurt because you're gunning for me."

Ward huffed. "And why exactly do you think I'd be
gunning for you?"

Tessa took a couple of moments to figure out the best
way to say this, but there was no best way. "I thought
you could be working with Joel."

A burst of air left Ward's mouth. Definitely not
humor but surprise. "Not a chance."

"Ditto," Tessa countered. "I don't work for him, either."

The silence came, and so did the stares, and it didn't
sit well between them. Tessa could almost feel the tension smothering her. It helped, though, when Landon's
arm brushed against hers. She wasn't even sure it was
intentional until she glanced up at him.

Yes, it was intentional.

Soon, very soon, they were going to have to deal with
this unwanted attraction between them.

"Did your memory return?" Ward asked her.

The question was so abrupt that it threw her for a
moment. "How did you know I'd lost it?"

"Word gets out about that sort of thing. Did you remember everything?" Ward pressed.

Everything but what mattered most to Landon—who'd murdered Emmett.

"My memory is fine," Tessa settled for saying, and she watched Ward's reaction.

At least, she would have watched for it if he hadn't dodged her gaze. "And the baby that was with you when Landon rescued you from that burning barn? How is she?"

Tessa decided it was a good time to stay quiet and wait to see where he was going with this. It was possible Ward thought she had indeed given birth, because they'd mainly dealt with each other over the phone and it'd been months since she'd seen him in person.

"The baby's okay, too," Landon answered.

Ward volleyed glances between them, clearly expecting more, but neither Landon nor she gave him anything else. If they admitted the baby wasn't theirs, the word might get back to Quincy. She didn't want him to have any more fodder for trying to get custody of the baby.

Ward's glances lasted a few more seconds before he turned his head toward Grayson. "Could we get on with this interview? I also want to read Tessa's statement on the attacks."

"We're still processing the statement," Grayson volunteered.

Since Tessa had made one the night before, she doubted there was any processing to do, but she was thankful that Grayson seemed to be on her side. About this, anyway.

Landon put her hand on her back to get her moving. Not that he had to encourage her much. Tessa figured she'd personally gotten everything she could get from Ward.

"You believe him?" Landon asked. "Do you trust him?" he amended. He didn't take her back into the squad room but rather to the break room at the back of the building.

"No to both. I believe he could have been set up with that phone call from the gunwoman. Just as someone set me up with that phone call to him. But I'm not taking him off our suspect list."

Our.

She hadn't meant to pause over that word, and it sounded, well, intimate or something. Still, Landon and she had been working together, so the *our* applied.

"I should call the ranch and check on the baby," she said. She'd already walked on enough eggshells today, and besides, she did want to check on Samantha.

Landon took out his phone, made the call and then put it on Speaker when Mason answered. "Anything wrong?" Mason immediately asked.

"Fine. We're just making sure Samantha is okay."

"Yeah, I figured that's why you were calling. Are you sure you aren't the parents? Because you're acting like the kid is yours."

Landon scowled. "I'm sure. And just drop the subject and don't make any other suggestions like you did last night."

She couldn't be sure, but she thought maybe Mason chuckled. She had to be wrong about that. Mason wasn't the chuckling type.

"Quincy's not backing off the custody suit," Landon explained. "He's the kind of snake who'd try to sneak someone onto the ranch to steal the baby."

"The hands have orders to shoot at any trespassers— even one who happens to be in a wheelchair."

"Good. Tessa and I won't be much longer, and we'll

head back to the ranch as soon as Grayson finishes his chat with Ward."

Landon ended the call, but as he was putting his phone away, his gaze met hers. "What?" he asked.

Tessa hadn't realized she was looking puzzled, but she apparently was. "What suggestions did Mason make?" But the moment she asked it, Tessa wished she could take it back, because Landon looked even more annoyed than he had when Mason had brought it up.

"Mason thinks you and I are together again," Landon finally said.

Tessa wasn't sure how to feel about that. Embarrassed that Mason had picked up on the attraction or worried that what she felt for Landon—what she'd always felt for him—was more than just mere attraction.

"He suggested…" But Landon stopped, waved it off. "He suggested, since it already looks as if we're together, that we should raise the baby. If Quincy is the father, that is, but isn't granted custody."

She figured Mason had suggested a little more than that. Maybe like Landon and her becoming lovers again. Which was the last thing Landon wanted. She hadn't heard any part of his conversation with his cousin, because he'd stepped outside the guest cottage to take the call, but now Tessa wished she'd listened in.

But then she was the one to mentally wave that off.

She didn't need to be spinning any kind of fantasies about Landon, even ones that included the baby's future.

"That kiss shouldn't have happened," Landon said, and his tone indicated it wouldn't happen again. It did, though.

Almost.

He brushed a kiss on her forehead, and his mouth lingered there for a moment as if it might continue. But then they heard something that neither of them wanted to hear.

Joel.

"I have to see Landon and Tessa now," Joel practically shouted. "It's an emergency."

Mercy. What now?

Landon cursed again, and he stepped in front of her as they made their way back to the squad room. Considering the volume and emotion in Joel's voice, Tessa halfway expected to see the man hurt and bleeding. Maybe the victim of another attack. Or the victim of something staged to look like an attack. There didn't appear to be a scratch on Joel, though.

"What do you want?" Landon snarled, and he didn't sound as if he wanted to hear a word the man had to say.

Joel went toward them. His breath was gusting, and he held out his phone. At first Tessa couldn't tell what was on the screen, but as Joel got closer, she saw the photo of the woman.

Oh, God.

"That's Courtney," she said, snatching the phone from Joel.

Now, here was someone who looked hurt and bleeding, and Courtney's blond hair was in a tangled mess around her face.

A face etched with fear.

"Look at what she's holding," Joel insisted, stabbing his index finger at the screen.

But Joel hadn't needed to point out the white sign that Courtney had gripped in her hands. Or the two words that were scrawled on the sign.

Help me.

Chapter Ten

Landon groaned and motioned for Dade to have a look at the picture Joel had just shown them.

"You're sure that's the missing woman?" Dade asked Tessa.

"I'm sure it's Courtney," Tessa answered, though she had to repeat it for her response to have any sound. She was trembling now, and some of the color had drained from her face. "Where is she? How did you get that picture?"

The questions were aimed at Joel, and Landon was about to put the guy in cuffs when he shook his head. "I don't know who or where she is," Joel insisted. "Someone texted me that picture about twenty minutes ago."

Hell. Twenty minutes was a lifetime if Courtney truly did need someone to help her. Landon hoped that *if* wasn't an issue and that the woman wasn't faking this.

"That looks like the bridge on Sanderson's Road," Dade said after he studied the photo a moment.

It did, though it'd been years since Landon had been out there. There were two routes that led in and out of town, and Sanderson's Road wasn't the one that most people took.

"I'll call in Gage and Josh to head out there now," Dade added. He took out his phone and stepped away.

Joel moved as if to step away, as well, but Landon grabbed him by the arm. "Who's the *someone* who texted you that picture?"

"I don't know. Whoever it was blocked the number."

Landon would still have the lab check Joel's phone to see if there was some way to trace it. Or maybe there was even some way to figure out who'd taken the picture. It clearly wasn't a selfie, because he could see both of Courtney's hands, but whoever had snapped the shot was standing close to her.

"Why would someone text you about Courtney?" Tessa asked.

Joel lifted his hands in the air. "None of this makes sense, but what I don't want you doing is blaming the messenger. I did the right thing by bringing you this photo, and I don't want to be blamed for anything."

Landon would reserve blame for later, but Joel could be just as much of a snake as he was a messenger.

Dade finished his call and motioned for Landon to step into Grayson's office with him. Since Landon didn't want Tessa left alone with Joel, he took her with him.

"Gage said someone was spotted near the fence at the ranch," Dade explained.

That didn't help the color return to Tessa's face, and Landon had to step in front of her to keep her from bolting.

"The baby's okay," Dade assured her. "Everyone is. The person ran when one of the hands confronted him, but all of this is starting to feel like a trap."

Landon made a sound of agreement. "Have Josh and

Gage stay put at the ranch. I'll get Joel and Ward out of here, and then while Grayson stays with Tessa, you and I can go look for Courtney."

Tessa was shaking her head before he even finished. "Courtney won't trust you. If I go with you, maybe we can get her out of there."

Now it was Landon's turn to shake his head. "You're not going out there."

"I agree," Dade said and then looked at Landon. "But I don't think you should go, either. The two of you are targets. I'll call in the night deputies, and Grayson and I can go after Courtney."

His cousin didn't wait for him to agree to that. Probably because Dade knew he was right. He went to the interview room to fill in Grayson, and Landon returned to the squad room to tell Joel to take a hike. But it wasn't necessary.

Because Joel was already gone.

Normally, Landon would have preferred not having Tessa around a creep like Joel, but it gave him an uneasy feeling that the man had just run out like that.

"I demand to know what's going on," Landon heard Ward say. "Someone's trying to kill me, and I need to know everything about this investigation."

"We'll fill you in when we know something," Grayson said. "Now leave. I'll have someone call you and reschedule the interview."

Ward came out of the interview room, but he didn't head for the exit. He stopped in front of Landon and Tessa. "Tell me what's going on." Then he huffed, and Landon could see the man trying to put a leash on his temper. "I can help," he added as if they would agree to that.

They didn't.

Landon didn't want help from one of their suspects.

"Just go," Landon insisted.

Ward glanced at Tessa. Why, Landon didn't know. She certainly wasn't going to ask him to hang around, and while mumbling some profanity, Ward finally turned and stormed out.

Almost immediately Tessa's gaze started to fire around the room. No doubt looking for something she could do to help save her friend. Or at least, the woman she thought was her friend. As far as Landon was concerned, the jury was still out on that.

"Courtney's alive," Landon assured Tessa. "Hang on to that."

She shook her head. "Courtney was alive when that photo was taken. Just because someone sent it to Joel twenty minutes ago, doesn't mean that's when it was taken."

No, it didn't, and there was no way to assure Tessa otherwise.

"Dade and I will leave as soon as the night deputies arrive," Grayson said as Dade and he gathered their things. That included backup weapons.

Hell. Landon wanted to go with them. He wanted to help if his cousins were walking into a trap, but he caught a glimpse of something that reminded him of why he should stay put. Or rather a glimpse of someone.

And that someone was Quincy.

The timing sucked. It usually did when it came to Quincy, but this was especially bad. Landon didn't want Quincy to find out Courtney's last known location, since the woman was on the run, probably because of him.

"I need to see you, Deputy Ryland," Quincy said the moment his goon helped him maneuver the wheelchair through the door.

"I don't have time for you right now," Landon fired back. "You need to get out of here."

But Quincy wasn't budging. He had some papers in his hand, and he waved them at Landon. "Here's the proof for me to take my daughter. Now, hand her over to me."

Landon really didn't want to deal with this now, but he was hoping that Quincy's proof was bogus.

"This is the result of the DNA test I had run yesterday," Quincy went on. "I paid top dollars to have the results expedited so I'd know the truth. You lied about the baby being yours, and you'll both pay for that lie. Did you honestly think you could keep my daughter from me?"

That was the plan, and Landon wanted to continue with that plan.

He went to Quincy and took the papers, and Tessa hurried toward them so she could have a look, as well. Grayson and Dade stayed back, watching, but both his cousins knew how this could play out if the test results were real.

And they appeared to be.

Appeared.

Landon handed off the paper to Dade so his cousin could call the lab and verify that a test had been done.

"Where did you get the baby's DNA?" Landon asked.

"From Courtney's place in Austin. There was a pacifier in the crib, and I had it tested."

Landon glanced at Tessa to see if that was possible, and she only lifted her shoulder. So, yeah, it was possible. But Landon had no intentions of giving Quincy an open-arms invitation to take a child he'd fathered. Any fool could father a baby.

"Did you just admit that you broke into your ex's house?" Landon pressed.

Clearly, Quincy didn't like that. He leaned forward and for a moment looked ready to come out of that chair and launch himself at Landon. "You can't keep my daughter from me," Quincy snarled.

Maybe not forever, but he darn sure could for now. "A DNA test is a far cry from a court order. I'm guessing even with that so-called proof, which can easily be faked, by the way, that you'll have trouble getting custody. Plus, you haven't proven that the DNA from the pacifier even belongs to the baby we have in custody. So leave now and come back when and if you have a court order."

Quincy would have almost certainly argued about that if the two trucks hadn't pulled to a stop in front of the building and the deputies hadn't hurried inside.

"What's going on?" Quincy asked.

Landon didn't answer, but he did motion for the goon to get Quincy moving. "Either you can leave or I'll arrest you both for obstruction of justice." A charge like that wouldn't stick, of course, but at least Quincy would be locked up.

Quincy glanced at all of them, and while it was obvious he thought this was somehow connected to him, he didn't argue. He said something under his breath to the hired goon, and the guy wheeled him out of the sheriff's office.

"This isn't over," Quincy said from over his shoulder. It sounded like the threat that it was.

"He'll try and follow you," Landon reminded Dade and Grayson.

Grayson nodded, and Dade and he headed out the back.

"I'm not giving Quincy the baby," Tessa insisted.

Just lately they hadn't been in complete agreement, but they were now. Landon put his hand on her back to get her moving to Grayson's office, but they'd hardly made it a step when Landon heard a sound of glass shattering behind them.

He turned to step in front of Tessa, but it was already too late.

The blast tore through the building.

ONE SECOND TESSA was standing, and the next she was on the floor. It took her a moment not only to catch her breath but to realize what had happened. Someone had set off some kind of explosive device.

Oh, God.

Just like that, her heart was back in her throat, and her breath was gusting. Someone was trying to kill them. Again.

Cursing, Landon drew his gun, and in the same motion, he crawled over her. Protecting her again. But not only was he putting himself in danger, Tessa wasn't even sure it was possible to protect her. The front door had been blasted open and one of the reinforced windows had broken.

"Car bomb," she heard Landon say, though it was hard to hear much of anything with the sound of the blast still ringing in her ears.

The words had hardly left his mouth when there

was a second explosion, and even though Tessa hadn't thought it possible, it was louder than the first.

Landon caught on to her, scrambling toward Grayson's office, and he pushed her inside. But he didn't come in. He stayed in the hall with the gun ready and aimed.

"The deputies?" Tessa managed to say. She wasn't sure where they were, though she could hear them talking.

"They're fine."

Good. That was something at least, but another blast could bring down the building. Plus, they had Grayson and Dade to worry about. They were outside, somewhere, and while they'd gone out through the back, that didn't mean someone hadn't been waiting there to ambush them.

If so, the photo of Courtney had been a trap.

That sickened Tessa, but if that was indeed what it'd been, that didn't mean Courtney had wanted this to happen. Courtney would have likely been forced to have that picture taken. Which meant she was innocent.

"Stay down," Landon warned her when Tessa lifted her head.

She did stay down, but Tessa crawled to the desk, opened the center drawer and found exactly what she'd hoped to find.

A gun.

She wasn't a good shot, but she needed some way to try to defend herself if things escalated. And they did escalate.

"There's a gunman!" Grayson shouted.

Tessa couldn't tell where the sheriff was, but the sound of the gunshot confirmed his warning. And from the sound of it, the gunshot came through into the squad room. It wasn't a single shot, either.

More came.

"Hell, there's more than one gunman," Landon grumbled.

Tessa was about to ask how he knew that, but it soon became crystal clear. Bullets started to smack into the window just above her head. The reinforced glass was stopping them. For now. But whoever was firing those shots was determined to tear through the glass.

But how had the shooter known Landon and she were inside the office?

Maybe their attackers had some kind of thermal scan or were on the roof of one of the nearby buildings. Not exactly a thought to steady her nerves, because it was daylight and any one of those shots could hit an innocent bystander.

"One of them is using an Uzi," Grayson called out. "Everybody stay down."

Tessa certainly did, but Landon didn't. He scurried toward her and maneuvered into the corner so that the desk was between the window and her. Not that it would do much good. The Uzi could fire off a lot of shots in just a few seconds, and it wouldn't be long before those bullets made it through the glass, and then Landon and she would be trapped. He must have realized that, too.

"We have to move," he said. "Stay low and go as fast as you can."

Tessa barely had time to take a breath before Landon had them moving. He stayed in front of her as they barreled out into the hall, and he didn't waste a second shoving her into the interview room where Ward had been just minutes earlier.

She caught a glimpse of the shooter then. One of them, anyway. The man had on a ski mask and was behind a car parked in front of the café across the street. The position gave him a direct line of sight into the sheriff's office, especially now that the door was open. And the shooter made full use of that.

He fired at Landon.

The bullet came too close, smacking into the wall right next to Landon's hand. Tessa latched on to his arm and pulled him into the room with her, and she prayed the deputies were doing something to stay out of the path of those shots. There was another hall leading to the holding cells on that side of the building, so maybe they'd used that.

More shots.

Maybe some of them were coming from Grayson or Dade, though it was hard to tell. Though it wasn't hard to tell when Landon fired. He leaned out the doorway, took aim and pulled the trigger.

"The shooter got through the window," Landon growled.

Mercy. That meant he was in the building, and if this was the gunman with the Uzi, he could mow them all down.

Landon fired another shot. Then another.

It was hard for Tessa to see much of anything, but she did catch a glimpse of a man peering out from Grayson's office. He, too, wore a ski mask and what appeared to be full body armor.

Landon had no choice but to duck back into the interview room when the guy started firing, but there was no way they could let this monster get any closer. Though she knew Landon wasn't going to like it, she lifted her head and body just enough to fire a shot.

She missed.

The bullet tore into the office doorjamb, but it must have distracted the guy just enough. Landon cursed—some of the profanity aimed at her—and he fired again. This time at the guy's head.

Landon didn't miss.

Tessa heard the shooter drop to the floor. Thank God. But she also heard someone else.

The shots stopped.

The relief washed over her. Until Grayson shouted out something she didn't want to hear.

"The second gunman's getting away!"

Chapter Eleven

Landon wanted to kick himself. Two attacks now at the Silver Creek sheriff's office. And either attack could have killed Tessa, his cousins or the other deputies. They'd gotten damn lucky that there hadn't been more damage and there had been no injuries.

Of course, one of the shooters hadn't had much luck today.

The guy was dead, but that wasn't exactly a dose of great news for Landon. Just like the gunwoman from the day before, dead shooters couldn't give them answers, but maybe Grayson and the others would be able to find the gunman who'd gotten away. While Landon was wishing, he added that the moron would cough up a name of who was behind the attacks.

And that they'd find Courtney.

The last might not even be doable. When the deputies had finally made it out to the bridge, there'd been no sign of the woman. If someone was holding her captive, then it was possible that person had taken her far away from Silver Creek.

Tessa got out of the truck and went into the guesthouse ahead of Landon. As instructed, she hurried, and that precaution was because of the stranger one of the hands had seen in the area just minutes before the attack at the sheriff's office. Landon doubted that was a coincidence, and because of the possible threat and the attacks, everyone was on high alert.

By the time Landon got inside, Tessa was already at the bassinet and was checking on the baby—who was sleeping. At least Samantha was too young to know what was going on. That was something.

Tessa sighed and touched her fingertips to the baby's hair. She didn't have to tell him that she was worried about both Courtney and the little girl. There were threats all around them, and not all of those threats came from armed thugs. The biggest threat could come from the child's own father.

Landon thanked the nanny and Gage for staying with the baby, but he didn't say anything to Tessa until the two had left. Since he was essentially planning a crime, it was best not to involve his cousin and the nanny.

"If Quincy gets the court order," Landon told her, "we'll take the baby from the ranch. I know a place we can go."

"A safe house?"

"Not an official one. I don't want to go through channels for that, but it'll be a safe place." He hoped. And not just safe. But a place they could stay until they managed to stop Quincy from taking the newborn.

She nodded, and Landon nearly told her to go ahead and pack. Then he remembered Tessa didn't have much to take with her. It wouldn't take them long at all to get out of there if Quincy showed up with the law on his side.

"Why don't you try to get some rest?" Landon suggested. "You've been through a lot today."

"You've been through worse," Tessa quickly pointed out. "You had to kill a man."

Yeah, a man he would kill a dozen times over if it meant neutralizing the threat. Except there was more to it than that, and even though Landon tried to push it aside, the thought came anyway.

He'd kill to protect Tessa.

Hell.

This was about that blasted attraction again.

"I'm sorry about all of this," she added, and when she turned away from him, Landon knew there were tears in her eyes.

She was coming down from the adrenaline rush, and soon the bone-weary fatigue would take over, but for now there was no fatigue. Just her nerves firing. Landon's nerves were doing some firing, too, but unfortunately, his body was coming up with some bad suggestions as to how to tame those nerves.

"This isn't your fault," Landon said.

They weren't just talking about the danger now. Somewhere in the past couple of seconds, they'd moved on from nerves, danger and gunmen to something so basic and primal that he could feel it more than the nerves.

"I'm sorry about this, too," Tessa whispered, and she went to him, sliding right into his arms.

And Landon didn't stop her. Heck, if she hadn't come to him, he would have gone to her. That meant this stupid mistake was a little easier to make.

Landon hated that she landed in his arms again. Hated it mainly because it was the only place he wanted her to be. Along with giving her some comfort, it was doing the same thing to him. But it was also playing with fire. Having her in his arms made him remember how much he wanted her, and sadly, what he wanted was a whole lot more than a hug.

"Don't," he said when she opened her mouth, no doubt to remind him, and herself, that this was a bad idea.

Since he'd stopped her from putting an end to this, Landon decided to go for broke. He lowered his head, brushed his mouth over hers.

Oh, man.

There it was. That kick of heat. And it wasn't necessarily a good kick, either. It made him go for more than just a mere touch of the lips. If he was going to screw up, he might as well make it a screwup worth making.

He kissed her, hard and long, until he felt her melt against him. Of course, the melting had started before the kiss, so it didn't take much for him to hear that little hitch in her throat. Part pleasure, part surprise. Maybe surprise that they were doing this, but Landon figured it was more than that. Every time he kissed Tessa, he got that same jolt, the one that told him that no one should taste as good as she did.

Especially when she had trouble written all over her.

But it wasn't trouble on her face when she pulled back a fraction and looked up at him. "This can't go anywhere," she said.

The voice of reason. It couldn't go anywhere. He couldn't lose focus, couldn't get involved with someone in his protective custody. Plus, there was that whole thing about not wanting his heart stomped on again.

All of that didn't stop him, though.

Worse, it didn't stop Tessa.

She slipped her hands around him and inched him

closer. Of course, the closeness only deepened the kiss, too, and the body-to-body contact soon had them grappling for position. Landon knew what position he wanted—Tessa beneath him in bed. Or on the floor. At the moment, he didn't care.

But the baby had a different notion about that. Samantha squirmed, made a little fussing sound, and that was enough to send Tessa and him flying apart. She turned from him but not before Landon saw the guilt.

Guilt that he felt, too.

He would have mentally cursed himself about it if his phone hadn't buzzed. Maybe this would be good news to offset the idiotic thing he'd just done. No such luck, though. Landon didn't recognize the number on the screen.

While Tessa tended to the baby, Landon answered the call, but he didn't say anything. He just waited for the caller to speak first. He didn't have to wait long.

"It's me, Courtney Hager," the woman said. Her words and breath were rushed together. "Is the baby okay?"

"She's fine. Safe."

"You have to get a message to Tessa for me," she said before Landon could add anything else. "Please."

"Where are you? Are you all right?"

His quick questions got Tessa's attention, and she hurried back toward him. However, he also motioned for her to stay quiet. If someone was listening and had put Courtney up to this, he didn't want to confirm to that person that Tessa was with him.

"I'm just outside of town," Courtney answered after several snail-crawling moments, "but I won't be here much longer. I have to keep moving. If I don't, they'll find me."

"Tell me where you are, and I'll send a deputy to get you," Landon insisted.

"You can't. Not now. They know the general area where I am, and if they see a cop, they'll find me. Just tell Tessa that I need her to meet me on the playground of the Silver Creek Elementary School. And don't bring the baby. It's not safe."

You bet it wasn't. "It's not safe for Tessa and you, either," Landon pointed out.

"I know." A hoarse sob tore from her mouth. "But I don't have a choice. You can come with Tessa, only you, but don't bring more cops or else it'll just put us all in even more danger."

"Who'll put us in danger?" Landon pressed.

"I'm not sure, but I need to give Tessa something. Only Tessa. She's the only one I trust. If she doesn't come, I'll have to keep running. Tell her to meet me tonight after dark. And tell her to be careful to make sure she's not followed."

"Where are you right now?" Landon didn't bother to bite back the profanity he added at the end of that.

Another sob. "Please have Tessa come." No sob this time. Courtney gasped. "Oh, God. They found me again."

As much as Tessa wanted to get Courtney out of harm's way, she prayed she wasn't trading her friend's safety for Landon's. Nothing about this felt right, but then it'd been a while since Tessa had felt right about anything. Someone wanted her dead, and that someone might want Courtney dead, too.

And Tessa didn't know why.

But maybe Courtney could help with that.

Courtney had said she wanted to give Tessa something. Evidence maybe? Whatever it was, it could turn out to be critical. Or it could lead to Landon and her being in danger again.

"I really wish you'd reconsider this," Landon repeated to her, and Tessa knew even when he wasn't saying it aloud, he was repeating it in his head.

Landon didn't want her going into town, where they'd already been attacked twice, but like Tessa, he also wanted to find Courtney and get some answers. If they could protect the woman and if Courtney was innocent in all of this, then she could eventually take custody of the baby, and that meant Quincy wouldn't stand much of a chance of getting custody.

She hoped.

Of course, there were a lot of *ifs* in all of this.

Tessa wasn't sure where Courtney had been for the past few days, and it was possible the woman was involved in something criminal. After all, why hadn't she just gone to the cops instead of asking to meet Tessa?

Then there was the matter of the phone Courtney had used to call Landon. When Landon had tried to call her back, she hadn't answered, and it hadn't taken him long to learn that it was a prepaid cell. Of course, it was possible Courtney had lost her own phone. Tessa had. But then whose phone had she used to make that critical call to Landon?

They found me again.

Tessa had heard the terror in Courtney's voice and that wasn't the voice of someone faking her fear. At least, Tessa didn't think it was.

"You trust Courtney?" Landon asked as they drove toward town. He was an uneasy as Tessa was, and both of them looked around to make sure no one was following them.

"I want to trust her," Tessa settled for saying.

It wasn't enough, and that was why Landon had arranged for some security. There was a truck with two ranch hands following them. Two of his cousins, Gage and Josh, had been positioned on the roof of the school building for hours. Added to that, there were two deputies waiting just up the street. If anything went wrong, there'd be five lawmen and two armed ranch hands to help.

But that wouldn't stop another sniper with an Uzi.

Yes, this was a risk, and if Tessa could have thought of another way, she would have done this differently.

Landon had instructed the deputies and the hands to stay back and out of sight. Of course, anyone looking for Courtney would also be looking for any signs of the cops. If the person or Courtney spotted them, it might put a quick end to this meeting, but Tessa had no intention of doing this without backup.

"Remember, when we get there, I don't want you out of the truck," Landon instructed as they approached Main Street. "I'll meet with Courtney, get whatever it is she wants to give you and then talk her into coming back with us so I can put her in protective custody." He paused. "Any other ideas as to what it is Courtney wants to give you?"

They'd already speculated about the obvious—some kind of evidence. Evidence perhaps linked to the attacks. Or maybe even Emmett's murder. After all, Courtney had been at Tessa's place the night Emmett was killed, so maybe Courtney had seen something. Maybe she had even picked up a shell casing or something the killer had left behind.

Tessa had to shake her head, though. If she'd found something like that, then why hadn't she just gotten it to the cops somehow? Unless…

"Maybe Courtney saw the person who killed Emmett," Tessa speculated. "Or maybe she found out Ward had hired the killer. If she saw Ward's badge, she might believe she can't trust anyone in law enforcement."

Landon made a sound of agreement, but his attention was already on the school just ahead. "If anything goes wrong, I want you to stay down."

Tessa wanted to tell him to do the same thing, but she knew he wouldn't. Landon believed that badge meant he had to do whatever it took to make sure justice was served. Even if this was just another trap.

"Someone could be holding Courtney," Tessa said, talking more to herself than Landon. She remembered the photo of Courtney's bruised face.

"That's my guess, too, but if someone's with her, Gage will let us know. He'll let us know when he spots her, as well."

Since there'd been no calls or texts from any of his cousins or the deputies, Courtney probably hadn't arrived yet. Or else she was hiding and waiting for Tessa to show.

At least there was one silver lining in this. The baby was at the main ranch house with Mason and Grayson. Both would protect the baby with their lives. Tessa just hoped it didn't come down to that.

Landon pulled to a stop next to some playground equipment, and he fired glances all around them. Tessa did the same, but the only thing she saw was the truck with ranch hands parking just up the road from Landon's own vehicle. When they didn't spot Courtney, Landon took out his phone, and Tessa saw him press Gage's number.

"See anything?" he asked Gage.

"Nothing. You're sure she'll show?" Even though the call wasn't on Speaker, Tessa had no trouble hearing him in the small cab of the truck.

"I'm not sure of anything. If she's not here soon, though, I'm taking Tessa back to the ranch."

"Agreed," Gage said, and he ended the call.

Landon hadn't even had time to put his phone away when it buzzed, and he showed her the screen. It was the same number Courtney had used for her earlier call. Landon pushed the button to take the call and put it on Speaker, but he didn't say anything.

"Is the baby safe?" Courtney asked the moment she came on the line.

"Yes. Now, help us to keep it that way."

"I tried. I'm *trying*," she corrected. "I told you to come alone with Tessa," Courtney continued. "There are two cops on the roof. Send them away, and we'll talk."

"We'll talk right now," Landon snapped. "Someone's trying to kill Tessa, and you put her at risk by having her come out here. The cops on the roof are my cousins. They're men I trust, and that's a lot more than I can say for you right now. Tell me why you dragged us out here."

Tessa pulled in her breath, waited. Courtney could just hang up and disappear. And that was why she had to do something.

"Quincy's trying to take the baby," Tessa blurted out. "He's getting a court order."

"Oh, God," Courtney said, and there was no way that emotion was faked. Tessa could feel the pain. "You can't let him have her."

"Then come out of hiding," Landon insisted. "Let us protect both Samantha and you."

"I can't," Courtney said, and this time Tessa heard more than just the fear. She heard the woman sobbing. "I'd hoped they wouldn't still be on my trail, that I could meet you face-to-face, but I can't. They're following me, and I'd just lead them straight to the baby."

"Who's following you?" Tessa and Landon asked at the same time.

"Gunmen. There are two of them. They caught me by the bridge and forced me to take a picture with a sign that said Help Me. I'm guessing they did that to lure you out to help me, but when they tried to shove me in a car, I managed to get away."

Tessa and Landon exchanged glances. "Why would those men send the picture of you to Joel Mercer?" Landon asked.

The moments crawled by before Courtney said anything else. "Are you sure the men didn't send the photo to Quincy? I figured they'd send it to him, that maybe they were trying to get money from him because Quincy would pay lots of money to find me."

That knot in Tessa's stomach got even tighter. She didn't like that Courtney had dodged the question about Joel. To the best of Tessa's knowledge, Courtney didn't know Joel. Or at least, Courtney hadn't said anything about knowing Joel, but if she didn't know him, then why hadn't she just come out and said that?

"So you don't think these men work for Quincy?" Tessa pressed. Later she'd work her way back to the subject of Joel, but for now she wanted to get as much information as possible, and she didn't want Courtney clamming up.

"I don't know. But it's possible they used to work for him. They could have gotten greedy and figured they could use me to get him to pay up. But it's not me Quincy wants. It's the baby."

"So he's Samantha's father," Tessa said.

Courtney didn't jump to answer that, either, and she gave another long pause. "How is he getting a court order to get custody? He's a convicted felon."

"He claims he's got DNA proof," Landon explained.

"No. He couldn't have," Courtney insisted. "Where does he claim he got it?"

"He says it's from a pacifier that he took from your house."

"Samantha never used a pacifier, so whatever he's saying about it is a lie. Have the cops already run a DNA test on Samantha?"

"Yeah. We're waiting on the results now. Anything you want to tell us about that?" Landon challenged. Probably because Courtney hadn't confirmed that Quincy was indeed the baby's father. In fact, her friend hadn't confirmed much at all at this point.

That made Tessa glance around again, and she tightened her grip on the gun Landon had given her. She reminded herself that if this was a trap, Gage and Josh would see an approaching gunman. Ditto for seeing Courtney, too, but it was possible the woman wasn't anywhere near the elementary school.

"When you called, you said you wanted to give Tessa something," Landon reminded Courtney.

"I left it underneath the slide on the playground."

Of course it was in the middle of a wide-open space. A space where a shooter could gun them down.

"What is it?" Tessa asked.

"I can't say over the phone in case someone is listening. Just take it and use it to protect my baby."

Tessa hoped there was indeed something to do that, but the only thing that would make it happen was for Courtney to have the evidence needed for them to make an arrest. But if it was that simple, why hadn't she just said what it was?

"We want to protect you, too," Landon said to Courtney. "Tell me where you are, and I can arrange for Samantha and you to be together at a safe house."

Tessa couldn't be sure, but she thought Courtney was crying again. "I can't risk him finding me in a safe house. For now, just protect my little girl. I'll call you again as soon as I can. I have to go."

"Wait," Landon snapped, but he was talking to himself because Courtney had already ended the call.

As Landon had done with her earlier call, he tried to phone her right back, but she didn't answer. Tessa listened to see if she could hear a ringing phone nearby but there was nothing. Not a sound. Of course, it was possible that Courtney had put that so-called evidence beneath the slide before she even made the original call to them.

Landon called Josh and filled him in on what Courtney had told them. Judging from Landon's tone, he was just as frustrated with what Courtney had said, and hadn't said.

"Josh is wearing body armor," Landon explained once he was off the phone. He's going out there to retrieve what Courtney left, and Gage is going to keep watch from the roof to make sure no one comes in here with guns blazing."

That jangled her nerves again. She hated that Josh had to put himself out there like that, but whoever was behind this wasn't after Josh. They were after Landon and her. And Courtney. Well, they were if Courtney was telling the truth.

"Stay in the truck," Landon told her, and he opened the door.

Tessa caught on to his arm. "It's not a good idea for you to be out in the open."

"I won't be." He got behind his truck door, using it for cover. "But I want to be in a position to give Josh some backup if he needs it. Just stay down."

She did because Tessa didn't want to distract Landon, but she also kept her gun ready. It seemed to take an eternity for Josh to make his way from the roof to the playground, though she figured it was only a few minutes. With each step he took, her heart pounded even harder and her breath raced. Maybe, just maybe, there'd soon be an end to the danger.

Josh was being diligent, too, his gaze firing all around him, and he hurried to the huge slide that was in the center of the playground. She watched him stoop down and pick up what appeared to be a manila envelope. He didn't look inside. Instead he hurried back to the cover of the building.

Time seemed to stop again, and even though she was expecting the call, Tessa gasped when Landon's phone buzzed. Unlike with the other call, she wasn't close enough to hear what Josh said to him.

"Does it have a name on it?" Landon asked. Again, she couldn't hear, but whatever Josh had told him caused Landon's forehead to bunch up. "Go ahead and get in touch with the lab," Landon added. "Then text me the lab's number in case I need to talk to them, too."

Landon got back in the truck in the same motion as he put away his phone. "It's DNA results," he said.

Tessa's mind began to whirl with all sorts of possibilities. "Whose DNA?"

Landon shook his head. "There are file numbers, but the lab should be able to give us a name. It might take a court order, though."

Which meant more hours, or possibly even days, when they didn't have answers. Was the DNA connected to the baby or did this have something to do with Emmett's murder?

Landon started the engine just as his phone buzzed again, and Tessa was hoping that Josh had found something else in that envelope. But it wasn't Josh. Tessa saw Mason's name on the screen. This time Landon put the call on Speaker.

"We got a problem," Mason said. "Two men just tried to trespass onto the ranch. And Tessa heard something she didn't want to hear from the other end of the line.

Someone fired shots.

Chapter Twelve

Landon cursed, threw the truck into gear and started driving—fast. His first instinct was to head to the ranch, but that would be taking Tessa directly into enemy fire. Instead, he could drop her off at the sheriff's office so he could go and help Mason. Maybe he wouldn't get there too late.

"Are they shooting at the guesthouse?" Landon asked. Beside him, Tessa was trembling, and she had a death grip on the gun.

Mason didn't answer for such a long time that Landon had his own death grip on the steering wheel. "No," Mason finally said. "That was Grayson and Nate who fired, and they weren't anywhere near any of the houses. They shot the intruders. Both men are dead."

Landon figured that was the best possible news he could hear right now. "Are there signs of any other gunmen?"

"Doesn't appear to be, but the ranch hands will patrol the grounds all night to make sure. I'll also give Gage and Josh a call, but it might be a good idea for all of you to stay away from here until we give you the all clear."

Yeah, Landon agreed. The ranch was essentially on lockdown and needed to stay that way. "We'll be at the sheriff's office until we hear from you. Is the baby okay?"

"She's fine, but she peed on me. Went right through the diaper. I'm not sure why that keeps happening to me whenever I'm around kids."

If this had been another cousin, Landon might have thought Mason was saying that to give them some comic relief, but Mason wasn't the comic-relief type.

"Is Courtney alive?" Mason asked.

"For now. But she didn't show up for the meeting. She did leave us something, though. The results of a DNA test. I'll let you know as soon as we know exactly what it is."

Landon ended the call and raced back to the sheriff's office—though the place no longer felt exactly safe. The boarded-up front of the building had something to do with that. The explosion hadn't done any structural damage, but it would be a while before things returned to normal. That included any peace of mind. They weren't going to get that until this snake was captured and put away.

As soon as they were in the building, Landon moved Tessa back to the interview room. No windows in there, unlike Grayson's office, which also had some parts of it boarded up. He waited in the hall, and it didn't take long for Josh to come through the door. However, Landon could tell from his cousin's expression that it wasn't good news.

"The lab wouldn't give you the DNA results," he said to Josh. Tessa stepped into the hall with Landon.

"Bingo," Josh confirmed. "It's a private facility and can't release them. Hell, they can't even tell me who submitted the test or whose DNA it is."

Tessa nodded, let out a long breath and pushed her hair from her face. He hated to see the fear and frustration on her face. Hated even more that those feelings, especially the fear, were warranted.

"Maybe if you tell the lab it's connected to a murder investigation?" Tessa suggested.

"I already tried that," Josh assured her. "They still want the court order. But I'll get started on it right away."

Since this might take a while, Landon had Tessa sit at the interview table, and he brought her back a bottle of water from the break room fridge. It wasn't much, especially considering she'd hardly touched the sandwiches they'd had before leaving for the meeting with Courtney, but he figured Tessa's stomach had to be churning. His certainly was.

"Stating the obvious here, but Courtney's covering up something," Tessa volunteered.

It was obvious. Too bad the answers weren't equally obvious. "Any idea what?"

She took a deep breath first, then a long sip of water. "Keep in mind that I don't know Courtney that well, but she certainly didn't confirm that Quincy was her baby's father."

Landon nodded. "And she was adamant that Quincy couldn't have gotten Samantha's DNA from a pacifier."

Tessa made a sound of agreement. "Granted, I wasn't around the baby much before Courtney left her with me, but I never saw her with a pacifier. So why would Quincy claim something like that?"

Landon could think of a reason. "A shortcut. Maybe Samantha really is his child, but since he can't get a real DNA sample, he created a fake one."

Of course, that would have taken the help of someone who worked in a lab, but considering Quincy was a criminal, he wouldn't have had any trouble paying someone off to help him out.

"Did Courtney ever mention being with Quincy or any other man, for that matter?" Landon asked.

"No." Tessa didn't pause, either. "She just said things weren't good between her and Samantha's father and that she didn't want him to see the baby."

Hearing that gave Landon a bad feeling. If Courtney knew about Landon's connection to Tessa, the woman could have purposely concealed her involvement with Quincy. Or maybe Quincy had been the one to put Courtney up to meeting Tessa.

But why?

What could Quincy have hoped to gain by having his lover get close to Tessa? As sick as Quincy was, maybe he'd planned on trying to seduce Tessa or something so he could sway her into getting revenge against Landon. That was such a long stretch, though, that he didn't even bring it up to Tessa. Besides, Tessa obviously already had too much to worry about.

"Don't say you're sorry again," Landon warned Tessa when she opened her mouth.

Since she immediately closed her mouth, Landon figured he'd pegged that right.

"I've made a mess of your life," she said. Not an apology but it was still too close to being one, so Landon dropped a kiss on her mouth.

She didn't look surprised by the kiss. Which was probably a bad thing. They shouldn't be at the point where he could just give her random kisses and have

Tessa look content about it. But that was exactly how she looked—content.

Then she huffed.

No explanation was necessary. The attraction was there, always there. And they didn't even need a little kiss to remind them of it. This time, though, the attraction didn't get to turn into anything more than a heated look and the half kiss. That was because Landon heard someone talking in the squad room. Someone he didn't want to hear talking.

Because it was Ward.

"What did you find?" Landon heard the man ask. Except it wasn't a simple question. It was a demand.

That got Landon moving back into the hall again, and he didn't bother to tell Tessa to stay put. Whatever reason Ward was there, it would no doubt involve her anyway.

"What are you talking about?" Josh asked.

Ward huffed as if the answer were obvious. "What did you find on the playground? And don't bother to lie and say you weren't there, because I had someone watching the sheriff's office, and he followed you."

Josh looked about as uneasy with that as Gage and Landon. Landon went closer, and he made sure it was too close. Since he was a good three inches taller than the man, Landon figured it was time to use his size to do a little intimidating. But even if he hadn't been taller, he would still have been mad enough to spit bullets, and he was about to aim some of that anger at Ward.

"What the hell do you mean, you had someone watching us?" Landon demanded.

Ward's chin came up, but the confidence didn't quite

make it to his eyes. "I told him to stay back, not to interfere with your investigation, and he didn't."

No, but what was disconcerting was that no one had noticed this shadow. Of course, since it was probably a federal agent doing the spying, he could have used some long-range surveillance equipment.

Ward pointed to Josh. "He saw him pick up something, and I want to know what it was."

"Trash," Landon said with a straight face. "We don't like litterbugs around here."

If looks could kill, Ward would have blasted Landon straight to the hereafter. "It was something about Tessa, wasn't it? Or the woman you're looking for—Courtney."

Landon just stared at him. "If you're waiting for me to make some kind of buzzer sound to let you know you've got a right or wrong answer, that's not going to happen. The Silver Creek sheriff's office has jurisdiction over the investigation into the recent attacks, and if we found anything, we don't have to share it with the feds."

"This is my investigation!" Ward didn't shout exactly, but his voice was a couple of notches above normal conversation. This time he pointed at Tessa. "She's working for Joel. Can't you see that?"

Tessa came forward and faced Ward head-on. "I've had a very bad day," she said. No longer shaky, just pissed off. "And I'm tired of you accusing me of working for Joel. I loathe the man and nearly got myself and others killed because I was trying to find evidence to have him arrested."

"I don't believe that," Ward argued.

"Tough." Tessa's index finger landed against his chest. "Because until you have some kind of proof, I want you to stay far away from me and anyone connected to me." She turned to go back toward the interview room.

"I can't do that," Ward said. "Because I need to find Courtney Hager."

That stopped Tessa in her tracks, and she turned around slowly to face him. "Why? How do you even know Courtney?"

The muscles got to working in Ward's jaw. He put his hands on his hips and lowered his head a moment. "I can't tell you. But she's part of a federal investigation."

Mentioning federal was probably a dig at Landon since he'd just played the local-jurisdiction card on Ward.

"A word of advice when it comes to Courtney," Ward continued a moment later. "Don't trust her and don't believe a word she says."

"Why?" Tessa repeated.

But Ward only shook his head. "If you find her, turn her over to me. I'm the only one who can stop her from being killed."

And with that, Ward turned and walked out. Landon didn't bother to follow him and press him for more. They might both have badges, but that was where the similarities ended. They clearly were on opposite sides here, but Landon had to repeat Tessa's *why*.

"If he knows Courtney," Tessa said, "then maybe all of them are connected somehow—Joel, Quincy, Ward and Courtney."

Yeah, but how?

"I'm calling Kade," Landon explained, taking out his phone. "He's still with the FBI, and he might be able to find a link if there is one."

When his cousin didn't answer, Landon left him a message to find out if Courtney was in some witness protection program or was a criminal informant. Those two were the most obvious connections, but when people like Joel and Quincy were involved, it was possible this was a plain and simple criminal operation.

And that Courtney was part of it.

"We can't keep letting this go on," Tessa said. "And I've got an idea how to stop it."

That got not only Landon's attention but his cousins' attention, as well.

"I'm sure it's all over town that I was drugged," she continued. "Everyone probably knows I can't remember all the details of what happened the night Emmett was killed."

"Because someone drugged you," Josh provided.

Tessa nodded. "But what if we spread the word that I am remembering, and the memories are becoming clearer. We could even say I'm planning to go through hypnosis or take some kind of truth serum so I can identify Emmett's killer."

Landon was the first to curse, but Josh and Gage soon joined in, all of them telling her variations of no way in hell was that going to happen.

Landon huffed after he finished cursing. "You would make yourself an even bigger target than you already are."

She lifted her hands, palms up. "Someone wants me dead. I can't imagine that target can get any bigger."

"Well, imagine it," Landon snapped. "This killer will stop at nothing to come after you."

"Apparently, he, or she, will come after me anyway. The killer, the person who hired him or both think I saw something that night. I don't think I did, but hypnosis couldn't hurt. Heck, I might remember exactly what we need to catch this person, and if I don't, the mere threat of me remembering could lure him or her out."

"And you could be killed." Hell. Landon didn't need to say that aloud. Especially since she could be killed with or without the hypnosis, but he wanted to find another way. One that wouldn't put a bull's-eye on Tessa's back.

"You don't want to hear this," Josh said to him, "but Tessa is right. This could work."

"You're right. I don't want to hear it." Landon cursed some more. It didn't help. Because damn it, Josh was right. It could work. Still, Landon couldn't make a call like that.

And that made him stupid.

Because he had done exactly what he'd said he wouldn't do—he'd gotten personally involved with Tessa. He'd lost focus. That could be doubly dangerous for Tessa, the baby and anyone else around them.

Gage went closer, tapped Landon's badge. "You need to be thinking with this right now. We could use the next twelve hours to get everything ready, and this time we could maybe get ahead of an attack."

Hell, Gage was right, too, but that still didn't make this any easier to swallow. Landon was about to do what he didn't want to do. Give in. But before he could do that, his phone buzzed, and he saw Grayson's name on the screen. He got an instant punch of fear because this call could be to tell them that there was another intruder at the ranch.

"What's wrong?" Landon said the moment he answered, and he hoped he was just jumping to conclusions.

He wasn't.

Landon could tell from Grayson's pause. And Tessa must have been able to tell from Landon's expression, because she hurried to him.

"Is it the baby?" she asked.

In case it was, Landon didn't put the call on Speaker. He just waited for Grayson to continue.

"The sheriff over in Sweetwater Springs called," Grayson continued. "They found a body."

"Courtney?" Landon managed to say.

"No. It's a man, and there's no ID yet, but there was a note."

Everything inside Landon went still. Everything except that gut feeling that he was about to hear something he didn't want to hear.

"The sheriff sent me a picture of a note," Grayson explained, "and I'm sending it to you now."

It took but a couple of seconds for Landon's phone to ding, indicating that he had a text, and it took a few more seconds for the photo to load.

Yeah, this was bad. And not bad just because the note was on a dead man's chest. But because the note was addressed to Landon. *This is for you, Landon. Keep protecting Tessa, and there'll be another dead body tomorrow.*

Chapter Thirteen

Tessa didn't regret putting this plan into motion. Especially after seeing the photo of the note that'd been left on a dead man. But it was hard to tamp down all the emotions that went with making herself bait for a killer.

At least the baby was safe. That was something. Before Landon and the other deputies had leaked the news about her impending hypnosis, they'd made arrangements for a safe house and moved Samantha from the ranch. Along with two lawmen and a nanny. Considering there'd been two attempts by intruders, that was a wise thing to do anyway. It got not only Samantha out of immediate danger but also everyone else on the ranch.

Judging from Landon's expression, though, that was the only thing he thought was *wise* about this plan.

But they'd taken other precautions that Tessa felt fell into the wise category. After Grayson and Landon had hashed out the details, they'd agreed that it would be too risky to actually bring in a hypnotist. The killer might try to stop that before the person could even get inside the building. Instead, Grayson had put out the word that the hypnosis session would be done via the computer with an undisclosed therapist.

While Tessa was at the sheriff's office.

That would keep the hospital staff safe, but what it wouldn't do was get Tessa the session that might truly end up helping her recover any lost memories. At least, she wouldn't get the session today. There hadn't been enough time to set that up, but if this trap didn't get them the killer, then that was the backup plan.

"All the reserve deputies are in place," Grayson said when he finished his latest phone call. All of the Ryland lawmen at the sheriff's office—Grayson, Dade, Josh and Landon—had been making lots of phone calls to set all of this up. All doing everything possible to make sure she was safe.

Maybe it would be enough.

"Where are the reserves?" Landon asked.

"Both ends of Main Street, and I've got the other two positioned on the roofs of the diner and the hardware store."

Good. That would stop someone from launching an attack like the previous two. Tessa also knew that security had been beefed up at the ranch just in case the snake after them hadn't gotten the word that the baby had been moved.

"The reserves have orders to stay out of sight," Grayson added. "I've also put out the word that most of the deputies are tied up with the two intruders who were killed at the ranch."

Tessa approved of that, as well. Their attacker might not come after them if he or she sensed this was a trap. Of course, the person had been pretty darn bold with the other attacks, so maybe that wouldn't even matter. Whoever was behind this had no trouble hiring thugs to do their dirty work. That was the reason Landon had insisted on having her wear a bulletproof vest, but she'd put it beneath her shirt in case someone had been watching her go into the sheriff's office.

"We struck out on the dead guy in Sweetwater Springs," Dade said, joining the others and Tessa in the center of the squad room. "He was a homeless guy and doesn't seem to have a connection to any of our suspects."

Which meant he'd been killed just to torture and taunt Landon. And it was working. Every muscle in his body was tight to the point of looking painful, and Tessa figured that wouldn't get better until this was over.

"What time is the hypnosis session supposed to take place?" she asked.

Grayson checked the time. "Right about now. Why don't you go into the interview room and pretend to get started?"

That room had been chosen because there were no windows to guard, and the only way to get in was through the door. A door that Landon was personally guarding.

Tessa sank down at the table to wait. She wasn't certain how long a real hypnosis session would take, but it was possible the killer would try to put a quick end to it. Which meant bullets could start flying at any moment. Or this trap might fail. After all, the killer could just go after her when she finally left the office, but then he or she wouldn't be able to put an end to those possible memories before she could tell anyone else about them.

"You can still back out of this," Landon assured her.

Yes, but everyone in the building knew that wasn't going to happen. Tessa only shook her head. "This could all be over this morning. And then your life can get back to normal."

Of course, it would never be normal for Landon or the rest of his family, because even if they caught Emmett's killer, Emmett would still be dead. It wouldn't even matter why he died, because it would always be such a senseless killing.

She heard the footsteps coming toward the interview room, and Tessa automatically went on alert. But it was just Josh, and he had a very puzzled look on his face.

"Something's going on with the baby's DNA test," Josh said. "I just got off the phone with the lab, and they told me the test results have been suppressed."

"Suppressed?" Tessa and Landon repeated together.

Josh shook his head. "Apparently the feds have removed both the DNA sample and the test results from the lab, and they aren't making them available to anyone else in local law enforcement."

Tessa had no idea what that meant. "Why would they do something like that? And what about the other DNA results Courtney gave us?"

"Those are being released," Josh explained. "Well, partially, and only to us. According to those tests, Quincy isn't the father." He paused. "Emmett is."

That brought Grayson and Dade into the hall with them, and the cousins were as stunned as Tessa was. But it was more than just being stunned. This didn't seem right.

"Emmett and Annie were in love," Tessa said. "Before Annie died, they were trying to start a family. They were happy. I can't believe Emmett would have cheated on his wife, much less gotten Courtney pregnant."

All of the lawmen made sounds of agreement, but she could also feel the doubts. They looked at her as if she might have solid information about this. She didn't.

But it did jog something in her head. Something Tessa hadn't remembered until now.

"Courtney and Emmett were talking when she came to my house that night he was killed. I didn't hear what they said, but the conversation was tense. Maybe even an argument."

Landon cursed. "Why didn't you tell us this sooner?" However, he immediately waved that off because he already knew the answer. He'd asked that question only out of frustration. Frustration that Tessa was certainly feeling, too. "Think hard. Did Courtney ever mention Emmett?"

"No. But Courtney wasn't exactly volunteering anything about her personal life." Which was too bad, because details, any details, would have helped now.

Landon looked at his cousins. "Any idea if Emmett was romantically involved with Courtney?"

Grayson and Dade shook their heads, but Josh shrugged. "You know how Emmett was—not one to spill much about his job or his personal life."

Tessa knew that. It was because as a DEA agent, Emmett often worked undercover assignments that he couldn't discuss, and it was possible that Emmett had wanted some information from Courtney about Quincy.

But she kept going back to Annie.

The one thing Tessa was certain of was that Emmett and Annie had had a good marriage and that he had been torn to pieces when she'd been killed eight months ago in that car crash.

Except…

"What else are you remembering?" Landon pressed.

Landon didn't appear to be fishing with that question, either. He was studying her expression, and that was when Tessa realized her forehead was bunched up.

"It's probably nothing," she said. And hoped that was true. "Annie and Emmett were going through fertility treatments, and Annie was desperate to have a child. Maybe Emmett wasn't as desperate as she was."

No one disagreed with that, and it put a knot in her stomach.

Grayson scrubbed his hand over his face. "Emmett was worried about what the treatments were doing to Annie. But that doesn't mean he would cheat on her. Their marriage was solid."

No one disagreed with that, either. So that meant there had to be some other explanation.

"Maybe the results Courtney gave us are fake," Dade suggested. "Maybe Courtney thinks we'll do more to protect the baby if it's a Ryland."

That could be true, though they were already doing everything humanly possible in that department. "Or maybe Courtney just wanted to make sure Quincy didn't get the baby, and this was her way of making sure of that." Tessa paused. "But that doesn't explain why the feds would suppress the DNA test."

Everyone stayed quiet a moment. "Perhaps the feds aren't suppressing the baby's DNA but rather Courtney's," Landon said.

"Why would they do that?" Though she'd no sooner thrown out that question than she realized why. "You think Courtney is a federal agent or some kind of informant?"

Landon lifted his shoulder. "She could be. If she was a deep-cover operative—a Jane, they call them—then her DNA wouldn't be entered into the system."

True. Because it could get her killed if someone she was investigating got access to the database and ID'd her as an agent. But Courtney hadn't given her any indications that she was in law enforcement.

And there was something else that didn't make sense.

"If Samantha is Emmett's baby, then why would Quincy believe the child is his?" Of course, Tessa knew the most obvious answer—that Courtney could have been sleeping with both Emmett and Quincy at the same time. No way would she want to tell Quincy that.

The conversation came to a quick halt when Grayson's phone buzzed, and a message popped up on the screen.

"One of the reserve deputies spotted Joel making his way here," Grayson relayed. "He's alone and doesn't appear to be armed."

That didn't mean he wasn't carrying a concealed weapon.

Landon snapped in the direction of the front door. "Hell," he said under his breath.

She certainly hadn't forgotten about Joel, and he was still a prime suspect, but Tessa hadn't expected him to show up. He was more the sort to send hit men to do his dirty work.

"We're busy," Landon snarled. "You'll have to come back."

"Yes, I heard about the busyness going on. Tessa's hypnosis. It's all over town, and I'm guessing you did that to draw out the person trying to kill her."

"Is that why you're here—to try to kill her?" Landon fired back.

"No." Joel stretched that out a few syllables. "I don't want Tessa dead."

She couldn't see his face, but Tessa could almost see the smirk that was surely there. She stood to confront the man herself, but Landon motioned for her to stay put, and he pulled the door nearly shut so there was a crack of only an inch or so. That meant she would still be able to hear the conversation, but Joel wouldn't be able to see that she wasn't going through a hypnosis session.

"Did you miss that part about me saying you'll have to come back?" Landon snapped to Joel.

"No, I didn't, but you'll want me to stay when you see what I've brought you. You wanted proof that Quincy was up to his old tricks. Well, here it is."

Tessa hurried to the door and looked out as Joel handed Landon a piece of paper. She was too far away to see what it was, but it certainly got not only Landon's attention but also his cousins'.

"Where did you get this?" Landon asked.

Joel wagged his finger in a no-no gesture. "I can't reveal my source."

"And that means we can't use this to arrest him." Landon cursed. "Who gave this to you?"

"I meant it when I said I can't reveal my source," Joel insisted. "Because I don't know where it came from. Someone sent it to my office in an unmarked envelope."

Landon glanced back at her to see if she was watching, and Tessa didn't duck out of the way in time before Joel spotted her.

"Did you remember who killed Emmett?" Joel immediately asked her.

But Tessa didn't answer. She went back into the interview room and kept listening, though she knew Landon would fill her in on what was on that sheet of paper as soon as Joel left. Which would no doubt be soon. No way would Landon want one of their suspects hanging around.

"According to this, Quincy is into gunrunning and drugs," Grayson said, reading through the paper.

"Complete with dates of the transactions and those involved with Quincy," Joel bragged. "I'm not sure exactly who Quincy pissed off, but clearly, the person who sent this is out to get him."

Yes, and it made her wonder why that person hadn't just sent it to the police. Of course, all of this could be some kind of ploy on Joel's part to get the suspicion off him. In fact, Joel could very well be the one behind the gunrunning and drugs, and the names on that paper could be people he wanted to set up to take the fall.

"Say, do you smell smoke?" Joel asked.

Tessa immediately lifted her head and sniffed. She couldn't smell anything, but judging from the way Landon and the others started to scramble around, they did.

Oh, God.

Was this the start of another attack?

Her heart went into overdrive, and even though she'd tried to prepare herself for this, maybe there was no way to prepare for something like that.

"Get the hell out of here," Landon ordered, and it took her a moment to realize he was talking to Joel.

Joel obeyed, and as soon as he was out the front door, Landon hurried to her.

"Is there really a fire?" she asked, but Tessa soon got the answer, because she smelled the smoke.

"The reserve deputies didn't spot anyone other than

Joel near the building," Grayson called out to them. "But there's definitely a fire in the parking lot."

Maybe someone had put some kind of incendiary device on a timer. And maybe it wouldn't stay just a fire once the flames reached a car engine. They could have another explosion.

"Hell," Grayson added a moment later. "There are two fires. Landon and Josh, go ahead and get Tessa out of here. We can't wait around here for the killer to show up."

She reminded herself they'd planned for this just in case they had to evacuate. Landon had parked a bullet-resistant cruiser directly in front of the sheriff's office, and he'd already told her if anything went wrong, he'd be taking her to a safe house. Not the one where they were keeping Samantha but another one so they wouldn't lead the killer straight to the baby.

"Are the reserve deputies sure there are no gunmen in the area?" Landon asked Grayson.

"They don't see anyone."

But that didn't mean someone wasn't out there. Someone hiding in a place the deputies couldn't see.

"You know the drill," Landon told her. "Stay low and move fast."

She did, and Tessa figured she was out in the open only a couple of seconds since she literally stepped right out the sheriff's office and through the back door of the cruiser that Landon had opened for her.

Josh and Landon, though, were outside longer—and therefore in danger—since Landon got behind the wheel and Josh got into the front seat with him. Landon took off right away, but that didn't mean they were safe. In fact, this could be playing right into the killer's hands.

"The reserve deputies will follow us," Josh relayed, and he handed her a gun that he took from the glove compartment. "But they're using an unmarked car."

Good. That meant they'd be close enough to provide backup but without completely scaring off the person responsible for the attacks.

"Where's the killer most likely to come after us?" she asked.

But Landon didn't answer. That was because his head snapped to the left, and Tessa saw the black SUV a split second later.

Before it smashed right into them.

The jolt slammed her against the side of the door so hard that it knocked the breath out of her. Tessa gasped for air all the way, praying that Landon hadn't been hurt or worse. After all, the SUV had slammed into the driver's side. But she couldn't see his arm or shoulder. Couldn't tell if he was bleeding.

"Hold on," Landon shouted, and he gunned the engine.

At least they were able to move and the collision hadn't left them sitting ducks. As soon as Landon sped away, Tessa heard the sound of other tires on the asphalt.

The SUV was in pursuit.

"There's not even a dent in the SUV's bumper," Josh growled, and he turned in the seat to keep watch. He also kept his gun ready, though it wouldn't do any good for him to fire, since the windows on the cruiser would stop his bullet.

That also meant it would stop the bullets of their attackers, but since they must have known that, Tessa figured they had something else in mind.

And they did. The SUV crashed into them again.

This time Tessa went flying into the seats in front of her, and she barely managed to hang on to the gun. Though it was too late, she grappled around and managed to get on her seat belt. Just as the third impact came. She looked behind her and saw that Josh was right—the SUV bumper was still in place, which meant it'd been reinforced.

Landon drove as fast as he could, no doubt trying to get away from Main Street so that no one would be hurt. Plus, they were headed in the direction of one of the reserve deputies though she wasn't sure what he would be able to do. If the bumper on the SUV had been reinforced, then the windows probably had been, as well.

"Hell," Landon growled.

Tessa looked behind her and saw why he'd cursed. The passenger's-side window of the SUV had lowered, and she saw someone stick out the barrel of a big gun. Except it wasn't just a gun. It was some kind of launcher.

Oh, God.

Were they shooting a grenade at them?

She heard the loud swooshing sound and tried to brace herself for an explosion. But it didn't happen. Instead, something smacked onto the back of the cruiser. Definitely not a grenade. It looked like a lump of clay.

"Get down on the seat!" Landon shouted to her.

Not a second too soon, because they hadn't avoided an explosion after all. The clay must have been some kind of bomb, because the blast tore through the car, shattering the windows and lifting the rear of the cruiser into the air. It smacked back down onto the pavement, stopping them cold.

Tessa hadn't thought her heart could beat any harder,

but she was wrong. It felt ready to come out of her chest, but she forced her fear aside because they were about to have to fight for their lives.

The first shot came at them before she could even lift her gun and get it ready to fire. Thank God that Landon didn't have that problem, though. He pushed her down on the seat and fired out the gaping hole in what was left of the back window.

Whoever was attacking them didn't waste any time, either. More shots came, and even though Josh and Landon were using their seats for cover, she knew that bullets could easily go through those.

She didn't dare lift her head, since the SUV was just a few yards from her, but Tessa could see the vehicle in the cruiser's side mirror. And what she saw sent her heart dropping to her knees.

The person in the passenger's seat stuck out that launcher again, and he aimed it right at the cruiser. Sweet heaven. The cruiser wouldn't be able to withstand another direct hit, and that was probably why both Landon and Josh started firing at the guy. He pulled the launcher back inside the SUV. For only a couple of seconds.

Then he took aim at them again.

Tessa prayed this wasn't it, that the three of them wouldn't all die right here, right now. But then she heard a welcome sound.

Shots.

Not ones coming from Josh or Landon. These shots were coming from up the street. Either the reserve deputies had arrived or this was Grayson and Gage coming to help. She hated they were now all in harm's way, but without their help, Landon, Josh and she wouldn't get out of this alive.

She cursed the men trying to kill them. Cursed the fact that she was so close to dying and didn't even know why.

Landon scrambled over the seat, covering her body with his. What he didn't do was fire. Probably because he didn't want to risk hitting his cousins or the other deputies. Josh did fire but that was only when the thug tried to put the launcher out the window again.

The shots outside the cruiser continued, one thick blast after another until they blended together into one deafening roar. But even over the roar, Tessa could still hear another sound.

The squeal of the tires, followed by the stench of the rubber burning against the pavement.

The gunmen were getting away.

Chapter Fourteen

Landon knew they'd gotten darn lucky, but it sure didn't feel like it at the moment.

He'd banged his shoulder when the SUV had first plowed into them, and it was throbbing like a toothache. Josh was limping from a bruised knee. And while Tessa didn't have any physical injuries, she had that look in her eyes that let him know she was on the verge of losing it.

Landon couldn't fault her for that. They'd come so close to dying. Hell, lots of people had since the attack could have turned into a bloodbath on Main Street. However, other than Josh's and his minor injuries, everyone was okay. Again, he qualified that. Everyone was physically okay.

Tessa finished her phone call with the nanny and turned to Landon. "The baby's fine. No sign of any gunmen at the safe house."

That was a relief even though he would have been shocked if attackers had found the location. They'd been careful when they'd moved the baby. Of course, Landon thought he'd been careful with the arrangements he'd made for Tessa, and look how they'd turned out.

Now all he could do was regroup and keep her safe. Not that he'd done a stellar job of that so far, and that meant he had to make some changes. Landon had brought her back to the Silver Creek Ranch guesthouse, but this would be their last night here. In the morning he would put her in Holden's protective custody, and Holden could take her to a real safe house. Then Landon could focus on catching this SOB who kept coming after them.

"Do I need to remind you that the fake-hypnosis plan was my idea?" Tessa said.

She sounded as weary and spent as Landon felt. Maybe even more. He was accustomed to dealing with nightmares like this, but Tessa wasn't. Though lately she'd had way too much experience in that department.

"I'm the one with the badge," Landon reminded her. "I should have done a better job."

"Right, because of those superhero powers you have."

At first he wasn't sure if her smart remark was an insult to point out his shortcomings, but then she lifted her eyebrow. "It was my plan," she repeated. "You got stuck with the mop-up."

"It was more than mop-up," he grumbled. But what he meant to say was that *she* was more than mop-up.

He didn't.

There was already enough dangerous energy zinging between them without his admitting that he'd been scared spitless at the thought of losing her.

"Besides, I have superhero powers," he added because he thought they could use some levity. "If we ever have to jump a ditch, you'll see what I mean. And I can open medicine bottles on the first try."

She smiled. Which was exactly the response he wanted. But it didn't last. He saw her bottom lip tremble, and just like that the tears watered her eyes. She blinked them back, of course. Landon stayed put, though. That whole dangerous-energy thing was still there.

"I guess you'll be leaving soon," she said, her voice not much louder than a whisper. "Who'll be babysitting me after you leave?"

Landon hadn't said a word to her about the arrangements he'd made shortly after the attack, and he was pretty sure she hadn't heard, because he'd made them when the doctor was checking her. Clearly, Tessa's superhero power was ESP.

"Holden," he admitted. "He'll be here first thing in the morning."

She didn't curse, but some of the weariness vanished, and he was pretty sure she wasn't happy about being traded off to another Ryland. Of course, there couldn't be much about this situation that pleased her, and it was clear he sucked at keeping her out of harm's way.

"You know with me tucked away, it'll be harder for you to catch Emmett's killer," she added.

Hell's bells. He didn't like the sound of that at all. "You're not thinking about making yourself bait again." And it wasn't a question.

"No. I doubt I could get you or any of your cousins to go along with that. Just reminding you that the killer might just disappear until the dust settles. Or until I come out of hiding." She paused. "Unless you're planning to put me in WITSEC."

Yeah, he was. And since Tessa also hadn't said it as a question, either she truly did have ESP or else she knew him a lot better than Landon wanted her to know him. It was best if he kept some of his feelings from her. Especially the feeling that he was afraid for her, and there weren't many times in his life he'd felt like this.

Tessa scrubbed her hands on the sides of her bor-

rowed dress. "Well, I should probably…do something."
She moved as if to go into the kitchen.

And Landon should have let her go. He didn't.

Landon was certain the only thing he didn't want
about this were the consequences. And there would be
a price to pay, all right. A huge one. Because not only
would this make him lose focus, it would take him back
to a place he swore he'd never go. A place where he had
Tessa in his arms. In his bed.

Knowing all of that didn't stop him from reaching
for her.

She was already heading toward him anyway, and
it would have been easy to slide right into this without
thinking. Landon wanted to think, wanted to remember
how he'd felt when she'd walked out on him.

He didn't think, though. Didn't remember.

One touch of his mouth to hers, and there was no
turning back. No remembering.

"You don't want to do this," she said, her voice not
even a whisper.

"You're wrong." And he proved it.

He slipped his hand around the back of her neck,
pulled her against him. Until they were body to body.
He'd already crossed a huge line, and there weren't
enough superhero powers in the world to make him
stop. Tessa seemed to feel the same way, because the
moment he deepened the kiss, he felt her surrender.
Heck, maybe the surrender had happened even before
this. All Landon knew was that this seemed inevitable.

And necessary.

If he'd been given a choice between her and the air
he was breathing, he would have chosen Tessa.

Of course, that was the logic of that brainless part

of him behind his zipper, but Landon went right along with it. If he was going to screw this up, he might as well make it worth it, even though just being with her seemed to fill the "worth it" bill.

Tessa was still trembling, probably from the adrenaline crash, but Landon upped the trembling by taking the kisses to her neck. Then lower to the tops of her breasts. Even though they had been together but that once, he remembered just how to fire her up.

But Tessa obviously remembered how to do the same to him.

He had her neck at an angle so she couldn't use that clever mouth on him, but she made good use of her hands. First on his chest. She slid her palm all the way to his stomach. And lower.

Definitely playing dirty.

He already had an erection, but that only made him harder. And hotter. To hell with foreplay. If she wanted that, he could give it to her after he burned off some of this fire that she'd started.

Landon enjoyed the sound of surprise, then pleasure, she made when he shoved up her dress and pulled it off her. Now the body-to-body contact was even better because her nearly bare breasts were there for the kissing. Landon fixed the "nearly" part by ridding her of her bra so he could kiss her the way he wanted.

Man, he was in trouble here.

Tessa was the source of that trouble. "I'm not the only one who's getting naked here." And she robbed him of his breath when she shimmied off her panties. "Please tell me you have a condom."

"In my wallet," he managed to say.

Tessa obviously took that as a challenge to get it out, and since Landon was distracted by her naked body, he lost focus long enough for her to go after his wallet. Either she was very bad at that task or else she was doing her own version of foreplay, because by the time she was done, Landon was already lowering her to the sofa.

The moment she had his wallet, she went after his clothes. Landon let her because it gave him a chance to kiss some places he'd missed the first time they'd had sex. It slowed her down a little, and she made a sound of pure pleasure that Landon wished he could bottle. But it still seemed to take only the blink of an eye for her to get off his shirt and boots and get him unzipped.

Landon helped with the jeans and his boxers. Even though this was mindless wild sex, he didn't want anything in between him and her.

And so that was what he got.

He took hold of her, pulling her onto his lap, and in the same motion, he went inside her. Of course, she was familiar, but he still felt that jolt of surprise. Still felt both the relief and the building need. The relief wouldn't last.

The need would.

"We are so in trouble here," she whispered.

Even if he'd had the breath to answer, he wouldn't have argued with her. Because they were. This might be the last time they ever saw each other, and here they were complicating it with sex.

Great sex, at that.

It didn't take long for them to find the right rhythm. Landon caught on to her hips, and Tessa used the rhythm and motion to slide against him.

Yeah, definitely great sex.

He went deeper, faster. Until he could feel Tessa close. That was when he kissed her. It slowed them down a little, but it was worth it. Worth it, too, to watch her as she climaxed. Definitely not a trace of fear or weariness. Only the pleasure.

Tessa gave it right back to him. She kissed him and gave him exactly what he needed to finish this. Landon gathered her in his arms and let go.

"HELL," LANDON SAID under his breath.

Even though it was barely a whisper, Tessa heard it. She'd figured it would at least be a couple of minutes before Landon started regretting this, but apparently not. *Hell* wasn't exactly the postsex mutterings she wanted to hear.

"Phone," he added.

And that was when Tessa heard the buzzing. A buzzing she'd thought was in her head, but apparently not. Landon moved her off him, frantically dug through the pile of clothes that they'd practically ripped off each other and took his phone from his jeans pocket.

She saw Grayson's name on the screen along with the words Missed Call.

Now it was Tessa who was cursing. This could be something important, a matter of life and death, even.

While he was calling back Grayson, Landon went into the bathroom. She didn't follow him, and he didn't stay in there long. By the time he made it back into the living room, Grayson had already answered.

Tessa hurried to get dressed, and she braced herself to hear that there was another intruder on the grounds. Thankfully, Landon put the call on Speaker, but he probably did that to free up his hands so he could get dressed.

"Everything okay?" Grayson asked.

"Yeah," Landon lied. "What's wrong?"

"Nothing. Well, nothing other than all the other

wrong things that have been going on, but we might have gotten a break."

Tessa was so relieved that her legs went a little weak. Of course, that reaction might have had something to do with having a half-naked hot cowboy just a few inches from her. It was wrong to still notice that with the danger all around them, but her body just couldn't forget about Landon.

"That info Joel gave us panned out," Grayson went on. "Though we can't use it as evidence to get Quincy, Dade was able to find a criminal informant who verified that the illegal arms transactions did happen on the dates that were on that paper. Even better, the CI gave us the name of a witness. The transaction happened in San Antonio PD's jurisdiction, so Nate's on his way now to question the witness."

"How credible is this witness?" Landon asked.

"Credible enough. He's a businessman, no record. It appears he didn't know what was going on with the deal and that he got out of it as soon as he realized it was illegal."

It took Tessa a moment to process that, and while it wasn't a guarantee that it would get Quincy out of their lives, it was a start.

"As a minimum," Grayson went on, "this witness can put Quincy in the company of known felons, and that means he can be arrested for a parole violation. If we get lucky, we could have Quincy behind bars tonight, where he'll have to finish out the rest of a twenty-year sentence."

That would mean one of their suspects was off the streets. But Tessa immediately felt the sinking feeling in the pit of her stomach that even that wouldn't help.

So far their attacker had only sent thugs after them, and Quincy could still certainly do that from behind bars.

"Is that troubled expression for me or for something else?" Landon asked her the moment he ended the call.

"You and everything else," Tessa admitted. She sank down on the sofa to have "the talk" with him. "What just happened between us doesn't have to mean anything."

He didn't say anything. Landon just waited, as if expecting her to add a *but*. She didn't, because Tessa didn't want him to feel hemmed in, especially since her life was in the air right now.

Landon dropped down on the sofa next to her, took his time putting on his boots and then turned to her. She tried to prepare herself for anything from a thanks to some profanity for what Landon might see as a huge lapse in judgment.

That didn't happen, though.

He kissed her. Not a quick peck of reassurance, either. This was a real kiss. Long and scalding hot. A reminder that what'd just happened did mean something. Well, to her, anyway. It was possible that the kiss was just a leftover response to the attraction.

"Questions?" he asked after he finished that mind-numbing kiss.

Plenty. But she kept them to herself. Good thing, too, because his phone buzzed again. Not Grayson this time. It was Courtney. Landon answered it right away.

"What the hell is going on?" he demanded before Courtney even got a word in.

"I'm sorry," Courtney said after a long pause. "Is Samantha okay?"

"Yes. She's at a safe house. Now, talk."

Courtney didn't do that. Not right away, anyway. "Everything I've done has been to protect my daughter, and I hate that I put you in danger. But I'd do it again if it kept her safe."

"What did you do?" Tessa asked. "And is Emmett really Samantha's father?"

She heard Courtney take a long breath. "I don't want to get into this over the phone. Meet me and we'll talk."

"Talk first and then we'll consider meeting you," Landon countered, and he sounded very much like the lawman that he was. "But I'm not taking Tessa anywhere until I know what's going on, and maybe not even then. You know someone tried to kill her again?"

"Yes, I know. And I'm sorry. So sorry."

"I'm not looking for apologies," Landon snapped. "Answers. *Now.*"

Courtney took another deep breath. "I'm a Justice Department operative." And that was all she said for several long moments. "But you might have already guessed that."

"It was one of the theories. I figured that might be why you had Samantha's DNA results suppressed."

"It was. Partly," Courtney added. "And I also had them suppressed because the DNA sample you took from Samantha will prove that Quincy is her father."

Landon didn't say anything, but Tessa could see the relief Landon was feeling because this meant Emmett hadn't cheated on his wife. But she could also see the confusion.

"Right before Emmett was killed," Courtney went on, "he agreed that he would say Samantha was his so that Quincy couldn't get her."

That sounded like something Emmett would do, and that might have been what Emmett and Courtney had been discussing when she'd seen them together.

"You knew Emmett well?" Landon asked.

"Yes. We'd worked together on some investigations. I'm so sorry he's dead."

They all were. But Tessa hoped Courtney could give them some answers. "Do you know who killed him?"

"No," Courtney quickly answered, "and if I did, I would be figuring out a way to make sure his killer gets some payback."

Hard to do that with killers on their trails. "How the heck did you ever get involved with Quincy?"

"I was on a deep-cover assignment, and he helped me make some contacts. Ward introduced us."

That was not a connection that Tessa wanted to hear. "Ward knows you're an agent?" Tessa asked.

"No." Courtney groaned. "Maybe. But he's not supposed to know. I was posing as a criminal informant when I met him. I'm a Jane operative, and there aren't any records about me in any of the regular Justice Department databases, but it's possible Ward hacked into the classified files and found out my real identity. Maybe that's why all of this happened."

"What *did* happen?" Landon pressed.

Again, Courtney paused. "A little over nine months ago, Quincy arranged a meeting with me, and he drugged me. Rohypnol, I think. I blacked out, and when I woke up, I was naked and in bed with him."

Landon cursed, and Tessa couldn't quite choke back the gasp that leaped from her throat. Courtney had been sexually assaulted.

"I would have killed Quincy on the spot, but his thugs came in. At that time he was paying some motorcycle gang to play bodyguard and do his muscle work for him. So I left to regroup, to figure out a way to bring him down. And then I found out I was pregnant."

"You're sure the baby is Quincy's?" Tessa said, though it was a question she hated to ask.

"I'm sure. I had a real DNA test done, but those test results have been destroyed. Emmett was helping with that, and that's why I saw him the night he was killed. He's the one who had those fake results created."

Landon jumped right on that. "You think that's why Emmett was killed, because he was helping you?"

"I hope not." The sound Courtney made was part moan, part groan. "But I don't know for sure. Quincy could have found out Emmett was helping me and sent this hired muscle after him. I can't rule out Joel, either, because Emmett was investigating him. Both Joel and Quincy certainly have the resources to hire guns not only to kill Emmett but to go after you."

"And Ward?" Landon asked. "Can you rule him out?"

"No," Courtney said without hesitation. "I don't have anything on him, though. I don't have anything to bring anyone to justice. That has to change. I have to make sure Samantha is safe. That's why I gave you those fake DNA results—to protect my baby. I knew Emmett would have done the same thing if he'd been alive."

"He would have," Landon assured her. "But why leave the fake DNA results on the playground like you did?"

"I was hoping Quincy would get word of it. After the fact," she quickly added. "I certainly didn't want him showing up on that playground. I also thought if you believed Samantha was a Ryland, that you'd do everything within and even beyond the law to protect her."

"That was a given," Landon assured her. "She doesn't need Ryland blood for us to do that."

Tessa made a sound of agreement. They were a family married to the badge, and they wouldn't have let a snake like Quincy take the baby. She'd learned that firsthand, but then, Courtney probably felt she needed some insurance with those altered DNA results.

"What do you know about the body that turned up in Sweetwater Springs?" Landon asked. "It had a note similar to the one left on Emmett's body."

"I have no idea." And it sounded as if Courtney was telling the truth. "But that goes back to Quincy, doesn't it? I mean, he's the one with a personal vendetta against you."

Yes, but either Ward or Joel could have used that to set up Quincy. Of course, after what Courtney had just told them about Quincy sexually assaulting her, Tessa wanted the man to pay and pay hard. But she also wanted the same for the person behind the attacks. That way they could get double justice if that person turned out to be Quincy.

"We don't have anything to help with pinning this on Ward or Joel," Landon explained, "but we might have something on Quincy. There's a witness who could possibly help us nab Quincy on a parole violation."

"That won't help. He'll still send someone after Samantha."

Neither Landon nor Tessa could argue with that.

"I'm still weak from the delivery," Courtney added. "That's why I've had such a hard time keeping out of the path of these thugs."

"If you're weak, that's even more reason to let me help you," Landon insisted.

"I do need your help," Courtney agreed. "I have a plan to draw out Quincy. A plan that will put him behind bars for the rest of his life. I'll text you the details. And, Landon, please come. I'm begging you to help me."

Chapter Fifteen

As plans went, there was nothing about this one that Landon liked. Because it stood a good chance of getting Courtney killed. It was also a plan he couldn't stop, since Courtney had already set things in motion.

And that *motion* involved Landon.

"Let me get this straight," Grayson said, sounding as skeptical as Landon and Tessa were, and Landon had no trouble hearing every drop of that skepticism from the other end of the phone line. "Courtney wants you to pretend to bring her baby to the playground at the elementary school so that Quincy's hired guns will believe that she now has the child?"

That was it in a nutshell, and it would put a huge target on Courtney. "She said that Quincy knows Tessa and I have the child, so it'll make it more believable if I show up. Of course, it won't be the real baby. Courtney suggested a doll wrapped in a blanket."

Grayson cursed a blue streak—which had been Landon's first reaction, as well. "And then what? Quincy's men gun her down and take the 'child'?"

This wasn't going to sound any better than the first part of the plan. "Courtney believes they won't shoot her, because they won't risk hurting the baby." Maybe that would happen. After all, Quincy seemed determined to get his hands on his daughter.

"Then what?" Grayson snarled.

"Then she can use the child to draw out Quincy. When he tries to kill her and take the baby, then she can arrest him for conspiracy to commit murder, rape and other assorted felonies."

Grayson stayed quiet a moment, obviously processing that. "How much time do you have?"

"Not much. Courtney said she'll be at the playground in about thirty minutes from now. If I'm not there with the fake baby, then she said she'll just try to deal with the hired guns to draw Quincy out, that one way or another she's putting an end to this tonight."

More profanity. "And how does she know the hired guns will even be there?"

"Because they've been following her, and she's barely managed to escape them several times." Obviously, once they'd managed to capture her, because that was when the photo of her had been taken. "She said if she steps out into the open, the gunmen will be on to her right away."

"Call her back. Stop this plan," Grayson insisted.

"Already tried. Multiple times. She's not answering her phone."

Courtney probably didn't want Landon trying to talk her out of this, and part of him couldn't blame her. She was a desperate mother trying to protect her baby, but Courtney was taking a huge risk that might not pay off.

"Where are Tessa and you now?" Grayson asked.

"On the way to the sheriff's office. I wanted to leave Tessa behind, but—"

"If this is a trap, I don't want to have gunmen come

to the ranch," Tessa interrupted. It was an argument Landon had had with her from the moment they'd read the text with Courtney's plan.

Grayson clearly wasn't pleased about that, either. Welcome to the club. If there was a pecking order for displeasure here, Landon was at the top of it. Taking Tessa out in the open like this was dangerous.

"You're coming here to the sheriff's office?" Grayson asked.

"Yeah." Though that was a huge risk, too, considering everything that'd happened there in the past couple of days. "I have two armed ranch hands and Kade following me into town. I thought it best if the others stayed at the ranch. Just in case."

Though the ranch would probably be the safest place in the county since Tessa, he and the baby wouldn't be there.

"The two night deputies are here," Grayson explained. "Tessa can stay here with Kade and them. I'll go with you and the ranch hands to drop off the doll. I just wish I had more time to bring in backup."

So did Landon, but since Courtney wouldn't even answer her phone, there was no chance of putting a stop to this meeting. "I'll see you in ten minutes." Well, he would unless they encountered gunmen along the way.

"Stay low in the seat," Landon instructed Tessa. This was a farm road, no streetlights and only the spare lights from the ranches that dotted the area. It would be the perfect place for an attack.

"You think this will fool Quincy's men?" she asked.

She was looking down at Kimmie's doll, which they'd wrapped in a pink blanket. Landon was thankful it had been at the guesthouse or they would have had to go looking for one. When the little girl had brought over the gift for Samantha, Landon hadn't known it would come in so handy.

"It's dark," Landon answered. "And I'll make sure the blanket covers the doll's face."

It was a little precaution, but he'd taken a few bigger ones, too. Like Tessa and him both wearing Kevlar vests. And asking Kade and the ranch hands for backup. Landon had asked them simply because they'd been outside the guesthouse at the time. Patrolling. Right now every minute mattered.

"If shots are fired," Tessa said the moment he made the final turn for Silver Creek, "swear to me that you'll get down."

"They won't fire shots. Not as long as they think I have the baby."

"Swear it," she repeated.

Landon figured the little white lie he was about to tell might steady her nerves. "I'll get down."

And that was partly true. He would indeed get down if he could, but it was a playground. Not exactly a lot of places to take cover. And then there was Courtney to consider. He couldn't just leave her out in the open to be gunned down.

He saw the lights from Main Street just ahead and knew they had only a couple of minutes before he had to drop her off. "If this doesn't work," he added, "you're going into WITSEC first thing in the morning."

Tonight if he could arrange it.

But even that was a lie. Because either way, she'd have to leave. Catching Quincy wouldn't put an end to the danger if it was Joel or Ward who was after them.

However, it could get Courtney and the baby out of harm's way.

"So this is goodbye," she said, though judging from the slight huff she made, Tessa hadn't intended to say that aloud.

Landon considered another white lie, but after everything that had happened between them, he couldn't do that to Tessa. "Yes. More or less, anyway. If we get Quincy, I'll be tied up with that, and Grayson can finish up the WITSEC arrangements."

She nodded and glanced at him as if she wanted to say more. She didn't. Not for several long moments, anyway.

"I'm in love with you," Tessa blurted out, and that time she looked as if that was exactly what she wanted to say.

Hell.

Landon sure as heck hadn't seen that coming.

"I don't expect you to feel the same way," Tessa added, "and I don't expect you to do anything about it."

But she probably did expect him to give her some kind of response, and he would have done just that—even though he didn't have a clue what to say.

But something caught his eye.

They were still several blocks from the sheriff's office, on a stretch of Main Street with buildings and businesses on each side, but he saw the woman.

Courtney.

Landon got just a glimpse of her before she darted into an alley. But he got more than a glimpse of the two men who were running after her. One of those men lifted his gun, aimed it at Courtney.

And he fired.

"GET DOWN!" LANDON SHOUTED to Tessa.

He pushed her lower to the seat, but she was headed in that direction anyway. She also threw open the glove compartment and took out a gun. But before Tessa could even get the gun ready to fire, another shot rang out.

The bullet slammed into the windshield of Landon's truck.

So much for their theory that these goons wouldn't fire because they wouldn't want to risk hitting the baby. If Samantha had been in the truck with them, she could have already been hurt. Or worse.

That gave Tessa a jolt of anger. Not that she needed the thought of that to do it, but it helped. She was fed up with someone putting Landon and the others in danger. Fed up with all these attempts to kill her. She wanted to shout out, demanding answers, but the gunmen obviously didn't have answers on their minds.

They fired more shots into the truck.

"Hold on," Landon said. "I'm getting us out of here."

He threw the truck into Reverse, hit the accelerator and just as quickly had to slam on the brakes. He cursed, and it took her a moment to realize why. The truck with Kade and the two ranch hands was behind them.

But so were two more gunmen.

There was one on each side of the street, and they were shooting into Kade's truck. While in Reverse, as well, Kade screeched out of there, getting out of the path of those bullets, but Tessa figured he would double back to help them.

"Text Grayson." Landon tossed her his phone. "He needs to stay the hell back for now. I don't want him hit with friendly fire."

Neither did she, and while she did the text, she got

a dose of what could be friendly fire. Landon leaned out from his truck window and fired at the guys behind them.

That was like turning on a switch. Suddenly, shots started slamming into the truck, and they were trapped with gunmen both in front of and behind them. Landon put the truck back in gear, jerked the steering wheel to the right and drove into one of the alleys.

But it was a dead end.

"Come on," Landon told her. He took his phone and shoved it in his pocket. "Move fast."

She did. Tessa hurried out of the truck, but she had no idea where they were going. She knew all the shops on Main Street, but she certainly didn't know the back alleys. Thankfully, Landon did. With his left hand gripping her wrist, they ran toward a Dumpster, and he yanked her behind it.

Just as the next shot came.

This one smacked into the Dumpster, the bullet pinging off the metal, which acted like a shield for them. But it wouldn't be a shield for long if all four of those thugs came in there with guns blazing. For now the four stayed back, using the fronts of the buildings for cover.

"Shoot them if they try to come closer," Landon told her, and he began to kick at a wooden fence on the left side of the Dumpster.

Tessa kept watch and tried to tamp down her breathing. Hard to do, though, because she felt ready to hyperventilate. It didn't help when one of the men darted out. She fired.

Missed.

And she fired again.

She wasn't sure if she winged him or not, but at least it got him scurrying back behind the building.

Landon gave the fence a few more kicks, and it gave way. Tessa had no idea what was on the other side, but it was behind the secondhand store run by a local charity group. The area wasn't very wide but was littered with all sorts of discarded furniture and another Dumpster. That was where Landon took her.

There wasn't much light at the back of the building. The only illumination came from Main Street and a pale moon, and there were enough shadows that it would be easy for a gunman to be right on them before she saw him.

"Keep watch there." He tipped his head to the alley between the store and a hair salon. The alley where she'd seen Courtney running. But there was no sign of her now.

What had gone wrong?

Had Quincy realized this was a trick and sent his thugs after her? Probably. This plan had been so risky right from the start, and now Courtney was running for her life again. But then, so were Landon and she.

While he kept watch of the area they'd just left, he also texted Grayson. No doubt to let him know their location. The moment he did that, though, he eased his phone into his pocket and put his finger to his mouth in a "stay quiet" gesture.

And Tessa soon knew why.

She heard the footsteps, and they were coming from both sides of the thrift store. Either the four gunmen had separated and were now in pairs or else this was someone else.

Tessa pulled in her breath. Held it. Waiting.

Other than the footsteps, everything was so quiet. At least for a couple of heart-stopping seconds.

"Ryland?" someone called out. She didn't recognize the person's voice, but it was likely one of Quincy's hired guns. Or whoever's hired guns they were. "Do the smart thing and give us the kid. That's all we want."

So definitely Quincy's men.

Well, maybe.

Unless this was yet another attempt to set him up.

"The kid's not in your truck," the guy continued. "We checked. So tell us where you have her stashed and you and your kin won't die."

Maybe it was out of frustration or maybe just to let the jerk know he wasn't cooperating, but Landon fired a shot in the direction of the voice.

The man cursed, calling Landon some vile names.

"It's me you want," someone else shouted.

Courtney.

Tessa couldn't tell where exactly she was, but she was close. Maybe just one building over.

Now Landon cursed. "Stay down!" he yelled to Courtney.

"No. I'm not going to let Tessa and you die for me. Just promise me you'll take care of my baby."

And then it was as if the world exploded.

The blast came like a fireball to their right. In the same area where Courtney had just been. It was deafening, and the flurry of shots that followed it didn't help. Tessa couldn't tell where the gunmen were, but she had no trouble figuring out where they were aiming all those shots.

At Courtney.

"Don't get up," Landon told her.

But that was exactly what he did. He leaned out from the Dumpster and fired two shots. Even over the din of the other bullets, Tessa could hear that the last one he fired sounded different.

"I got one of them," Landon snarled.

Tessa hated that he'd been forced to kill a man, but she wished he could do that to all four of them.

The fact that one of their comrades had fallen didn't stop the other three from firing. And running. They were heading away from Landon and her and were almost certainly in pursuit of Courtney.

"Stay behind me," Landon instructed. "I need to get you to Grayson so I can help Courtney."

Tessa wanted that. Well, she wanted part of it, anyway. She wanted Landon to save Courtney, but Tessa wasn't certain she'd be any safer with Grayson than she was with Landon.

Landon got them moving again. This time toward the back of the hair salon. It was also the direction of the sheriff's office. Of course, that was still buildings away. To Tessa, it suddenly felt like miles and miles, and it didn't help that the shots were still ringing out.

And getting closer.

God, were those men coming back?

Part of her hoped that meant they'd given up on chasing Courtney, but her mind went to a much worse scenario. They could have already killed Courtney and were now doubling back to take care of the other lawmen, Landon and her. Since Kade, Grayson and heaven knew who else were out here, the thugs could be firing those shots at them.

There was no Dumpster at the back of the salon, so Landon pulled her into the recessed exit at the rear of the building. It wasn't very deep, just enough for them to fit side by side, and like before, Landon instructed her to keep watch. She did, and Tessa listened.

The shots had stopped, and she could no longer hear footsteps. In fact, she couldn't hear anything, and that caused her heartbeat to race even more. Something was wrong.

And she soon realized what.

The door behind them flew open, and someone put a gun to Landon's head.

"Move and you die," the man growled.

IF IT WOULD have helped, Landon would have cursed, but it wouldn't have done any good. One of the thugs had a gun pointed at him, and that meant Landon had to do something fast before the thug killed him and then turned that gun on Tessa.

"Drop your guns," the man ordered. "Do it!" he added, and this time he put the gun against Tessa's head.

Landon couldn't risk it, so he did drop his gun, but he didn't drop it far. Just by his feet. Tessa did the same, and hopefully, that meant he could grab them if it came down to it. Of course, in the small space, Landon might be able to overpower the guy.

"Who hired you?" Landon asked.

Though he figured getting an answer, much less a truthful one, would be next to impossible. Still, he had to try while he also came up with a plan to get Tessa out of there.

The guy didn't say a word, but Landon could hear some chattering. Probably from a communications earpiece he was wearing. Landon wished he could hear the voice well enough to figure out who was giving these orders.

Landon's phone buzzed in his pocket. Likely Grayson. But he didn't dare reach for it. Grayson would take his silence as a sign he needed help.

"There's no reason for you to keep Tessa," Landon tried again.

"Shut up," the man barked. Judging from the earpiece chatter, he was still getting his orders.

Landon looked at Tessa. He expected for her to be terrified, and she probably was, but that wasn't a look of terror in her eyes. It was determination.

And something else.

She didn't move an inch, but Tessa angled her eyes to the left. It was Landon's blind side because of where he was in the recessed doorway, but Tessa must have seen something. Grayson maybe? Then, she lowered her eyes to the ground for a second.

Landon hoped like the devil that he was making the right interpretation of what she was trying to tell him—to get down—and he readied himself to respond.

But nothing happened.

The moments just crawled by with the thug behind him getting an earful from his equally thuggy boss. And with Tessa and him waiting. Landon didn't want to wait much longer, though, because there were two other hired guns out there somewhere, and he didn't want them joining their buddy who had a gun on Tessa.

"Now!" Tessa finally said. She didn't shout it, but she caught hold of Landon's arms and dragged him to the ground with her.

Just as the shot blasted through the air.

Even though he'd been expecting something to happen, his heart jumped to his throat, and for one sickening split second, he thought maybe Tessa had been hit. But she wasn't the one who took the bullet.

It was thug number two behind them.

Both the thug and his gun clattered to the ground, and Landon didn't waste any time gathering up their weapons and getting Tessa the heck out of there. Since he figured it was an ally who'd killed the guy, he followed the direction of the shot, and he got just a glimpse of Courtney as she ran away. She was the one who'd fired the shot.

But now someone was firing at her.

The bullets blasted into the walls of the building as she disappeared around the corner. Landon needed to disappear, too, or at least move Tessa out of what was to become a line of fire. It didn't take long for that to happen. The shots came, and Landon pulled her between the hair salon and the barbershop.

It was darker here than in the back and other side alleys. That was because the perky yellow window awnings on the side of the salon were blocking out the moonlight. Landon could barely see his hand in front of his face, and that definitely wasn't a good thing. He didn't want to run into one of the two remaining gunmen.

Of course, there could be more.

Since that wasn't exactly a comforting thought, he pushed it aside and pulled Tessa into a recessed side exit of the barbershop. They couldn't stay there long, but it would give him a chance to check in with Grayson.

"See who texted me," Landon said, handing Tessa his phone and her gun. Since he didn't want anyone crashing through the door as the other thug had done, he volleyed glances all around him. And listened for footsteps.

"Grayson," she verified. "He wants us to try to get to the bakery shop just up the street. He says we should go inside because the other deputies and he are creating a net around the area. They're closing in to find the gunmen, and they don't want us caught in cross fire."

Landon didn't want that, either, but the bakery had been closed for months now and was probably locked up tight. It was also three buildings away from the barbershop. Not very far distance-wise, but each step could be their last.

"What should I text Grayson?" she asked.

Her voice was shaking. So was she. But then, she'd just had a man gunned down inches behind her. Thank God Courtney was a good shot or things could have gone a lot worse. Though Landon hated that Courtney was having to fight a battle when she'd given birth only a week earlier. It didn't matter that Courtney was a federal agent; her body couldn't be ready for this.

"Give Grayson our location and tell him we're on our way to the bakery." Landon hoped they were, anyway.

It was too risky to head to the street. The lighting would be better there, but it would also make it too easy for the thugs to spot them. Instead, he led Tessa to the back of the building again, and he stopped at the corner to look around.

Nothing.

Well, nothing that he could see, anyway.

He doubted Courtney was still around to take someone out for him, and that meant he had to be vigilant even though he couldn't see squat. However, he could hear. Mainly Tessa's breathing. It was way too fast,

and Landon touched her arm, hoping it would give her
a little reassurance. It was the best he could do under
the circumstances because he had to keep her moving.

Landon dragged in a deep breath, hooked his arm
around Tessa's waist and hurried out from the cover
of the building. No shots, but Landon knew that could
change at any second. As soon as he reached the other
side of the barbershop, he stopped again and made sure
there wasn't anyone in the alley ready to ambush them.

He cursed the darkness and the shadows, and he
moved himself in front of Tessa, racing across the open
space to the next building. Two more and they'd be at
the bakery. Landon only hoped by the time they made
it there, Grayson would have it secured.

"Let's move," Landon whispered to her, and they
started across the back of the next building. But they
didn't get far before Tessa stumbled.

Landon tightened his grip on her to try to keep her
from falling, but she tumbled to the ground anyway.
Then he darn near tripped, as well. That was because
there was something on the ground. And Landon immediately got a sickening feeling in the pit of his stomach.

Because that something was a dead body.

Chapter Sixteen

Tessa barely managed to choke back the scream in time. A scream would have given away their position, but it was hard not to react when she fell onto the body.

The person was still warm. And there was blood. But Tessa had no doubt that the person was dead, because there was no movement whatsoever.

"Courtney," she whispered on a gasp.

"No, it's not," Landon assured her. But he did more than give her a reassurance. He got her back to her feet and moved her into the alley on the side of a building. Probably because the person who'd done this was still close by.

The light was so dim in this part of the alley that it took Tessa several heart-racing moments to realize Landon was right. It wasn't Courtney. It was a man.

Quincy.

His wheelchair was only a few feet from his body and had been toppled over. There was also a gun near his hand.

What had happened here?

Tessa could think of a couple of possibilities. Maybe he'd been shot in cross fire by the thugs he'd hired? Or maybe the thugs worked for someone else? It was also possible Courtney had done this. After all, Quincy was a threat to the baby, her and maybe anyone else who crossed his path.

It was hard to mourn the death of a snake like Quincy, but Tessa realized the goons were still around because she heard several more shots. If they did indeed work for Quincy, maybe they didn't know their boss was dead.

"We need to keep moving," Landon told her under his breath.

They did, and Tessa forced herself to start running. Landon helped with that again. He took hold of her, and they ran through the back of the alley to the next building. They were close now to the old bakery where Grayson wanted them to go, but it still seemed miles away.

More shots came.

And these were close. Too close. One of them smacked into the wood fence that divided the alley from the town's park, and the shot had come from the area near Quincy's body.

Tessa hoped that once the thugs saw that Quincy was dead, they'd back off, that no more bullets would be fired. But almost immediately, another shot rang out. Then another.

Landon slipped his arm around her, but it wasn't preparation to get them running again. He pulled her deeper in the alley, and his gaze fired all around them. He stepped in front of her when they heard some movement near Quincy's body, and Tessa got just a glimpse of not one of the gunmen but Courtney.

The woman was leaning over Quincy and touched her fingers to his neck. It seemed as if she was making sure he was dead.

"Courtney," Landon whispered.

Tessa glanced out again and saw Courtney's head whip in their direction. She got to a standing position and turned, heading their way.

Just as there was another shot.

This one smacked right into Courtney's chest, and Tessa heard her friend gasp in pain as she dropped to the ground.

Oh, God.

Courtney had been hit.

The new wave of adrenaline slammed into Tessa, and she would have bolted out to help her if Landon hadn't stopped her. Landon cursed and stepped out from the building, but he almost certainly couldn't see the shooter, since the bullet had been fired from the alley of the building over from them.

Courtney groaned, the sound of sheer pain, and while she was gasping for breath, she was also trying to lift her gun. No doubt trying to stop the gunman before he put another bullet in her.

"She's wearing Kevlar," Landon said.

Because her instincts were screaming for her to help Courtney, it took Tessa a moment to process that. The bullet had hit the Kevlar, not her, and that meant she might not die. Not from that shot, at least, but the next one went into the ground right next to her. The only reason it didn't hit her was that Courtney managed to roll to the side. But Courtney was still writhing in pain, still gasping for air and clearly couldn't get to her feet to run.

Landon's phone buzzed, and Tessa saw Grayson's name on the screen. He passed it back to her so she could answer it.

"What's your position?" Grayson asked.

"We're still two buildings away from the bakery. We need help. Can you get to us?"

"Not right now. We're pinned down. There's a sniper on one of the roofs, and every time we move, he fires a shot. He hit one of the reserve deputies."

That didn't help steady her heart. "Courtney's been hit, too."

Grayson belted out some profanity. "We'll get there as soon as we can." And he ended the call.

Tessa knew that he would, but soon might not be soon enough. Plus, there was no way an ambulance could get anywhere near the scene. Not with all the gunfire.

"I've got to help Courtney," Landon whispered, but Tessa heard the hesitation in his voice. He made a split-second glance at her as she slipped his phone back into his pocket. "Stay put and keep watch around you."

That was the only warning Tessa got before Landon stepped out. He pivoted in the direction of the shooter, and he fired. Tessa prayed that would put an end to the immediate threat.

It didn't.

She saw the gunman's hand snake out, but this time he didn't fire at Courtney. He fired at Landon. Her heart nearly went out of her chest as Landon scrambled to the ground, using a pair of trash cans for cover.

As Landon had told her, she kept watch around her, but Tessa also tried to do something to stop that thug from gunning down both Courtney and Landon. Courtney was in the open, an easy target, and bullets could go through the trash cans where Landon had ducked down. She had to help. She couldn't just stand there and watch them die.

She waited, watching, and when she saw the gunman's hand come out again, she took aim and fired. Almost immediately, the guy howled in pain, and while she certainly hadn't killed him, at least she'd managed to injure his shooting hand. However, that didn't stop him from firing.

Again and again.

The man was cursing, and he was making grunting sounds of someone in pain, but that didn't stop him from pulling the trigger, and he was shooting at Landon. Maybe because he thought Landon had been the one to fire that shot at him.

Courtney moved again, managing to get on her side. And she even tried to take aim, but she was clearly in too much pain to defend herself. The gunman's next bullet slammed into her again, and Tessa heard Courtney's gasping sound of pain.

Mercy, she'd been shot, and this time Tessa didn't think the bullet had gone into the Kevlar. Landon must not have thought so, either, because he came from behind the trash cans and he raced out. Not toward Courtney.

But toward the alley where the gunman was getting ready to send another shot right into Courtney. To finish her off, no doubt.

Landon put a stop to that.

He pulled up, pivoted and double-tapped the trigger.

Even though there had been so many shots fired all around them, those two sent Tessa's heart into overdrive. Because now both Landon and Courtney were in the open, and if Landon's two shots didn't work, then the gunman would try to kill them both again.

Tessa was ready to do something to make sure that

didn't happen when she heard the movement behind her. She started to whirl around, bringing up her weapon in the same motion, but it was already too late. Before she could even see who was behind her, someone hooked an arm around her neck. Stripped her gun from her hand.

And whoever it was put a gun to her head.

HELL. THE GUNMAN wasn't down.

Landon didn't know how the guy had managed to stay on his feet, not after Landon had put two bullets in him. He'd aimed for the guy's chest, figuring he, too, was wearing a vest, but two shots at this close range should have sent the guy to the ground. They didn't.

The man was gasping just as Courtney was doing, but he not only stayed upright but also pulled the trigger. Thank God the shot was off or Landon would have been a dead man.

Another shot came in Landon's direction, and he scrambled to the side. This time when he aimed, he went for the kill. As much as he would have liked to have this guy alive to answer questions, that wasn't going to happen. Landon put two bullets in his head. This time it worked, and the guy didn't manage to get off another shot before he collapsed onto the ground.

Just in case there was some shred of life left in the clown, Landon kicked away the man's weapon. There was no time to check and see if he was truly dead, because he didn't want to stay out of Tessa's line of sight for another second. Plus, he could still hear gunshots just up the street, which meant Grayson and the others were fighting for their lives.

He hurried to Courtney to see how bad her injuries were. There was blood, but from what Landon could tell, the injury was to her shoulder, a part of her that the Kevlar hadn't protected. She would live. Well, she would if she didn't bleed out, and that meant he had to clear the area so they could get her an ambulance.

"Clamp your hand over the wound," he instructed Courtney.

He dragged the wheelchair in front of her so she'd have some cover, and then he turned to check on Tessa.

Landon's heart slammed against his chest.

Tessa was barely visible at the back corner of the building where he'd left her. But she wasn't alone. Landon couldn't see who was with her, but whoever it was had a gun.

"I'm sorry," Tessa said. "I didn't see him in time."

Landon hated that she even felt the need to apologize. With all the bullets flying and the chaos, it would have been hard to hear someone coming up behind her. Besides, they hadn't even known the locations or even the number of the other gunmen. With this guy and the sniper on the roof, there were at least two, but Landon figured there could be others waiting to strike.

For now, though, he had to figure out how to get Tessa away from this goon before one of his comrades showed up to help. To do that, he had to stay alive, so he, too, ducked behind the wheelchair. It was lousy cover, but it was metal and might do the trick. Besides, he didn't plan to be behind cover for long. Not with Tessa in immediate danger.

Even though the timing sucked, Landon thought of what she'd said to him in the car.

I'm in love with you.

Landon hadn't had a chance to react to that, hadn't even had much time to think about it, but now those words troubled him. Because if Tessa was indeed truly in love with him, she might do anything to try to keep him safe. That might include sacrificing herself.

"I don't know what you want," Landon said to the guy, "but tell me what it'll take for you to release Tessa."

Nothing. For some long heart-pounding moments. Then Landon saw the person lean forward and whisper something in Tessa's ear. He couldn't hear what the guy said, but he got a better look at him. He was wearing a ski mask like the other thugs who'd been trying to kill them.

Not good.

Because it was hard to negotiate with someone who would murder for money.

"He wants Courtney," Tessa relayed. Her voice sounded a lot steadier than Landon figured she actually was. Trying to put on a good front.

Or maybe it was more than that.

She sounded angry. Perhaps because the guy had managed to sneak up on her, or maybe he'd added something else to that whisper.

"Courtney?" Landon questioned. "Why her?"

Landon figured he wasn't going to get a straight answer to that question, and he didn't. In fact, he didn't get an answer at all.

But it did make him think.

All along they'd believed the attacks were about Tessa, about what she possibly saw the night Emmett was murdered. The other theory they'd had was the attacks were connected to him, that Quincy was behind them. But maybe Quincy was after only Courtney and the baby, and Tessa and he just got in the way.

"Quincy's dead," he told the thug in case he hadn't

noticed the body. "I hope he paid you in advance or you're out of luck."

The guy whispered something else to Tessa. "He still wants Courtney. He wants you to step aside."

Well, hell. Quincy must have left orders to kill Courtney even if something happened to him.

"If you kill Courtney, you'll make the baby an orphan," Landon tried again. "Whatever Quincy paid you or planned to pay you, I'll give you double. All you have to do is let Tessa go."

Of course, that might just prompt the guy to take her hostage, but every second he had a gun to her head was a second that could take this situation from bad to worse.

And it got worse, all right.

Landon heard the sound of an engine. Not a car. But rather a motorcycle. And it was coming at them fast. It didn't take long for it to come barreling up the alley, and Landon saw yet one more thing he didn't want to see.

Another ski-mask-wearing thug.

He brought the motorcycle to a stop right beside Tessa and his partner in crime. Landon wanted to send a shot right into the guy's head, but the thug holding Tessa might retaliate and do the same to her.

"I can pay you off, too," Landon told the second thug. He practically had to shout to be heard over the motorcycle engine. "With Quincy dead, wouldn't you rather have all that money than end up dead?"

"I got no plans to die," the one on the motorcycle shouted back. He was bulky, the size of a linebacker and armed to the hilt.

He killed the engine and climbed off, and Landon could have sworn his heart skipped some beats when he saw what was happening. The thugs switched places, and the whispering one who was holding Tessa dragged her onto the motorcycle with him.

Hell. Time was up. Landon couldn't let the guy just drive off with Tessa, because he was certain he'd never see her alive again.

"When you're ready to give us Courtney," the bulky guy said, "then you'll get Tessa back."

Landon doubted that. No way would they leave Tessa alive. "Take me instead," Landon bargained.

Tessa frantically shook her head and moved as if ready to cooperate with this stupid plan that would get her killed. Yeah, she'd been right about that *I'm in love with you*. She was putting her life ahead of his, and that wasn't going to happen.

"Lawmen don't make good hostages." The bulky guy again, though the other thug, the whisperer, said something else to Tessa. Something that Landon couldn't catch.

But whatever it was caused Tessa's shoulders to snap back.

"Landon, watch out!" she shouted.

The bulky guy took aim at Landon, and Landon had no choice but to fire.

Chapter Seventeen

The man who still had hold of Tessa yanked her to the side of the motorcycle. Just as the sound of two shots cracked through the air. One of those shots had come from Landon. The other, the thug who'd ridden up on the motorcycle.

Tessa hit the ground, hard, so hard that it knocked the breath out of her, but she fought to get up because she had to stop the big guy from shooting at Landon again. She managed to catch on to his leg, and it off-balanced him just enough to cause his next shot to go up in the air.

Landon's didn't.

His bullet went into the guy's shoulder. It didn't kill him, but it sent him scrambling for cover.

The uninjured gunman didn't do anything to help his partner. He latched on to Tessa's hair, dragging her back in front of him. Once again, she was his human shield, and Landon wouldn't have a clean shot to put an end to this.

"Get down!" she shouted to Landon.

He didn't, but at least he hurried back behind the wheelchair next to Courtney. Courtney was still moaning in pain. Still bleeding, too, from the looks of it, but at least she was alive. For now. And so was Landon. Tessa needed to do something to make sure it stayed that way.

"I'll go with them," she called out.

"No, you won't!" Landon answered. "They'll kill you."

Almost certainly. Tessa didn't want to die, but at least this way, Landon would be safe, and he would be able to get Courtney to the hospital. Samantha wouldn't be an orphan. Of course, if these men killed her, it wouldn't end the danger to Courtney, Landon or the baby, but maybe Landon could get them all to a safe house before the gunmen could regroup and attack again.

Tessa tried to hold on to that hope, and since she was hoping, she added that she could find a way to escape. Maybe she could do that once they had her wherever they were going to take her. All she would need was some kind of distraction.

The injured thug crawled to his partner and whispered something to him that Tessa didn't catch, but whatever it was, it got her captor moving. He had his left hand fisted in her hair, and with the gun jammed against her temple, he hauled her to her feet, keeping behind her. He then began to back his way to the motorcycle.

"We'll trade Tessa for Courtney," the wounded man shouted out to Landon. "You've got thirty seconds to decide."

Tessa knew that wasn't going to happen. No way would she make a trade like that, even though Courtney immediately tried to sit up. Tessa got so caught up in trying to figure out how to stop this that she nearly missed something.

Something critical.

Why was the wounded man doing all the talking? He was having trouble breathing and couldn't stand, and yet the whispering guy had let him bark out the order for the trade.

Why?

Was it because she might recognize his voice?

Even though her mind was whirling, she tried to recall those whispers, but he'd purposely muffled his voice, and that meant this was likely either Joel or Ward. Too bad the men were about the same height and build, or she would have been able to tell from that.

So Tessa went with a bluff. Except in this case, she figured her bluff had a fifty-fifty chance of succeeding.

"The man holding me is Ward," she shouted.

Bingo.

Even though it'd been a bluff, she knew she was right when she heard him mumble some profanity under his breath. Then he cursed some more, much louder.

Yes, definitely Ward.

This time it was Landon who cursed. "How the hell could you do this? You're supposed to uphold the law, not break it."

"Breaking it pays a lot more than upholding it," Ward answered. "Now, bring Courtney to me, or I start shooting."

"You're going to start shooting no matter what I say or do," Landon countered, but Tessa saw him readjusting his position. Probably so he could take the shot if he got it, but Ward was staying right behind her.

But Ward wasn't staying put, either. He was inching her backward, but Tessa couldn't tell if he was trying to get her on the motorcycle or simply closer to his hired gun. Yes, the guy was injured, but that didn't mean he couldn't kill her.

"Who killed Quincy? You?"

"Possibly. He got in the way. He was here to get Courtney, but I never had any intentions of letting him have her."

"Because you want to kill her yourself," Landon concluded.

"She knows too much."

"About what?" Courtney asked, her breath gusting through the groans of pain.

"You don't really want me to go into that here, do you? Because then I'd have to kill Landon."

"I already know," Landon assured him.

It was a lie, but Tessa could feel the muscles in Ward's arm turn to steel.

"This is about your dirty dealings with Joel," Landon went on. "Both Tessa and Courtney were investigating him, and you believed they were on to you. They weren't, but I was."

Tessa hadn't thought it possible, but Ward's arm stiffened even more. "Joel will turn on you," she said.

"Joel's dead," Ward whispered. "Or soon will be. Before he dies, he'll confess to all of this. Including Courtney's murder. And yours."

She was pretty sure that wasn't a bluff. In fact, Ward had no doubt already arranged for Joel's death, and with Ward's connections in law enforcement, he could indeed set up Joel. Then Ward could walk away a free man with all the money he'd made from his business deals with Joel.

Well, he could walk if Landon, Courtney and she were dead.

That meant no matter what Landon and she did, the bottom line was that Ward would kill them. And he would do that before Landon got a chance to tell anyone else. That meant Tessa had to do something fast.

But what?

She went with the first thing that popped into her head. "Landon, did you record Ward's confession with your phone?" she called out.

"Sure did," Landon answered. She doubted he had, but judging from the way Ward started cursing, he didn't know it was a lie. She could see Landon put his left hand in his pocket. "And I just sent it to Grayson. Now every lawman in Silver Creek knows you're a dirty agent."

A feral sound came from Ward's throat, and Tessa knew he was about to shoot her in the head. She didn't waste a second. She dropped to the ground. Or rather that was what she tried to do, but Ward held on to her hair, yanking it so hard that she couldn't choke back a scream of pain.

Not good.

Because her scream brought Landon to his feet. He bolted toward them, firing a shot at the wounded gunman. Tessa wasn't at the right angle to see where his bullet had gone, but since the gunman didn't return fire, she figured Landon had hit his intended target.

Ward moved his gun, too. Aiming it at Landon. But Tessa rammed her elbow into his stomach. It didn't off-balance him, definitely didn't get him to drop his gun, but he had to re-aim, and that was just enough time for Landon to make it to them.

Landon plowed into them, sending all three of them to the ground.

Tessa felt the jolt go through her entire body, and while she didn't lose her breath this time, Ward's gun whacked against the side of her head. At first she thought it was just from the impact, but he did it again.

The pain exploded in her head.

But even with the pain, she heard Landon curse the man, and he dropped his own gun so he could latch on to Ward's wrist with both hands. It stopped Ward from hitting her again. Stopped him from aiming his gun at either of them, but Ward let go of her hair so he could punch Landon with his left hand. And he just kept on punching and kicking him.

Tessa tried to get out of the fray just so she could find some way to stop Ward, but it was hard to move with the struggle going on. She fought, too, clawing at Ward's face, but the man was in such a rage that she wasn't even sure he felt anything.

However, she did.

Ward backhanded her so hard Tessa could have sworn she saw stars. She fell and landed against the hulking hired gun—and yes, he was dead—but before she could spring back to her feet, Landon and Ward were already in a fierce battle. Landon was punching him, but Ward was bashing his gun against Landon's face.

Mercy, there was already so much blood.

Tessa frantically looked around and spotted the dead guy's gun. She wasn't familiar with the weapon and prayed it didn't go off and hit Landon. Still, it was the only thing she had right now. She scooped it up and tried to aim it at Ward.

But she couldn't.

Ward and Landon were tangled together so that she

couldn't risk firing. Someone else had no trouble doing that, though. In the distance she heard a fresh round of gunfire. Grayson, the deputies and that sniper. Maybe she could try to put an end to this so she could help them. Until the area was safe, the ambulance wasn't going to be able to get to Courtney to save her life.

Maybe Landon's, too.

In that moment she hated Ward so much that she wanted to jump into that fight and punch him. But that wouldn't do Landon any good. He was battling for his life. For Courtney's and her lives, too, and Tessa was powerless to help him.

She waited, praying and watching for any opening where she would have a shot. But then she saw something that caused her breath to vanish.

Ward quit hitting Landon with the gun.

And Ward managed to point it at him.

He fired.

Tessa thought maybe she screamed. She screamed inside her head, anyway, and the scream got louder when Landon dropped back.

Oh, God. Had he been shot?

She'd heard that when some people died, their lives flashed before their eyes, and even though she wasn't dying, it happened to her. Tessa saw everything. Her time with Landon. All the mistakes she'd made. All the chances she'd lost to have a life with him.

Ward could have just taken all of that away. He was trying to make sure he killed Landon. He took aim at him again.

Everything inside her went still. And then the rage came. Even though Landon was still too close to fire, she shot the gun into the ground next to the dead man.

Ward whipped his head in her direction, turning his gun toward her. But Landon reacted faster than Ward did. Landon lunged at the man, twisting his wrist so that the gun was pointed at Ward's chest.

Ward fired.

Like his hired thugs, Ward was wearing a bullet-proof vest, so Tessa expected him to make the same groan of pain that she'd heard from Courtney. But what she heard was a gurgling sound. Because Ward's bullet hadn't gone into his vest but rather his neck.

He was bleeding to death right in front of them.

Tessa didn't care. If fact, she wished him dead after all the hurt and misery he'd caused. Instead, she looked at Landon and was terrified of what she might see.

His face was bloody. So was his left arm.

"The bullet just grazed me," he said.

It looked like more than a graze to her, but at least he wasn't dead or dying.

The relief came so hard and fast that she probably would have dropped to her knees if she hadn't heard Courtney groan again.

"Check on her," Landon instructed. "I'll watch this snake."

Tessa nodded, and she somehow managed to get her feet moving. Though she'd made it only a few steps when she heard Ward speak.

Or rather he laughed.

"You think you got Emmett's killer," he said, his voice not much louder than a whisper. Still, Tessa had no trouble hearing it. "You didn't. He's still on the roof, and he's probably killing more Rylands right now."

And with that, Ward drew the last breath he'd ever take.

Chapter Eighteen

Landon didn't want to be stitched up. Hell, he didn't want to be in the hospital ER. He wanted to be out there with Grayson and the rest of his cousins so they could catch Emmett's killer. At least, he was dead certain he wanted that until he took one look at Tessa.

She was staring at him as if she expected him to keel over at any moment.

He was probably looking at her the same way, though.

She'd already gotten a couple of stitches on her forehead where Ward had hit her with his gun. Half of her face was covered in bruises, and there was way too much worry in her eyes. Of course, none of that worry was for her own injuries. It was for Courtney's and his.

"I'm fine," Landon told her, something he'd already said a couple of times. Judging from the way she was nibbling on her lip, he might have to keep repeating it.

"You were shot. Courtney was shot. And Emmett's killer is still out there."

"The only thing that you left out is that Courtney and I are going to be fine."

The doctor had already told them that. Courtney had lost plenty of blood, but the bullet was a through-and-through, so she wouldn't even need surgery. She'd been admitted to the hospital, though, for a transfusion, and Landon had made sure the security guard was posted outside her door. If that sniper, aka Emmett's killer, managed to get away from Grayson's team, Landon didn't want the snake slithering into the hospital to try to finish off a job for his dead boss.

"Are you going to be fine?" Landon asked Tessa the moment the nurse stepped away from him.

She nodded, but he wondered if that was the biggest lie of the night. This nightmare was going to stay with her for the rest of her life, and it wasn't even over yet.

Landon got up from the examining table, trying not to wince. He pretty much failed at that. It felt as if he'd just gotten his butt kicked, but if he could have pretended he wasn't aching from head to toe, he would have. Each wince caused Tessa to look even more worried.

He shut the door and went to her. Not that he thought they needed the privacy, but his mind was still on that sniper showing up. Or at least it was on the sniper until Tessa leaned in and kissed him.

Gently.

Both of them had busted lips, so anything long and deep would have caused some pain. Even that light touch seemed to cause her to flinch, just a little.

"Sorry," he said.

"Don't be. You saved my life." There were tears in her eyes now.

"You saved mine, too."

And since he wanted to do something to rid her of those tears, he risked the pain and kissed her for real. There probably was some pain involved, but his body must have shut it out. Tessa's, as well. Because the sound she made wasn't one of pain. It was that silky little purr of pleasure.

Landon might have just kept on kissing her if the door hadn't opened and Grayson hadn't walked in. Tessa tried to move away from Landon as if they'd been caught doing something wrong, but Landon kept his arm around her.

"Are all the deputies okay?" Landon immediately asked.

"Everyone's fine. We caught the sniper," Grayson said.

Those six words made Landon feel as if a ten-ton weight had been lifted off his shoulders. And his heart. Even though one of the reserve deputies had been injured, none of his cousins had been hurt in this fiasco, and they had Emmett's killer.

Landon cleared his throat before he spoke. "The sniper's alive?"

Grayson nodded. "And he's talking. His name is Albert Hawkins, a former cop. Once he heard Ward was dead and had fingered him for Emmett's murder, I guess he figured if he talked, it might get him a plea deal with the DA or at least get the death penalty off the table."

Landon wasn't sure he wanted deals to be made with his cousin's killer, but as long as he spent the rest of his life behind bars *and* gave them some answers, then he could accept it. Well, he could accept it as much as he could anything about Emmett's murder. And while he didn't like that a killer would be giving them those answers, the man who'd orchestrated all of this—Ward—was past the point of being able to explain the hellish plan he'd set in motion.

"Did Ward have Emmett murdered because of me?" Landon asked, and he hoped it was an answer he could live with.

Grayson took a moment, probably because this was as hard for him as it was for Landon. "No. It wasn't because of you. Ward sent Hawkins to kidnap Tessa so they could use her to find Courtney. Emmett showed up to talk to Tessa about Joel, and when he tried to stop the kidnapping, Hawkins killed him."

Tessa shuddered, shook her head. "So I'm the reason Emmett was killed."

Landon wanted to nip this in the bud. "No, he died because he was doing what was right." Landon would have done the same thing in Emmett's place. But it might take him a while to convince Tessa that this wasn't her fault.

"I wish I could remember," she whispered.

Landon hoped she didn't get that wish. Judging from Grayson's expression, he felt the same way.

"Hawkins gave you a huge dose of drugs that night," Grayson explained. "He said you were fighting like a wildcat, so he hit you on the head and drugged you and he's the one who put that tracking device in your neck."

Landon gave that some thought. "So the plan was to let her go so that she'd lead him to Courtney?"

Grayson gave another nod.

Landon had to hand it to Ward—it was a plan that could have worked. Even if Tessa had remembered who'd murdered Emmett, she wouldn't have necessarily connected the killer to Ward. Plus, Tessa had the baby with her, so Ward must have believed that Courtney would come for the child.

But something didn't fit.

"Then who put Tessa in the burning barn?" Landon asked.

"Hawkins. On Ward's orders, though. After Tessa didn't lead him to Courtney, Ward figured it was time to cut his losses and get rid of her. He didn't want Tessa coming to any of us for help in case we figured out what was going on. So he used the tracking device to find her, drugged her again and put her in the barn."

"Any idea why he didn't just kill me?" Tessa's voice wasn't exactly steady with that question.

"Again, Ward's orders. He wanted your death to look as if it was connected to Landon. That's why he wrote what he did on the boulder."

It turned Landon's stomach to think about how close Ward had come to making this sick plan work. If Landon hadn't seen the burning barn, he might not have gotten to them in time.

"Hawkins also admitted to putting the note on Emmett's body," Grayson went on. "That was Ward's idea, too, he says. He also says Ward staged those injuries he got and murdered the other guy just so he could leave another of those taunting notes."

It was a good thing Ward was dead, because Landon wanted to pulverize the man for that alone. It'd been torture for Landon to believe he was the reason Emmett had died.

"Please tell me you've arrested Joel for this deadly partnership with Ward," Tessa said. "Or was Ward telling the truth when he said he was going to kill him?"

"No, he's dead, all right. It was set up as a suicide, but I think Ward was tying up loose ends."

And those loose ends included committing more murders tonight. Or rather trying to commit more. It was stupid that so many people had died to cover up a dirty federal agent's crimes.

"The cops did find something interesting near Joel's body," Grayson continued. "Proof of payment for the hit on a man named Harry Schuler."

Landon knew the name, and clearly, so did Tessa. She touched her fingers to her mouth for a moment. "One of the reasons I was investigating Joel," she said, "was because I believed he murdered Schuler."

"And he apparently did," Grayson verified. "I figure Ward had the proof all along and decided to leave it next to Joel's body."

They might never know why Ward had done that. Perhaps to "prove" that Joel had been overcome by guilt from all the illegal things he'd done. But Joel wasn't a man with that kind of a conscience. He might have had no conscience at all.

"So with Joel and Ward dead, the danger is really over," Tessa said. But she didn't sound overjoyed by that as much as just relieved.

"It is," Grayson verified, and he checked the time. "By the way, as soon as we caught Hawkins, I called the safe house and asked them to bring the baby. They should be here soon. I figured Courtney would want to see her daughter."

"She will," Landon agreed.

But Courtney wouldn't just want to see the baby. She would take custody of her. As she should. After all, Courtney was the baby's mother, and she'd been through hell and back to make sure Samantha was safe. Still, Landon felt a pang of a different kind. Not just because they'd all been through this nightmare but because the baby would no longer be part of his life.

Oh, man.

When had that happened?

When had he gone from being married to the badge to missing holding a newborn? For that matter, when had his feelings for Tessa deepened?

And there was no mistaking it—they had deepened. But just how deep were they? Deep, he decided when he glanced at her.

"Are you okay?" Grayson asked him.

Landon didn't want to know what had prompted Grayson to ask that, but he hoped he didn't look as if he'd just been punched in the gut. Though it felt a little like that. A gut punch that made him also feel pretty darn happy.

Grayson tipped his head to Landon's arm, which the nurse had just stitched. "You're sure? You both look beat up."

They were, but Tessa and he nodded. Being beaten up wasn't something Landon wanted to experience again anytime soon, but it could have been a lot worse.

Grayson volleyed glances at both Tessa and Landon and hitched his thumb to the door. "I need to get back to the office. Will you let Courtney know the baby's on the way?"

They assured Grayson that they would, and Tessa and Landon went out into the hall as soon as Grayson walked away. Courtney wasn't far, just a couple of doors away, but Landon had something on his mind, and he didn't want to wait any longer.

"Before all hell broke loose, you told me you were in love with me," Landon said to Tessa.

A quick sigh left her mouth. "I'm sorry about that."

His stomach dropped, and he stopped, caught on to

her shoulder. "You're sorry?" And yeah, his tone wasn't a happy one.

"I know how your mind works," she explained. "Hearing that will make you feel obligated in some way, and that's not what I want you to feel."

She would have started walking away if he hadn't held on. He did remember to hold on gently, though, because her shoulders were probably bruised, too.

"What do you want me to feel?" he came out and asked. Except it sounded like an order. So Landon softened his tone and repeated.

And he kissed her, too, just in case she needed any help with that answer.

When he pulled back from the kiss, she was looking at him as if he'd lost his mind. Which was possible. But if so, this was a good kind of mind losing.

She kept staring at him as if trying to gauge his mood or something. So Landon helped her with that, too.

"Tessa, do you want me to be in love with you?"

Still more staring, but her mouth did open a little. "Do you want to be in love with me?" she countered.

Hell. This shouldn't be this hard. He was fumbling the words. Fumbling *this*. So he went with his fallback plan and kissed her again. This time he made it a lot longer, and when he felt her melt against him, Landon thought this might be the time to bare his heart to her.

He was in love with her.

Desperately in love with her.

However, he didn't get out the words before he heard the commotion in the hall. He didn't draw his gun, though, because this commotion was from laughter. He soon saw the source of the laughter when Gage and

Kade came into sight. Kade had the baby bundled in his arms.

"Told you," Gage said before they even made it to Landon and Tessa.

Kade chuckled. "Yep." Then Kade glanced at Landon and smiled. "Gage and I were just saying that it wouldn't be long before you two were back together."

"And that caused you to laugh?" Landon asked.

Gage shrugged. "We were just wondering if you'd have that thunderstruck look on your face when you realized you couldn't live without Tessa. You got that look. And Tessa's got that same look about you."

Landon glanced at Tessa, and he frowned. And not because he didn't feel that way about Tessa. He did. But he wasn't especially pleased that his cousins and Tessa had figured this all out before he did. Because Tessa did have that look on her face, and that meant he did, too.

Well, hell.

What now?

Landon got that question answered for him because the baby started to fuss, and besides, Courtney had already waited too long to be with her daughter.

"We can talk about this later," Tessa said, taking Samantha from Kade. Gage dropped kisses on both Tessa's and the baby's cheeks, and his cousins strolled away, still smiling like loons.

Landon gave the baby a cheek kiss, too. His way of saying goodbye. Tessa did the same before they opened the door to the hospital room. Courtney was clearly waiting for them, because the moment she spotted the baby, she got out of the bed. Since she still had an IV in her arm, Landon motioned for her to stay put, and they brought the baby to her.

He could see the love, and relief, all over Courtney's face.

"Thank you," Courtney said, her voice clogged with
the emotions. "Grayson had the nurse tell me that the
danger was over, but I didn't know I'd get to see Samantha so soon." Tears spilled down her cheeks, but
Landon was certain they were happy tears. She tried
to blink back some of those tears when she looked at
them. "I can't ever thank you enough."

"No," Landon teased, "but you can let us babysit
every now and then."

The moment he heard the words leave his mouth, he
froze. It was that "us" part. It sounded a lot more than
just joint babysitting duties.

And it was.

A lot more.

"I'm in love with you," Landon blurted out, causing
both Tessa and Courtney to stare at him.

"I'm guessing you're not talking to me," Courtney
joked. She snuggled her baby closer, pressing kisses
on her face.

Since Courtney needed some time alone with the
baby and since Landon didn't need an audience for the
more word fumbling and blurting he was about to do,
he gave the baby another kiss. After Tessa had done
the same thing and hugged Courtney, Landon led Tessa
back into the hall.

"You don't have to tell me that you love me," Tessa
tossed out there before he could speak.

"I have to say it because it's true," he argued.

She stared at him as if she might challenge that, so
he hauled her to him and kissed her. It was probably a

little too rough considering their injuries, but Tessa still made that sound of pleasure.

Landon suddenly wanted to take her somewhere private so he could hear a lot more of those sounds from her.

"Here's how this could work," Landon continued after the kiss had left them both breathless. "We could be sensible about this, and I could just ask you out on a date. One date could lead to a second, third and so on—"

"Or I could just remind you that I'm crazy in love with you, and we could skip the dates and move in together."

He liked the way she was thinking, but Landon wanted more. Heck, he wanted it all.

"We could have lots of sex if I move in with you." She winked, nudged his body with hers.

He liked that way of thinking, too. Really liked it after she gave him another little nudge, but Landon wanted to finish this before his mind got so clouded that he couldn't think.

Landon looked her straight in the eyes. "How long will I have to wait to ask you to marry me?"

Tessa didn't jump to answer, but she did smile. Then she kissed him. "Two seconds," she said with her mouth against his.

"Too long. Marry me, Tessa."

Landon let her get out the yes before he pulled her back to him for a kiss to seal the deal. This was exactly the *all* that he wanted.

* * * * *

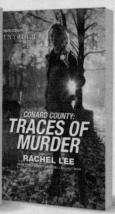

*After forensic investigator Lena Love is attacked and
left with a partial heart-shaped symbol carved into her
chest, her hunt to find a serial killer becomes personal.*

*Read on for a sneak preview of
The Heart-Shaped Murders,
the debut book in A West Coast Crime Story series,
from Denise N. Wheatley.*

Lena Love kicked a rock out from underneath her foot, then
bent down and tightened the twill shoelaces on her brown
leather hiking boots.

The crime scene investigator, who doubled as a forensic
science technician, stood back up and eyed Los Angeles's
Cucamonga Wilderness trail. Sharp-edged stones and ragged
shards of bark covered the rugged, winding terrain.

"Watch your step," she uttered to herself before continuing
along the path of her latest crime scene.

Lena squinted as she focused on the trail. Heavy foliage
loomed overhead, blocking out the sun's brilliant rays. She
pulled out her flashlight, hoping its bright beam would help
uncover potential evidence.

An ominous wave of vulnerability swept through her
chest at the sight of the vast San Gabriel Mountains. She spun
around slowly, feeling small while eyeing the infinite views
of the forest, desert and snowy mountainous peaks.

The wild surroundings left her with a lingering sense of
defenselessness. Lena tightened the belt on her tan suede
blazer. She hoped it would give her some semblance of
security.

It didn't.

Lena wondered if the latest victim had felt that same vulnerability on the night she'd been brutally murdered.

"Come on, Grace Mitchell," Lena said aloud, as if the dead woman could hear her. "Talk to me. Tell me what happened to you. *Show* me what happened to you."

A gust of wind whipped Lena's bone-straight bob across her slender face. She tucked her hair behind her ears and stooped down, aiming the flashlight toward the majestic oak tree where Grace's body had been found.

Lena envisioned spotting droplets of blood, a cigarette butt, the tip of a latex glove…*anything* that would help identify the killer.

This was her second visit to the crime scene. The thought of showing up to the station without any viable evidence yet again caused an agonizing pang of dread to shoot up her spine.

Grace was the fifth victim of a criminal whom Lena had labeled an organized serial killer. He appeared to have a type. Young, slender brunette women. Their bodies had all been found in heavily wooded areas. Each victim's hands were meticulously tied behind their backs with a three-strand twisted rope. They'd been strangled to death. And the amount of evidence left at each scene was practically nonexistent.

But the killer's signature mark was always there. And it was a sinister one.

Look for
The Heart-Shaped Murders *by Denise N. Wheatley,*
available June 2022 wherever
Harlequin Intrigue books and ebooks are sold.

Harlequin.com

HIEXP0422

Get 4 FREE REWARDS!

We'll send you 2 FREE Books plus 2 FREE Mystery Gifts.

KENTUCKY CRIME RING — JULIE ANNE LINDSEY

TEXAS STALKER — BARB HAN

FREE Value Over **$20**

UNDER THE RANCHER'S PROTECTION — ADDISON FOX

OPERATION WHISTLEBLOWER — CYNTHIA EDEN

Both the **Harlequin Intrigue®** and **Harlequin® Romantic Suspense** series feature compelling novels filled with heart-racing action-packed romance that will keep you on the edge of your seat.

YES! Please send me 2 FREE novels from the Harlequin Intrigue or Harlequin Romantic Suspense series and my 2 FREE gifts (gifts are worth about $10 retail). After receiving them, if I don't wish to receive any more books, I can return the shipping statement marked "cancel." If I don't cancel, I will receive 6 brand-new Harlequin Intrigue Larger-Print books every month and be billed just $5.99 each in the U.S. or $6.49 each in Canada, a savings of at least 14% off the cover price or 4 brand-new Harlequin Romantic Suspense books every month and be billed just $4.99 each in the U.S. or $5.74 each in Canada, a savings of at least 13% off the cover price. It's quite a bargain! Shipping and handling is just 50¢ per book in the U.S. and $1.25 per book in Canada.* I understand that accepting the 2 free books and gifts places me under no obligation to buy anything. I can always return a shipment and cancel at any time. The free books and gifts are mine to keep no matter what I decide.

Choose one: ☐ **Harlequin Intrigue Larger-Print** (199/399 HDN GNXC)   ☐ **Harlequin Romantic Suspense** (240/340 HDN GNMZ)

Name (please print)

Address   Apt. #

City   State/Province   Zip/Postal Code

Email: Please check this box ☐ if you would like to receive newsletters and promotional emails from Harlequin Enterprises ULC and its affiliates. You can unsubscribe anytime.

Mail to the **Harlequin Reader Service:**
IN U.S.A.: P.O. Box 1341, Buffalo, NY 14240-8531
IN CANADA: P.O. Box 603, Fort Erie, Ontario L2A 5X3

Want to try 2 free books from another series! Call 1-800-873-8635 or visit www.ReaderService.com.

*Terms and prices subject to change without notice. Prices do not include sales taxes, which will be charged (if applicable) based on your state or country of residence. Canadian residents will be charged applicable taxes. Offer not valid in Quebec. This offer is limited to one order per household. Books received may not be as shown. Not valid for current subscribers to the Harlequin Intrigue or Harlequin Romantic Suspense series. All orders subject to approval. Credit or debit balances in a customer's account(s) may be offset by any other outstanding balance owed by or to the customer. Please allow 4 to 6 weeks for delivery. Offer available while quantities last.

Your Privacy—Your information is being collected by Harlequin Enterprises ULC, operating as Harlequin Reader Service. For a complete summary of the information we collect, how we use this information and to whom it is disclosed, please visit our privacy notice located at corporate.harlequin.com/privacy-notice. From time to time we may also exchange your personal information with reputable third parties. If you wish to opt out of this sharing of your personal information, please visit readerservice.com/consumerschoice or call 1-800-873-8635. **Notice to California Residents**—Under California law, you have specific rights to control and access your data. For more information on these rights and how to exercise them, visit corporate.harlequin.com/california-privacy.

HIHRS22

Love Harlequin romance?

DISCOVER.

Be the first to find out about promotions, news and exclusive content!

Facebook.com/HarlequinBooks

Twitter.com/HarlequinBooks

Instagram.com/HarlequinBooks

Pinterest.com/HarlequinBooks

YouTube.com/HarlequinBooks

ReaderService.com

EXPLORE.

Sign up for the Harlequin e-newsletter and download a free book from any series at **TryHarlequin.com**

CONNECT.

Join our Harlequin community to share your thoughts and connect with other romance readers!
Facebook.com/groups/HarlequinConnection